SEMANTIC ERROR

THE NOVEL

1

J. Soori

Illustration by

Angy

NEW YORK

SEMANTIC ERROR

1 J. Soori

Translation by PUBLANG
Cover art by ANGY

Ize Press
150 West 30th Street, 6th Floor
New York, NY 10001

Visit us at izepress.com • facebook.com/izepress • twitter.com/izepress • instagram.com/izepress

First Ize Press Edition: January 2026
Edited by Ize Press Editorial: Won Young Seo
Design by Ize Press Design: Wendy Chan

Library of Congress Cataloging-in-Publication Data is available.

ISBNs: 979-8-4009-0316-8 (paperback)
979-8-4009-0317-5 (ebook)

10 9 8 7 6 5 4 3 2 1

TPA

Printed in South Korea

SEMANTIC ERROR

TABLE OF CONTENTS

SEMANTIC ERROR

<0>

More than half the students in the lecture hall were asleep. Keeping over a hundred college students engaged in a lengthy lecture would be a near-impossible task for even for the most seasoned professor. To make matters worse, the presenter at the podium didn't have a single distinctive feature that commanded attention. He wore a loose plaid shirt, dark jeans that ignored all fashion trends, and a black cap that hid his facial features.

It was only when he clicked the button on the laser pointer to bring up his presentation slides that the droopy eyes of the audience snapped wide open in horror. There, on the screen, were the words:

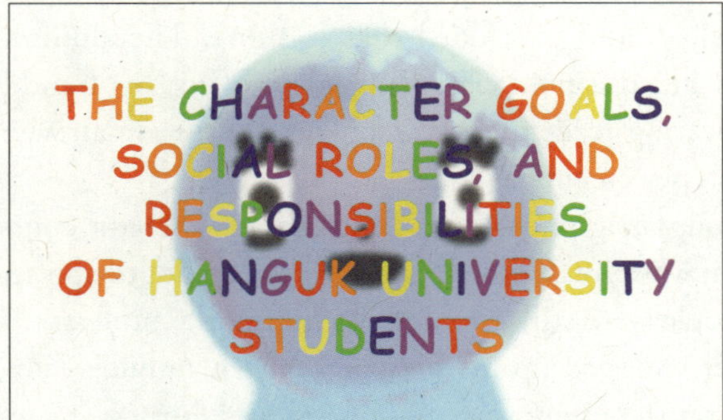

The font size alone—at least 93 point—was shocking enough, but the choice of Comic Sans was especially alarming. In addition, each letter had been painstakingly changed to different colors of the rainbow, while behind the text loomed a blurred illustration.

"I will now begin," the presenter said, his blank, indifferent expression in stark contrast to the audience's shock. He clicked to the next slide.

This time, the image that appeared on the screen was composed of only a single line of text against a black background. The ugly font and alarmingly large text size, however? It remained unchanged.

"Over the course of this lecture," the presenter began, "I will examine the effectiveness of Hanguk University's attempts to bestow their core values—honesty, creativity, and passion—upon their students through an investigation of the reputations of our most distinguished alumni, during which I will redefine the archetype of the model student and explore what roles and responsibilities current students should aspire to in the future, through which..."

The students who had been jolted awake soon slipped back into a stupor, the shock of the presentation's visuals quickly wearing off. It didn't help that the voice of the presenter was low and monotonous, with no pitch variation whatsoever, or that his first sentence seemed to go on forever.

"For honesty, I focused on the following alumni..."

The lecture content was surprisingly in-depth, and the logic was solid. The presenter had conducted a thorough investigation into whether the university's talent development system—as described on its website—actually worked, and concluded that it didn't. The alumni he cited as examples included a politician stripped of office for fraud, a professor caught fabricating academic research, and a businessman who'd accepted bribes for job placements.

For a group assignment done for a mere two-credit course, the level of dedication was rare. Unfortunately, by the end of the presentation, less than ten people were still listening, including the professor. Thus, when the presenter wrapped up his presentation ten minutes later with some final words on the importance of honesty and fairness, he was met with only a small, haphazard round of applause.

"Thank you for listening," he concluded, then flipped to the last slide.

Gasps immediately burst from the lips of the few who'd still been paying attention. Even the students who'd been dozing abruptly shot up in their seats, staring at the screen in disbelief.

Group Leader: Sangwoo Choo
Presentation: Sangwoo Choo
Part 1 Research: Sangwoo Choo
Part 2 Research: Sangwoo Choo
Data Compilation: Sangwoo Choo
Slides: Sangwoo Choo
Participants: Sangwoo Choo

As the room erupted in whispers and murmurs, the professor pushed his glasses up his nose, visibly bewildered.

The presenter—Sangwoo Choo—briefly observed the stir that had broken out among his audience. *That illustration I used in the background must have really brought the presentation together,* he silently concluded.

return 0;

A student wearing a baseball cap pulled low over his eyes entered the office to meet with the professor, who looked slightly troubled as he gestured for the student to sit.

"Thanks for dropping by, Sangwoo," the professor began. "I wanted to talk about your presentation from earlier today."

"Was there some kind of issue with it?" Sangwoo asked.

"The content was impressive, but…" The professor trailed off, flipping through the attendance sheet. "Did none of your group members participate?"

Sangwoo had delivered a remarkably in-depth presentation on his own, but it was, after all, a group project. There were supposed to be three other people in his group.

"No," Sangwoo replied without a hint of emotion.

The professor rubbed his forehead with a sigh. "Could you expand on that, please?"

"Originally, I was only responsible for the first part of the research and the presentation slides," Sangwoo explained. "However, the person assigned to the second part of the research didn't send their material to me by 6 PM yesterday, as he had promised to do, so I completed it instead. As for the designated presenter, he said he couldn't attend class due to grief over his great-aunt's passing, so I filled in for him as well."

"What about the last one, then?"

"I never even met them."

The professor nodded silently and made three marks on the attendance sheet. Then he peered at the paper closely, as if he had just discovered something. "It seems there's a graduating senior in your group. He emailed me in advance to let me know he wouldn't be able to attend class this week, as he'd won an award and would be traveling abroad to accept it."

"Yes, I did hear about someone entering a competition."

The professor studied Sangwoo for a moment. "Given the circumstances, don't you think leaving his name off the project might be a bit harsh?"

"No, I do not," Sangwoo answered simply, his tone unwavering.

"How come?"

"If he had only missed class today but participated in every other instance, I would be willing to be more considerate of his situation. But he never attended any of the in-class meetings for the project, let alone contributed."

The professor pushed the attendance sheet toward Sangwoo. "Take a look. It shows he attended every single class, aside from today's and last week's."

Sangwoo didn't even blink. "Perhaps he had someone else mark him as present."

A peculiar expression flickered across the professor's face. "I see. Thank you, Sangwoo. Have a good rest of your day."

"Yes, Professor."

Sangwoo bowed politely and exited the office, his face just as impassive as it had been when he first walked in.

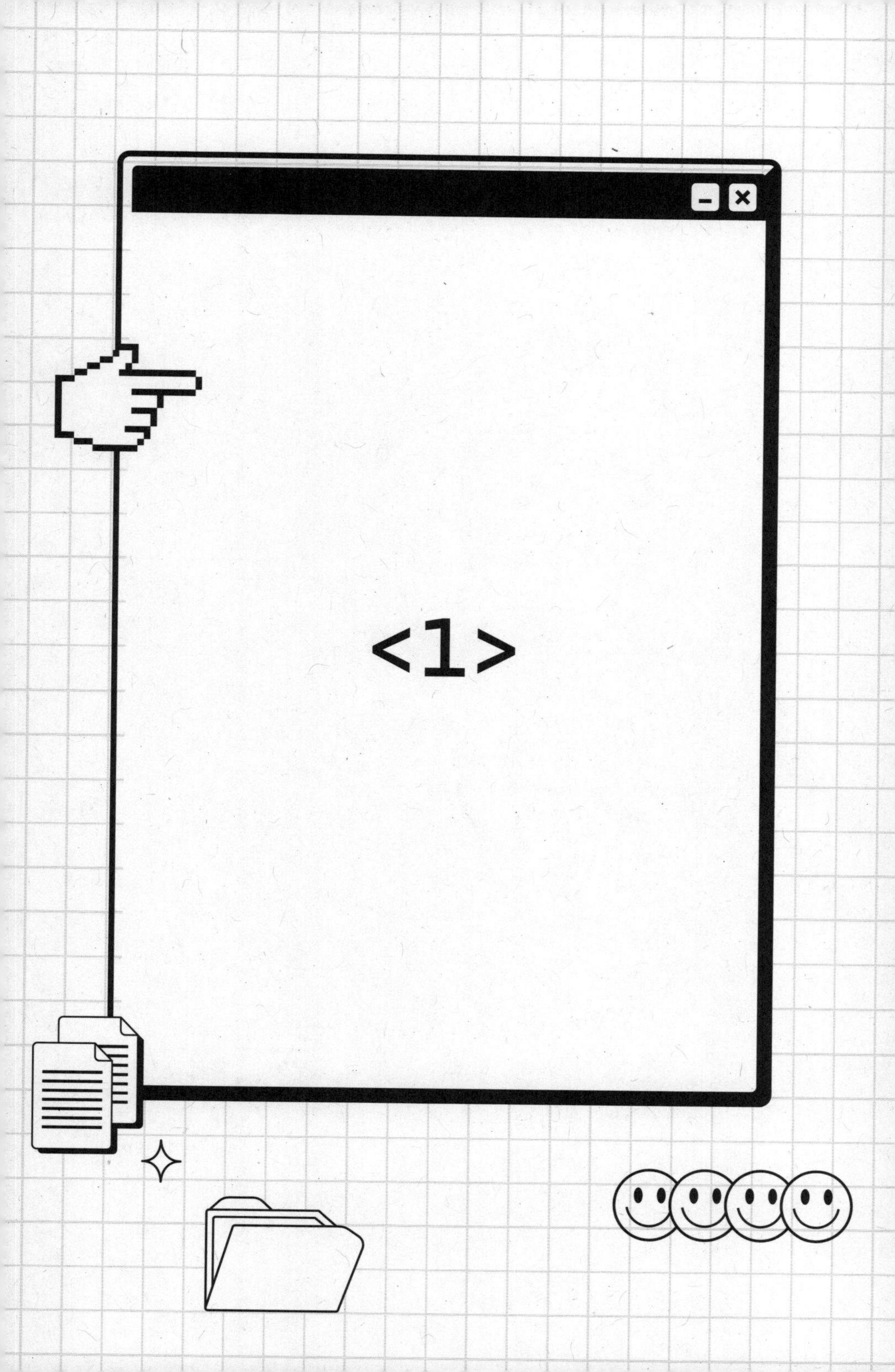
<1>

The first semester of Sangwoo's junior year had finally come to a close. His schedule had been jam-packed with twenty-one credits worth of notoriously difficult classes, but he'd managed them just fine. It was the two-credit core curriculum required course that'd worn him down in the end.

The class, Ethics for Hanguk University Students, consisted of weekly lectures and several simple group projects. Indeed, the topic of the final presentation had seemed so straightforward to Sangwoo that, at first, he hadn't taken it seriously. Even when he'd found out one of his group members would be skipping class entirely for a competition, he hadn't thought much of it. But then another member had suffered a family emergency, and yet another ghosted him the day before the presentation. What'd once been a task Sangwoo could've easily finished alone in a day had subsequently turned into a time-consuming hassle as he chased down teammates and waited on their materials.

Annoyed as he'd been, Sangwoo put it behind him once the presentation was over—at least until the grades came out, and a minor issue surfaced.

The day the grades were posted, Sangwoo's phone was bombarded with messages. Two people sent a single message and left it at that, but one kept pestering him with texts and calls—demanding that they meet in person to talk—until Sangwoo finally blocked the number.

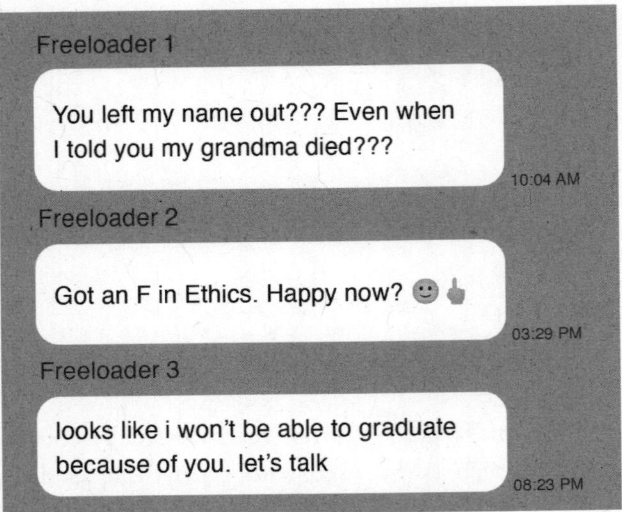

Then came winter break. Sangwoo planned to reduce his course load the following semester to focus on developing a mobile game. To prepare, he had been teaching himself programming languages during the week and working part-time at an internet café on weekends. His life was going smoothly, save for one nagging distraction.

It happened on a Saturday like any other, which meant he was in the middle of his shift. Two undergraduates were on their way out after gaming the day away, and standing by the register as he was, Sangwoo couldn't help but overhear their conversation.

"Did you hear that Jaeyoung isn't going to be able to graduate this semester?" one of them asked.

"Huh? How come? I thought he was gonna study abroad."

The first student sighed. "It's because of that core class, Ethics or whatever. Some guy told the professor that Jaeyoung was having someone else mark attendance for him, so he got an F."

"Oh, shit! And he can't make up for it or anything?" the second student asked. He clicked his tongue.

"Apparently, the professor didn't wanna compromise for the sake of the guy who snitched."

"Oh… So he's basically telling Jaeyoung to talk to the dude himself."

The story sounded way too familiar. Sangwoo continued to eavesdrop while pretending to be busy behind the counter.

"I heard the guy's not picking up his phone, though."

"Really? What's his major?"

"Not sure. Mechanical engineering? Computer science? Anyway, Jaeyoung has been trying to figure out where the guy lives. He's seriously pissed… Nobody knows, though, so he's screwed big-time."

There was a pause. "I'm honestly kinda impressed that he snitched. Must be one of those goody-two-shoes types, huh…?"

It seemed Sangwoo had found himself tangled up with yet another jerk. Still, this wasn't the first time he'd gotten caught up in some sort of conflict during his university years. He'd always managed to handle things well enough.

During his freshman year, for example, he'd almost gotten into a fist-fight with an older student who tried to force him to down a soju bomb. Another time, he'd made it into the school newspaper for refusing to pay the student council fee. He'd even gotten into a scuffle with a stranger on the street over bumping shoulders, and had once ended up at a police station after a heated argument with someone who'd cut in line. But none of those incidents could be compared to possibly ruining someone's graduation.

Sangwoo seriously considered changing his phone number, but ultimately decided against it. He hadn't done anything wrong, so it would be silly to act scared. Still, after that, he couldn't stop himself from going rigid every time a notification popped up on his phone.

Visual Arts Suyoung Han

Hey, Mr. Developer! So sry but I don't think I can do the project anymore, just got a job offer… I asked a really talented classmate to take my place

12:31 PM

Sangwoo was sorely disappointed by the first message he'd received in a while. Despite Suyoung's slow pace—the consequence of a busy schedule—her illustrations had been absolutely fantastic. Sangwoo had already designed the game around her style, so having to replace her with another artist was far from ideal.

This school is full of irresponsible people, Sangwoo thought. At least she'd bothered to find someone to replace her before disappearing—though there was no guarantee this replacement would be any good.

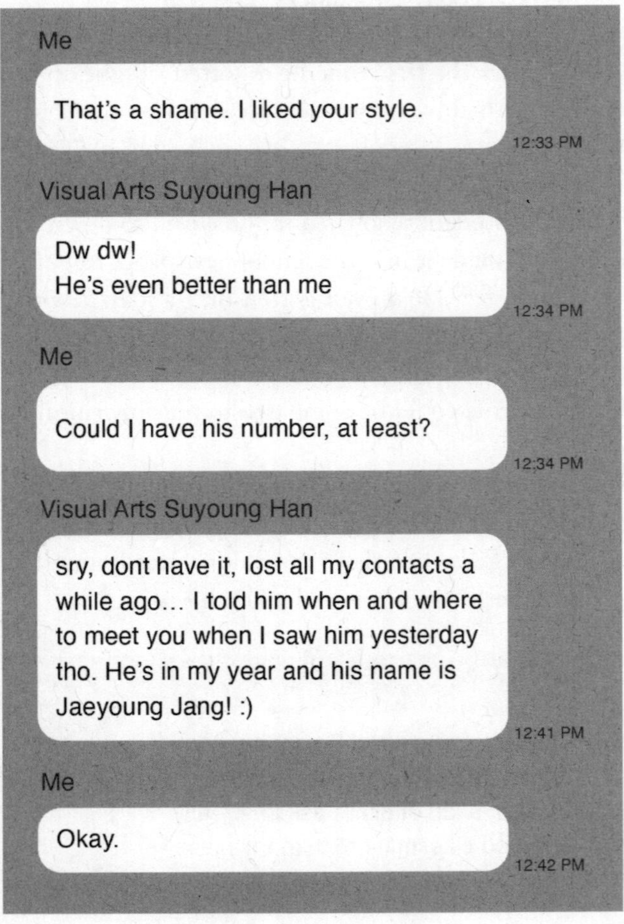

After wrapping up the conversation, Sangwoo headed to campus. The meeting was scheduled for 4 PM, but he arrived three hours early to organize character drafts and sketches.

Visual design major Jaeyoung Jang, huh? he pondered. Aside from the vague promise of talent, Sangwoo was completely in the dark about the person in question. He didn't even know whether they were male or female, much less what their art style was like. Would they be as busy as Suyoung, or as willing to leave the project half-finished to chase after some job?

For now, he'd just have to give them a chance and see for himself.

At 3:55 PM Sangwoo packed up his things and headed upstairs. He arrived at the small meeting room he'd reserved on the third floor of the library just one minute before the meeting. He took out his notebook and pen, ready.

However, the replacement didn't show.

If it had been any other appointment, Sangwoo would've left without a second thought. But his project needed a designer. He couldn't do it alone. He killed time by playing a game on his phone for ten minutes.

Still, no designer.

Maybe they'd mixed up the time, or something urgent had come up. It was also possible that Suyoung had given them the wrong information—or that they'd simply changed their mind about coming at the last minute. Sangwoo's mind ran through all the possibilities as another ten minutes passed.

And still, no designer.

What a total scumbag, Sangwoo thought. In his experience, anyone who couldn't bother to be punctual rarely turned out to be decent. Working with someone like that was bound to lead to trouble. His frustration simmered as another ten minutes ticked by.

And yet, no designer.

"This is it. Last chance," Sangwoo muttered. Purely out of respect for Suyoung, who had been both skilled and kind to him, he decided to wait for just ten more minutes. But though he sat there with the patience of a monk, the other person didn't show.

Gritting his teeth, Sangwoo pushed himself up from his chair. He despised all forms of waste, but nothing irritated him more than wasting time. He had just begun to reach for the doorknob, ready to leave, when the door swung open abruptly.

"Is this the right place?" the person on the other side of the door mumbled under his breath.

Sangwoo continued to scowl as he looked at the newcomer. He was wearing a loose black beanie and had oversized glasses perched on the bridge of his nose. Three metal piercings glinted along one ear.

With the attitude of the truly unapologetic, the man sauntered into the room and casually flopped down in the seat across from Sangwoo. Though they were supposed to be having a meeting, his hands were notably empty when he pulled them from his pockets. He rubbed them together before finally glancing up.

The man's eyes widened as they met Sangwoo's. He pointed a finger at him. "Oh!"

"Can I help you?" Sangwoo asked. He reflexively reached up to feel his own cheek, wondering if there was something on his face.

The man looked momentarily taken aback, but he soon regained his composure. His wide eyes returned to normal size.

Though Sangwoo had already lost all interest in working with the man in front of him, he decided to go through the motions for the sake of protocol. He forced himself back into his seat and gripped his pen.

"Are you the designer?" he asked curtly, avoiding eye contact.

"I sure am."

"Are you aware of what the project entails?"

The man, who was apparently the Jaeyoung Jang he'd been waiting for, hummed distractedly. "Kinda."

Suppressing a wave of frustration, Sangwoo explained patiently, "I'm developing a 2D action-adventure game geared toward children. It uses the Creator2d-x framework, and the story is in first-person point of view."

Jaeyoung didn't seem to be listening to a word Sangwoo said. He was slouched in his chair, bouncing his legs up and down. Then, without bothering to ask for permission, he suddenly picked up Sangwoo's notebook and started flipping through it.

"Someone's done their homework," he commented.

Sangwoo snatched the notebook back, flipped to a blank page, and set it down on the table before pulling a folder from his bag and handing it to the man. The documents within detailed his game's title and overall concept, accompanied by the preliminary character designs Suyoung had created.

Jaeyoung glanced down, silently examining the papers. "Man, this sucks," he mumbled under his breath, though it was plenty loud enough for Sangwoo to hear. Lifting his eyes away from the meticulously organized *Veggie Man* drafts, he added, "Suyoung's usually pretty good, but I can see she half-assed this. The concept's unoriginal, and the sketches are lazy."

With a flick of his hand, he sent the folder flying back in Sangwoo's direction—the corner clocked Sangwoo right in the nose.

Sangwoo placed the folder on top of his notebook, his expression hardening. He had planned to at least go over the details of the project out of courtesy, but his patience had already worn thin. Realizing that exerting any more effort would only drain his energy further, he decided to cut the meeting short.

"I don't think we're a good fit," Sangwoo declared, gathering up his notebook and folder. "I'll look for another designer."

"Are you really *that* good at coding?" Jaeyoung asked out of nowhere. "Like...if I asked you to implement something, would you be able to?"

"I can implement almost any feature that would be necessary for a 2D action-adventure game, as long as it's been designed properly."

"You sound pretty sure of yourself," Jaeyoung remarked.

The dismissive tone stung at Sangwoo's pride. Was the guy underestimating him because he was just a student? Or because he'd only recently returned to school after finishing his mandatory military service?

"I'm especially skilled in debugging and optimization," Sangwoo clarified. "In high school, I built a budget-tracking app, and I even developed an HTML5-based arcade game—"

"That stuff doesn't matter," Jaeyoung said, cutting him off. Pushing his glasses up the bridge of his nose a little, he tapped a finger on the *Veggie Man* concept sheet. "It's not enough for a game to just run without errors. It's gotta be *fun*. How smooth the animations are, how satisfying it is to hit an enemy—those are the real selling points. And it's not just the graphics; background music matters, too. Which makes me wonder: Can I really trust your judgment when you okayed a garbage concept like this? Is this project going to be worth the time I invest in it?"

The man was totally unpredictable. He couldn't care less one moment and was all business the next.

Sangwoo instinctively tensed. "If you put your faith in me, I will do my best."

As soon as the words left his mouth, frustration bubbled up inside him. He wasn't some subcontractor who had to grovel for work—he was the one *hiring* for this project.

"But I have to ask..." Sangwoo straightened up and crossed his arms. "Do you have any experience working on mobile game projects?"

It was a well-timed counterattack. If this man turned out to be all talk and no skill, Sangwoo was ready to walk out the door without a second thought.

"No," Jaeyoung responded easily.

"Then, goodbye."

"But I do have quite a bit of experience in web design..."

Sangwoo paused in the middle of rising from his seat. If this man was skilled at crafting website UI, designing an app shouldn't be much of a stretch. Beyond the smaller object sizes and additional optimization requirements, the fundamentals were the same. Plus, Suyoung had spoken as if this deadbeat was exceptionally talented.

"May I see your portfolio?" Sangwoo asked.

Jaeyoung smirked, pulling a tablet from his coat pocket. A few taps later, he handed it over to Sangwoo.

Sangwoo studied the screen before him. A list of projects had been arranged in a horizontal scroll, displayed against a clean white background like paintings at an art gallery. Carefully examining each piece, he zoomed in to check the details.

From websites to posters, logos to illustrations, this guy could seemingly do it all. And the quality was far above what you'd typically expect of a college student. *He's even better than most pros*, Sangwoo concluded. UI efficiency—check. Conciseness of interface—check. Effective color usage—check. And his illustration skills? They were excellent. His art style was distinct, lively, and full of character.

Internally, Sangwoo had already discarded the sketches he'd previously adored, his mind moving on to something better.

"Yeah, I'm no slouch," Jaeyoung said, catching a glimpse of Sangwoo's reaction.

"You did all of these yourself, correct?"

After dismissing Sangwoo's question with a snort, the designer began to sketch something with a pen into Sangwoo's discarded notebook. After twenty seconds, he'd produced a drawing of a carrot character. It was nothing like Suyoung's work. His carrot was rebellious, edgy, and… incredibly cool. It was absolutely amazing.

Sangwoo couldn't help but be impressed; the man clearly had every right to be confident in his skills. Sangwoo's heart raced with excitement, though he forced himself to keep it in check. He still had a few lingering doubts.

"Can you dedicate your time to this project throughout the entirety of next semester?" Sangwoo asked.

"Yeah. I happen to have a ton of free time because my graduation plans got screwed up."

"What if you get a job offer halfway through the project like Suyoung did?"

Jaeyoung shrugged. "I always finish what I start."

Only minutes ago, Sangwoo had inwardly sworn that he would never trust someone who was forty minutes late to a meeting, but this man was making him change his mind. With talent like his, Sangwoo could overlook a little tardiness. That was saying a lot, considering Sangwoo usually held punctuality—and diligence—above all else.

"Could I have your contact information, then?" Sangwoo asked, respectfully offering the man his phone.

Jaeyoung took it and began to enter his number. Then abruptly, his expression shifted. His brows furrowed as he slowly tilted his head to look up at Sangwoo.

"It's already in here."

"No, that can't be right," Sangwoo objected.

Jaeyoung's voice grew sharper. "Here, look."

Confused, Sangwoo took his phone back—and saw that it was already calling someone.

Calling Freeloader 3...

Sangwoo and the man stared at the screen in silence as the number dialed. Then, from somewhere within the room, a ring sounded.

Jaeyoung pulled his phone from his coat pocket, his expression cold. He let out a dry, disbelieving laugh as he stared at the screen. Sangwoo also glanced at it and saw the name he'd been saved under.

Incoming call from Douchebag!

Shocked, Sangwoo bolted out of the meeting room, leaving his notebook and pen behind. He didn't dare look back, so he had no idea if Jaeyoung called after him, chased him, or just stayed where he was.

The next twenty minutes were a blur. When Sangwoo finally made it home, he only paused to catch his breath after he'd secured the door using all three of its locks. His knee was throbbing, aggravated after he'd tripped while rushing up the stairs.

Sangwoo staggered over to the fridge and gulped down a bottle of water. "This can't be happening," he muttered to himself.

For the longest moment, he stood rooted to the spot, dazed. Then he finally mustered the courage to pull out his phone. No missed calls or messages.

With trembling fingers, Sangwoo unblocked "Freeloader 3," and a string of unread texts and missed calls immediately popped up. Five days ago, Jaeyoung Jang, aka Freeloader 3, had sent him a lengthy text, apologizing and asking to meet.

In the message, Jaeyoung admitted he'd made a mistake in not reaching out to Sangwoo directly about his absences since Sangwoo was the group representative. He claimed he'd explained everything to another group member instead. There were also several follow-up texts, some of which felt borderline threatening.

That was the last message.

As Sangwoo scrolled through the texts, his initial shock began to fade. The man he'd thought was a talented game designer had turned out to be nothing more than a shameless, self-centered scumbag with zero integrity. In a way, he was lucky to have found this out before they'd started working on the project together.

A part of him was disappointed, especially after seeing Jaeyoung's impressive illustrations, but Sangwoo knew it was in his best interest to move on. There was no way he'd ever work with a punk like Jaeyoung, and he doubted the guy would want to work with him, either.

I did nothing wrong, Sangwoo reassured himself. The conflict had been unexpected, but in the end, it was entirely Jaeyoung's fault—not his.

Even so, an uneasy feeling lingered in the pit of Sangwoo's stomach. He kept glancing at his phone until, in the early hours of the morning, exhaustion finally overtook him and he fell asleep. When he woke up, a new message was waiting for him.

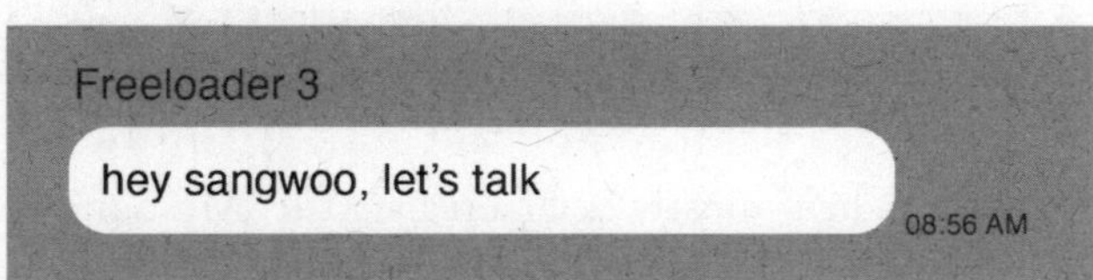

Sangwoo tried to rub the sleep from his eyes, then stared at the screen for a long moment. When he was a kid, he'd only ever been called by his childhood nickname. He'd practically gone through his entire life without hearing his first name.

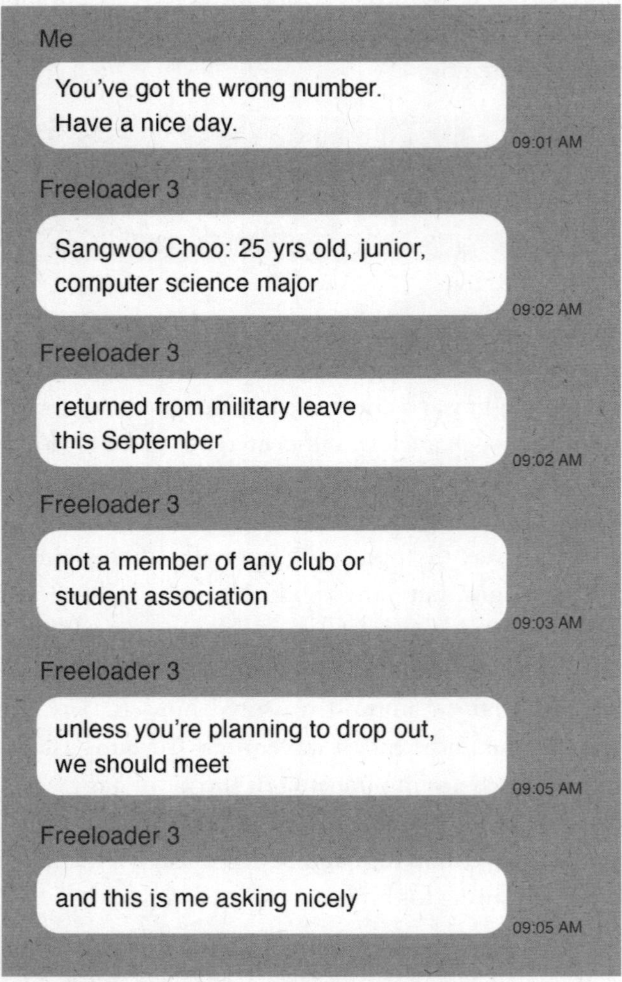

Then, in college, he'd mostly been a respectful "Mr. Sangwoo Choo." During his military service, it'd been "Private Choo," "Corporal Choo,"

and finally "Sergeant Choo." The only people who ever called him just "Sangwoo" in such a casual manner were his parents.

The responses were unsettling—menacing, even. Sangwoo stared intensely at the screen, reading them over and over. As he did, two new texts came in.

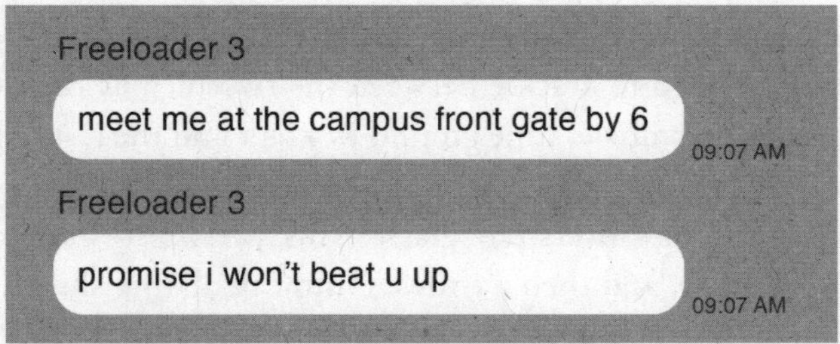

Sangwoo scoffed, clenching his phone tightly. "As if."

He hadn't done anything wrong; there was no reason for him to listen to the guy. So what if Jaeyoung had done some digging on him? What was he going to do, report Sangwoo to the police? If anyone was going to do that, it was Sangwoo—he was all for relying on police authority when in a difficult position. He knew exactly what kind of situation would be best to call upon them.

He reread Jaeyoung's message, slowly this time. Whatever the guy's intentions were, his text was clearly a threat.

Still, Sangwoo wasn't perturbed in the slightest. Jaeyoung had no real power over him. Sangwoo diligently attended classes, but otherwise kept his involvement with campus activities to a minimum, which meant his professors were the only ones who could affect him in any way.

`return 0;`

After three days, Sangwoo assumed that the ridiculous feud between himself and Jaeyoung had finally fizzled out. In hindsight, this was an entirely and painfully incorrect assumption. But given the internet café's proximity to their school, all it took was a little critical thinking to realize that the likelihood of running into Jaeyoung there was relatively high.

On that fateful day, Sangwoo was restocking cabinets with bags of chips when a pack of college students rushed through the internet café's front door. The tallest one was saying, "I told you, there's nothing going on between us. We just grabbed a meal, that's…all…" He trailed off when he saw Sangwoo, and his footsteps slowed.

Lightning seemed to crackle between the two men as their eyes met. Just like a scene in a movie, time ground to a halt and the rest of the world faded away.

Behind Jaeyoung's oversized glasses, his previously impassive eyes widened in surprise, and then narrowed into calculating slits. If it hadn't been for the intensity in his gaze, Sangwoo honestly might not have recognized him.

Even though he hadn't really done anything wrong, Sangwoo's fingers went stiff with anxiety. The bag of chips he'd been holding dropped to the floor, and a number of thoughts flashed through his head, including *Damn it, this is going to be annoying,* and *Get me out of here!*

Although Sangwoo was silently readying himself for a fight, Jaeyoung simply walked right past him and disappeared into the smoking-allowed room with his four friends. Sangwoo returned to his chair behind the counter and tried to get some studying done, but he found he couldn't focus on his textbook or class notes at all.

Sangwoo glanced up from his book, noted where Jaeyoung's head was peeking over the PC, then turned to look at a window on the screen of his own computer. It showed a list of users in the internet café and what programs they were using. Jaeyoung—seat number thirty-two—was playing an online RPG when Sangwoo looked first. He eventually switched to an FPS game, then an MMORPG. Meanwhile, Sangwoo was stuck on the same page.

Maybe I was worried about nothing, Sangwoo mused. He'd honestly thought Jaeyoung would throw a punch or two, based on the threatening texts he'd sent, but now it seemed like he was going to act his age and drop it. This was probably the best possible outcome Sangwoo could've asked for.

However, his hopes were dashed when he saw a message pop up on his computer screen.

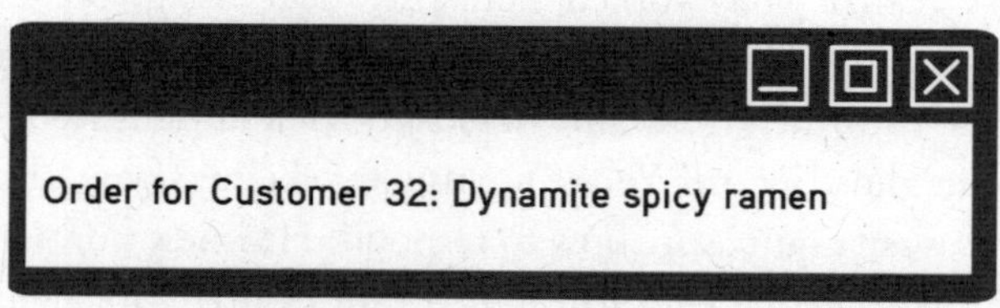

Of course. With a long sigh, Sangwoo rose to his feet and began to prepare the noodles according to the recipe, pouring precisely 450 mL of water into the pot. Although it only took minutes to boil, it felt like hours.

As he methodically cracked the dried noodles in half, placed them in the pot, and sprinkled the soup base on top, Sangwoo thought back on how he'd resolved past conflicts. As far as he could remember, he'd always fought with logic, choosing to point out other parties' faults instead of letting his emotions overcome him. They, on the other hand, most commonly dealt with their anger by swearing at him or even occasionally taking a swing in his direction. When violence of that sort broke out, he preferred calling the police rather than reciprocating with his own fists.

Deciding he might as well follow the same protocol when dealing with Jaeyoung, Sangwoo headed over to the room the other man was in. When he pushed the door open and stepped inside, he found the space hazy with cigarette smoke.

Carefully balancing the bowl of instant noodles on a tray, Sangwoo walked over to seat number thirty-two. Jaeyoung reclined comfortably in the chair with a cigarette between his lips. When Sangwoo set the plate down, Jaeyoung spun the chair to face him and stared with a strange look on his face. He was wearing a red sweatshirt with an extremely obnoxious pattern on the chest, making him look more like a common thug than anything else.

Disgusting, Sangwoo thought. He began to turn around, but Jaeyoung's leisurely voice brought him to a halt.

"I didn't realize you worked here, my dear Sangwoo." Frowning slightly, Jaeyoung stubbed out his cigarette on an ashtray. As a thin wisp of smoke rose into the air, he slowly looked back at Sangwoo. "So, why have you been ghosting me? You're hurting my feelings, you know."

Sangwoo wasn't quite sure how to respond. He knew how to stand his ground against someone who threatened him or used violence, but he'd never encountered anyone who picked a fight in such a calm manner.

"Answer me, Sangwoo."

Jaeyoung's voice was very gentle, especially considering that he was harassing someone. Sangwoo decided he would hold back until the man showed his true colors.

When Sangwoo finally responded, it was with a "Can I help you?"

"Yeah. Look me in the eyes when I'm talking."

This was a request that Sangwoo could easily fulfill. He lifted his head to meet Jaeyoung's eyes, and the other man glanced away to light another cigarette. For a long moment, he just sat there with smoke occasionally puffing out through his lips. Then he looked back at Sangwoo and abruptly extended his right hand.

"Let's make up," he demanded. "We're going to make that game together, right?"

Sangwoo stared at the large hand that had been offered to him, unsure if he was seeing things. Concluding it was indeed reality, he blinked curiously.

"How can we make up if we've never fought? Furthermore, I am not planning on making anything with you."

Jaeyoung dropped his hand back onto his lap and chuckled incredulously. "Why do you think I was asking to meet up, huh?"

"I have no idea."

"Well, maybe you should try being a bit more imaginative."

Sangwoo shrugged. "Talking with me won't change your grades. As someone who evidently possesses a high enough IQ to be accepted into a university, I hope you know that."

Jaeyoung crossed his arms, lips turning up in a cold smile. "You think this is about my damn grades? The correction period ended weeks ago."

"Why do you keep harassing me, then?" Sangwoo asked flatly.

"Nobody's *harassing* anyone. I figured I would talk to you since Suyoung introduced us and there's a potential project on the line. I was gonna listen to what you had to say and try to resolve any misunderstandings between us, okay?"

"But I have no interest in talking with you."

Jaeyoung's tone immediately grew sharper. "Would it have been too much trouble to text me that? Huh?" he asked in a low voice. "Where are your fucking manners?"

Sangwoo, who had been quietly massaging the phone in his pocket just in case things escalated, noted that Jaeyoung possessed an uncanny skill for cussing someone out while maintaining an incredibly even tone. That was not reason enough to call the police, however.

Sangwoo suddenly felt a bit lost, unsure how to react. A part of him knew that a simple apology might be enough to smooth things over, but he was following his typical protocol—and the *hostile* command had already been activated.

"How was I supposed to deduce that you truly just wanted to talk?" he finally responded. "From all accounts, you are still actively suffering from the false belief that your inability to graduate is my fault. It would be odd if you *weren't* holding a grudge. With that in mind, I don't know how you can conclude that I'm the one in the wrong."

Back when Sangwoo had been in middle school, a teacher had slapped him across the face after he'd talked back to them in a similar tone. *"You can't keep talking to people like that when you're out in the real world,"* he'd been told countless times, and he'd made an effort to fix his speech patterns as a result. With Jaeyoung, however, he found that he couldn't keep the venom out of his voice.

Strangely enough, Jaeyoung remained completely nonchalant as he said, “I *would* have graduated if you hadn’t run your mouth to the professor. Two damn credits, and now I can’t go to grad school abroad.”

“I still fail to see how that was my fault.”

“Sangwoo—,” Jaeyoung began, but Sangwoo cut him off.

“Stop acting like we’re friends. And did you really think you would be able to graduate after making someone answer the roll call for you? Why do you think other students go to class every day? Moreover, do I seem like a dimwit who would include some deadbeat’s name as a contributor on the project?”

Despite the barrage of words, there was no hint of surprise on Jaeyoung’s face. “Yeah… I figured you’d be like this.”

“Now, may I be excused?”

“No, I’m not done yet.” Jaeyoung took a deep drag of his cigarette and exhaled the gray smoke, then spat, “You think you’re some kind of saint? Or upholder of the law? Don’t try to lecture me, asshole. You don’t get to be the judge of my actions.”

“Fine. You can continue being a lowlife if you wish, but please do refrain from contacting me.”

“Shit… You’re a real piece of work, aren’t you?” Jaeyoung’s eyes were cold as he put out his cigarette. “I’m just trying to be friendly, okay? It’s not like I asked you to grovel for forgiveness or beg the professor to reverse his decision. The least you could do is act a bit embarrassed instead of trying to judge me for my sins.”

Although the anger in Jaeyoung’s voice was obvious, Sangwoo was a little lost as to what he was trying to get across. In the end, he responded, “I’m not quite sure what you mean. If there’s something you want from me, just say it outright.”

He hadn’t meant to offend, but Jaeyoung looked like he’d just been attacked. Dumbfounded, he gaped at Sangwoo like a fish, opening and closing his mouth a few times, before crossing his arms and leaning further back into his chair. His face twisted into a scowl.

“Repeat after me: ‘I’m sorry that you can’t go on your awesome study abroad program because of me.’”

It was an easy task. Sangwoo opened his mouth confidently, but...the words stuck in his throat. Jaeyoung's sentence contained a glaring error, or perhaps two.

"Only if you correct both errors in that sentence. Firstly, I'm not the reason you couldn't graduate. It was because you missed too many classes and you didn't get points from the project. Secondly, I am not sorry."

Once the feedback was applied, his new task would be to say, "You can't go on your awesome study abroad program." That was the truth, so he had no issue speaking it aloud.

"Shit, you're such a weirdo," Jaeyoung snapped, his voice full of derision.

The name-calling didn't affect Sangwoo in the slightest—it was an insult he had already heard many times.

Jaeyoung turned his chair back to face his monitor, then stirred his bowl of instant noodles with a pair of chopsticks. "Damn, the noodles are all soggy," he muttered. He shoved the tray back at Sangwoo, snapping, "Take it back."

Sangwoo wordlessly obeyed, but as he turned around to walk out of the room, Jaeyoung called out to him yet again.

"Hey!"

"Yes?" he responded calmly.

"I never wanna see your face again, you hear me?"

In terms of results, Sangwoo couldn't have asked for anything better. Somehow, it appeared that he had unintentionally defeated his opponent. Jaeyoung was shooing him away with an exasperated expression.

Sangwoo nodded. "My shift ends at 10 PM. Make sure to leave the building after I'm gone."

"You crazy asshole..."

You're one to talk, you sleazy scumbag, Sangwoo thought to himself as he walked out of the smoking room.

return 0;

Sangwoo's life returned to normal after the conclusion of his and Jaeyoung's ridiculous feud. He diligently studied in the school library every single day, even though he was on break. However, he was still facing a serious issue: he had yet to find a new designer for *Veggie Man*. He'd made another post on the school forum, saying he was looking for a designer to make graphics for an action game, but his inbox remained empty. This was quite problematic, since he'd intentionally scaled back his schedule for the next semester, anticipating that he'd be dedicated to working on the game. If he couldn't find a designer, he'd end up wasting all that precious time. Other than that, the rest of his life was going well.

That was until, on a day like any other, Sangwoo decided to head over to the dining hall after meeting his studying quota. On his way, he beheld a large box walking toward him, a smaller one perched on top of it. They were being carried by a student who was obviously struggling and unable to see anything in front of her.

Sangwoo glanced at her feet. Then, after a brief examination of her walking patterns, he concluded that she had only a few seconds left before tripping on a protrusion. Moments later, he heard her shout, "Nooo!"

The smaller box fell, spilling a variety of random items, including a reading stand, a roll of tape, and several bags of snacks. Unfortunately, the spot where they landed was on an incline, and they began to roll downhill.

The girl desperately reached out with one arm and chased after the items, but it seemed to be a lost cause. Though he found her rather pitiful, Sangwoo continued on his way. After all, his objective was to reach the dining hall.

As he walked past her, the girl called out, "Excuse me!"

Sangwoo immediately stopped walking.

"I-I'm really sorry, but could you help me out? These boxes are killing me. I'll treat you to a meal in return!"

"Where are you headed?"

"The lockers on the third floor of the library!"

Gears began to turn in Sangwoo's head. At a brisk walk, he could reach the library in about seven minutes. He didn't even have to refer to the meal prices at the dining hall—it was a deal that would pay him far above minimum wage.

Giving the girl an affirmative response, Sangwoo turned his focus to helping her gather up all the fallen items and put them back in the smaller box. Once that was done, he proceeded to lift the bigger one with both hands.

The girl began to fidget with embarrassment. "Sorry, it's super heavy, right? I'll take the smaller one."

"Yes, it really is. What's inside?"

"Oh, you know… Just some books."

The box was indeed "super heavy," as the girl had put it. Even though Sangwoo took two breaks along the way, he still had to remove his puffer jacket to avoid getting too sweaty. What he'd thought would be a seven-minute trip ended up taking fifteen minutes, and by the time he reached the third floor of the library, he was limp from exhaustion. It was clear that the energy he had exerted was worth far more than a single meal, and he regretted making such a foolish choice.

"Thanks so much, Sangwoo! You're my savior," the girl, who introduced herself as Jihye, exclaimed. In the fifteen minutes it'd taken to get the boxes upstairs, she'd not only learned Sangwoo's name, age, and major, but she'd also swiftly shifted from speaking to him like a stranger to addressing him like a close friend.

Most people, especially underclassmen, didn't try to strike up a conversation with Sangwoo since he had a naturally standoffish look about him, but Jihye seemed to be built differently.

As the two of them walked out of the library, she asked, "Is there anything you wanna eat?"

"You can just buy me a meal ticket. It's fine."

Jihye gasped dramatically. "No way! I'm not letting you eat at the school dining hall. I *have* to buy you a really nice meal to express my undying gratitude, okay? C'mon, follow me."

"All right."

"Oh, and stop acting so stiff! We're friends now, not strangers."

"If you say so…"

Jihye swore that it would only take ten minutes to get to the restaurant she had in mind, but Sangwoo could already tell that the trip would be considerably longer. He was slightly peeved that he was going to have to walk so far just for a single meal, but he decided he wouldn't complain. He'd been the one who'd agreed to let Jihye pick their destination, after all.

It turned out that Jihye loved to talk. Even though Sangwoo didn't respond to most things she said, she kept chattering on.

"I'm telling you, this Italian place is *the best.* The pasta's amazing, of course, but the pizza dough is super thin and crispy, too. I love it! I got Alfredo pasta in one of their bread bowls last time, and it was so good I practically ate the freaking plate! Oh, and they give a ten-percent student discount, and every single worker there looks like a celeb…"

As Jihye continued to describe their destination, they left campus and walked down a street lined with bars, all swarmed by undergrads. Jihye confidently led Sangwoo into a quieter alley and pointed to the second floor of a building. There was a sign with a single tree drawn on it. The simplicity of its design gave the sign a quiet aura of elegant confidence, as if to vouch for the restaurant's quality.

The stairs below led to a large door, and a small bell rang as Sangwoo pushed it open. Dim lights illuminated the spacious interior, and the furnishings added to the space's warm and welcoming ambience.

A hostess greeted them, then asked if they had a reservation and how many people were in their party. Shortly after, they were shown to an empty table.

"The only requirement to work here is being smoking hot, I swear," Jihye said in a hushed voice as she glanced around.

Ignoring her, Sangwoo took a seat and immediately began to analyze the menu. *Am I seeing this right?* he wondered, doubting his eyesight. Even the lowest-priced item was more than three times the amount he usually paid for food of any kind. It was completely unreasonable in his opinion, especially since most of the dishes on the menu were primarily composed of some sort of starch. It was *definitely* not the kind of compensation he deserved for just lifting a couple of boxes.

After a pause, he asked, "Are you sure you can afford this?"

"Eh, it's a special occasion! I'll just starve a bit at the end of the month," Jihye replied cheerfully.

The logic for making such a decision escaped Sangwoo, but there was no reason for him to concern himself with the status of someone else's bank account. Instead, he turned his eyes to the menu as Jihye began to shower him with praise for basically saving her life. *Fresca* citrus salad, *cacciucco alla livornese, calamari fritti*... The list of unfamiliar items went on and on. Sangwoo pronounced each one in his head, eyes narrowed in concentration.

Suddenly, a kind voice broke into his thoughts. "Are you ready to order?"

Before Sangwoo could say anything, Jihye piped up, "One *spaghetti alle vongole* for me, please!"

"I'll get...," Sangwoo began, fully prepared to order the most expensive pasta dish on the menu. However, his words trailed off when he made eye contact with the server.

Maybe the restaurant *did* value the workers' looks above everything else—even Sangwoo had to admit the server was an unusually handsome man, even though he did not normally pay attention to others' appearances when interacting with them.

The man's hair was combed over neatly, keeping his hair out of his slim, smiling face. His monolid eyes were bright and large, and his nose was straight and perfectly shaped, perking up just a bit at the tip. Overall, his appearance was neat and dashing, his white shirt and black apron only adding to the effect.

Have I seen him before? Sangwoo wondered as he stared intently at the man. *Maybe he's some kind of model and I came across him in an ad...?* He was still deliberating when the server's lips curled up into an icy smile.

"Sangwoo? Hello?" Jihye urged Sangwoo impatiently, snapping him out of his thoughts.

He quickly ordered some pasta with lobster, and the server jotted down their orders on his notepad.

"One *spaghetti alle vongole* and one lobster tortellini—got it. Can I get you anything else?"

"You guys do discounts for Hanguk University students, right?" Jihye asked.

"Of course. Actually, I'm also a student there," said the server as he smiled and marked something on his notepad.

Jihye's voice grew more excited as she took out her student ID from her wallet and showed it to him. "I already knew that! I've seen you a few times while passing the art department. I saw that play last year, too—*The Salesman*! It was crazy difficult to get those tickets."

The server took her ID and examined it closely before handing it back to her. "A French major?" he noted. But strangely, he directed a somewhat unfriendly gaze right at Sangwoo when he continued, "I guess it makes sense. Some of you have pretty *unique* tastes."

Completely oblivious to the biting undertone, Jihye laughed and said, "I'm the only French major here. Sangwoo, what was yours again?"

Sangwoo had no desire to share details of his life with a stranger, and he thought it was completely unreasonable for the server to glare at him even though they had just met. So he simply asked, "You got our orders, right? I suggest you get back to work."

Silence washed over the table. Jihye looked like she was watching a horror movie unfold in front of her, but the server's smirk just grew even more bitter.

"It's nice that you're so consistent," he muttered quietly, picking up his notepad and pen. After announcing that it would take about twenty minutes for the food to be ready, he walked away.

Jihye glanced at Sangwoo nervously. "Are you upset?"

"No."

Jihye chewed on her lip nervously, as though she didn't believe Sangwoo's honest answer. "I—I swear I didn't mean to make you mad. I'm so sorry… My stupid tongue just slips up sometimes."

"I told you, I'm fine."

"I'm so, so, so sorry!" Jihye bowed her head and began to grovel like she had committed some awful crime.

"Stop that. I said I'm fine."

"I—I know, but still…"

"That's enough."

Sangwoo sighed in annoyance and turned his head slightly, only to accidentally lock eyes with the server who had taken their order. Instead of looking away like most people would, the man stared intently back at Sangwoo as he wiped a wine glass with a cloth.

After a moment of intense eye contact, Sangwoo decided to look away first. "That server keeps glaring at me," he commented.

"Huh? No way!" Jihye discreetly glanced in the server's direction. "Oh, you're right."

"I don't think he likes me."

"Aw, I'm sure it's not that."

They filled the next twenty minutes with meaningless chitchat. Jihye asked in a low whisper if Sangwoo thought he could beat the server in a fight, and Sangwoo responded that he did not enjoy violence—if they ended up getting into a scuffle, he would simply let the server get a punch in and then call the police.

Hearing this, Jihye laughed loudly. "You're so funny. You don't look like the type..."

"What do you mean by that?"

"I mean, I didn't think you would make a joke like that."

"It wasn't a joke."

Jihye fell silent, nodding awkwardly.

After that, they sat quietly until the server came by with their food, carrying two plates on one arm. His face was strangely stiff as he set down Jihye's plate and walked around the table to place Sangwoo's dish right in front of him.

Then, talking so quietly that only Sangwoo could hear him, the server whispered, "I wasn't planning on doing this, but the more I thought about it, the more pissed off I got."

"Excuse me?"

"Why the hell are you here? You trying to pick a fight or what?"

Sangwoo blinked in surprise and finally looked up at the server, who was glaring at him with venom in his eyes. It seemed unlikely that the man would be so angry just because of a single comment.

After a brief moment of contemplation, Sangwoo decided the server had mistaken him for somebody else. "Do we know each other?" he asked.

The server's lips fell open in shock. For a long moment, he just stared at Sangwoo in disbelief, then a caustic laugh escaped him. His glare never wavered as he took out a pair of glasses from his apron and put them on.

A flash of realization struck Sangwoo like lightning when their eyes met through the oversized lenses. The deadbeat trash he'd encountered in the library meeting room had been wearing similar glasses, and the height seemed to match as well. Although he wasn't wearing any of the earrings or the painful-to-look-at clothes, Sangwoo figured the two of them had to be the same person.

"You're…the Kim dude." Belatedly, he added, "Youngjae Kim."

The server's face had already gone tight with anger. He bent over slightly and whispered right in Sangwoo's ear, "I told you I never wanted to see your face again."

"I didn't know you worked here."

"Sangwoo…"

The sugary sweet tone sent a shiver down Sangwoo's spine, and he pushed his chair back slightly to put some space between himself and the server. Unfortunately, the man shifted forward at the same time, so his handsome face remained as close as ever.

"C'mon, bro. Can't you hear me talking to you?"

"I only have a sister," Sangwoo responded curtly, his voice cracking slightly.

At this, the server scoffed. "Okay, you're just asking for it now. So, what's something you dislike?"

"You," Sangwoo answered honestly.

The server didn't even bat an eye. "Least favorite color?"

"Red." Sangwoo didn't particularly like or dislike most colors, but he *hated* red—it was the color of an error.

"Least favorite animal?"

"*Homo sapiens.*" In Sangwoo's opinion, humans were the most imperfect creatures to walk the planet. They didn't have strong claws, thick skin, or lethal venom, and were easily swayed by impulses and emotions. He silently glared at the personification of irrationality standing in front of him.

"Least favorite food?"

"Pasta." He wasn't a picky eater by any means, but at this very moment, he despised everything that had anything to do with this man.

"Least favorite place?"

"Anywhere within ten meters of you." *So please get lost,* he thought, but let the rest of his sentence go unsaid.

The server laughed coldly, breaking the brief silence that had settled after their dry exchange. Then, in that same soft tone from before, he whispered, "I was planning on just ignoring you, since you didn't seem...*normal.* But I've changed my mind. You should really look forward to next semester."

"Sure, feel free to put a hit out on me. I'll keep the police on speed dial."

"Your imagination really needs more work."

By the time Sangwoo came up with a good comeback, the server was long gone.

"Are you friends with him?" Jihye asked brightly, already halfway through her food.

"Not at all."

"Oh, I guess I should have known, since you got his name wrong. It's Jaeyoung, not Youngjae."

Sangwoo silently stabbed his pasta with his fork, but he'd entirely lost his appetite.

"He's in the drama club, and he's super popular. I know a lot about him because my friend audited a bunch of graphic design classes after watching him in a play. Apparently, J.S. Entertainment wanted to recruit him as an actor when he was twenty—"

"Stop."

Jihye blinked in confusion. "Sorry...?"

"Talk about something else."

Jihye fell silent, her face dejected. She'd maintained a stream of constant dialogue no matter the situation prior, so Sangwoo hadn't expected this sort of response. Feeling a tinge of anxiety, he began to shovel pasta into his mouth. Somehow, the food seemed to taste worse than what he typically ate at the university dining hall.

What did he mean, he "changed his mind"? Sangwoo wondered. He tried to steer his mind in another direction but ultimately found it impossible. *I just hope I never cross paths with that deadbeat again, in any way, shape, or form.*

`return 0;`

Sangwoo remained faithful to his schedule of studying during the week and working part-time over the weekend. Time flew, and before he knew it, the new semester was about to begin.

All engineering students were required to take at least two liberal arts courses, since it was apparently important for them to possess a general knowledge of the humanities. Sangwoo had chosen to take both this semester and had utilized his free time to study the textbooks and materials they would cover. The rest of his schedule only consisted of major requirements, which would give him no trouble.

	Mon	Tues	Wed	Thu	Fri
9					
10	Intermediate Chinese 10am - 11am	Embedded Systems 10am - 11am	Pop Culture and Cultural Theory 10am - 12pm	Intermediate Chinese 10am - 11am	Embedded Systems 10am - 11am
11	Engineering Math 2 11am - 12pm	Algorithms 11am - 12pm		Engineering Math 2 11am - 12pm	Algorithms 11am - 12pm
12					
1					

Up until now, he'd made sure to take more than twenty credits every single semester, but this one was different. He'd intentionally created an easy schedule for himself so that he could develop his game in peace, though, thanks to the string of inconveniences he'd run into, he was still lacking a decent designer.

Unfortunately, the class adjustment period had ended a long time ago, and Sangwoo didn't particularly feel like messing with his perfect timetable. He'd specifically arranged it so every single day of the week was perfectly balanced, and he would be able to grab lunch right after class.

When the first day of the new semester finally arrived, Sangwoo went about his day as per usual: wake up at 8:30 AM, do a brief workout, shower, then eat some cereal with milk. The next tasks on his list were to brush his teeth, then get changed.

Sangwoo's closet was divided into two sections: shirts went on the top shelf and pants went on the bottom, organized in the order they were washed. Today, he decided on a black T-shirt and black cotton pants with his usual belt. He then combed his fingers through his hair before pulling on his customary black cap. A black padded jacket, scarf, and backpack completed the ensemble. By the time he got downstairs to his bicycle, it was 9:16 AM on the dot.

When he arrived on campus and walked through the front gates, he was satisfied to find that it was exactly 9:24 AM. Sometimes he ended up being a minute or two late due to traffic conditions, which never failed to irritate him. Thankfully, this rarely ever happened.

Sangwoo put his bicycle in the bike parking area first, then headed to the humanities building. The doors opened to reveal a staircase. It had sixty-four steps in total, with short corridors located at every sixteen-step interval. It took precisely 0.9 seconds to climb one step, which meant that all combined, it took exactly sixty-one seconds to reach lecture hall 403, the classroom on the fourth floor where his Intermediate Chinese class was located.

Sangwoo entered the room thirty minutes before class started, though a brief glance revealed that a student was already sitting in one of the front rows. Not thinking much of it, Sangwoo immediately headed over to the fourth row.

"What the...?" he muttered.

There was a strange sight in front of him—more specifically, there was a bag sitting on the desk farthest to the right. He blinked in surprise, struck speechless. During the past six semesters, he had always sat in the exact same seat without anybody managing to steal it from him. The idea of sitting somewhere else felt absurd.

Fourth row, farthest to the right. It was the perfect seat. From there, he could make direct eye contact with the professor without having to crane his head back to see the podium, and whatever materials were on the board, whether a presentation or something written, were perfectly visible. In addition, it was in a spot where the air from the vents wouldn't make direct contact with his skin, and there were no windows nearby, which meant thermal conductivity was low. Furthermore, being right next to a wall made him feel much more comfortable compared to being surrounded by other students.

Whose bag could that be? Sangwoo thought with a twinge of annoyance. But it was the unfortunate truth that people could sit wherever they wanted, since there wasn't a reservation system for classroom seats like the library had.

Even as he begrudgingly headed over to the seat right next to his original choice, Sangwoo couldn't help but glance at the bag on the desk. He opened his textbook, but his attention was scattered. At last, he decided to politely ask the person if they would be willing to switch spots once they'd returned.

Immediately, Sangwoo felt a bit calmer. He wasn't a superstitious person, but he wasn't overjoyed at the thought of sitting somewhere other than his "perfect" seat for the first lecture of the new semester.

It was almost time for class to start, and the rest of the room gradually began to fill up. A male student who looked younger than Sangwoo nodded at him in recognition. "Good morning," he said.

The student's face wasn't familiar, so Sangwoo ignored him.

A moment later, a female student greeted him with an upbeat, "Didn't expect to see you here again!"

Of course, he didn't recognize her, either.

Students continued to stream into the room, but nobody took the seat with the bag. Sangwoo glared at it, noting that it was made of leather and had a single long strap so it could be worn on one's shoulder. If only he could just push it aside and reclaim his rightful place… But Sangwoo repressed the urge. Even he knew that putting a bag on a seat was an unspoken way of laying claim to it.

The professor walked into the room just three minutes before 10 AM and passed around some handouts. She said a few casual greetings, then glanced around curiously.

"It looks like the TA is running late," she said.

Given that this class was an elective, Sangwoo had to admit he was slightly impressed. Most people didn't have the passion required to volunteer as a TA outside of their major courses. Though the job came with extra credit and was a great opportunity to get to know a professor better, it was also accompanied by a list of tedious chores—the main reason most people weren't particularly motivated to take the position.

As the students looked around the room curiously, somebody walked in through the back door and raised his hand. "I'm right here, Professor," he said cheerfully.

"There you are, Jaeyoung! I haven't seen you in a while. This is the last class that I'd expect you to volunteer for."

"I still need some credits to graduate, and I figured I'd brush up on my Chinese a bit."

"Excellent," she said, nodding in approval. "Everyone, meet Jaeyoung. He will be our TA for the semester. Jaeyoung used to live in Hong Kong, so feel free to go to him with any questions you might have! He'll be collecting all your assignments for this class as well."

Sangwoo, who had been scanning the handout, flinched in surprise. But it was probably somebody else—Jaeyoung wasn't exactly a rare name.

At that moment, he heard the leather bag being lifted off the desk to his right as somebody dropped into the seat. Sangwoo genuinely didn't want to look, but his head turned before he could stop himself.

Jaeyoung Jang was wearing a red beanie and puffer jacket; they stood out so much they were nearly offensive to look at. To add insult to injury, he was wearing a red sports jersey underneath the jacket and clutched a red can of soda in one hand. It was a very small relief that he wasn't wearing red pants as well.

Sangwoo's mouth fell open in disbelief.

"I didn't realize you were in this class," Jaeyoung commented shamelessly as he took a sip of soda.

And he had the gall to call me a weirdo.

Sangwoo remained speechless even as the professor began her lecture.

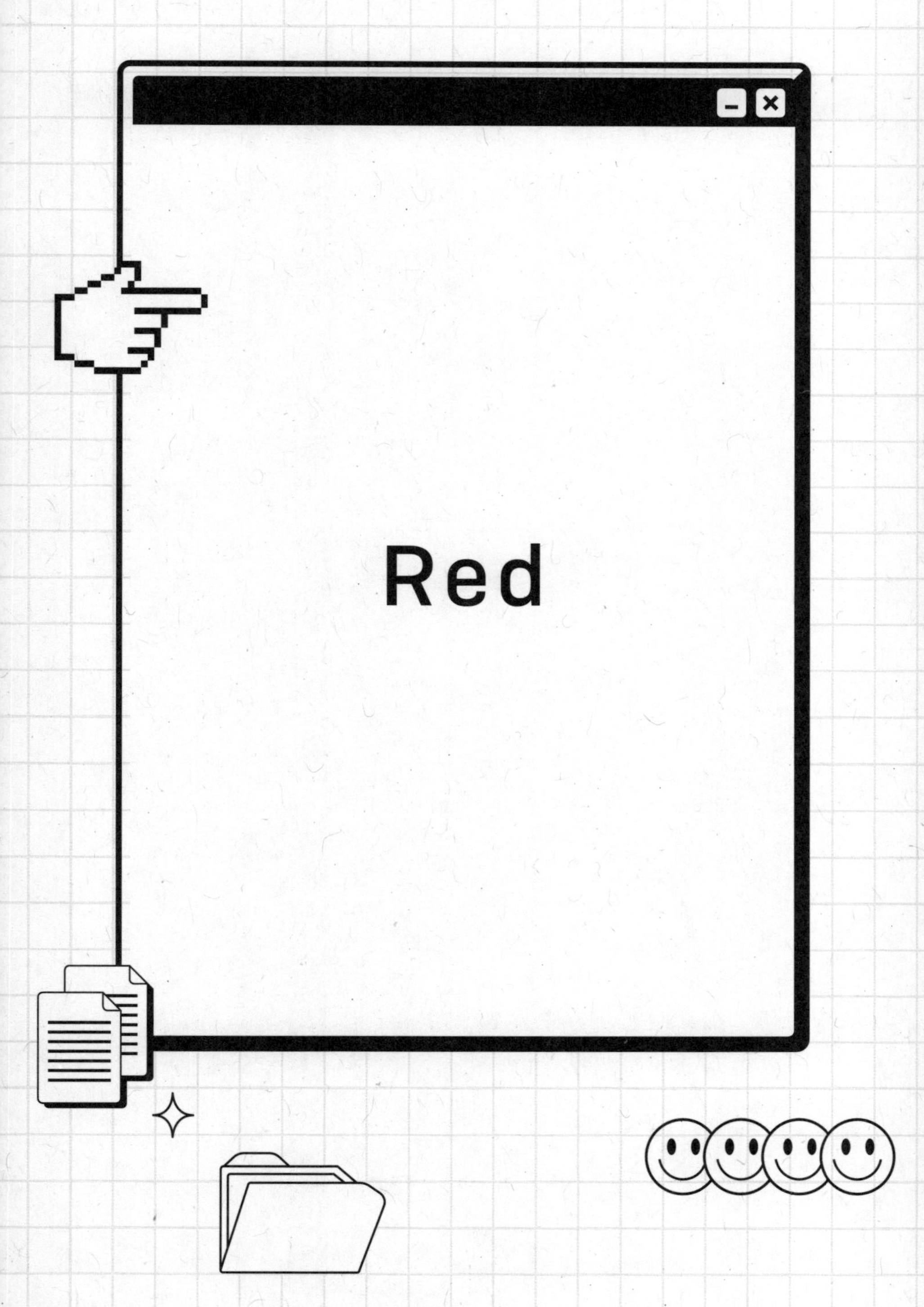

Red

The first time Jaeyoung had encountered him was four years ago, during the first semester of his junior year. For some reason, the visual arts and computer science departments had decided to have a joint welcoming party for freshmen, so they'd ended up at the same barbecue place with just a few tables separating them.

Although they were all around the same age, the two groups of students couldn't have been more different. The visual arts majors were a sea of vivid colors, every one trying to stand out over the rest. On the other hand, every article of clothing at the computer science table was monochrome, like there was some rule against wearing anything but black, white, and gray. Just judging by the meager few who'd dyed their hair compared to visual arts students, it was obvious that the word "self-expression" had an entirely different definition depending on which side of the restaurant you found yourself.

(1)

Jaeyoung remembered sitting at a table, offering drinks to freshmen and getting slightly tipsy himself, when he suddenly heard somebody say, "No."

He'd always prided himself on being good with faces, but even he couldn't recall the exact appearance of someone from years prior. On top of that, the weirdo didn't exactly stand out in the looks department. Even now, Jaeyoung would simply describe him as an average guy who looked like he had a chip on his shoulder. Still, one thing about the weirdo had caught his eye back then: his notably slender neck.

"Why not?" someone else asked. "You can't hold your drink? Is it some religious thing?"

"I *can* drink, but I don't want to at this particular moment," the first voice said firmly.

Jaeyoung discreetly looked over and saw the student representative for computer science arguing with a freshman. The computer science rep seemed to be trying to get the younger guy to down a soju bomb that had been mixed in a *makgeolli* bowl.

Word spread about a new weirdo over among the computer science majors, so even the visual arts reps put down their drinks to watch the disaster unfold.

"Hey, I'm older than you! Show some damn respect!" the computer science rep exploded.

"It has nothing to do with you," the freshman responded matter-of-factly. "Like I said, I'm just not interested in consuming any alcohol right now."

Jaeyoung shook his head in disbelief, knowing the student rep wouldn't give two shits about what a freshman had to say. Given that nearly 90 percent of computer science majors were men, it was culturally expected that any underclassman would bend over backward to follow an upperclassman's orders. Honestly, it made sense that the student rep was pissed—sure, there was the occasional oddball who refused to drink because of their religion or some allergy, but it sounded like this particular freshman had no good reason to turn down the bowl.

Unfortunately, the situation only got worse when the student rep, drunk and angry, yelled at someone to bring him a baseball bat to teach the insolent kid a lesson.

Unlike most people, the weirdo refused to back down. He pulled out his phone instead.

"Who the hell are you tryna call?" the computer science rep snapped.

"The police."

From there on out, it was total chaos. People tried to snatch the phone out of the weirdo's hand, but he ran around the restaurant, neatly evading them. The entire time, the computer science rep continued to screech at random people to bring him a baseball bat.

Jaeyoung remembered being content to watch it all from a distance until shit really hit the fan. In the end, he'd been the one who ripped the phone out of the weirdo's hand and chucked it on the floor. Then he'd helped the guy get away before his oh-so-respectable upperclassman succeeded at braining him with a frying pan. Jaeyoung might've even taken a punch to the face in the process, but he couldn't recall all the details.

The welcome party had been completely ruined, but the students had still managed to stuff themselves and get wasted after the weirdo escaped. For the remainder of the night, the guy had been the talk of the room, and definitely not in a good way. Jaeyoung remembered the computer science rep declaring that he'd throttle the asshole with his bare hands. But given the weirdo was still alive, it seemed that had proven harder than expected.

Realistically, it made sense that nobody had been able to torment the guy; he wasn't involved in any clubs or the student council. He literally only showed up for class, nothing more. Still, from what Jaeyoung had heard, the computer science rep had bullied him in every form and fashion he'd been capable of as a sophomore, but the freshman hadn't been affected in the slightest. Apparently, he hadn't cared if he had to eat alone in the dining hall, or if someone insulted him to his face. And if things started to get violent or people tried to physically block him from going to class, the guy would just call the police.

Honestly, the most surprising part about the whole thing was that the weirdo happened to be an extremely diligent and talented student. In spite of the numerous efforts to bring him down, he'd ended up with the highest GPA in his entire department. The prominent theory among the computer science majors was that he could write in programming languages like they were his mother tongue because he was a machine himself.

The only one who'd ultimately suffered from the entire fiasco was probably the computer science rep. Facing such a complete, utter defeat must have left some lasting scars.

Jaeyoung never imagined he'd end up interacting with the weirdo directly—

(2)

...or so he'd thought, but there they were, taking the same elective the following semester.

Around that time, Jaeyoung had been the furthest thing from an early bird, spending his evenings and nights getting absolutely hammered. As a result, he was always late to class, which meant he always sat at the very back of the room. And the other guy? He'd sat in the same seat every single class: the one right in front of Jaeyoung.

Despite how hungover he'd been back then, Jaeyoung could still remember thinking that the weirdo's neck was strangely pretty, and that he had really pale skin for a man. That stupid neck had frequently distracted him from the lecture, although he wouldn't have paid close attention regardless.

However, the two of them had never talked, and the weirdo had soon faded from Jaeyoung's memory after, in the middle of the semester, the older man decided he couldn't be bothered to keep going to class.

(3)

The next time Jaeyoung encountered the then-freshman, the guy had been standing in front of a convenience store.

He'd looked at Jaeyoung with eyes that were both indifferent and slightly upturned. Then, without any preamble, he'd declared: "I loaned you 850 won precisely three days ago. I would like it back."

Though caught off guard, Jaeyoung grabbed a thousand-won bill from his wallet, probably because he felt a little guilty about staring at the weirdo's neck during class. The guy took the money from him and carefully scanned it, as if he suspected that Jaeyoung had given him a fake bill.

Weirdly enough, Jaeyoung found himself marveling over how thick the guy's lashes were. He glanced at the baseball hat—apparently a permanent part of the guy's daily outfit—wishing he could take it off and get a better look at the other man's eyes.

Finally, he muttered, "I need to provide some change, but I don't have any coins."

"Oh, don't worry about it."

The weirdo ignored Jaeyoung and quickly ran into the convenience store. After a few seconds, he came back and placed exactly 150 won into Jaeyoung's palm.

At that moment, a tall, well-built man came up to them and greeted the freshman. The computer science major looked between him and Jaeyoung in visible confusion.

"By the way, I borrowed money from you, right? Or was it somebody else?" asked the tall student.

"Yes, it was me. I loaned you 850 won."

"Here. Just take this."

The weirdo accepted the thousand-won bill, then diligently passed it to Jaeyoung. "I mistook you for somebody else," he said. "Please return the 150 won to me."

Jaeyoung admittedly felt a bit stupid as he took the offered cash and returned the coins to the freshman, who then handed the coins to the tall student and disappeared in a blink. It took him a few minutes to finally realize what had just happened. Although the other student had looked nothing like Jaeyoung, they both had brightly dyed hair, which was why the weirdo had mistaken the two.

By the time Jaeyoung completed the second semester of his junior year and enrolled for his mandatory military service, the shock and confusion of that day had faded away, along with any thoughts of the weirdo. When he'd returned to school after being discharged, his schedule had been filled with classes, freelance work, playing sports, and drama club activities.

The second semester of his senior year had been particularly busy, to the point he'd barely had time to eat and sleep. Still, when an underclassman had begged him to be the MC for the school festival, Jaeyoung hadn't been able to turn the desperate kid down. In the end, he'd wound up moderating several events and had walked around campus interviewing students with the broadcasting club's cameraman.

(4)

It was during one of those interviews that Jaeyoung ran into the weirdo again, this time right in front of the engineering building.

He was wearing his black baseball cap, a dark-green checked flannel, dark straight-legged jeans, and a pair of worn sneakers. He was a bit tanner and more muscular compared to how he'd looked in his freshman year, probably because of his own military service. But his eyes, totally cool and indifferent, hadn't changed one bit.

Jaeyoung's next action had been more impulsive than anything else. For some reason, he'd been happy to see the guy again after so long, so he'd walked right up to him and said, "Hey! How are you enjoying the festival?"

But Jaeyoung had made a critical mistake—he'd assumed the other man would recognize him. Instead, the guy didn't even glance at him as he responded, "No, I'm not interested."

A surge of annoyance created a lump in Jaeyoung's throat, though he wasn't quite sure where the emotion had come from. But when the weirdo began briskly walking away, he followed, refusing to give up.

Pushing the microphone closer to the guy's face, Jaeyoung said insistently, "Come on, you're on camera! Anything to say about this wonderful festival?"

"I hope all universities get rid of festivals in the future. I find them both uninteresting and unenjoyable, so kindly stop trying to force me to enjoy myself."

While Jaeyoung had stood there, trying to process what he'd just heard, the weirdo had strode off far into the distance. Jaeyoung had turned to the underclassman holding the camera and laughed over how absurd the comment was, but he'd been silently boiling with anger.

That being said, his life had been too amazing back then for such a minor incident to put a dent in his mood. Just a few months before his graduation, Jaeyoung had won the grand prize at an international branding competition, subsequently attended the award ceremony in Singapore, and was accepted to a master's program at a top design school in the U.S. thanks to his awards and stand-out portfolio. In the latter half of the semester, he'd started skipping most of his classes, choosing to hang out with his friends and prepare for his last drama club play instead.

To put it simply, his life had been good. "Had" being the operative word, since before long, he'd received horrifying news.

Ethics for Hanguk University Students (Required course) — FAIL
Verdict — Graduation Prohibited

He'd genuinely had no idea he could get so completely screwed over by an elective, let alone one that was only two credits. Plus, everybody knew Ethics was a complete waste of time. Each semester, the hundred-plus students that signed up got crammed into a classroom, forced to listen to a series of useless lectures, and ordered to put together bullshit presentations so the professor had something to do for the last few classes. Although passing it was a requirement to graduate, nobody gave a shit since all you had to do to pass was show up.

Obviously, Jaeyoung had never gone for a variety of reasons—he was basically allergic to classes with such a stupid topic, not to mention that he'd been too busy with his competitions and drama club to care. Above all, he'd blindly trusted an underclassman's promise to answer roll call for him and take care of the group project.

To be fair, he'd learned much later that very underclassman had gotten dragged down on the same sinking ship he had.

"I'm so sorry, Jaeyoung," the underclassman had told him. "If it makes you feel any better, I'm screwed, too... I went to every single class, but I still got an F because the professor gave me a zero for the group project. The leader is such a heartless asshole. I can't believe I have to deal with this on top of my great-aunt's funeral."

Jaeyoung had scrambled to buy a premium green tea set from Jeju Island to present to the professor, along with a whole spiel about how sorry he was. He'd made sure to mention the amazing grad school opportunity that he'd been given, and that he was planning to serve as a good representative of both Hanguk University and South Korea itself while studying abroad.

Unfortunately, the professor hadn't budged. He'd just said in a tired tone, "I do think it's quite unfortunate, but there's nothing I can do for you. I told the head of the arts department the same thing when she dropped by to go to bat for you. Honestly, you should have informed me that you wouldn't be coming to class because you're about to graduate. Forging attendance has been a hot topic recently, so I'm afraid I can't just sweep it under the rug. Maybe if nobody had ever found out..." He'd trailed off with a shrug. "That student really was quite stubborn."

It had almost sounded like the professor would be willing to overlook the issue of Jaeyoung's attendance if he managed to change the group leader's mind. Thus encouraged, a fuming Jaeyoung had gotten the guy's number from his underclassman buddy, but that dipshit had never responded to any of his texts or calls. Eventually, Jaeyoung had realized he'd probably been blocked.

At that point, it was winter vacation, which meant Jaeyoung would have to go and talk to the guy in person. Unfortunately, the asshole's address had been harder to find than a damn unicorn. Jaeyoung had looked through the member directories of the movie club, a cappella club, judo club, and countless others, but not a single one of them contained the name "Sangwoo Choo." The mysterious group leader was a returning student who didn't participate in extracurriculars, so even the admin staff of the computer science department wasn't much help. The grade-correction period had ended during this wild goose chase.

Jaeyoung's initial despair had worn off within a few days, mainly because he'd brought the situation upon himself with his own laziness. In fact, once he'd come to terms with his new reality and being the laughingstock of every single social gathering he attended, he found it pretty hilarious. Though that didn't mean he hadn't talked shit about this so-called "Sangwoo" with his friends.

The fact was, Jaeyoung could afford to laugh at his own misfortune. Sure, he was graduating later than he expected, but compared to some of the guys who were just returning from the military, the timeline for his future had barely been affected at all. Furthermore, his portfolio was so solid that he'd definitely be able to study abroad or get a job despite the unplanned half-year delay.

That'd been when Suyoung came into the picture. She was a fellow Hanguk University student who was the same age as Jaeyoung, and was graduating at the end of the current semester after several gap years. She'd been planning to stay at Hanguk Uni for her graduate degree, but had recently gotten a job offer from a large overseas company and been left scrambling.

"Hey! I heard all about how your graduation plans got screwed up," was the first thing she said upon seeing Jaeyoung. "Wanna work on a mobile game instead?"

"A game? Like a student project?"

"Yeah! The developer is supposed to be some kind of computer science prodigy, and I think it'll be fun! Plus, you have a ton of free time, don't you? If you ask me, working on it would be better than being a total bum."

Jaeyoung had raised an unimpressed eyebrow. "Basically, you want me to do your job."

"Yeah… Something like that," Suyoung had muttered, then looked at him with large, pleading eyes. "Could you *please* do this for me? I just don't have the time for this right now, and the developer is a bit…particular, if you get what I mean. Even if you end up turning it down, please just go to the meeting for me and explain that I can't do the project anymore. C'mon, I'm begging you!"

"I don't work for free."

Suyoung gave a desperate nod. "Of course! I'll buy you drinks as soon as my schedule frees up a bit."

Although Jaeyoung had pretended to accept her request reluctantly, the truth was that he was so free that he'd been wasting away his days gaming in the clubroom. But what Suyoung didn't know couldn't hurt her.

* * *

(5)

When Jaeyoung had walked into the meeting room, he'd thought he was dreaming. There he was: the same idiot who'd tried to square up against an upperclassman as a freshman, had an unusually pale neck, and never managed to remember Jaeyoung's face. True to form, the punk didn't recognize him yet again.

To say that the meeting had turned out to be more entertaining than Jaeyoung had expected would have been a colossal understatement. The other guy's initial air of caution had fallen away when Jaeyoung showed off his portfolio, and Jaeyoung had found himself becoming more and more excited about the guy's coding skills, since they were rumored to be nothing short of mythical. This anticipation nearly overshadowed the extreme irritation he'd been feeling about his botched graduation plans.

At some point, the weirdo had even signaled his willingness to share his contact information with Jaeyoung by asking, "Could I have your number, then?"

Unfortunately, things had gone downhill from there. By the time Jaeyoung realized the weirdo was *the* group leader, the little shit had already disappeared from the meeting room, leaving only a notebook behind.

The frustration over his delayed graduation plans because of two damn credits bubbled up inside him anew. He'd tried to get the weirdo to meet with him again, thinking he might feel better if he gave the guy a good scolding, but the weirdo ghosted him once more.

Jaeyoung had been angry—like, truly, honestly, *fuming* mad. But he'd also known that it was too late to correct his grade, so beating the shit out of the weirdo wouldn't fix anything. And anyway, he still didn't have a clue where the guy lived.

In the end, he'd been forced to move on.

(6)

That is, until one peaceful weekend when Jaeyoung encountered the weirdo once more. He'd gone to an internet café to play games with his friends, only to see the weirdo manning the counter. Immediately, he'd thought of a variety of ways to make the guy's life miserable, but he'd also known that he'd need a *special* form of torture if he truly wanted to torment him. After all, the list of people who'd failed to bully the guy was long.

Ultimately, he'd forced himself to be calm. To be patient. But unfortunately, it'd been nearly impossible to focus on gaming when the weirdo's mere presence pissed Jaeyoung off.

More impulsively than anything else, Jaeyoung had ordered some ramen. It's not like he had any intention of harassing the weirdo by forcing him to remake it over and over until it was "just right" or something like that. All he'd wanted was to see a hint of apology or discomfort in that robotic face of his.

But the weirdo had remained completely shameless until the very end. Jaeyoung had gotten so pissed off he'd cussed the guy out, feeling an odd sense of solidarity with the students who'd tried to bully the weirdo in the past.

"Fine. You can continue being a lowlife if you wish, but please do refrain from contacting me," the guy had told him.

Did this guy get raised by wolves or something? Jaeyoung had wondered, fighting the urge to punch him in the face. He'd only held himself back because he knew he wouldn't get an ounce of satisfaction from it. The weirdo would just call the police without so much as a wince.

The truth was, Jaeyoung had kind of grown fond of the guy after observing him for several years despite what others said about him. It made sense, since Jaeyoung had always been drawn to outcasts and rebels.

Now that he'd been forced to deal with the weirdo *personally*, however, those feelings had been washed entirely away by a flood of irritation and disgust.

I hope I never see that asshole again.

(7)

The weirdo had made it crystal clear that he never wanted to see Jaeyoung. Therefore, it'd come as a rather nasty surprise when he'd walked right into the restaurant where Jaeyoung worked, and with a pretty girl in tow.

It was a well-known fact that Jaeyoung worked there—the place was owned by one of his close friends who'd asked him to be a server. He'd been a fixture of the establishment since the day it opened.

Unsurprisingly, he'd felt his blood boil the moment the weirdo walked through the door. His heart had been pounding away in his chest as he walked over to the little dipshit's table to meet his challenge head-on. But then, to Jaeyoung's shock, the weirdo had simply ordered pasta. Even worse, there had been absolutely no recognition in the guy's eyes when he'd glanced at him.

In that moment, a strange emotion had swept over Jaeyoung like a wave, powerful enough that it swept away even the immense anger he'd felt at the computer science student ever since the younger man had screwed him over.

Which made him wonder: Why *did* the weirdo rile him up so much? As the kitchen prepared the order, Jaeyoung had carefully tried to pinpoint the answer. When he really thought about it, the answer had been obvious—Sangwoo Choo treated him like he was a tiny, insignificant rock on the side of the road.

To be fair, some of their encounters—from the freshman welcome party, the 850-won incident, and the campus festival interview—had happened a long time ago. Jaeyoung wasn't unreasonable; he understood if the weirdo didn't remember those incidents. But not recognizing the very person he'd screwed out of graduation? That was crossing the line.

Any normal person would have the basic human decency to pretend to be embarrassed, especially since Jaeyoung had extended an olive branch first. However, it was clear that Sangwoo felt he'd done nothing wrong. He'd just wanted Jaeyoung to get the hell out of his life.

When that weirdo had looked at him and said, "You're...the Kim dude. Youngjae Kim," his tone had made it obvious that he thought of Jaeyoung's displays of anger as mere tantrums. It was no wonder a simple outfit change had been enough to make the guy think he was someone else.

Never in his life had Jaeyoung met anybody with the ability to make him feel so insignificant and meaningless. While that feeling had driven the computer science rep years ago to try and crush the weirdo under his foot, Jaeyoung's anger had taken a different form. He just wanted Sangwoo Choo to *notice* him. He wanted the other student's nonchalant face to crumple with some kind of intense emotion. He wanted to open that meticulously organized skull and carve his name there.

"What's something you dislike?" he'd asked the weirdo.

"You."

Too easy, Jaeyoung had thought. He'd come up with a master plan the moment he got off work that day. First, he'd used the weirdo's schedule, which was in the notebook left behind after their interview, to rewrite his own. After that, he had done some reconnaissance.

He'd talked to the security guards at the front and back gates, the servers at the dining hall, the dining hall nutritionist, the owner of the convenience store, the administrative work-study employees, the librarian, the construction workers at the futsal court, and all the students who'd taken a class with the weirdo in the previous semester. He asked them all the same question: "Do you know Sangwoo Choo? He's a student here, and he's usually dressed in black clothes with a black baseball cap."

The results had been quite interesting, to say the least.

"Yes, I know him. He rides his bike to school at the exact same time every day," the security guard had said.

"Oh, him?" the convenience store owner had responded with a nod. "He buys the same kind of coffee at the same time every single day. He's never purchased anything else."

"Last semester, he came to the library at exactly 4:02 PM every single day without fail," the librarian had observed. "It's like he has some kind of internal clock..."

The construction worker had chuckled and asked, "The guy who's always walking around by himself, you mean? I noticed he always walks past us at exactly forty-one minutes to the hour. Then he walks around that corner and throws away his coffee in the second trash can. Maybe he doesn't like the other ones."

As for the students, one had told Jaeyoung thoughtfully, "I remember him sitting in the same seat every single day for the entire semester."

Basically, Sangwoo Choo was much more abnormal than Jaeyoung had ever imagined. And given those who'd tried their hand at annoying the guy beforehand had demonstrated he couldn't be affected through normal means, Jaeyoung would have to come at this from the weirdo's perspective.

With that in mind, he'd poured all his energy into coming up with a plan that would ruin the weirdo's precious, perfect daily routine. The day before classes began, Jaeyoung was excited to return to campus, his plan ready to be set into motion.

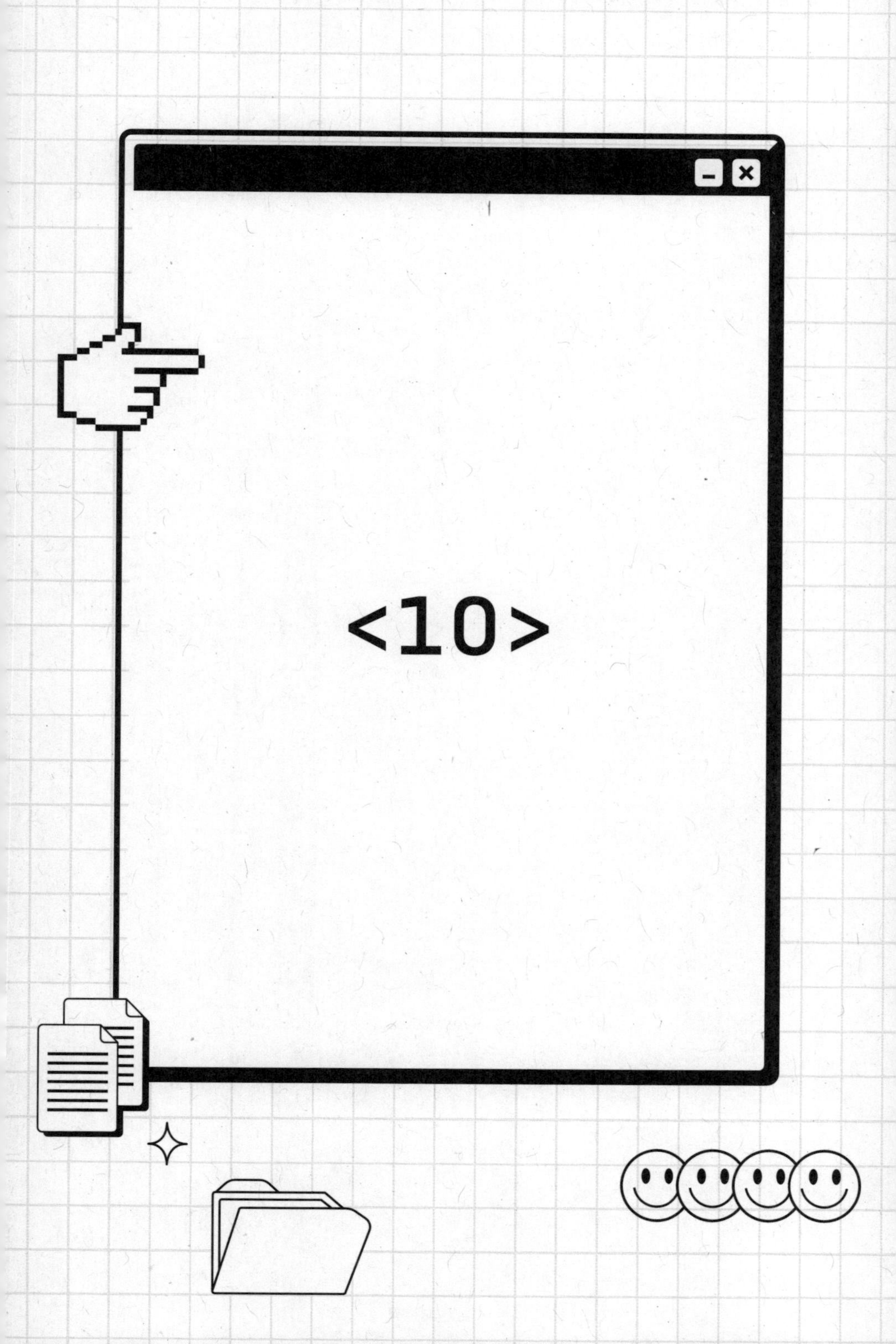
<10>

No matter how hard Sangwoo tried to focus on his Intermediate Chinese class, his efforts were thwarted by the irritating presence seated next to him. He couldn't help but notice when Jaeyoung would spin a pen around his fingers, bounce his leg, or occasionally bump against Sangwoo with his elbow. Although the class was only fifty minutes, it felt like five long hours.

When the professor dismissed everyone, a huge wave of relief swept over Sangwoo. He sprang to his feet and practically ran out the door without a backward glance, leaving behind Jaeyoung, who was carefully coloring the corner of his desk with a pen.

"I was planning on just ignoring you, since you didn't seem... normal. *But I've changed my mind. You should really look forward to next semester,"* Jaeyoung had said. Had he been implying he'd do his best to disrupt Sangwoo in all his classes?

A ball of anxiety began to form in Sangwoo's chest, but he forced it away. It was much more plausible to assume that their schedules had coincidentally overlapped. Anything more sinister was extremely unlikely.

But when he arrived at his next classroom in a frantic rush, Sangwoo once again found a bag occupying the seat that had always been his. This time, it was a navy backpack.

Sangwoo tried to calm himself by taking several deep breaths. Someone else must have caught on to how perfect that seat was. It was simply an unfortunate coincidence.

He sat down next to the spot that should have been his, then forced himself to open up his textbook. But he was so angry he couldn't even process the letters. Sweat began to dampen the page that his fist was resting on.

He was going to have to see that demon every single Monday morning, which meant he wasn't going to be able to focus on the contents of the lectures *at all*. It was unbelievable.

As Sangwoo cursed inwardly, the owner of the backpack arrived. He wasn't the least bit interested in seeing who it was, but his head still turned before he could stop himself. His eyes jumped from one item to another: a red puffer jacket, a red sports jersey, a red hat, and finally, a red can of soda.

It was his archnemesis.

Jaeyoung Jang slung his leather shoulder bag and navy backpack across the back of his seat and sat down. For about thirty seconds, Sangwoo just sat there and stared at him like he was an alien.

Jaeyoung took a sip of his soda and grinned at him.

This couldn't be happening. Sangwoo immediately rose to his feet, but he couldn't skip this class. Instead, he went and put the greatest distance possible between himself and Jaeyoung.

After a few minutes, the professor walked in and began to take attendance. When he reached Jaeyoung's name, he raised an eyebrow and pushed up his glasses.

"Jaeyoung Jang, visual arts major… Are you sure you're in the right class?"

"Yes, sir. I happen to love math," Jaeyoung responded enthusiastically.

"That's well and good, but this class isn't just regular math—it's geared toward engineering. Do you still want to take it?"

The professor sounded pleasantly intrigued, which was in stark contrast to Sangwoo's utter dismay. He dropped his head into his hands, clutching at his hair and gnashing his teeth. So intense was his despair that he ended up missing four whole minutes of the lecture.

It didn't get any easier for him to focus after that. Not only did looking at the professor from such an unfamiliar angle throw him off, but the professor's voice sounded oddly distant for some reason. To make things worse, he felt unsettled by everything around him.

When the lecture finally concluded, Sangwoo shot out of the classroom like a bullet from a gun. He'd really been hit where it hurt, and it triggered such an overwhelming level of rage in him that his composure was completely shattered.

Sangwoo nearly sprinted to the dining hall and lined up for food. As he caught his breath, bent over with his hands on his knees, he caught a glimpse of that eyesore of a red puffer jacket. Jaeyoung was chatting with the students who had lined up behind Sangwoo.

Sangwoo suddenly felt a chill run down his back. Jaeyoung wasn't paying any attention to him, but simply being within ten meters of him made Sangwoo feel like he was about to break out into hives. The line couldn't move quickly enough.

When Sangwoo finally reached the Korean food station and got his lunch, he ended up being two minutes earlier than usual. Despite that, his body shook, vibrating with anxiety.

"Oh, look at that! There are empty seats over there!"

Over there? Where? A terrible feeling settled in Sangwoo's gut.

Jaeyoung, who had been making a show of walking past the other empty tables, sat down right next to Sangwoo, who was eating by himself in the corner.

Sangwoo had two options available:

```
  i) Go somewhere else: If Jaeyoung followed him and
repeated his actions, then it would be a waste of
time.
  ii) Stay where he is: Nothing more would happen.
```

According to Sangwoo's quick calculations, it would be best if he just ignored Jaeyoung. So that was exactly what he did, silently shoveling his food into his mouth.

Moments later, he got to witness a fascinating phenomenon.

"Whoa, Jaeyoung! Haven't seen you at the dining hall in a while!"

"Oh, hey! It's good to see you, dude," Jaeyoung replied.

"I heard they're not letting you graduate because you cussed out a professor."

"Who the hell said that?"

Despite Sangwoo's deliberate choice to sit in an empty, isolated corner of the dining hall, people quickly filled up the seats around him simply because of Jaeyoung's presence. Sangwoo mechanically continued to shove spoonfuls of food into his mouth, uncomfortable with the bustling students and cacophony of noise surrounding him. His head spun.

Once his plate was clear, he glanced at the clock: 12:22 PM. He was six minutes ahead of schedule. Sangwoo quickly stood from his seat to put his emptied tray away, then drank five cups of water at the fountain. He'd definitely eaten way too fast; it felt like there was a rock sitting in his stomach.

Making his escape via the back door, Sangwoo then walked over to the convenience store. He always had a Black Holic canned coffee after lunch, as it was the cheapest option, and it had just the right amount of liquid. He drifted past the snacks, instant noodles, and ice cream before stopping in front of three beverage fridges. His target was the fifth shelf of the third fridge.

But there was nothing there.

Maybe he had missed something? But no matter how carefully he searched, Sangwoo couldn't find any Black Holic canned coffees. This was completely unprecedented, and Sangwoo never did well in such situations. For the longest time, he just stood there, staring in despair. Then he approached the middle-aged woman who managed the store.

"Do you not sell Black Holic canned coffees anymore?" he asked with a note of desperation in his voice.

"Oh! Um…" She awkwardly averted her eyes. "Somebody bought out our entire stock yesterday afternoon."

The truth hit Sangwoo like a sledgehammer to the head. He didn't bother asking about the culprit's identity—there was only one person who could have committed such an atrocity. He had to focus on finding a solution instead.

"When are you going to restock them?"

"Hmm. It'll be at least two weeks. They're not very popular, so…"

In the end, Sangwoo was left with no choice but to purchase a drink that seemed similar enough. He staggered out of the convenience store, clutching the coffee to his chest. His day had been a complete, total mess. Nothing had gone according to plan.

Feeling dazed, he headed over to the entrance of a small trail that led up to the mountain behind the college. He always walked this particular path while drinking his coffee after lunch. It took eleven minutes to navigate from beginning to end, and it was a way to keep himself energized throughout the day.

He trudged down the road as he recalled the unsavory events from earlier in the day. Now that he thought about it, several oddities stood out to him. How had Jaeyoung known his schedule so thoroughly? How had he known where Sangwoo liked to sit and what coffee he usually bought?

He was almost like…a stalker.

Just as Sangwoo's thoughts reached that conclusion, he was met by yet another obstacle.

"Sorry, you can't go that way," someone called out.

Sangwoo stopped in his tracks. "Why not?"

"The drama club reserved it."

Just as the man had said, the entrance to Sangwoo's usual walking trail was blocked off. It wasn't too absurd a happening in the grand scheme of things, but it was certainly something that had never occurred before. And though Sangwoo couldn't help but find it suspicious that the space had been reserved on that particular day, he wasn't going to stand there and argue about it.

With a sigh, Sangwoo turned around and took another path that would take him through the campus. The new canned coffee that he'd bought ended up being so sweet it made him grimace. And strangely, when he walked past the futsal court, one of the construction workers who'd been taking a short break in front of the work site called out to him.

"That's not your usual route! What's the occasion?"

Puzzled by the query from a complete stranger, Sangwoo ignored the man entirely. *Too many bizarre things have happened today.*

After pouring the rest of his coffee down the gutter, he walked over to the School of Natural Sciences, where he knew he would find three trash cans placed in a line. He always tossed his coffee in the second trash can, since it was always empty. Today, however, it was completely full.

Sangwoo gritted his teeth and threw the empty can at the third bin, only to be even more infuriated when it bounced off the lid and fell on the ground. After picking it up and properly disposing of it, he headed to the library, practically shaking with anger.

He can't get to me here, he thought as he stormed into the library. Finally, he felt safe. Since he always reserved a study carrel as soon as spots opened at midnight, nobody could take his spot away from him.

After requesting a book that he would need later through a public computer, he located another one that would prove useful on the shelf for newer titles and checked it out. Next, he walked into the reading room and sat down at his chosen desk: the rightmost seat of the eight-seater booth in the theology corner. It was his favorite spot, and for a good reason. Most people didn't come over to this section of the library, and there were no windows that could serve as a distraction. He'd never sat anywhere else.

Glancing to the side, Sangwoo caught sight of a bag in the chair next to his. His heart skipped a beat, but it was a white tote, not a backpack or a leather shoulder bag. Relieved, he opened his computer science textbook and began his regularly scheduled study session. At some point, he got up to use the restroom.

When he came back to his seat, he found a can of Black Holic coffee on the table.

```
i) Did I purchase it? N
ii) Is the owner around? N
iii) Is it something of use to me? Y (Reason: It's Black Holic)
```

* * *

The three-step algorithm only took a few seconds, but just as Sangwoo reached out to open the drink, he saw a sticky note on the can. The handwriting was so awful that it looked like a toddler had written it with their non-dominant hand.

Property of Jaeyoung Jang

As Sangwoo scowled in disgust, a hand emerged from over his shoulder and snatched up the can. Slowly, Sangwoo looked up to meet a pair of smiling eyes, framed by large glasses, staring right back at him.

"Fancy seeing you here," Jaeyoung said cheerfully. He then picked up the white tote that had been sitting in the chair of the desk next to Sangwoo and slung it over the chair's back. His backpack and leather bag soon followed.

For a moment, Sangwoo could only gape at him in disbelief. Apparently, the asshole had carried around three entire bags just to make Sangwoo's life miserable.

Without further ado, Jaeyoung placed his red beanie on his desk and walked away. Sangwoo tried his best to focus on his textbook, but his grip was so tight on his mechanical pencil that he broke the lead twice. To him, Jaeyoung was like a cockroach—more unsettling when he was out of sight than in it. Sangwoo couldn't stop thinking about what the older man might be doing after dropping off that stupid beanie.

A moment later, Jaeyoung returned carrying three books in his hands. Sangwoo glanced at the titles: *The History of Sex*, *The Nature of Orgasms*, and *The Beauty of the Naked Form*. They were exactly the kind of books he expected a lowlife like Jaeyoung to read.

After plopping the books on top of his desk, Jaeyoung leaned back in his chair and began to flip through the pages. Whenever there was an illustration, he stopped and peered closely at it.

He really is the scum of the earth.

Although Sangwoo did his best to avoid looking over at Jaeyoung, he kept getting distracted by the sound of pages turning. Jaeyoung also kept bumping the table as he shook his leg. It was a shame that Sangwoo was the only other person sitting there—if anyone else was around, it would have been much easier to silently pressure Jaeyoung to stop.

Unfortunately, it was apparent the asshole was hell-bent on making Sangwoo's life miserable. Why else would he choose the seat right next to him and continually rattle a table that sat eight when there were six other seats farther away?

```
Express anger = Defeat
Ignore him = Victory
```

Sangwoo had encountered a guy similar to Jaeyoung in high school. At the end of the day, attention seekers like them just wanted to catch people off guard and fulfill their disgusting desire for notoriety. It was obvious that the asshole was waiting for Sangwoo to lose his cool and start cussing him out.

Sangwoo didn't want to give the asshole what he wanted, but his patience was wearing thin. He tried to force himself to reach some kind of nirvana, but when the desk shook so violently that the lead in his pencil snapped yet again, he'd had enough. He sprang to his feet, quickly grabbed his writing utensils, shut his textbook, shoved his belongings into his backpack, and began to walk away. He didn't get far, however, before Jaeyoung stretched and rose from his seat, following Sangwoo as if it were the most natural thing.

At this point, Sangwoo was too tired to feel surprised. He told himself again that it was best to ignore the asshole, but his anger just kept growing as he briskly headed down the library staircase. When Jaeyoung nearly ran into him from behind, he completely lost it. Scowling, Sangwoo spun to face him.

It was like a scene from a Western movie—two cowboys standing in a field, ready to duel to the death. For all intents and purposes, Sangwoo looked like the angry villain trying to attack Jaeyoung, the smiling, confident hero. When he glowered at him, a gust of wind even blew between them, like a set animation in a video game.

If only we were in an RPG... Sangwoo thought wistfully. If they had been, he could've taken out a weapon and stabbed Jaeyoung right in the heart. Instead, he could only attack with words.

"Have you lost your mind?" he snapped.

The blow didn't land. In fact, Jaeyoung looked more satisfied than anything else.

Sangwoo figured he would take another swipe. "Are you a stalker?"

"What a wild accusation to make. Have you ever considered that you're just too predictable?" Jaeyoung let out a leisurely yawn, then slipped his hands into his pockets. "It wasn't exactly hard to find out that you do the exact same things at the exact same places every single day. Did you seriously think nobody would notice because you wear black? You stand out more than you think."

"How did you figure out my schedule?"

Jaeyoung took a familiar notebook out from one of his three bags and tossed it at Sangwoo, who recognized it immediately as the one he'd left in the meeting room—the one with his schedule in it.

As Sangwoo stood there, his mind racing, Jaeyoung took a few steps toward him. The closeness made their difference in height much more palpable.

Determined not to appear intimidated, Sangwoo glared at Jaeyoung fiercely. "Harassing me will not give you a diploma. This is a complete waste of your time."

"Yeah, I know. Trust me, this is pretty annoying for me, too… But you really had it coming."

"What do you stand to gain from doing this?" Sangwoo demanded through gritted teeth.

Jaeyoung gave him an evil grin. "It'll make me feel better."

A chill ran down Sangwoo's spine. Initially, he'd believed he might be able to reason with Jaeyoung, but he'd been entirely incorrect.

To tell the truth, nothing Jaeyoung was saying made any sense to him. Didn't people usually hurt others in order to obtain something they desired? How was Sangwoo supposed to handle a total sadist whose only desire was to torture him?

Finally, Sangwoo asked, "What can I do to get you to stop?"

"Hmm..." Jaeyoung glanced up thoughtfully. "I dunno. Haven't thought that far ahead. Maybe you could try being a bit more polite, or repent for being such a rude asshole."

"I have nothing to *repent* for."

"Fine, then. You can just wait until I have a sudden change of heart. It happens pretty often."

"You know, I initially thought you were just a scumbag. I was unaware that you're insane."

"Thanks. I hear that a lot."

For a moment, they glared at each other silently, invisible sparks flying through the air.

Sangwoo's lips twisted into a sneer. "You must think I'm a spineless idiot. Well, you're wrong. I'm not scared of anything, and I've faced all sorts of jerks, scumbags, and freaks in the past." He injected confidence into his voice. "You're nothing more than a pest to me."

Jaeyoung shot him a bright grin. "Good to know! I do *love* a challenge."

"Do your worst, you scumbag."

"Oh, I happen to have a ton of free time on my hands, thanks to a certain asshole."

Scowling, Sangwoo turned around sharply and approached his bicycle, which he'd secured to the railing in front of the library. He made sure to obscure the code to the bike lock just in case Jaeyoung was trying to take a peek, then quickly swung himself onto the seat.

What if he deflated my tires? Sangwoo wondered suddenly. If Jaeyoung had messed with his bike, he could call the police on him right away. But despite his initial suspicions, nothing seemed amiss.

Sangwoo ended up getting home earlier than usual. He secured his bicycle to a post in front of his building, then quickly climbed the stairs to the fourth floor.

It was only when he finally stepped into his apartment that all the built-up tension drained from his body. He collapsed onto the bed without bothering to change his clothes and lay there for a long time, letting himself recover.

That was awful, he thought. It had been a horrible, horrible day. He'd been distracted during class, had eaten his lunch so quickly that it'd given him a stomachache, hadn't been able to take his usual walk, and had his library study session ruined.

Although he'd forced himself to sound confident when he was facing Jaeyoung, Sangwoo felt the exact opposite. Jaeyoung was different from the villains he'd faced in the past. The asshole was meticulous and sly, and it was unlikely that he would do something illegal that Sangwoo could use against him.

Which left him with only one solution: Withstand the torture until Jaeyoung got tired of it. The asshole's behavior so far had been bizarre enough to totally catch Sangwoo off guard, but there was one thing he knew—there was no way the jerk would stick with a class like Engineering Mathematics 2. Not only was it incredibly difficult, but he wouldn't benefit from it in any way. That meant Jaeyoung's harassment would last for two weeks at the most, since that was the duration students had to drop classes.

Two weeks. It would be a pain, but it wasn't very long in the grand scheme of things. Sangwoo could handle that; it would be an exercise in patience, nothing more. And once it was over, his world would be peaceful again.

Of course, that didn't make the situation any less annoying. A surge of anger and indignation rose in Sangwoo, but he had no one to vent them to. Not only did he suffer from a perpetual lack of friends, but most people wouldn't be able to empathize with the amount of stress he'd felt from simply having his seat robbed from him and being forced to sit next to someone else.

Needless to say, he didn't get much rest that night.

return 0;

On the second day of the new semester, Sangwoo stumbled out of his apartment an hour earlier than usual and weakly swung himself onto his bike. He usually made sure to get a full eight hours of restful sleep, but he was running on four today. He'd been snapped awake in the middle of the night thanks to a nightmare, and his entire body was now protesting as a result.

In said nightmare, a red puffer jacket had zipped open to reveal sharp teeth and tried to bite him. It felt pretty ridiculous upon waking, but in his dream, he'd only been able to run around in terror.

Sangwoo clenched his jaw and repeated his magic mantra to himself: *Just two more weeks.* It was important to steel himself against the strange, unwelcome sense of anxiety that kept whispering that his stable, peaceful life would soon collapse. All he could do was be patient; he wasn't about to drop his required courses, and even if he did, Jaeyoung would probably show up in his new classes as well. Taking a gap year wasn't an option—not for such a minor inconvenience.

When he rode his bike through the front gates of the school, the time on Sangwoo's digital watch read exactly 8:24 AM. To his relief, the campus was almost entirely empty. The only reason he'd gotten up so early was because he was determined to secure his rightful spot.

Sangwoo parked his bike in the designated area in front of the library and briskly walked to the engineering building for class. A few minutes later, he found himself standing at the door to his classroom. He pushed it open slowly, his heart pounding.

No! Sangwoo despaired. A leather shoulder bag was already placed on the rightmost desk in the fourth row. He ran over to the desk and examined the bag, but he couldn't figure out how Jaeyoung had managed to get to the classroom and take his seat so early.

Did he leave the bag here yesterday?

It was a disturbing idea, but it was much more plausible than the alternative, which was that Jaeyoung had come to school at the crack of dawn. Sangwoo was near certain that Jaeyoung was someone who'd rather die than wake up that early.

Defeat tasted bitter. Robbed of his rightful seat once again, he picked out another: the one farthest away from his original choice.

Given how early it was in the morning, the classroom heater hadn't been turned on yet, and the room was freezing. After some contemplation, Sangwoo decided he would keep his puffer jacket and scarf on.

Drowsiness began to creep in as he sat waiting. Although he had his textbook lying open on the desk, the letters were blurry. It made sense, really—he'd barely slept the night before. But he absolutely *could not* fall asleep during class.

In that case, maybe I should sneak in a short nap now instead. Sangwoo shut his textbook and put his head down on it, using it as a pillow for the first time in his life. His consciousness faded rapidly away.

When he came to, a monotonous voice was saying, "Each of your assignments is worth thirty percent of your grade, with the final project being worth the last twenty. My office and email address are listed on the syllabus. If you would like to request a meeting, reach out to the TA or send me an email. Now, let's take a look at this set of examples..."

Sangwoo blinked, only to find his vision filled with red. Jaeyoung was sitting right next to him, a mocking smile on his face, even after Sangwoo had made sure to distance himself from the asshole's stupid bag.

Sangwoo surged upright and glanced at his watch—class had started fourteen minutes ago. Every single student in the room except for him had a worksheet in front of them. Sangwoo turned back to see Jaeyoung waving one at him.

That insufferable ass...

Sangwoo frantically scanned the room, but he didn't see anybody with a spare worksheet. He entertained the idea of interrupting the professor and asking for one, but that probably wouldn't go well—it was a request he should have made at the beginning of class.

There was only one other option. Gritting his teeth, Sangwoo thrust his hand at Jaeyoung. "Give me my worksheet," he demanded in a low voice.

"*Your* worksheet? Sorry, but this is mine."

"So? I already know you won't be using it."

Jaeyoung narrowed his eyes and gave the worksheet another flap. Sangwoo reached out and tried to snatch it from him, but the older student pulled it back sharply and folded the paper in half once, then again. Sangwoo watched him, his throat tightening with anxiety.

"Did nobody ever teach you how to say 'please'?" Jaeyoung whispered, raising an eyebrow. In that moment, with his bright red outfit, he looked just like the devil. And clenched between his fingers was Sangwoo's printout—now a paper airplane.

"Give me that," Sangwoo hissed.

"Nope. I'm not hearing enough desperation."

"I said, hand it over."

The professor turned his back to the class to write something on the board, and the paper airplane flew from Jaeyoung's hand and out the back door, drawing a graceful arc through the air.

"Oops… Looks like you lost your chance."

Sangwoo stood from his seat. Rage bubbled up inside him, but he suppressed it with everything he had. He should have known better than to think that Jaeyoung would cooperate.

Trying his best to stay silent, he squeezed through the rows of desks and grabbed a worksheet from the pile on the podium. Unfortunately, the professor chose that exact moment to turn around.

"What do you think you're doing?" he demanded, giving Sangwoo a stern look.

"I'm sorry, Professor. I didn't receive a worksheet, but I thought it would be rude to disrupt the class by raising my hand."

"Well, maybe you *would've* gotten a worksheet if you weren't dozing off during your first class." The professor clicked his tongue, eyes filling with a strange mixture of exasperation and pity. "You might want to go to the bathroom before you sit back down."

"Pardon?" Sangwoo asked, confused.

"Bathroom. Now."

Slightly baffled, Sangwoo walked out through the front door, still holding the worksheet. He'd never been the type to be a teacher's pet, answering every question and making a point to visit during their office hours, but his high scores on exams and assignments were typically enough to earn his professors' trust by the end of a semester. Getting on a teacher's bad side on the first day of class was an entirely new experience. To make things even worse, Professor Choi was a well-regarded computer science teacher who usually taught advanced 400-level courses.

Questions still swirling through his mind, Sangwoo hurried into the bathroom. The sight that greeted him in the mirror was so shocking that he nearly shouted—somebody had drawn a thick, dark mustache under his nose. He frantically tried to wash it off, but he couldn't scrub it away no matter how hard he tried.

Judging his current efforts to be a waste of time, Sangwoo put some soap on his hands. His desperate rubbing seemed to yield some results, but the process was painfully slow. Precious minutes of the lecture were going down the drain along with the dirty water.

How did I end up in such a stupid situation? Sangwoo lamented. *Ugh, that asshole really lived up to his arts major and drew this on so well.*

In total, it took Sangwoo nineteen minutes to restore his face to normal. At that point, there were only five minutes remaining in class, and he didn't feel like getting another pointed look from the professor by walking back into the classroom.

What did I do to deserve this? he thought indignantly. Sure, he'd told the Ethics professor that he'd been the only one who'd worked on the group project, but that was the pure, honest truth. Jaeyoung might be bitter over his inability to graduate, but that wasn't Sangwoo's fault—the senior had brought it upon himself. And yet, despite Sangwoo's innocence, he'd been ousted from class and left with no other choice but to wait outside until the lecture was over. It wasn't fair.

"That damn error…!"

And Jaeyoung wasn't just any error, either: He was a *semantic* error. It was the worst insult that Sangwoo could come up with.

Not all errors were the same: syntax or formatting issues, for example, could be easily debugged. Errors in logic, however, were trickier to deal with since they tended to pop up in code that seemed to be done perfectly. They were so hard to catch that even a careful line by line inspection wasn't always enough to pinpoint where the issue was coming from. To Sangwoo, Jaeyoung was the human equivalent: an unwelcome intruder who'd inexplicably materialized out of nowhere to destroy his carefully built routine.

Students began to walk out of the classroom, signaling that class had ended. Sangwoo painstakingly cut through the crowd, finally returning to the desk where he'd been sitting. He saw Jaeyoung's horrible red jacket out of the corner of his eye as he picked up his backpack, but ignored it and swiftly made his way out of the classroom. He knew the asshole's goal was to piss him off, and he didn't want the enemy knowing he'd succeeded.

Now that Sangwoo had started the day off on the wrong foot, it felt like everything was crumbling around him—like he'd placed a semicolon in the incorrect spot somewhere in his code. During Algorithms, he had no other choice but to claim the leftmost seat in the second row, which left him blankly staring at a pillar that obscured his entire vision. The seat was so terrible that it essentially rendered attending the class pointless, but it was the only way Sangwoo could distance himself from Jaeyoung's desk-snatching self.

The rest of the day continued to play out like some kind of terribly written movie script. When Sangwoo had gone to the dining hall after class and sat at the most secluded table he could find, Jaeyoung had sat right next to him despite the literal *dozens* of other tables available and began to eat wordlessly. Feeling indigestion settling in, Sangwoo had put away the tray of Korean food he'd retrieved and had gone to the convenience store, only to find that his favorite canned coffee was still out of stock. And the path he typically used to take a walk? It was still cordoned off by the drama club.

By the time he finally plopped down at the library desk he'd reserved, Sangwoo was exhausted. It had only been two days since the harassment had begun, and already he wasn't confident he could endure eight more of the same.

Jaeyoung chose that moment to swagger up to Sangwoo like a villain, a fantasy novel clutched in one hand. "Hope you have a productive study sesh," he crooned, claiming the seat next to Sangwoo before leaning back and flipping the book open.

Sangwoo glowered at him. Just looking at Jaeyoung's face was enough to send his blood pressure through the roof. *Maybe I should report him,* he mused, silently listing out all of the crimes Jaeyoung had committed in his head.

```
List of Offenses:
-Walking around in red clothes (not illegal)
```

-Taking my preferred seat (not illegal)
-Sitting next to me (not illegal)
-Bouncing his leg (inconclusive)
-Spinning his pen (inconclusive)
-Buying up all the cans of Black Holic coffee (not illegal)
-Filling a trash can to the brim (not illegal)
-Refusing to provide me with a worksheet (not illegal)
-Drawing on my face (not illegal)
-Existing (not illegal)
-......

The longer the list went on, the more pathetic Sangwoo felt. Jaeyoung had never insulted him outright or laid hands on him—all the things he'd done were small and trivial, but they had made Sangwoo want to rip his own hair out.

He's like a bug in my code.

Glaring at the man next to him, Sangwoo watched as Jaeyoung flipped to the next page of his novel. The senior was lounging back in his chair with one of his legs propped up on his opposite knee, bouncing it up and down like an overly energetic child. Sangwoo felt a sudden, overwhelming desire to smack his stupid beanie-covered head.

Although Jaeyoung had managed to thoroughly distract him for quite a while, Sangwoo finally got a moment of respite when the asshole yawned and fell asleep on the desk. To Sangwoo's profound relief, his enemy never snored, ground his teeth, or muttered in his sleep.

Some students—presumably Jaeyoung's friends—came by and took pictures of him as he slept, snickering quietly. A few girls had hung around too, whispering among themselves, but Sangwoo hadn't minded. They hadn't been loud enough to prove a bother, so by the time two hours had passed, he found he'd actually been able to accomplish some of the objectives he'd had in mind for the day's study session.

Sangwoo quietly put his books and pencil pouch back in his bag, trying not to wake Jaeyoung, but the moment he slid back his chair and stood up, the asshole sprang to his feet. Sangwoo could only watch in horror as Jaeyoung's elbow brushed against the pile of snacks and drinks that some students had placed next to him in some kind of strange ritual offering, knocking them onto the floor.

Ignoring the commotion, Sangwoo headed toward the exit of the library. He tried to move as quickly as possible, but it was no use—Jaeyoung caught up to him effortlessly. By the time they reached the stairwell that led down to the first floor, he found himself caught in some kind of idiotic competition, racing down the stairs like his life depended on it.

"I bet this is pissing you off, Sangwoo," Jaeyoung commented from behind him.

"Please do not talk to me. Your voice is grating."

"Well, too bad. You brought this upon yourself."

"How? I did nothing wrong," Sangwoo snapped as he marched out of the building and headed to his bicycle. "You're the one who's acting like a child. In fact, not even a child would do things like—"

"Oh, I see… You still think you're totally innocent, don't you? You think I'm some kind of stalker."

Sangwoo stopped dead in his tracks, as Jaeyoung's words had struck a chord. "Of course I do. What fault can you find in my actions? If the offense was having your name excluded from the presentation—"

"*Okay, enough*," Jaeyoung snarled.

Sangwoo spun around to face his enemy, only to find that Jaeyoung and his infuriatingly red beanie had gotten much closer to him than he had thought. Face uncharacteristically serious, Jaeyoung stared straight into Sangwoo's eyes as the last traces of sunlight disappeared behind him.

"Believe it or not," he said softly, "I wanted to be friends with you."

Sangwoo stared at him in silence. He'd seen Jaeyoung up close before, but beyond his questionable attire, he'd never taken the time to examine the man carefully. He'd never realized—or cared—that Jaeyoung's eyes were slightly downturned, that his nose was straight and high-bridged, or that his hair and eyes were closer to brown than black.

"Humans run on emotion, you know," Jaeyoung continued. "If you hadn't treated me like absolute shit, I wouldn't be so pissed over the group presentation."

"Will you leave me alone if I apologize, then?"

After a moment of visible disbelief, Jaeyoung laughed out loud. "How stupid can you be? I thought you were supposed to be a computer science genius! Though I guess your specialty is machines, not people..."

"I'm not sure what I'm supposed to take away from that."

"Think about it. If there was such a simple solution as apologizing, things wouldn't have spiraled into this mess."

Sangwoo had solved countless difficult problems in the past, but Jaeyoung's words sounded like total gibberish. He might as well have been speaking a different language. Fighting with Jaeyoung was the equivalent of trying to get a void function to return a value—impossible.

Finally, Sangwoo managed to say, "You can justify your actions all you want. At the end of the day, you are and will never be more than a lowlife, a deadbeat, sadistic piece of trash."

Jaeyoung smirked at him instead of getting angry or offended. "I love it when you compliment me."

"It seems you've truly lost your mind now."

"Sure have! See you tomorrow."

What a complete freak, Sangwoo thought, undoing his bike lock. He rode away without looking back.

return 0;

On Wednesday, Sangwoo had a two-hour-long block of Pop Culture and Cultural Theory. The class was infamous for being difficult, but it was the only liberal arts class that had been available during the time slot in his schedule he'd been looking to fill.

At a glance, the course's syllabus was filled with confusing concepts and phrases Sangwoo had never heard before, like "the Frankfurt School" and "Orientalism." He knew the material would be difficult for a computer science student like him. He'd read ahead in the textbook, but it hadn't particularly helped. And if he had to deal with Jaeyoung's harassment as well…

Sangwoo felt resigned before the class even began. That was why, when he walked into the lecture hall exactly nineteen minutes before it was set to commence at 9:30 AM, he immediately squeezed his eyes shut. It was his way of avoiding the inevitable sight of Jaeyoung's loathsome shoulder bag sitting in the most perfect seat in the room.

But to Sangwoo's surprise, when he finally opened his eyes, there was nothing there—both his chair and desk were pristine and unclaimed.

Am I dreaming?

Heart pounding from the shock of this unexpected turn of events, Sangwoo quickly claimed the spot. In that moment, he felt like an emperor sitting on his throne. But the initial rush of satisfaction was quickly overshadowed by fear of what Jaeyoung would do next.

Suppressing his anxiety, Sangwoo began to review the material that would be covered during class. For the first time that semester, he actually felt satisfied with his studying environment—something that seemed highly correlated with the reclaiming of his proper seat and the absence of a certain crimson devil.

Alas, he was a few pages in when somebody plopped a white tote bag on the desk next to him. Sangwoo heaved a giant sigh.

"You wake up on the wrong side of the bed today?"

His head whipped up at the unexpected voice—the higher pitch was not only infinitely more pleasant to the ear, but it also definitely didn't belong to Jaeyoung. Instead, a girl wearing a dark-green jacket stood beside the desk next to him. As his joy subsided, Sangwoo realized she looked oddly familiar.

As if she'd read his mind, the girl cheerfully announced, "It's me, Jihye!" as she took a seat. "You helped me with those boxes, remember? We even grabbed lunch together."

Recognition sparked in Sangwoo's mind. He hadn't caught on to who she was at first because she was wearing a ponytail now—her hair had been down last time.

Jihye turned to face him. "I didn't think I'd see you in this class! Are you interested in philosophy? I'm taking it because I wanted to learn about the theories of French thinkers like Lacan and Foucault."

"No, I don't particularly care for it. I'm only taking this class to fill a requirement to graduate."

"Oh… That makes sense. I'm actually required to take a computer science course, too. Can you tell me which one's the easiest? I heard that Information-Processing Theory and Intro to Computer Science are—"

Jihye fell abruptly silent as the professor walked in, saving Sangwoo from listening to her babbling any further. Still, overall, things weren't too bad; despite the fact that he was seated next to someone who seemed to take great pleasure in chattering the day away, Sangwoo had the best desk in the classroom and a professor who appeared both punctual and well-organized.

I haven't seen Jaeyoung so far, he abruptly realized. He wasn't dumb enough to think that the guy had given up—there was probably a reason behind this pleasant development. Still, it felt like a breath of fresh air.

return 0;

"Basically, he believed the world is divided into two categories: the elite and the working class," Jihye explained. "And the former is who controls society."

"But that's *the truth,*" Sangwoo shot back, "so what use is there in an opposing opinion that glorifies the masses? It should have been discarded a long time ago."

"No, no. Remember, the professor said it doesn't matter if a theory is true or not! You can't approach sociology with such a black-and-white way of viewing things."

The two of them were walking down the hallway of the humanities building, discussing what they'd learned in class. The infuriating red color Sangwoo had come to dread remained delightfully absent, and the joy of that fact drowned out any surprise he felt over Jihye's markedly high intelligence.

This was the way things were supposed to be. With how much suffering he'd gone through over the past two days, Sangwoo found that even the brief moment of normalcy felt like heaven.

Though Jihye had sat next to him for the entire class, she hadn't been distracting in the slightest, unlike a certain someone. To top it off, she'd even been kind enough to explain anything he hadn't understood from the lecture.

"Anyway, where's your next class?"

"I'm done for today."

"I'm so jealous… I have two more after this. What do you wanna get for lunch?"

She seemed to be operating on the premise that it was only natural for her and Sangwoo to eat together since they'd sat next to each other during class. Though he silently questioned the validity of her rationale, Sangwoo let it slide—either way, the dining hall was his next stop.

As they exited the building and walked through the campus, Sangwoo kept glancing around nervously, trying to predict where his enemy would attack from next. Then, just as Jihye asked him if there was anything wrong, he spotted a crowd of people pouring out of the humanities building. The only good thing about that damn red puffer jacket was that it was highly visible, even from a distance.

"We have to hurry," he said.

"Huh? Why?"

"Come on!"

Not bothering to check if Jihye was following him, Sangwoo basically sprinted to the dining hall and quickly got in line for the Korean food station. *Judging by the size of that crowd, he must have attended a large lecture,* he mused. Now that he thought about it, Jaeyoung had to be retaking Ethics for Hanguk University Students, which probably overlapped with Sangwoo's Pop Culture and Cultural Theory class.

Looks like I'll be getting a break on Wednesdays, Sangwoo concluded with satisfaction as he grabbed a dining tray.

To make things better, a bolt of genius struck him as he tried to decide where to sit. Walking over to a section of the dining hall that was much more crowded than he usually preferred, Sangwoo quickly scanned the tables until he located one that had only two vacant seats. His heart filled with joy as he sat down with Jihye—now, Jaeyoung wouldn't be able to harass him here, either.

"You look like you're in a good mood," Jihye commented, voice curious.

"Indeed."

With that, Sangwoo began to eat his food in total silence. Despite everything, he wasn't entirely relaxed—his eyes consistently scanned over the students in line to get food. The red puffer jacket was lurking among the people in the *tonkatsu* line, its owner's eyes sweeping over the dining hall in a fashion not unlike Sangwoo's.

It was only a few minutes later, when Jaeyoung walked over to the seating area along with a crowd of other students, that his gaze finally fell on Sangwoo. Sangwoo gave the asshole a triumphant look, and Jaeyoung's face twisted into a strange, almost mocking smile before he walked away to sit somewhere else. It was so minuscule a victory that it barely deserved to be called one at all, but Sangwoo felt euphoric.

"Are you going right back home after lunch?" Jihye asked.

"No. I'm going to the library."

"Oh, that's great! Wanna drop by the convenience store? I'll get you something to drink."

Sangwoo shook his head. "You can't."

"Huh? Why not?"

He paused in the middle of picking up a bite-sized chunk of marinated meat. How could he possibly explain the situation? The story was far too long and convoluted.

"This will sound very strange," he began, picking his words carefully, "but I'm being...harassed."

"*What?*" Jihye looked so shocked that Sangwoo fell silent for a moment. When it seemed obvious that he wasn't going to elaborate, she said worriedly, "Like, *actually*? Sangwoo, that's a huge problem! How exactly are they harassing you?"

He immediately regretted bringing it up. As he tried to figure out the best way to explain his predicament, Jihye's eyes filled with horror.

"It's okay," she said. "Whoever it is, there's free counseling available for students, and we can even go to the police if you need to. We'll get you help!"

Hearing the blazing determination in her voice somehow made Sangwoo feel even more uncomfortable. Silently, he decided it would be best just to focus on answering her initial question.

"He purchased every single one of the canned coffees that I always drink, so there are none left at the convenience store."

"Huh…? So, he bought out your favorite drink? Like in a buyer's monopoly?" Jihye said, blinking in disbelief before bursting out laughing. "Just order a box online, then! You can even express ship it!"

Sangwoo felt like he'd been hit over the head with a club. He'd never even considered the possibility of acquiring a Black Holic coffee somewhere else.

Despite his intelligence, thinking outside of the box was definitely not Sangwoo's strong suit. At one point during grade school, he'd actually gotten an incredibly low score on a school IQ test. His teacher had explained that, though he was quite gifted in the realm of logical-operational intelligence, he was far below average in the realms of applied reasoning and interpersonal intelligence.

Sangwoo stared at Jihye, starting to see her in a new light. "You're so smart," he said in wonder.

She laughed in response. "All right, so how else does this guy harass you?"

"This one will sound quite strange as well, but I can only focus during class when I'm sitting in a specific seat."

Jihye gasped dramatically. "Hey, I saw something like that in an American TV show! Hey, don't take this the wrong way, but…have you considered that you might have obsessive compulsive…?"

"No, the doctor said my symptoms aren't that serious. Anyway, this guy keeps taking my seat before I can. The farther away I sit from that spot, the harder it is for me to concentrate, but I can't bring myself to sit next to that assho—that *person*, because I dislike him so much."

"Hmm…" Jihye narrowed her eyes in contemplation, then snapped her fingers. "Just get a desk divider! You know, like the ones people use in grade school?"

Sangwoo contemplated this. If he used the method she was proposing, he'd be able to remain in close proximity to his preferred seat without making visual contact with the enemy. It was a good solution.

Impressed with Jihye's flexible problem-solving, Sangwoo found himself nodding. His voice was a bit more hopeful as he said, "He also bounces his leg in the library and is very rough with books. When he's reading, I can hear every time he turns a page."

"Try earplugs. They're, like, dirt cheap."

Jihye smiled at him, and he smiled right back.

"Thank you. I mean it. Let me treat you to a meal sometime."

"Yay! I'll be looking forward to it!" she said, beaming.

Sangwoo decided to go shopping at a home goods store instead of going to the library as he usually did. When he was done with his food, he stood up and glanced over to the other side of the room—Jaeyoung was still eating with his friends.

"Wait! I'm not done yet!"

The words didn't even register in Sangwoo's mind. Oblivious of everything but the excitement burning in his chest, he put away his tray and chugged a cup of water. There was a barely noticeable skip in his step as he exited the dining hall.

"Hey, wait up!" Jihye called out.

When Sangwoo glanced back, he saw her sprinting toward him, ponytail swinging.

"Can I help you?"

"Huh?" she gasped out, panting.

"What do you need?"

"N-nothing! I just thought it'd be nice to, you know...walk together. Also, I hate eating alone. It's so embarrassing."

Her perception of things was so different from his own that Sangwoo found himself intrigued. He ate alone every single day, but *he* had never felt embarrassed...

"We don't have to go to the convenience store," Jihye continued. "Can you just walk me to the humanities building? I have a class there."

"Why?" he asked. She seemed a bit old to need an escort. It wasn't like she was some little kid who might be kidnapped without supervision.

"Taking a walk after a meal is good for your health. It prevents all sorts of illnesses," she responded, a bit more stubbornly this time.

It was a sentiment he couldn't find fault with. For the first time in his life, Sangwoo found himself going on his post-lunch stroll with somebody else. He'd been planning on heading straight to the home goods store, but Jihye's proposal had proven pretty convincing—after all, he knew his morning regimen of bodyweight exercises wasn't enough to appropriately maintain his health. Sneaking some cardio in during his time at school by taking a walk or two was vital.

"Can I ask you something?"

"You just did."

"No, that was a rhetorical expression indicating that I *was* about to ask you something," she shot back right away. "Since your name is Sangwoo Choo, was your childhood nickname 'Sangchoo'? Y'know, like the word for 'lettuce'?"

He blinked. "How did you know?"

"I knew it!" Jihye doubled over laughing. "I've been thinking about it ever since you told me your name. I almost called you that a couple times!" She lost it again, only barely managing to contain herself a few moments later. "Um… Would you get mad at me if I called you 'Sangchoo'?"

"No," he replied—and he meant it. People had been calling him Sangchoo ever since he was a kid, regardless of his protests, and he was resigned to it at this point. On top of that, Jihye already acted very familiar, so her referring to him by a nickname didn't faze him.

People were going to call him whatever they wanted—it was a waste of energy to get worked up over it. It was definitely preferable to how a certain someone loved referring to him as "Sangwoo" in a snarky tone that irritated him to no end.

As if fate was playing a trick on him, the accursed red puffer jacket entered Sangwoo's vision the second he thought of its owner. Jaeyoung had just stepped out from behind a building, accompanied by two other guys.

As soon as their eyes met, Sangwoo spun around.

"Sangwoo…? You okay?" Jihye asked, sounding slightly confused.

But Sangwoo couldn't afford to waste time talking to her. "I'm going that way. See you next time."

"Sure! See you later!"

She'd barely finished talking before Sangwoo made himself scarce. His mind raced as he sped down the path before him. A Jaeyoung-less class, lunch, and short walk… The day had been perfect—despite the lack of his favorite coffee—but the appearance of that red jacket had ruined it all. Sangwoo found himself genuinely hating the color.

After speed-walking for a few minutes, he glanced back. Jaeyoung was about ten steps behind him, his buddies nowhere to be seen. Sangwoo's legs propelled him forward again before he could even think about it, his movements more instinctive than anything else.

He *had* to escape. Where his firewall had once been unassailable—even in the face of outside threats or potential violence—now an error had slipped in right under his nose and corrupted the whole program, rendering it inoperable. Calling the police or tattling to a teacher like he had in grade school would not be enough to save him this time.

Driven entirely by the horror of seeing Jaeyoung's face, Sangwoo found himself sprinting as fast as he could. He hadn't run with such vigor since his days in the military. Buildings flew by: the natural science building, the student union building, then the convenience store. Countless students, their faces completely unfamiliar to him, were left in his wake.

Finally reaching the school's front gate, Sangwoo turned around, huffing and puffing. *I must have lost him,* he thought. But unfortunately, fate had betrayed him once again.

"Geez, you're fast!" Jaeyoung gasped, flopping on the ground. "Shit, let me just…catch my breath for a second. I'm too old for this, I swear… What is this, a track meet?"

Internally, Sangwoo let out a howl of despair. He would have turned around and raced away a third time, but he was in a similar debilitating state. Instead, he stumbled away from Jaeyoung, plopped himself down on the sidewalk, and chugged the bottle of water that he'd put in his backpack.

After a moment, Jaeyoung huffed, "What the…hell…is wrong with you? Why did you run away?"

"Why does it matter if I ran away or not? You're the creep who chased after me," Sangwoo responded, also panting heavily.

"You were acting strange! I just followed without much thought."

"That's even stranger!"

A long silence followed the bizarre conversation.

Sangwoo waited until he'd caught his breath, then rose to his feet and headed over to the library to get his bike. Jaeyoung followed with an annoyed scowl, matching Sangwoo's pace regardless of how fast or slow he walked. At some point, Sangwoo decided to just ignore him and walk at his normal pace—he didn't feel like racing through the campus again.

"So...your girlfriend is pretty cute," Jaeyoung commented nonchalantly.

"I don't have a girlfriend."

The asshole raised an eyebrow. "Then who were you eating lunch with earlier?"

It was an easy question. "Jihye Kim."

"What's her major?"

"Philosophy...I think?" Sangwoo answered mechanically, all his attention focused on walking.

At this, Jaeyoung scoffed. "Her family name is Ryu, and she majors in French."

Sangwoo froze mid-step, then whipped around to stare at Jaeyoung in horror. "You've been stalking her as well? She's a nice person. She has nothing to do with me!"

Jaeyoung's lips twisted into a mocking smile. "Stalking, my ass," he spat. "The two of you came to the restaurant where I work, and I checked her student ID. After something like that, it'd be weirder if I *didn't* remember her name."

Deciding that this speech wasn't worth listening to, Sangwoo continued walking. Unfortunately, the pointless questions just kept coming.

"Do you even know my name?"

"Why should I?" he asked flatly.

"Aren't you supposed to be smart or something?"

"An efficient brain is programmed to delete worthless information."

"Well, you're definitely talented at making people feel like crap."

Jaeyoung reached out and grabbed Sangwoo's shoulder, forcing him to a stop. An instinctive scowl found its way onto Sangwoo's face at the feel of the asshole's fingers on him.

"Task: compose a three-line poem with the initials of my name," Jaeyoung said with a sly smile.

What the hell? Sangwoo slapped the asshole's hand away from his shoulder.

"Reward: I'll stop harassing you."

Sangwoo paused. It was a tempting offer. "Query," he replied after a brief moment of contemplation. "Are there any other conditions I need to meet in order to receive this reward? What exactly is your definition of 'harassment'?"

"Answer: you have to exhibit some level of artistic talent in your composition. And I'll leave the defining to you."

"Artistic talent" was a bit too vague for Sangwoo's liking, but he liked the fact that Jaeyoung was giving him the ability to determine the scope of his own reward. He decided he might as well play along.

"What are your initials?"

"Knowing that is *your* job, dipshit."

Sangwoo had been under the opposite impression, but thankfully, he already knew the asshole's full name: Jaeyoung Jang. Two J's and a Y.

He began the poem, silently fumbling for the right words. "J… Just like rain, you dropped into my life."

Glancing up at Jaeyoung, Sangwoo found him smirking arrogantly with his arms crossed. The next line wasn't too hard to come up with.

"J… Jackass is what you are."

It was the fabric of Jaeyoung's red jacket, glinting away in the sun, that inspired the final line.

"And Y… You should go piss off for the rest of time."

An odd expression came over Jaeyoung's face. Although there was a slight downturn to his lips, they seemed to keep twitching upward.

Sangwoo fell silent, wondering what was going through the asshole's brain. In his opinion, his poem had been pretty well-crafted—but as the seconds ticked by, he began to feel increasingly anxious. This might be a questionable contest moderated by an even more questionable judge, but he still wanted his hard work to be recognized.

Finally, Jaeyoung said with quite a bit of authority, "Score."

Sangwoo perked up and listened intently.

"Accuracy, ten out of ten."

"Hmm..."

"Emotional sincerity, ten out of ten."

"I didn't expect the scores to be so generous."

"Literary quality, three out of ten."

"Pardon...?"

"Narrative element, one out of ten."

Gaping indignantly, Sangwoo stared at Jaeyoung as he worked himself up to announcing his assessment of the final category. *If I get a perfect score here, maybe the reward is still in reach?*

"Originality, zero out of ten."

Sangwoo had to suppress a violent stream of cuss words. His archnemesis smiled at him brightly.

"That'll bring the score to...twenty-four out of fifty. Guess we'll be seeing each other tomorrow, Sangwoo!"

Gritting his teeth, Sangwoo hurriedly walked away from Jaeyoung. He should have known better. Why had he wasted his time on a bunch of Jaeyoung's crap?

To Sangwoo's relief, Jaeyoung had the decency not to follow him. But the senior still had to get in one last parting shot.

"I've gotten a pretty good grasp on what makes you tick now, don't you think?"

"What am I, a clock?"

"I mean, you're not that far off..."

The words weren't even worth responding to. Instead, Sangwoo turned his attention to following his original plan: going to the home goods store. Quickly undoing his bike lock, he swung himself onto the seat and sped past Jaeyoung.

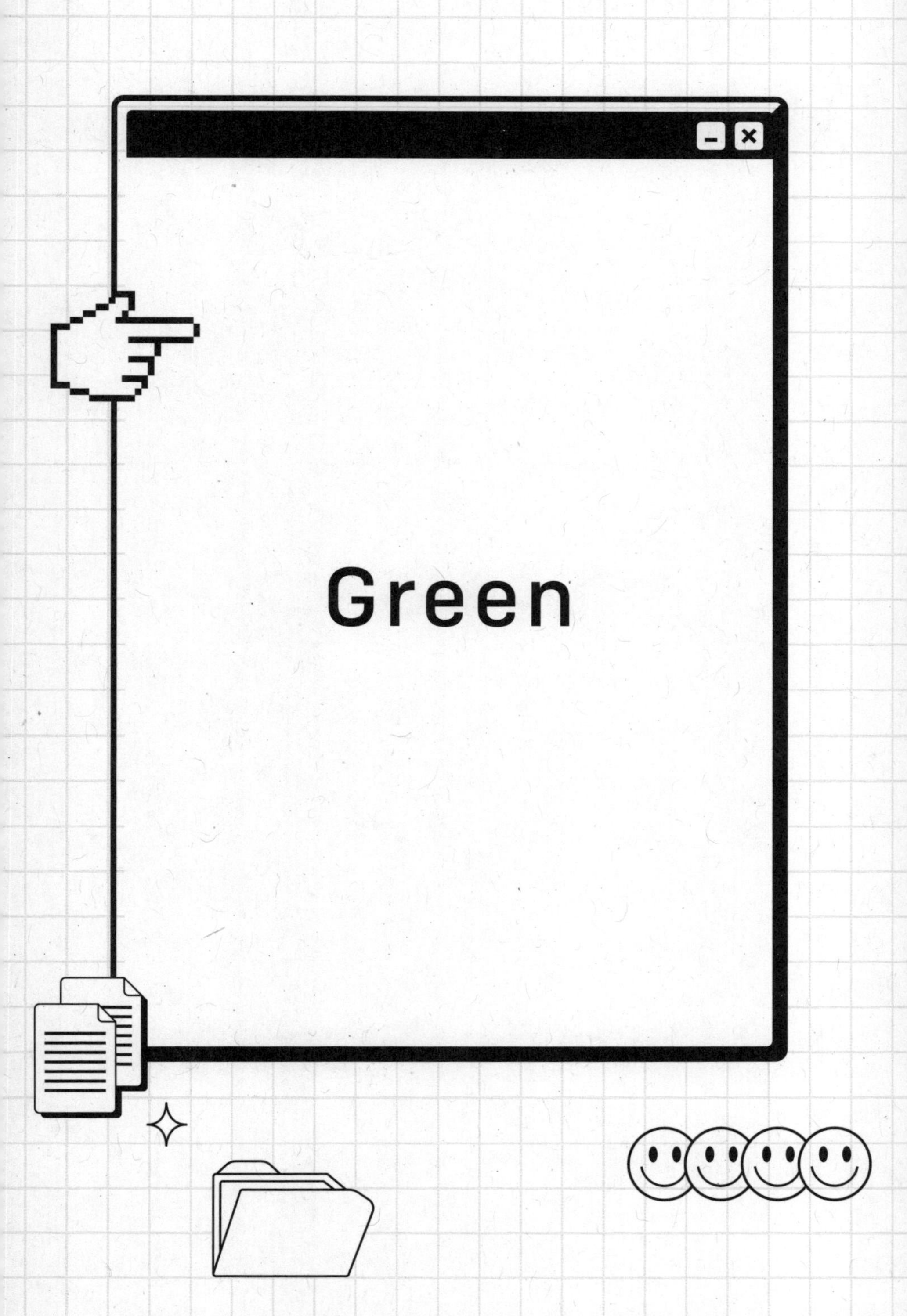

Green

For two entire days, Jaeyoung had harassed Sangwoo to his heart's content. He'd gotten his underclassmen friends to call dibs on all the weirdo's favorite desks, bothered him in his classes, and followed him around everywhere. Watching him bristle like a hedgehog had proven a truly lovely experience.

But that joyful sight wasn't the only reward Jaeyoung had won for himself.

First, he'd been given a plethora of delightful nicknames, "stalker," "lowlife," "sadistic piece of trash," and "deadbeat" among them. They weren't the most pleasant of monikers, of course, but having a label was always better than not having one—as a graphic designer, Jaeyoung knew the importance of branding all too well.

There was a reason why rich, handsome men in cliché TV shows went around looking for women who slapped them across the face and disappeared. It wasn't about romance, oh no. Negative impressions were much more impactful than positive ones—that was why outrage marketing was so successful. At any rate, it appeared the avenue of self-promotion he'd taken with Sangwoo had proven effective. Honestly, after observing the guy's near-clinical inability to remember who anyone was, having a variety of nicknames dedicated to him felt like kind of an honor.

Secondly, Jaeyoung had found that putting all those cracks and chips in Sangwoo's perfect defense was enough to offset the emotional damage the guy had caused him, at least somewhat. In fact, the utterly refreshing feeling of avenging himself was invigorating as chugging a can of soda.

Still, the pure, unadulterated entertainment Jaeyoung had gotten from tormenting Sangwoo was what had turned out to be the ultimate prize. Whenever that weirdo's emotionless face had crumpled in annoyance, he'd felt more exhilaration than pity. In fact, the whole thing had been so damn fun that Jaeyoung had even been willing to torture himself by waking up at the crack of dawn. He'd never thought of himself as a sadist, but... Well, it was never too late to discover new facts about yourself.

The original plan had been to follow Sangwoo around for the entire two weeks he had until he had to drop his classes, but Jaeyoung's resolve had already begun to weaken. Sangwoo's reaction to his harassment had been much more extreme than he'd expected, to the point he was beginning to worry the weirdo might run off and take a gap year. His goal had been to make Sangwoo slightly miserable, not bring his entire life crashing down on top of him.

It didn't help that Jaeyoung had a relatively short attention span. No matter how hard he tried, he just couldn't sit still in the quiet library. Not to mention, he hated eating the mediocre food in the crowded dining hall. The organization required to get underclassmen into place to steal Sangwoo's favorite desks had taken way too much effort, and every single minute that he'd had to spend in computer science classes where he didn't understand a thing had felt like torture.

Honestly, he'd known that he wouldn't be able to keep going for two whole weeks. He'd only made a project out of tormenting Sangwoo because he had way too much time on his hands.

Why did you do this to me, Sangwoo? Jaeyoung lamented, already cursing Sangwoo only three minutes into the class that he was being forced to retake, Ethics for Hanguk University Students. Even in the overly crowded lecture hall, he could immediately spot a handful of students who were answering roll call for someone else. How many of them would get screwed over like he had?

Jaeyoung despaired over the opportunity he'd lost—having a spot in a classroom in the U.S. where he could learn from the best designers in the world. It really was unfortunate that Sangwoo was the most rigid, inflexible asshole Jaeyoung had ever met. Now, thanks to that weirdo, he was stuck in this useless Ethics class. And since he was on the professor's radar for cutting class last semester, he had to actually show up this time.

While it would have been great if he hadn't been put in the same group as a damn snitch, Jaeyoung knew there was no point in thinking about what could have been. Instead, he let out a sigh and started scribbling on a piece of paper he'd borrowed from the person sitting next to him in the very back of the lecture hall. As he drew, he shot the professor the occasional glance.

When Jaeyoung exited the humanities building, he was relieved to find that the weather was objectively wonderful outside. It was nearly spring, the season of blossoming love. Had it already been six months since he'd broken up with his last girlfriend?

Jaeyoung was in the midst of pondering this, walking down the steps in front of the building with a crowd of other students, when he spotted Sangwoo in the distance. The weirdo was walking toward the dining hall with quick strides, accompanied by a girl wearing a green jacket. As always, Sangwoo himself was clad in the most inconspicuous, impossibly bland clothes Jaeyoung could imagine. It was a wonder he'd caught sight of the guy at all.

He's a real ladies' man, huh? Jaeyoung noted. Now that he thought about it, the weirdo had brought a girl along with him that time he'd come to the restaurant, too. He tried to imagine Sangwoo in a loving relationship for a brief moment, but found it was an impossible task. Given the guy's personality, it was hard to imagine he'd be able to get a girlfriend in the first place.

It was mainly curiosity that pulled Jaeyoung into the dining hall, which turned out to be as disgustingly full as usual. This time, it appeared Sangwoo had chosen to eat at a table that was already at full capacity instead of being a loner. It was a rather obvious—but valiant—bid to avoid Jaeyoung.

I'll let him savor the small victories, Jaeyoung decided, chuckling under his breath. For some bizarre reason, he found himself thinking that Sangwoo was *cute.* Shaking his head, he glanced at the girl accompanying Sangwoo and recognized her as Jihye Ryu, the one who'd been with him at the restaurant.

Jaeyoung sat down with his friends, then proceeded to eat the garbage that the cafeteria called "food." By the time he rose and walked out of the dining hall, he'd decided that the time to stop following Sangwoo around was long overdue—nothing was worth choking down food of that caliber.

Even the canned coffee he'd bought from the convenience store was absolutely vile. He'd only tried a single sip before throwing an entire can away, which left him with fifteen more to get rid of somehow. He'd left them on a table in the drama club room, but of course, none of the others had touched them.

A short while later, mid-journey across the campus with his friends, Jaeyoung caught sight of Jihye and Sangwoo yet again. *How adorable. They've got the perfect height difference, don't they?* he grumbled internally, sounding for all the world like some unnamed Thug A in a movie.

Studying the pair as they walked in their direction, Jaeyoung noted Sangwoo looked much happier after a day of not being relentlessly harassed. He figured the weirdo would walk right past him, too preoccupied with his girl to notice anybody else, but Sangwoo's eyes widened in recognition the moment he spotted Jaeyoung's approaching form in the distance.

Jaeyoung felt a strange surge of joy. Once upon a time, Sangwoo hadn't recognized him even though they were only a step apart. *Oh, how things have changed…*

Sangwoo immediately turned around and sped away, but Jaeyoung jogged after, intent on clinging to him as he had the two previous days. Jaeyoung was about ten steps away from his target when Sangwoo anxiously glanced back and saw him. The weirdo's eyes widened, and then—much to Jaeyoung's surprise—he began sprinting away. Judging from his reaction, one would've thought Jaeyoung was a serial killer out for his blood or something.

Naturally, Jaeyoung chased after him. Did he have a clue why he'd made that choice? No. Did he know how weird the whole thing would look? Absolutely. But he found himself running regardless.

As it turned out, Sangwoo was a practically a track star—Jaeyoung couldn't catch up to him no matter how hard he tried, even though Sangwoo was wearing a backpack. He'd never imagined the weirdo would be such an athletic guy, mainly because he acted and looked like such a nerd. Before Jaeyoung realized it, he was racing through the school's front gates. Other than during his time in the military, he couldn't remember the last time he'd sprinted such a long distance. He crouched, trying to catch his breath.

Seeing Sangwoo sprinting away from him had awakened something in Jaeyoung, snuffing out the workings of his rational mind under a wave of sheer determination. And now, in its wake, he was hit with an epiphany.

Because of his antics, the only thing he'd managed to do was get himself labeled as a critical bug in Sangwoo's simulation. He might have left a rather permanent impression on the weirdo's supercomputer of a mind, but at the end of the day, he was nothing more than a malfunctioning line of code to him.

Sure, whenever Sangwoo scowled at him, Jaeyoung felt a temporary rush of exhilaration, but he never felt truly satisfied. There was a desire burning in the back of his mind—a desire for Sangwoo to think of him as a cool, smart, funny upperclassman, just like how every other soul at the school did.

They do say that humans are inherently greedy creatures, Jaeyoung thought wryly. Maybe that was why he'd felt so strange hearing Sangwoo defend Jihye.

"You've been stalking her as well? She's a nice person. She has nothing to do with me!"

The words had created a rift between Jaeyoung and her. And now the temptation of claiming the moniker of "nice person" for himself hung before him like a forbidden fruit, just out of his reach.

Jaeyoung had long since looked through Jihye's social media profile in an attempt to dig up information that he could use to harass Sangwoo. It was all too easy nowadays to find someone online when you knew their name, major, and class year. Based on her posts, she appeared to be a diligent person, though not to the same insane degree as Sangwoo.

On the day they'd gone to the restaurant together, she'd posted:

he's a little intense, but I think he's a good person. hope i'll get to see him again.
#adorableweirdo #firstmeeting #excited

It was obvious she'd been talking about Sangwoo. As for the weirdo himself, the equation in his brain was clear:

* * *

Jihye = a nice person
Jaeyoung = a deadbeat, stalker, lowlife, sadistic piece of trash

The contrast between them was so stark, Jihye might as well have been a green-wreathed angel sent down from heaven, while Jaeyoung was some kind of crimson-drenched demonic entity that had crawled up from hell. Even thinking about it pissed him off.

Jaeyoung was fairly positive Sangwoo wasn't romantically interested in Jihye—after all, he didn't even know her last name or major. But innocent, naive guys like Sangwoo were easily swayed by kind gestures. Jaeyoung was willing to bet the luxury watch his grandfather had given him as a graduation present that the pair would end up dating within three months. The thought sent a sudden sense of dread sweeping over him, a vivid mental image following along with it.

It was about eight years in the future, on Sangwoo and Jihye's wedding day. Sangwoo was holding his beautiful bride's hands, thanking her for helping him stay strong back in college, when some dude named Youngjae Kim had taken his inability to graduate on time out on him. "I don't even remember what that piece of shit looked like, but he wore this red puffer jacket everywhere," the imaginary Sangwoo said.

Jaeyoung bristled. *Hell no. Over my dead body!*

At that moment, his plans changed—in a way, they underwent an upgrade. He wasn't sure what exactly made somebody a nice, respectable human being, and he wasn't going to become one anytime soon. Therefore, he had only one card left up his sleeve—his ability to make Sangwoo *see* him.

Jaeyoung might have known what made Sangwoo tick well enough to get the weirdo to remember his name, but his name was now associated with the following words: Jaeyoung Jang = red = villain = lowlife = piece of trash. He'd have to upend Sangwoo's perception of him entirely to get that to change.

Why am I putting myself through this? Jaeyoung asked himself with a tired sigh. *But also...why not? I have all the time in the world.*

Decision made, he began a careful analysis of the clothes in his closet.

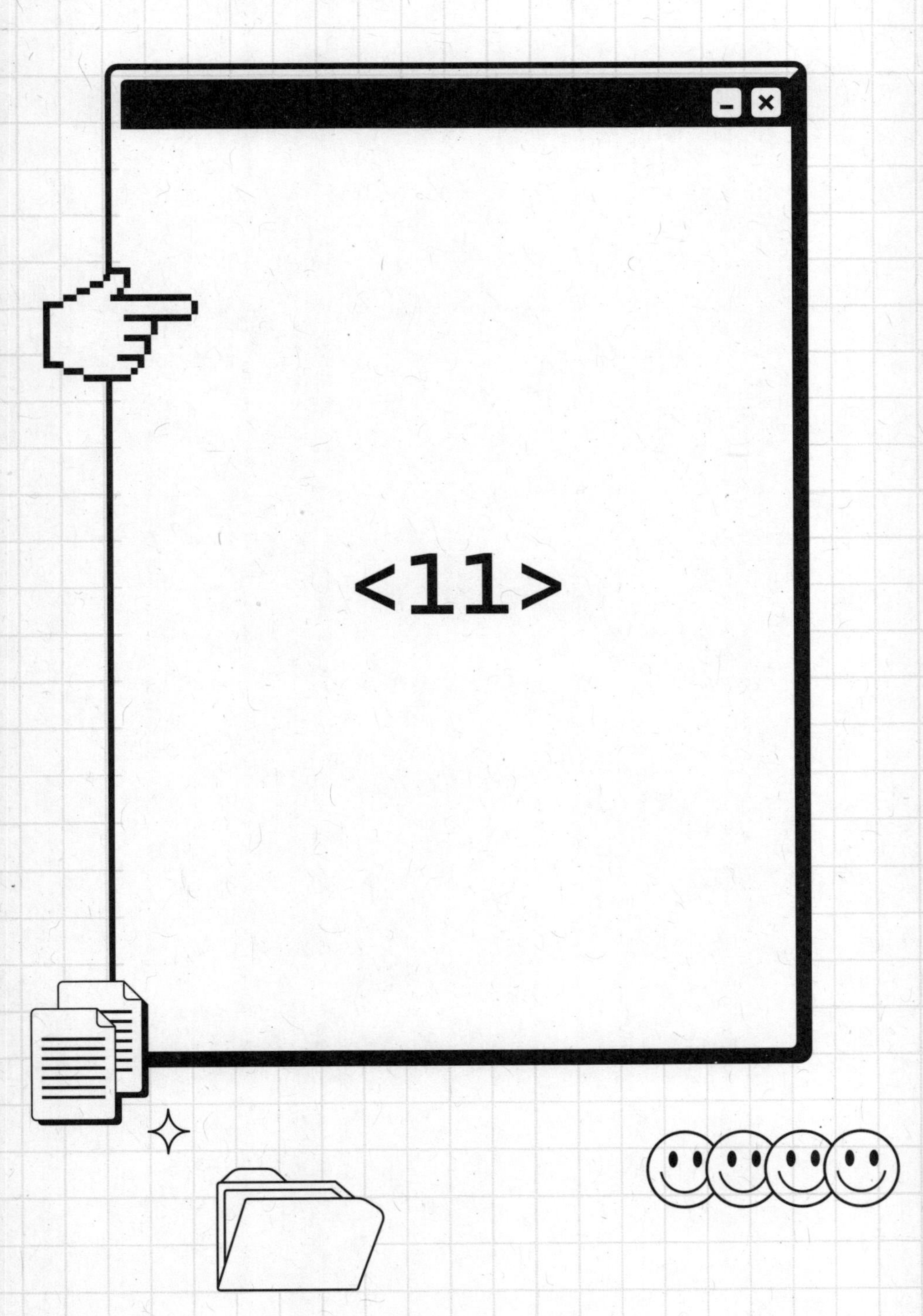
<11>

Sangwoo had never imagined that he would want to see Jaeyoung, but there he was, waiting for the asshole to walk into their classroom.

He'd chosen to sit in the fourth row in the second seat to the right, next to his preferred spot that had already been claimed by Jaeyoung's bag. His textbook was laid open on the desk in front of him, but he'd only placed it there out of habit—he hadn't looked at it once. Instead, he patiently watched for Jaeyoung, his mind reviewing the three avenues of attack he'd prepared. He couldn't wait to see Jaeyoung's face twist in surprise.

The professor walked into the classroom, but Jaeyoung was still nowhere to be seen, despite being the TA for the class. Sangwoo turned his entire body so that he could stare at the entrance at the back of the room, but there were no red puffer jackets among the swarm of hurrying students.

Just then, a voice asked, "What're you lookin' at? I'm right here."

Sangwoo froze. A man in a dark-green coat stood in front of him, his hands in his pockets. Even upon meeting his eyes—which were unobscured by glasses—Sangwoo still struggled to identify him as Jaeyoung. But he'd spoken with Jaeyoung's voice…

Still awash in a sea of confusion, Sangwoo watched as the man sat down in Sangwoo's favorite seat. All Jaeyoung had done was change a few aspects of his outfit, but that'd been enough to short-circuit Sangwoo's entire processing system.

Still, no matter what the man looked like, he was clearly Jaeyoung. Composing himself, Sangwoo took out a yellow desk divider—his first avenue of attack—and placed it on his right side, effectively obscuring Jaeyoung's face. Unfortunately, he could still hear the deadbeat's snort of laughter loud and clear.

"We'll start the skit presentations next Thursday, so I want everybody to start preparing now," the professor was saying.

The guidelines for the skit had been outlined in the class's syllabus. Students were to separate into pairs and write up a five-minute sketch in Mandarin Chinese, which they would then present to the entire class. It was an important assignment that would be worth 20 percent of their final grade.

As the professor passed out some worksheets to the first row, Sangwoo found himself wondering, *Isn't that the TA's job?*

But the professor had already begun to speak again. "The pairs and presentation dates have already been assigned, and are written here," she continued, projecting a list up on the board. "I'm aware that those of you presenting first might be at a bit of a disadvantage, but I'll make sure to take that into account when I'm grading."

Sangwoo's eyes quickly spied his own name on the list. However, they also quickly identified a glaring issue: the student he'd been paired with.

Sangwoo Choo (Computer Science), Jaeyoung Jang (Visual Arts)
Presentation: March 14 (Thursday)

Out of the thirty or so potential partners he could've had, he'd somehow ended up with Jaeyoung. Furthermore, it looked like they would be presenting on the following Thursday, which was the earliest possible presentation date.

Sangwoo's hand shot into the air, and the professor looked over at him.

"Yes? Do you have a question?"

"Professor, may I choose a different partner if the one I've been assigned is so objectionable that it'd be impossible for us to work together?"

The professor frowned at the question. "No. I'm sure some students will be more skilled than others, but the whole point of assigning the teams is to have you work through those differences. In fact, I specifically asked the TA to randomly select who would be paired with whom because I anticipated a question like this one. The process was totally fair. Now, does anybody have any questions that are *not* about changing partners or presentation dates?"

How can it be totally fair when he's *the one who assigned the pairs?* Sangwoo wanted to ask, but the professor had sounded so stern that he didn't have the courage to say anything else. He'd already made a bad impression on his Embedded Systems teacher—he couldn't let the same thing happen in another class.

Suddenly, the yellow desk divider limply fell to the floor to reveal Jaeyoung, chin in hand and a strange smile playing on his lips. "It'll be fine," he said smugly. "You can be a freeloader if you want. I got this."

Ugh, shut up! Sangwoo snarled inwardly, shoving the useless divider into his bag.

A few minutes later, the worksheets that had been going around the classroom reached Sangwoo's desk. He made sure to grab one before Jaeyoung could take it from him, then wrote his class year and name in the upper left corner.

"The sheet you just got contains expressions that you should have learned in Chinese 101, as well as some that are a bit more advanced. There should be a hundred of them overall. Please refer to them as you write your skit," the professor instructed. "Now, get together with your partner and discuss the assignment."

Sangwoo carefully read through the list. About 30 percent of the expressions were familiar, since he'd already memorized them. He'd taken Chinese 101 during freshman year and had gotten full marks for both attendance and the regular exams, but had lost a whole bunch of points on the skit and oral exam. Ultimately, he'd gotten an A- in the class, but he was aiming for an A+ in Intermediate Chinese—which meant Sangwoo needed to get a good grade on this group project.

Thanks to his fairly empty schedule, he'd likely have more than enough preparation time. The biggest challenge would be his partner, whom Sangwoo was sure would screw him over in any way possible.

Honestly, though, Sangwoo wasn't *too* worried. If need be, he'd just act out both sides of the skit. After all, the syllabus clearly stated that everybody would be getting graded on their individual performances.

Sangwoo opened his notebook and began to scribble down some ideas, fully prepared to do the project by himself. These expectations were upended, however, when Jaeyoung took his desk and placed it directly in front of his own.

Sangwoo didn't even look at the asshole as he said, "A good portion of the sentences are questions or answers concerning certain locations, so we can make the skit about a Hanguk University student, played by me, giving directions to a Chinese exchange student, played by you."

He hadn't been looking for any input, but Jaeyoung grumbled, "That's so cliché. I really dodged a bullet not developing that game with you."

He seemed to be making a habit out of criticizing Sangwoo's creative abilities. First, he'd said that *Veggie Man* was boring, then he'd given Sangwoo a zero out of ten in originality for his poem, and now he was attacking him about his idea for the skit. And that wasn't even bringing up the countless other snide comments he'd made.

"Let's hear your brilliant plan, then," Sangwoo said, tossing his pencil onto his notebook and leaning back in his chair like Jaeyoung always did. He crossed his arms, too, for good measure, and immediately found himself feeling much more powerful.

Jaeyoung skimmed through the handout full of Chinese sentences and said, "A Qing dynasty merchant turned phone scammer—that's our main character."

"Excuse me?"

"We'll start off with the merchant at a marketplace. 'How much are those?' 'It's a hundred thousand won for two bunches of grapes.' 'Th-that's way too expensive!' 'Please stop. Violence is illegal, you know. The exit is that way.' That'll take care of all the expressions listed for us to use when buying or selling something, so…"

Sangwoo, who had been fully ready to mock Jaeyoung's idea, couldn't help but get immersed in the story.

"Next, we can have the merchant say: 'Today, I earned zero won. I am very poor; I have no money…' Then we can shift to the scammer part of the storyline by using these: 'I sold all my items. Using the money I received, I bought a telephone. Now, I have nothing left…' Oh, and here's a good one: 'I am a scammer.'"

Sangwoo began to write down the plot in his notebook, referring to the worksheet to make sure Jaeyoung's expressions were included in the list.

"So he calls somebody with his phone: 'Ring, ring. *Wéi?* I am with your son. Give me ten billion won, and he can go back home.' Then the person on the other end says, 'I am not married. You are a scammer.'"

"So? How does it end?"

Jaeyoung shrugged. "How do *you* want it to end?"

Sangwoo mulled it over but couldn't think of any plausible action a Qing dynasty merchant would take after failing to scam someone over the phone. The best he could come up with was…

"He runs out of food and starves to death?"

"…Yeah, you *would* say that. It'll work with that idea, though: 'I'm hungry. Give me food.' The dying part doesn't fit any of the expressions on the list, but it should be fine to add. As his final request, he could ask that the telephone he bought be handed down to his brother."

Sangwoo read through the plot he'd jotted down in the notebook. It was definitely a bit strange, but it contained the perfect mixture of difficult and easy expressions. At that moment, a question flashed through his mind.

"Why a Qing dynasty merchant, of all people?"

"The professor is a Qing dynasty buff. I'm willing to bet she'll give us a perfect score if we show up wearing accurate clothes and a queue wig."

"If you really think—" he began, but Jaeyoung cut him off.

"Just look at this. The rating criteria says that visuals, humor, and preparation add up to twenty percent of your grade for this project."

Sangwoo had already noted that section and wondered why such a category would be included. Considering that tone, pronunciation, and fluency accounted for 50 percent, and level of difficulty, appropriateness of dialogue, and grammar made up 30 percent, the weight for performance seemed extraordinarily high.

Seeing the confused frown on Sangwoo's face, Jaeyoung added, "Trust me, she's my club supervisor. I know exactly what she likes."

"Which club?"

"Drama."

The lead of the mechanical pencil in Sangwoo's hand snapped, catapulting straight into Jaeyoung's face. Sangwoo didn't notice—not even when Jaeyoung lifted a hand to rub at his cheek with a frown. In his head, he was replaying the moment when his beloved walking path had been blocked off so the drama club could use it. Even that had been a part of the asshole's plan.

Sangwoo looked away from Jaeyoung, deciding to ignore his nemesis's presence in favor of writing out the skit's script instead. If he knew a certain Chinese phrase or saw it in the worksheet, he scribbled it down diligently. Otherwise, he just used Korean.

The entire time, Jaeyoung didn't say a word. He was so silent, it actually started to prick at Sangwoo's nerves. Based on the previous data he'd compiled, this was highly abnormal; Jaeyoung was someone who couldn't sit still for even a minute. He had to tap his pen on his desk, make snarky comments, or loudly flip the pages of his book.

Blinking in confusion, Sangwoo glanced up—only to jolt in surprise when he saw Jaeyoung staring at him, chin resting on his intertwined hands.

"Fascinating," the asshole muttered, eyes not pausing in their dissection.

Sangwoo immediately turned his gaze back to the paper and resumed working on the script. Unfortunately, this didn't do much to deter his nemesis.

"You wanna know *what's* so fascinating?" Jaeyoung whispered. "I just realized we have something in common."

Yeah, right. That's impossible. Sangwoo couldn't hide his frown, and Jaeyoung chuckled lightly.

"Geez, relax! I was talking about our handwriting."

Sangwo was utterly shocked. He had never considered his handwriting to be excellent by any means, but he knew it wasn't *nearly* as horrendous as Jaeyoung's. "Please stop distracting me."

"Sangwoo," Jaeyoung crooned in a low voice. "You're a pretty chill guy, aren't you?"

After two straight days of making Sangwoo's life a living hell, now the guy wanted to act like they were best friends? It was quite an interesting development, but Sangwoo had no intention of indulging him. He kept working.

"I mean, look at you! You're working on a project with a dude who's a deadbeat, sadistic piece of shit. Do you not know how to hold a grudge?"

Ignore him.

"Heyyy, Sangwoo…"

Ignore him.

"What are your thoughts on revenge?"

Ignore him.

"Personally, if I try to screw someone over, that means I care about them to some degree… But you don't feel any particular way about me, do you? You just want me to get lost, right?"

Ignore him.

"Come on, Sangwoo. It's not polite to ignore your partner."

"I can when said partner is an asshole."

Jaeyoung scoffed. "Damn… Is that seriously how you're gonna be?"

"Could you please be quiet? I'm in the middle of something."

"Fine, I will—*if* you do me a favor."

"I'll pass."

"Take off your hat."

Sangwoo glanced up, caught off guard, and found Jaeyoung in the same pose he'd been in before. His face was completely nonchalant.

It doesn't seem like he's trying to taunt or harass me… Sangwoo thought doubtfully. Either way, it would probably be best to ignore him.

Sangwoo went back to working on the script. As soon as he'd jotted down the last line, Jaeyoung snatched it up and proceeded to look over it himself. "I see," he murmured occasionally as he went, nodding to himself. "Not bad." He even grabbed Sangwoo's pencil and wrote down a few notes.

When Sangwoo got his notebook back, he found that all the blank spaces he'd planned to fill later were gone—Jaeyoung had come up with original lines in Chinese and had written them in.

What's wrong with him? Sangwoo wondered, completely baffled. Had the asshole finally decided to stop harassing him whenever he got the chance? It seemed so, given he was the one who'd come up with the final idea for their skit. He was being more helpful than annoying.

Sangwoo couldn't help but ask, "Why the sudden change of heart?"

"Huh? What do you mean?"

"Before, you were doing everything in your power to make my life miserable. What happened in these past two days?"

Honestly, Jaeyoung had to be the strangest guy Sangwoo had ever met. Everything about him was constantly changing. First, he acted like a deadbeat, then he popped up at a restaurant as a respectful waiter. He went from cussing Sangwoo out to smiling at him, as easily as if a switch had been flipped in his head. He'd even chased Sangwoo down like some kind of serial killer, only to make him compose a random poem! And now, after harassing him for days, the guy had decided to be a helpful collaborator for their group project.

The professor, who'd been roaming around the classroom and assisting other students, drifted over to them. "How are things going over here?" she asked, then raised a brow when she realized who Sangwoo's partner was. "Oh, so you're in this group, Jaeyoung! You two should be set, then."

"Actually, Sangwoo is the one who did the hard work," Jaeyoung responded with a smile.

Was the asshole glitching out or something? Sangwoo blinked at the guy in total disbelief, but the professor had already turned to him with a smile.

"Is that so? Let me take a look at the script."

If his partner had been anyone else, Sangwoo would have happily given them the credit for the outline. "I simply transferred their ideas onto paper," he would have said. But...he just couldn't do it. He couldn't bring himself to compliment Jaeyoung in any way. Instead, he respectfully handed the notebook to the professor.

"A merchant from the Qing dynasty?" She burst into laughter. "Oh, I love that. This will be a fun one for sure. But, wait. Some of these lines..." The smile slowly faded from her face. "I've never taught any cuss words in my class. Jaeyoung, are you the one who did this?"

The professor glared at Jaeyoung, but then realized Sangwoo was the one holding the pencil. She fixed a stern look at him.

"Fix those lines, or you get a zero on the entire assignment."

"Yes, ma'am," Sangwoo muttered, unable to say anything else under her piercing gaze.

She handed back the notebook and walked away, and Jaeyoung immediately began to snicker. Sangwoo gritted his teeth and ignored him in favor of erasing every single line the asshole had written, leaving behind bits of rubber in his fury.

As he brushed them away, Jaeyoung whispered, "Personally, I *love* holding grudges."

Sangwoo pressed the eraser down even harder.

`return 0;`

Seething at the fact that Jaeyoung had managed to catch him off guard once again, Sangwoo immediately headed over to the engineering building after the conclusion of Intermediate Chinese. His hopes of regaining his desk of choice were high: He knew for a fact he'd managed to get out of the room before Jaeyoung, and the asshole couldn't have reserved the seat in the middle of class. Alas, upon entering the room where Engineering Mathematics 2 was to be held, Sangwoo's mood plummeted into the abyss. Jaeyoung's navy-blue backpack, the one he usually used to steal Sangwoo's seat in his second class of the day, had already been placed in the rightmost spot of the fourth row.

Fortunately, Sangwoo had come prepared. He sat in the chair directly to the left of his favorite seat and put up the desk divider again, faithfully following Jihye's wonderful advice. He might've had no other choice than to talk to Jaeyoung during Intermediate Chinese, but all he had to do during Engineering Mathematics 2 was pay attention to the lecture and solve math problems.

Of course, Sangwoo had no doubt that his evil nemesis would try to annoy him around his defense. He'd already thought up several possible scenarios himself. Jaeyoung could "accidentally" knock the divider over, or tap relentlessly on his own desk, or just make weird noises throughout the whole class.

Sangwoo spent the first six precious minutes of the lecture waiting for Jaeyoung's first avenue of attack, but it never came. Finally, he crumbled. What the heck was that asshole up to on the other side of the divider?

Silently taking down the barrier between them, Sangwoo found himself staring at a sleeping Jaeyoung, head plopped onto his desk. It was the perfect chance to examine his nemesis. The asshole had been setting his nerves on edge for the entire day, but he couldn't quite put his finger on why. It wasn't just the lack of Jaeyoung's disgustingly red puffer jacket or glasses—it almost felt like a doppelgänger had taken his place, just like that time back in the Italian restaurant when Sangwoo hadn't been able to recognize him at all.

Taking a closer look, Sangwoo noted that Jaeyoung had taken out all three of his piercings, and his hair somehow looked much tamer. With his eyes closed peacefully, he didn't resemble the lowlife who'd made harassing Sangwoo his job.

It doesn't make any sense, Sangwoo thought, hit by a sudden, dizzying wave of discomfort and confusion. Until now, he'd thought of Jaeyoung as a deadbeat, sadistic piece of trash, but the man sleeping beside him would be better described as an orderly, mature, and stylish human. It was like Jaeyoung Jang had been saved as different, completely incompatible file types.

But no matter how shiny and handsome Jaeyoung was on the outside, Sangwoo knew the truth—on the inside, he was a disgusting, vile human. The most obvious proof of this was the fact that his visual arts ass was sitting in Engineering Mathematics 2 just so he could ruin Sangwoo's grades. Worse, his plan was proving so effective that he was achieving his insidious goal even in his sleep.

Clenching his fingers around his pencil, Sangwoo forced himself to focus on the lecture again. The professor had already moved on to another chapter while he'd been trying to figure out what Jaeyoung was scheming—now, Sangwoo could officially say he'd completely missed two entire chapters worth of material in Engineering Mathematics 2. Sadly, the same could be said for every single class on his schedule other than Pop Culture and Cultural Theory, the one class Jaeyoung couldn't barge into.

Sangwoo was reasonably confident that he could catch up on most of the content using textbooks and online lessons once Jaeyoung dropped the classes after the two-week period. Unfortunately, professors usually pointed out the content that would show up in exams during their lecture. There was no denying that he was missing out on some crucial information.

With Jaeyoung asleep, there was no better opportunity to actually concentrate. And yet, strangely enough, Sangwoo found his attention unerringly drifting back to his nemesis every few minutes.

Impressive, Sangwoo thought, doing his best not to look at Jaeyoung. *He's found a way to be distracting even when he is not actively harassing me.*

Pathetically, the rational side of his brain was overpowered by his impulses in just under a minute, and he couldn't stop his head from turning. Then there he was, sleeping right before Sangwoo's eyes: the most persistent error in the framework of his life.

Sangwoo found himself swept up by an emotion that he couldn't easily define, though he could confidently say he despised it. Thankfully, it dissipated pretty quickly once his mind turned to the slew of terrible things Jaeyoung had done to him while pretending to be a normal college student.

A rush of hostility surged in Sangwoo. Jaeyoung appeared to be suffering under the delusion that he wasn't the type to hold a grudge. But the thing was, Sangwoo was more than capable of getting revenge on someone, so long as certain conditions were met. It was just that, generally, he didn't think making someone's life miserable was worth the amount of time and energy it required. Also, he wasn't a complete weirdo.

But...what was the saying? An eye for an eye? In that moment, the concept sounded quite appealing.

Very carefully, Sangwoo extracted a black marker from his pencil pouch. Sliding closer to Jaeyoung, he took off the cap with all the solemnity of a soldier unsheathing his sword.

However, the tip of the marker froze midair, right before it touched Jaeyoung's forehead. It had been *years* since Sangwoo had last tried to draw something, and he found himself unable to use the canvas before him like he wanted to.

Of course, there was no unwritten rule that a person needed to possess a certain amount of artistic talent to doodle on somebody's face, but an innate sense of inferiority still held him back. Memories flashed through Sangwoo's mind: his second-grade teacher scolding him because he hadn't been able to come up with anything to draw in his notebook; losing his first-place academic ranking in his third year of middle school due to his arts evaluation...

After a long moment of hesitation, Sangwoo decided leaving a single dot would be better than nothing. He carefully studied Jaeyoung's face for a long time, trying to pick the best spot. The asshole's eyebrows were dark with a natural arch to them, the slight dip before leading down to the straight line of his nose. His long eyelashes cast a shadow over his cheekbones, below which lay a set of slightly parted lips.

I have to just go for it, Sangwoo silently reprimanded himself, clenching the marker even tighter. *It doesn't matter where.* His hand was trembling—not only had he never done something like this before, but he was sacrificing precious class time to do it.

Steeling himself, Sangwoo slowly moved the marker forward. But the moment the tip touched the skin of Jaeyoung's forehead, his eyes met Jaeyoung's now open ones.

It was completely unintentional on Sangwoo's part when the marker slipped, drawing a thick line down Jaeyoung's face.

His heart fell to the bottom of his feet. He felt like a kid caught with his hand in the cookie jar. It was really nothing compared to the time when Jaeyoung had doodled on Sangwoo's face, but it was still something he'd never even dreamed of doing to someone else before. Maybe being a terrible person required practice, like everything else in life.

Jaeyoung simply stared at him, his eyes open wide. Sangwoo stubbornly ignored him, glaring at his textbook as he shoved the marker back into his pencil pouch. His head was blank, his heart pounding in his ears.

Sangwoo sat frozen in his seat for the rest of the class, his head a jumbled mess.

When he finally snapped back to awareness, the lecture had ended, and everybody was filtering out of the classroom. To think he'd let a momentary burst of anger overtake him like that... He'd allowed himself to fall down to Jaeyoung's level.

"Saaangwoo," a voice called.

A chill ran down Sangwoo's spine—was Jaeyoung about to lose it on him? He'd have some choice words for the asshole if he did. Still, deep down, Sangwoo had to admit he was incredibly ashamed of what he'd done to the guy. How could he have doodled on somebody else's face with a marker?

"Hey, Sangwoo," Jaeyoung said again. "I'm talking to you."

Reluctantly, Sangwoo responded, "Yes?"

"That was an act of revenge, wasn't it?"

The asshole's cheerful tone made Sangwoo glance to the side, revealing a laughing Jaeyoung with a thick black line stretching all the way down his nose.

"Wow! Seriously, this is awesome," he continued, not even a trace of anger in his voice. "I feel like my robot vacuum cleaner baked a little treat for me!"

Jaeyoung reached over and patted the top of Sangwoo's capped head.

Sangwoo was so thoroughly baffled that he didn't even snap at the asshole for touching him without permission.

"Come on, let's go eat," Jaeyoung said with a big grin. "It's on me."

Even after a long pause, all Sangwoo could manage was a mumbled, "I thought I made it clear that we're not close enough for that..."

Jaeyoung ignored him, standing up and grabbing him by the wrist. Still disoriented, Sangwoo allowed himself to be pulled along.

Jaeyoung was the picture of a social butterfly as they left the engineering building, stopping to chat with what felt like every single person who walked by. Sangwoo's artwork didn't go unnoticed—Jaeyoung's friends laughed at the sight of it.

"Jaeyoung, what's that on your nose?" one girl had asked. "Is it for your club?"

"You like it? He did it for me."

The next time, it had been an upperclassman who waved at Jaeyoung. "Didn't expect to see you anywhere near the engineering building," he'd commented. "Oh, what happened to your face?"

"Just dropping by. As for my face, he's the artist."

Every single time Jaeyoung had announced that Sangwoo was the face-doodling culprit, he'd pointed at him as if he were citing a research reference. He seemed completely unembarrassed by the whole thing. Sangwoo, on the other hand, felt more humiliated than ever before. By the time they reached the first floor, his mind was in tatters from the endless "introductions."

Still, Jaeyoung wasn't done with him. The senior kept dragging him along until, somehow, they ended up in front of a pizza parlor on campus.

"Hope you like pizza," Jaeyoung said—but only after they'd already taken a seat.

At this point, Sangwoo couldn't even find the energy to point out that the words had come a few minutes too late. Instead, he said flatly: "I don't mind it."

"You're being awfully cooperative..."

"Can you erase the thing on your face?"

"Nope! I'm keeping it." Jaeyoung gave him a wide smile and scanned the menu, then ordered a pizza and two risottos without even asking Sangwoo's opinion. "I didn't order any pasta, since you hate it so much."

Sangwoo internally scoffed at the asshole's audacity. Who was he trying to fool by acting all considerate? And anyway, he'd only made that comment about the pasta because Jaeyoung worked at an Italian restaurant. Sangwoo didn't have any preferences when it came to food. He'd never even bothered to categorize the dishes he'd eaten based on taste. After all, the whole purpose of eating was to attain the energy and sustenance needed to stay alive and functioning. What was the point in being picky about appearance or taste as long as what you were consuming met the proper nutrient requirements?

In that sense, Sangwoo firmly believed that the goofball sitting across from him with a black line on his nose was wasting his money. They could have eaten at the dining hall for much cheaper.

"Sangwoo, did you understand anything from that lecture?"

"I would have if *you* weren't there."

"That's pretty wild, considering you have trouble even remembering my name."

"Personally, I find it more fascinating that the same person who went out of their way to get someone else to answer roll call for them would take a nap in a class they have no reason to be in."

At some point during this back-and-forth, the server had brought their food to the table. Sangwoo turned his focus to mechanically churning through pizza and risotto, not speaking another word. Jaeyoung tried to get a rise out of him by making a comment about his "unappetizing" way of eating, but he ignored it.

The moment he felt he'd eaten enough, Sangwoo rose to his feet and left. He felt slightly irked, perhaps because he'd been forced to dine at a place outside of his usual routine. Though it could have just as easily been the guy sitting across from him, smiling like an idiot despite the marker on his face.

"Hey, Sangwoo," called a voice from behind him. Jaeyoung must have paid for the meal in record time—he'd already caught up. "Look at the sky! Isn't it pretty? Personally, I think it'd do you good to stop and smell the roses."

Just fly away into the sky and quit bugging me, Sangwoo groaned inwardly, not deigning to lift his gaze from the ground.

The pair hadn't been walking for long when Jaeyoung took something out of his leather bag. When Sangwoo glanced at it, his gaze was immediately drawn to a familiar logo placed against a black background—it was a Black Holic canned coffee. Immediately, he knew that Jaeyoung was planning on taunting him by sipping away at the drink, keeping it out of his reach.

It was the moment Sangwoo had been waiting for: the moment where Jihye's second bit of advice would come into play. He'd already asked the owner of the convenience store when the next shipment of Black Holic coffee would arrive, and been informed it was coming the Monday after next. Since he only drank one can a day on weekdays, he only needed seven cans to hold him over—and he'd already purchased them all from his local grocery store. Even better, one of them was stored away in his bag.

Alas, he never even got to unzip his bag before Jaeyoung did something that stopped him in his tracks. The asshole reached out a hand and *offered him the coffee.*

"Here. Coffee delivery."

Error. Error. File not found.

Unsure why Jaeyoung wasn't chugging the coffee and taunting him, Sangwoo instinctively took the can, then held it up to his eye to confirm that the seal hadn't been broken. This elicited some murmurs from the asshole about how weird he was, but Sangwoo chose to ignore them in favor of continuing his inspection. However, even after he'd thoroughly inspected the can and shaken it back and forth, he didn't find any leaks or evidence of the drink having been tampered with.

"Geez… Just drink the damn thing."

"You must have done *something* to it," Sangwoo said firmly.

"What, like poison it? Relax. I'm just trying to get rid of it because I bought sixteen cans worth of the stuff, and it's nasty as hell."

Sangwoo seriously began to doubt his nemesis's state of mind.

Nothing he'd done today made any sense. It was like looking at a totally normal sequence of numbers, only for a $\sqrt{55}$ to pop up out of nowhere.

"How about this?" Jaeyoung asked in an impassive voice. "If you take off your hat, I'll give you the other fifteen."

"I'm not sure what me wearing headwear or not has to do with you," Sangwoo shot back. But inwardly, he couldn't help but wonder why the asshole was so obsessed with his hat.

The canned coffee opened with a satisfying, refreshing pop. Sangwoo carefully lifted the opening to his lips and tilted the can, letting the lukewarm liquid inside trickle into his mouth.

Jaeyoung, who had been watching from the side, suddenly asked, "Do you actually enjoy drinking that stuff?"

That wasn't something Sangwoo had ever considered. He simply found the taste of the familiar drink comforting, since it had always been a part of his daily routine. And speaking of that routine…maybe he could actually start rebuilding it right now.

Ignoring Jaeyoung's question, Sangwoo headed toward the humanities building. When he reached his walking path of choice, he found the "Drama Club - Filming in Progress" sign still stuck in the ground. That lie might have worked the past three days, but he knew the truth now. Without hesitation, he gave the sign a swift kick, then stuffed it in the garbage can.

Peace filled Sangwoo's heart as he began walking down his favorite path for the first time in forever. Not even Jaeyoung's presence could spoil his mood. He sipped on his canned coffee, his feet leading him down the trail with practiced ease.

"Well, this is pretty brave of you," Jaeyoung commented.

Unwilling to let the asshole spoil his walk, Sangwoo picked up his pace. Unfortunately, Jaeyoung was more than capable of keeping up.

"I mean, think of all the things I could do to you on this quiet, isolated forest path…"

"What are you, a damn thug?"

Jaeyoung scoffed. "Tsk, tsk. Watch your language."

Sangwoo shrugged. "If you're not, what is there for me to worry about? I was simply confirming whether it was worth my time to be concerned or not. What, did my question hit too close to home?"

"Watch it," Jaeyoung snarled through gritted teeth. "Even your friends over at the police station can't get here right away."

Sangwoo's lips twitched. While Jaeyoung was much taller than average—a trait his nice coat accentuated quite well—he didn't look like he'd be all that good at fighting.

Deciding to voice his observation, Sangwoo commented, "You don't strike me as a good fighter."

"Oh, yeah? Sounds like we got an athlete over here."

During grade school and middle school, Sangwoo had consistently taken tae kwon do lessons. He'd started prioritizing his studies once he entered high school, however, and now he didn't do much exercising except riding his bike to and from school and doing push-ups at home.

"I used to exercise consistently, but not anymore."

"We should shoot some hoops together sometime, just me and you. I guarantee that your hands will never even touch the ball."

"I'll pass. Also, stop acting so chummy with me."

As they neared the end of the path, Sangwoo saw the construction area on the route. Walking past the nearly complete futsal field and over to the natural science building, he stood right at his usual spot, took aim, and tossed his coffee at the second trash can. When it tumbled inside, a wave of satisfaction hit him. It felt like he was reconstructing a tower of cards that someone had carelessly knocked over.

His next stop was the library. Sangwoo took his reserved seat, and Jaeyoung once again sat right next to him. This time, however, the asshole decided to take out a pen and spin it around with his fingers instead of borrowing a bunch of books like he usually did.

Sangwoo took out his textbook and notebook, then turned around to hang his bag on the back of the chair. But when he returned to his original position, he found that Jaeyoung had snatched up the second of the two items.

"Give it back. You're committing theft."

Jaeyoung rolled his eyes and flipped over the notebook to check the price, then took out his wallet and handed Sangwoo the exact amount.

Sangwoo blinked at him, rendered speechless. He would still have reported the asshole for his crime if he'd considered the notebook valuable, but he only ever used it as a scratch pad. In the end, he decided it would be much more efficient to get a new one than to waste his time arguing with Jaeyoung.

But despite his magnanimity, the distractions began almost immediately. Still, Jaeyoung could loudly flip through his stolen notebook all he pleased—Sangwoo had come fully prepared. In fact, he'd been waiting for this very thing to happen.

Reaching into his backpack, Sangwoo quickly took out the earplugs he'd brought—his third avenue of attack against Jaeyoung's harassment—and placed them in his ears. Immediately, the noises that had been driving him up the wall ceased.

At least I was able to make good use of one piece of Jihye's advice, Sangwoo thought. The earplugs were admittedly a bit uncomfortable, but wearing them was infinitely better than having to listen to Jaeyoung's fidgeting. For the first time in days, he felt like he could actually focus on studying.

Unfortunately, he hadn't even finished reading a single paragraph before he felt a piercing gaze start boring into the side of his face. Glancing over, Sangwoo found that Jaeyoung had turned his chair to face him, pen and stolen notebook in hand. He appeared to be drawing something. The concentrated frown on his face, coupled with his frequent glances between the notebook and Sangwoo, made him look absurdly professional.

This is ridiculous, Sangwoo thought. Without any further ado, he put up the divider between him and Jaeyoung and turned his attention back to his textbook. But his focus faltered only a minute later—and when he glanced to the side, the divider was gone. Clearly, a certain asshole had taken it down, but he'd missed it because of his earplugs.

Sangwoo put the divider back up, but Jaeyoung removed it again almost immediately. By the time they'd repeated the childish cycle three times, anger was bubbling away in the back of Sangwoo's throat. If things kept going like this, his study session would be ruined for a third time.

He put the divider up yet again, holding it firmly in place with one hand this time so that Jaeyoung couldn't topple it over. This was effective enough that, for the next few minutes, he was allowed to read his textbook in peace. But that didn't last long—soon, he felt Jaeyoung's intense stare land on his face once more.

Sangwoo turned his head to find that Jaeyoung had climbed to his feet. The asshole was still scribbling away in the stupid notebook, using his new position to peek over the barrier.

"What is *wrong* with this guy?" Sangwoo muttered under his breath.

For the first half of the day, Jaeyoung had actually been tolerable; he'd contributed to their group project, given Sangwoo one of the canned coffees he'd bought out from under him, and even let Sangwoo bust down the fake drama club sign without raising a fuss.

But that would be looking at the situation through rose-colored glasses. Jaeyoung had also tampered with their skit's script and tricked the professor into blaming the result on Sangwoo. And now, the asshole was staring at him so intently that he couldn't digest a single word of his textbook!

It appeared that, while the Jaeyoung in the green coat was significantly less annoying than his red puffer-jacketed counterpart, he certainly wasn't a relaxing person to be around, either.

There was nothing else for it—Sangwoo would have to go over his textbooks at home instead. The desk back at his apartment was much smaller than the ones at the library, and his lights were dimmer, meaning the studying environment was less than ideal, but it would be worth it just to escape Jaeyoung's endless distractions.

Sangwoo had already yanked his earplugs out of his ears and begun to pack up when the sound of ripping paper reached his ears. Slipping his textbook into his bag, he turned to find something hovering right in front of his eyes.

"I have a gift for you," Jaeyoung declared.

As it turned out, the sketch Jaeyoung had been working on so intently for all that time was a caricature of Sangwoo's face.

It was even more exaggerated than the political cartoons in American newspapers. Sangwoo's cheekbones jutted out, his eyes slanted up, and prominent dark circles lurked under his lower lash line. On top of that, his lips were downturned, and his neck was so thin it resembled a stick more than anything else. Worst of all, the head of the hideous replica of him had been crowned with a gigantic black hat.

Sangwoo shredded the drawing into small pieces.

"That's a bit harsh," Jaeyoung muttered.

Sangwoo ignored him, making sure to brush every last piece of paper into his hand. He neatly deposited them in a trash can on his way out.

Of course, the asshole followed him. "Do you have any idea how much people are willing to pay for my illustrations?"

"I fail to see what the pricing of your art has to do with me."

"I'm just saying, that drawing didn't deserve to get ripped up like that."

"I didn't destroy it because it was of bad quality. I destroyed it because you're the one who drew it."

Jaeyoung scoffed. "Why'd you drink the coffee, then?"

"You didn't make the coffee."

"That...is true. Whatever."

By the time they left the library, it was 1:32 PM, which meant Sangwoo had wasted a truly absurd amount of time trying and failing to study.

As he swung himself onto his bike, Jaeyoung yelled, "Sangwoo!"

"What?"

"I know it's a bit early, but...good night!"

It was a pointless thing to say in the middle of the day, but it would've probably pissed Sangwoo off just as much to hear it right before he went to bed.

"I hope you have a nightmare," he responded, then rode away downhill.

`return 0;`

Sangwoo's routine saw a slight improvement the following day. Both of his Friday classes were requirements for his major, so Jaeyoung spent the duration of the lectures napping instead of harassing him. Sangwoo had felt slightly tempted to look over at the asshole on occasion, but forced himself to focus on his professors instead, reminding himself of the disaster that had befallen him after he'd tried to doodle on Jaeyoung's face.

At the end of his second class, he was pleased to find he'd done fine despite having the guy stuck to him like a leech.

As they walked out of the building, Jaeyoung casually said, "I can treat you to another meal, if you want."

It was yet another nonsensical offer to provide expensive food for free. Sangwoo would have accepted without a second thought if the proposition had come from anyone else, but the fact that his nemesis had delivered the words made him hesitate.

Sangwoo let the possible results play out in his brain.

```
i) Accept invitation
Financial gain Y, Stress Y = Slight loss
ii) Decline invitation – If Jaeyoung follows me to the dining hall
Financial gain N, Stress Y = Terrible loss
iii) Decline invitation – If Jaeyoung goes to eat somewhere else
Financial gain N, Stress N = No change to status quo
```

No matter what, if he accepted Jaeyoung's offer, he'd have to suffer through the painful ordeal of eating with the asshole. If he declined his offer, however, there was a possibility Jaeyoung would follow him, and he'd have to suffer the same agony without even getting free food. He had no choice but to take a gamble—it really all depended on how Jaeyoung would react.

"I'm good."

"Going to the dining hall again?"

"Yes."

"Geez, you must be their biggest fan. They should give you an award."

It was Sangwoo's lucky day: His decision resulted in the third outcome. Jaeyoung wandered off somewhere else, and Sangwoo entered the dining hall by himself. He followed his usual routine of getting his food, then finding a quiet section of the hall to sit. It proved a peaceful meal indeed, and, as an added bonus, he was only one minute off schedule when he finished eating.

Feeling only slightly bothered by his lateness, Sangwoo began to make his way out of the dining hall. His good mood was shattered all too soon, however, when he saw someone waiting for him at the entrance.

His nemesis.

"Here," Jaeyoung said, thrusting something at Sangwoo.

It was a can of Black Holic. Once again, Sangwoo only opened the coffee after giving it a firm shake and a thorough examination to prove to himself it was safe to drink.

As he took a sip, Jaeyoung asked, "You want a good grade on the skit, right?"

"Obviously."

"Come with me, then."

Getting a good grade equals going somewhere with him? Sangwoo wondered. It seemed a strange equation.

"To where?"

"To get costumes, of course."

"Why would we do that?"

"Come on… A Qing dynasty merchant can't just wear some T-shirt with English written all over it!"

"But…it's time for my walk."

"You can go on a stroll later," Jaeyoung snapped, irritation seeping into his voice.

When Sangwoo showed no signs of budging, the asshole grabbed his wrist and began to drag him off somewhere.

"This is assault!" Sangwoo yelled, lifting his phone with his free hand. "I will call the police. I *said*, I will call the police!"

Alas, it turned out that Jaeyoung was much stronger than he looked. He snatched Sangwoo's phone away with a frown and slipped it into his own pocket before Sangwoo could follow through with his threat.

Sangwoo scowled. "Just taking my phone away won't stop me. I hope you enjoy having a criminal charge on your record."

"Stop being so stubborn! I'm trying to help, okay? You can report me all you want if you still think I assaulted you when we're done. I won't try to stop you."

Though Sangwoo found it hard to believe, he figured he might as well *try* to trust him. Reluctantly, he agreed to Jaeyoung's terms.

Finally releasing Sangwoo's wrist, Jaeyoung asked, "You okay with being the merchant?"

"Yes."

Why wouldn't he be? The merchant had significantly more lines in the skit, which meant taking the role significantly raised his likelihood of receiving a high score.

"Okay. Then I'll be the customer and the person being scammed."

Staunchly refusing to reveal their destination, Jaeyoung led Sangwoo across campus. Eventually, they arrived at the student center and went up a flight of stairs, where they stopped in front of a door with a sign that read "Drama Club."

The door swung open to reveal a room that was filled with haphazard piles of props, costumes, and masks. There was a pile of Black Holic coffee cans—definitely purchased by Jaeyoung—sitting on top of a mini fridge, and posters of old plays covering the walls.

Two guys sat on a couch, playing some kind of soccer game on a gaming console. They both perked up as soon as they saw Jaeyoung.

"Oh, good afternoon, Jaeyoung!"

"Carry on. Don't worry about me," Jaeyoung said, not even glancing at them as he moved a mannequin aside to reveal a door. He beckoned Sangwoo forward, and the two of them walked inside.

The space they entered was awfully tight. Two-tiered hangers lined three of the four walls, displaying a wide assortment of costumes. While Jaeyoung rummaged through them using a long garment hook, Sangwoo tried to find something that looked like it could have come from the Qing dynasty. But with all the clothes packed onto the hangers, it was a difficult mission.

"How about this one?" Jaeyoung asked excitedly, extracting a long blue ensemble from a jumbled mess of costumes. It had a high-neck collar and was long enough to cover the wearer's ankles. Gold bands wrapped around the waist and sleeves, and a complex pattern was sewn onto the chest area.

After another brief search, Jaeyoung found a purple one of a similar design and held it up to himself. "Which one suits me better?"

"They look the same."

"Dude, the hems are totally different."

Sangwoo sighed. "Pick whichever one you like. I don't understand why you're so concerned over what to wear for a skit."

"Hey, I'm just trying to get a hundred," Jaeyoung responded. He held up a yellow piece that looked similar to the other two—identical, if you were asking Sangwoo. "Oooh, I like this one. Now we've just got to find you a queue wig."

Nodding, Sangwoo crouched and tried to locate one in a large box, only to come up with nothing. He dragged another box closer, but Jaeyoung surprised him by hunkering down right next to him, his face suddenly swooping in much closer than ever before.

"Back up, please."

"Sure, sure," Jaeyoung said easily. But he didn't move an inch.

Fidgeting uncomfortably, Sangwoo began to look through the second box. A few minutes had passed when he suddenly realized something had gone missing: his hat. He looked up to see Jaeyoung clutching it in his hands, staring at Sangwoo like something was lagging in his brain.

What is he planning now? Sangwoo wondered, but couldn't come up with a plausible answer. The only thing he could think of was that Jaeyoung had decided he wanted his hat for some reason. After all, he'd been going on and on about the thing since the previous day.

"You would be better off buying a new one," Sangwoo informed him resolutely. "I've been wearing that since high school."

Jaeyoung just continued to stare at him, not saying a word.

Thinking that an if-then statement might be more effective, Sangwoo tried: "If you stop harassing me, then I will buy you the exact same one."

He didn't particularly expect the words to trigger Jaeyoung to give him the ragged old hat back. As the asshole had said once before, the problem likely wasn't that simple.

But Jaeyoung didn't react how Sangwoo had guessed he would, either. There was no laughter, no joking, no plopping the hat on his own head. Instead, he caught Sangwoo entirely off guard by reaching out to him with his free hand and murmuring, "You've got something right… here."

Jaeyoung's long fingers advanced toward him very slowly, very carefully. Sangwoo could have backed away from them if he wanted to, but a strange tension gripped his limbs, holding him in place as Jaeyoung's hand brushed over his bangs and drifted to his forehead.

The second Jaeyoung's fingertips touched his skin, fireworks went off in Sangwoo's head. The disturbing sensation had him jerking backward so abruptly that he crumpled the prop box and sent Jaeyoung's hand flying.

"Give me the hat."

"But you look so much better like this! Why not try going without it?"

"Whether I do or do not is none of your concern," Sangwoo said flatly, extending his hand.

Despite the clear request, Jaeyoung made no move to return the hat. Abruptly, rage surged up in Sangwoo.

"Give. It. Back."

"Come on, I just wanted to see what you actually looked like!"

"I said, *give it back*!"

Sangwoo didn't usually raise his voice at upperclassmen, but he couldn't help himself. He lunged forward and snatched the hat out of Jaeyoung's hands, his chest colliding with the other student's. Jaeyoung fell backward, arms waving, but Sangwoo didn't wait around to see if he was okay. Instead, he sprang back to his feet and raced out of the costume room. The two students on the couch glanced up with wide eyes when he slammed the door shut behind him.

Sangwoo's heart was pounding, and he could feel blood rushing to his face. *That crazy asshole has to stop taking other people's belongings!* he thought angrily, seething as he marched out of the room. Jaeyoung had been completely correct when he'd described himself as unpredictable; helpful one moment, and incredibly irritating the next, he was as unpredictable as the weather.

As he continued walking, Sangwoo's footsteps gradually slowed. Embarrassment trickled in, gradually drowning out the anger that had overwhelmed him. Why had he yelled at Jaeyoung? Sure, the asshole had stolen his hat, but his reaction had been way over the top. It had also been deeply out of character for him.

In Sangwoo's defense, Jaeyoung's closeness—not to mention the unexpected and unwanted physical contact—had made it impossible for him to think logically. But that was a problem in and of itself, wasn't it? It wasn't like the asshole was a member of the opposite sex. Naked men sat in the same tub in public bathhouses all the time, and nobody batted an eye when men touched each other all over during a wrestling match. Even in football, tackles weren't much different than aggressive hugs. None of it meant anything because they were *all men*.

Reluctantly, Sangwoo reached the conclusion that his actions had been completely irrational. When Jaeyoung finally caught up to him, he found that he couldn't even look into the asshole's eyes out of sheer embarrassment.

Jaeyoung handed Sangwoo the blue costume, the queue wig, and his phone. "I really wasn't trying to make you mad," he said. "I only took off your hat to put the wig on you. I didn't know you'd get upset."

"I'm not upset."

It was a lie. Even now, Sangwoo's heart was pounding with anger, despite it being more than clear that he'd misinterpreted Jaeyoung's attempt to be helpful. *Apparently, that asshole has a talent for stressing me out, even when he's not doing it intentionally.*

"Let's try to get along, Sangwoo. We've gotta do our best to get a good grade on that skit."

Ignoring him with an ease that only came with practice, Sangwoo shoved his costume and wig inside his bag and walked out of the building. When he heard Jaeyoung following him, he spun around.

"Your new strategy isn't going to work on me. Stop acting like we're friends."

A smile crept onto Jaeyoung's previously emotionless face. "What strategy? I don't know what you're talking about. I'm just following my heart."

"Furthermore, you need to stop following me. I'm going home to study, since it's impossible to do so at the library with you."

"You know, telling someone not to do something… That's the perfect way to get them to do it."

"Please follow me, then."

"Sure! If you say so."

Gritting his teeth, Sangwoo nearly jogged over to the library, then got on his bicycle. He figured leaving Jaeyoung behind in a cloud of dust as he sped down his usual downhill path might lift his mood, but when he glanced behind him, the asshole was still there. In fact, he was riding a bright neon skateboard.

"What are you doing?" he called over to him, gaping in shock.

"I thought you wanted me to follow you?"

Sangwoo was struck speechless. He stared at Jaeyoung's skateboard, unable to even begin to fathom how Jaeyoung's brain functioned. Did the man not value his own time? He simply couldn't comprehend why the asshole would do something like this when he could be doing something infinitely more productive.

Sangwoo shook his head and tried to focus on riding his bike, but his gaze kept being drawn back to Jaeyoung like the other man was a damn magnet.

He hated to admit it, but Jaeyoung was obviously good at skateboarding. On top of that, he had a way of drawing people's attention. Nearly every single passerby looked at him with fascination and exclaimed in wonder.

Jaeyoung not only seemed well aware of their admiration, but reveled in it—whenever he passed through a particularly crowded area, he'd send his skateboard catapulting into the air, grinning like he was a celebrity as he gave out high fives to every kid he passed.

Watching him, Sangwoo couldn't help but think Jaeyoung's wild, free attitude resembled that of a video game character. He'd always known the two of them were very different from one another, but the sight of Jaeyoung skateboarding, wind blowing through his hair and a smile on his face, really drove the truth home: They were polar opposites.

Whereas Sangwoo only did what was absolutely necessary, Jaeyoung did as he pleased. He moved through life like he wasn't tied down by anything, grinning like a kid seconds away from getting in trouble, while Sangwoo was eternally emotionless and always stuck to the same routine. Even worse, in stark contrast to Sangwoo's complete lack of friends, Jaeyoung seemed to stumble across one wherever he went. The asshole's closet was probably bursting with colors, while Sangwoo's was a drab, relentless black.

The two of them might breathe the same air, but they lived in two very different worlds. If it hadn't been for "the incident," their paths would likely have never even crossed.

When Sangwoo took a turn and entered an alley, Jaeyoung sped up so they were cruising along, side by side. Despite the fact that no one else was around, Jaeyoung still jumped high into the air, did a half-spin, and landed safely on the ground. It looked so effortless, Sangwoo had to wonder if the skateboard had been glued to his feet.

"Why are you following me?" Sangwoo called out to Jaeyoung once again. He didn't get it—the asshole would've had a better time skateboarding literally anywhere other than the unevenly paved alleyway they were currently traveling down.

"Got nothing else to do," came the nonchalant response.

It didn't exactly answer Sangwoo's question, but at this point, he understood there was no need to try and comprehend his nemesis's strange brain. Soon enough, the time he'd spent suffering would come to a close.

"Just one week left," he pronounced.

"Until what?"

"The deadline for dropping classes."

Instead of responding, Jaeyoung just laughed.

Not long later, the pair rolled to a stop in front of Sangwoo's apartment: a four-story building with mold crawling up the external walls. Sangwoo pulled his bike over to a canopied bike rack and secured it to the spot labeled "Unit 402."

Jaeyoung stared up at the building, absently pushing his skateboard back and forth with his foot. "So this is where you live," he commented mildly.

"The minimum sentence for home invasion is three years' incarceration."

"Yeah, yeah, I was waiting for you to say that."

"I will immediately call the police if you steal my bicycle. The same applies to the saddle and any other components."

He'd thought Jaeyoung would come up with some sort of sarcastic retort, but the asshole just smiled silently. Stepping on one end of his skateboard, he pressed down hard and sent it flying up into his left hand at the same time that he waved at Sangwoo with his right.

"Have a good weekend, Sangwoo."

There was no ill intent in the words. Left with no other choice, Sangwoo responded with a curt, "I will."

Finally looking away from Jaeyoung, he walked into his apartment building. But as he began to climb the stairs, unease sat in Sangwoo's stomach like a brick. Wondering why, he sank into careful contemplation. Then... *Oh. This is the first time we've ever parted ways like normal people instead of cussing at one another.*

A small part of him worried that Jaeyoung would chase him up the stairs or something, but the staircase remained silent even as Sangwoo reached the fourth floor and entered the code to his door.

As he stepped into his apartment, a heavy sigh left his lungs. After that, muscle memory took over. First, he placed his bag by the door and put his hat and coat on a hanger. Then he changed into sweats and washed his hands with soap. When he looked into the mirror, he was met with the reflection of a mundane-looking guy with hair slightly pressed down from wearing a cap.

Grabbing a textbook from his bookshelf, Sangwoo placed it on top of his desk. He then took his pencil pouch and notebook from his bag and put them right next to it.

The next step was to take a seat at his desk, but his feet carried him over to the window instead. When he lifted the edge of the curtain and peeked out, he found that Jaeyoung was still lurking down below. He'd left his skateboard on the ground, and was scratching a black cat on its belly.

Sangwoo was familiar with the feline—he'd encountered it on several occasions, but it had always angrily hissed at him or left him behind as it dashed away. For a moment, he stood there and watched as Jaeyoung took several pictures of the cat. Then he closed the curtain.

The first two days had definitely been the hardest, like the video game that was his life had gotten switched to hard mode. Then he'd been allowed a single day of rest, which had then been followed by two days of mild irritation. It was an irregular sequence, operating totally without pattern—just like Jaeyoung's personality.

Sangwoo *hated* things that didn't follow a pattern. How was he supposed to predict anything about them?

He opened his textbook and began to study.

return 0;

Unpredictability was always accompanied by inefficiency.

In this case, it was Jaeyoung's endlessly inconsistent actions that were driving Sangwoo up the wall. It was impossible to anticipate the asshole's weekend plans, so whenever anyone walked in through the glass door of the internet café—which was partially covered by a game poster—Sangwoo couldn't help but tense up. He'd only relax, letting out a sigh of relief, when he was sure the entering customer wasn't his nemesis.

Today, the café was pretty slow. Unfortunately, Sangwoo ended up spending almost his entire shift stealing glances at the door. Although he was simply trying to prepare himself in case Jaeyoung burst into his workplace, funnily enough, it was like he was waiting for him instead.

Even if he had been, Sangwoo had an argument to support his actions.

If there was one consistency in Jaeyoung's routine over the last week, it was that he'd found some way to interact with Sangwoo every single day. The asshole had even chased him down on Wednesday, the one day their schedules didn't overlap.

Still, contrary to Sangwoo's expectations, Jaeyoung remained nowhere to be seen even once the clock hit 10:00 PM. *He could be waiting in front of my apartment,* he theorized, battling a mixture of confusion and unease. After all, Jaeyoung was one of the most persistent people he'd ever come across, and the guy knew exactly where Sangwoo lived. It would be no surprise if he showed up unannounced.

When Sangwoo walked back to his apartment after clocking out of work, he found a black silhouette waiting for him in front of the building. *I knew it!* he thought triumphantly, but in the end, the figure turned out to be nothing more than a large trash bag.

Clearly, he wouldn't be seeing Jaeyoung today. The realization left Sangwoo slightly deflated as he unlocked the door to his apartment—he should've spent his time at work more efficiently rather than constantly glancing at the door.

```
i) There is a [100]% probability of Jaeyoung appearing on weekdays.
ii) There is a [x]% probability of Jaeyoung appearing on the weekend. (0 ≤ x ≤ 50)
```

This was the equation Sangwoo finally reached based on his existing data and what had happened on Saturday. It was basically useless, but he still told himself that Jaeyoung wouldn't appear on Sunday, to lift his spirits if nothing else.

Unfortunately, this resolute belief was shattered when the small bell above the café door rang and Jaeyoung walked through at precisely 7:33 PM. Sangwoo forced himself to make eye contact with the asshole—greeting customers was part of his job description. But even as he did, frustration swirled inside him. He'd been proven wrong *again*.

What's that asshole going to do now? Sangwoo thought anxiously as

Jaeyoung walked past him. He found himself grateful that there was a security camera on the ceiling. If Jaeyoung tried to harass him, Sangwoo could simply report him to the owner and ensure that he was banned from the premises. He had full faith that the owner would have his back—he had taken Sangwoo's side a long time ago when he'd gotten into a fight with a guy who wanted to run a tab.

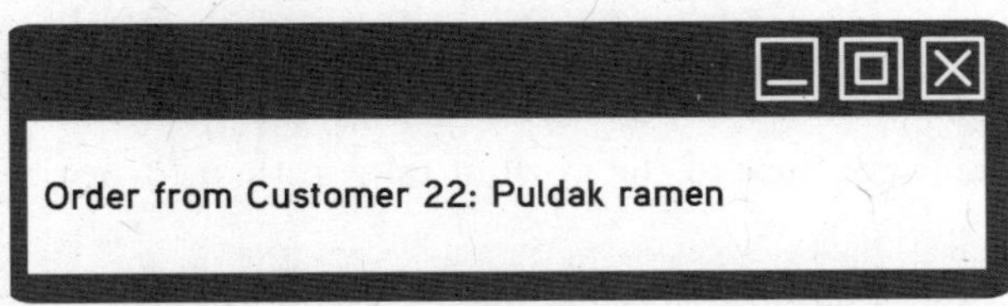

Sangwoo glowered at the notification. It had only been a minute since Jaeyoung walked past the counter, which meant he'd placed the order immediately after booting up his PC.

After measuring out the right amount of water, boiling it, and cooking the ramen according to the recipe, Sangwoo placed the plastic bowl on a tray and headed over to his nemesis. Jaeyoung was leaning back in his chair, bouncing his leg as he read a comic book.

Sangwoo put the bowl down, then left without stopping to chat. As he walked away, he heard Jaeyoung sigh behind him.

About three minutes after he'd returned to the reception desk, another notification popped up on his screen.

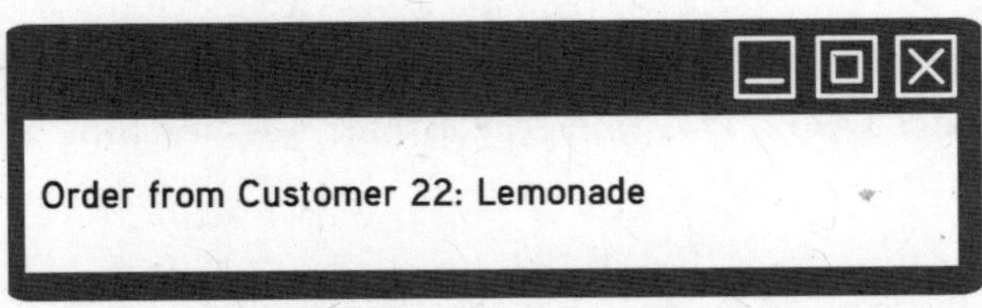

What, is he training me to fetch? Sangwoo wondered. Honestly, compared to the other things Jaeyoung had subjected him to, he didn't find it that objectionable. Not only was he getting paid to do it, but Jaeyoung's seat wasn't too far from the counter.

Filling exactly 80 percent of a cup with water, Sangwoo mixed in lemonade powder with a spoon. When he put in four ice cubes, the liquid reached the top of the cup.

Placing it on the same tray as before, he brought it over to Jaeyoung—who was now watching a video of people painting graffiti on a wall. The bowl of instant noodles was half empty.

The asshole let out a heavy sigh, but Sangwoo ignored it and placed the lemonade right next to the bowl of ramen, then turned around and left.

Another notification popped up just five minutes after he returned to the reception desk.

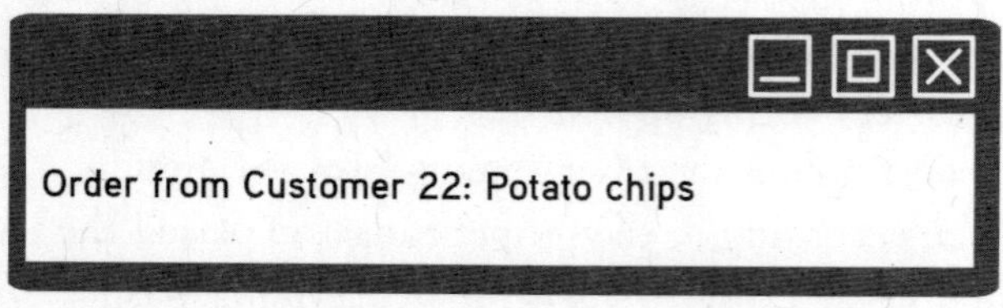

Sangwoo glared at the screen, a scowl contorting his lips. Though the system allowed customers to order any item on the menu, most people were sensible enough to come up to the desk and purchase chips on their own instead of ordering them through their PC.

It's fine, Sangwoo reminded himself. *I suppose I should be grateful for the exercise.*

Grabbing the chips from the cabinet, he headed toward Jaeyoung's computer once again. This time, the asshole was watching a basketball game.

"Haaah..."

It was possible he was mistaken, but Sangwoo had a sneaking suspicion that Jaeyoung's sighs were growing louder. But what business was that of his? He put the chips next to the other food and returned to the front desk, then crossed his arms and stared at the screen. He knew the asshole wasn't done just yet.

Just as he'd thought, it wasn't long before he got a fourth notification.

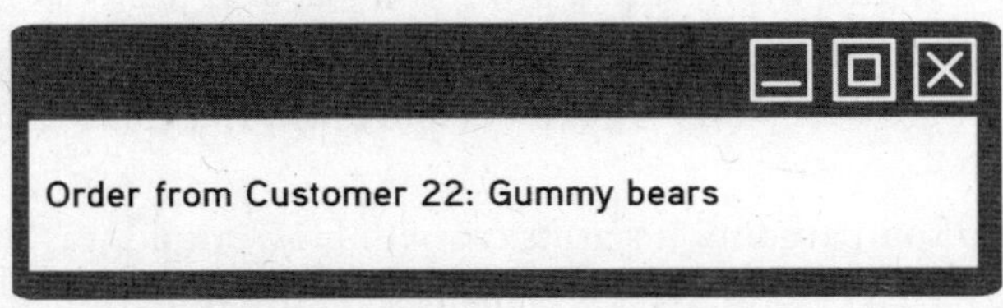

Sangwoo snatched the gummy bears from the shelf and brought them over to Jaeyoung, who released another long sigh as soon as he saw Sangwoo.

Scowling, Sangwoo tossed the bag full of candy at Jaeyoung's thigh. "Order them all at once next time."

"Haaaaaaaaah…"

"And stop sighing at me if you have something to say. Spit it out."

"This suuucks."

"I'm not sure what you expect me to do about it," Sangwoo muttered, turning around.

Behind his back, he heard Jaeyoung call out, "I'm not gonna stop ordering shit until you ask me why I'm sighing!"

Sangwoo scoffed in disbelief. Apparently, Jaeyoung was okay with wasting not only time but *money*, all because he couldn't bring himself to simply speak his mind.

"Fine. Why are you sighing?"

Immediately, Jaeyoung responded: "My laptop is broken."

Jaeyoung tried to pass it off as a casual comment, and it successfully piqued Sangwoo's interest.

"How? What is the issue?"

"No idea. It keeps beeping at me whenever I try to turn it on."

"The memory card might have come loose from the slot, or it may be an issue with the motherboard. If it's the memory card, you can simply open the body and put the RAM back in place. If it's the second, you'll have to take it in for repairs. The number of beeps will indicate what is going on."

"Ugh… I didn't understand a thing you just said. I *suck* at this stuff," Jaeyoung muttered glumly, then sighed yet again. "What should I do? Take it to a hardware store? That'd cost me, like, five hundred thousand won, right?"

Sangwoo spun around, his arms crossed. How stupid was this guy? If the asshole wasn't careful, he was going to get upsold to high heaven.

Jaeyoung stared up at Sangwoo from his chair, then mumbled, seemingly to himself, "I *did* bring it with me, but it's not like I can do anything to fix it. Maybe I'll look up a repair shop after I game a bit. It's probably too late in the day, though. What a disaster…"

Finally, Sangwoo gave in. "Give it to me."

It wasn't that Sangwoo felt bad for Jaeyoung in any way. No, no. He was simply allowing himself to follow his desires—and he'd gotten a whim to solve the asshole's problem.

"Oh! I *completely* forgot you were a computer science major!" Jaeyoung exclaimed, clapping his hands together and widening his eyes to a comical degree. "How convenient. You must have an affinity for fixing computers, right?"

"I'll just take a look."

Jaeyoung nodded and eagerly handed him a green laptop bag. When Sangwoo returned to the reception desk and unzipped it, he uncovered a silver fourteen-inch laptop. It had been released two years ago by a foreign brand, but that wasn't an issue. He'd used their products before and knew them well.

The laptop refused to boot up when he attempted to turn it on, but beeped twice. Two beeps instead of four—it was a telltale sign that something was wrong with the device's memory.

Sangwoo forced the laptop to shut down and began to take it apart with a screwdriver he grabbed from a drawer. When he got it open, he couldn't help but raise an eyebrow in disbelief. *How in the world…?* He'd imagined the RAM stick had just been jostled slightly out of place, but it was nowhere to be seen. Turning to his work PC, he sent a message to Customer 22.

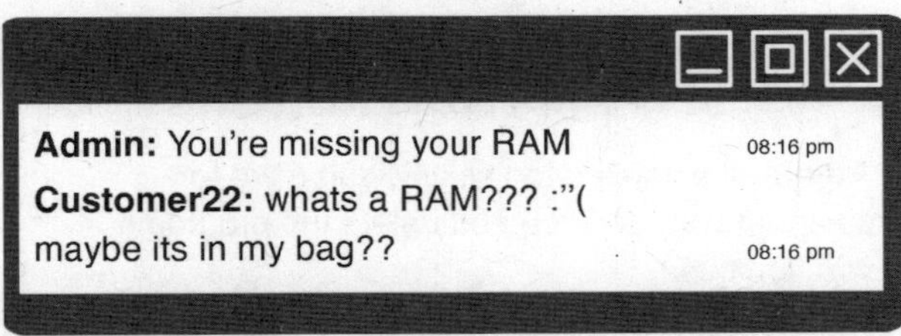

Why would it be in his bag? Sangwoo frowned slightly, but figured he had nothing to lose by looking. Lo and behold, after rummaging around the laptop bag's pockets for a while, he was able to locate the component. He scoffed silently.

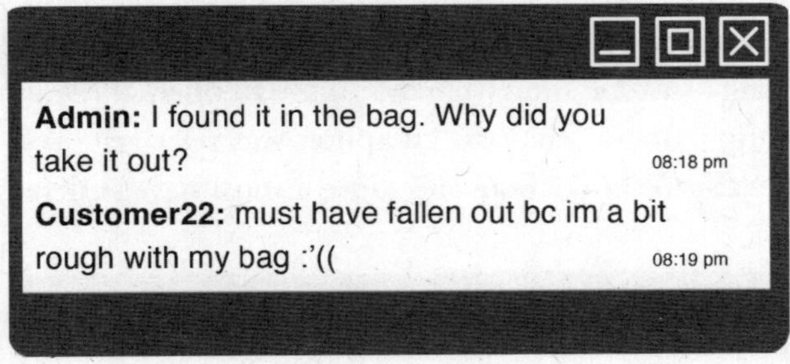

So I'm supposed to believe that not only did the RAM stick fall out by itself, but it also somehow slipped through the laptop's outer casing? Even for someone like Jaeyoung, it was a ridiculous thing to say.

Sangwoo plugged it back in, and the laptop finally turned on. Unfortunately, the hardware didn't seem to be the only issue. It took an abnormally long time for the system to boot up, and the screen that finally appeared after five excruciating minutes struck him speechless.

Nearly half the desktop was filled with icons for design programs, and the other half consisted of images, videos, documents, and various untitled folders. The messy array almost completely covered the female celebrity on Jaeyoung's wallpaper, which made recognizing her—an already difficult task for Sangwoo—nearly impossible.

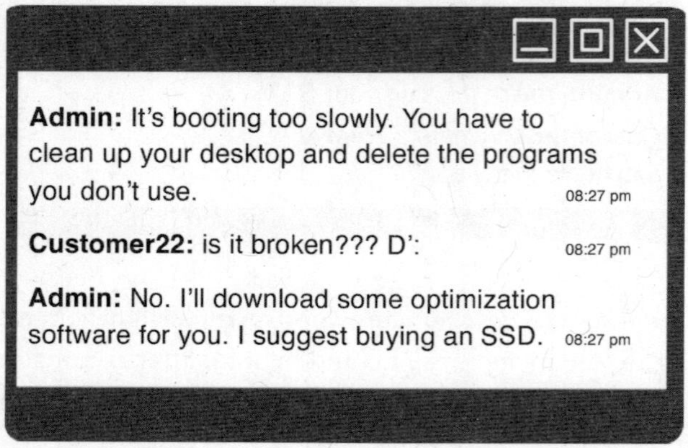

Alas, soon it became clear that the program he had in mind wouldn't solve anything—it took more than a minute to open a *web browser*. The most shocking part was that the computer was relatively new. Sangwoo didn't even want to think about the abuse it must have suffered.

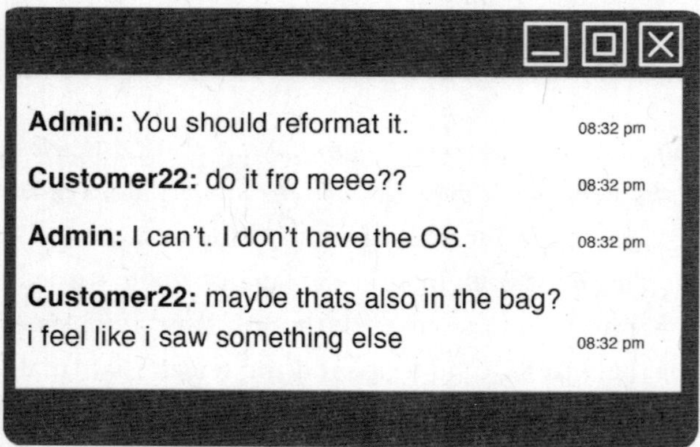

Who in the world carries around the OS for their laptop? Sangwoo thought dubiously. He was understandably shocked when he discovered a

USB drive in the back pocket of the laptop bag that, indeed, turned out to have the OS installed on it.

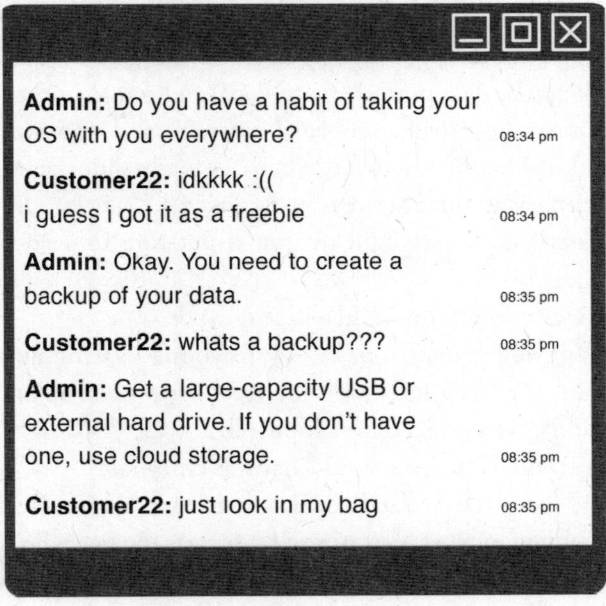

Sangwoo scoffed in disbelief when he found a one-terabyte external hard drive in the inner pocket.

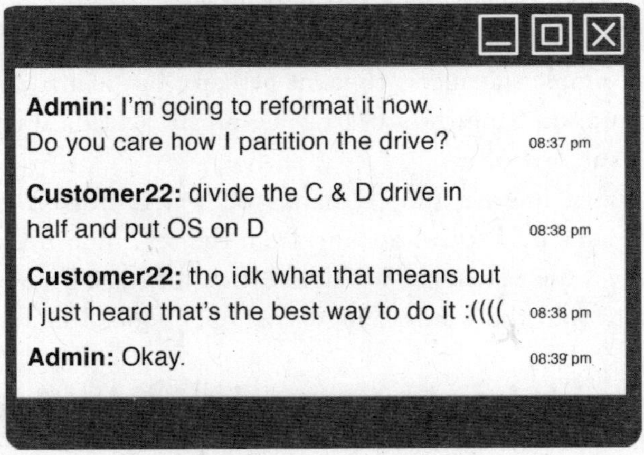

If Jaeyoung didn't even know what a backup was, how had he ended up with such a large-capacity hard drive in his bag? At this point, it was starting to feel like the bag had been enchanted to give whoever had it whatever they needed.

The laptop remained agonizingly slow, but Sangwoo eventually managed to back up the data onto the hard drive and reformat the laptop. He then went on to download some basic software and optimize things as best he could. Pride filled his heart when he finally shut the lid.

That feeling was the core reason he loved to stay productive—not only did it make time pass quickly, but it put him in a good mood as well.

"Your eyes are sparkling," said a nearby voice.

When Sangwoo glanced up, he saw Jaeyoung looking down at him, leaning against the reception desk with his chin propped up on his hands. Sangwoo hadn't even noticed him approach.

"And wait, you're done already? That was crazy fast!"

Belatedly, Sangwoo realized he'd wasted two hours on the laptop. There was nobody to blame but himself—he was the one who'd made the choice to repair the deadbeat's device, after all. To be fair, that deadbeat had been acting pretty nice recently for whatever reason…

Sangwoo scowled as he slipped the laptop back into the bag and shoved it at Jaeyoung. "Here. Don't try to run any graphic design programs. Your laptop doesn't have the specs for it."

"Thank you, Sangwoo."

It was a simple statement, flippant perhaps, but it made something strange stir inside Sangwoo's heart. The organ tickled, almost as if a feather had run over it.

Mentally, he knew a simple thank you wasn't suitable compensation for the time he'd spent. So why, from the very moment he'd heard Jaeyoung say those words, had he felt like his efforts had been worth it?

Unable to find the words, Sangwoo simply nodded mutely without making eye contact.

When the shift changed, Sangwoo quickly packed his things and put on his jacket. He walked out to find Jaeyoung standing in front of the door of the internet café with his laptop bag slung over his shoulder.

Sangwoo took off at a walk, still feeling slightly elated from his successful laptop repair. But after a bit of time had passed and the endorphin rush had faded, he realized that he'd been mindlessly strolling along with Jaeyoung at his side. The other man was humming some bizarre song, his hands tucked in his pockets.

Feeling as if it would be a good idea to be more cautious, Sangwoo kept a careful eye on Jaeyoung for the next few minutes. But, contrary to his expectations, the guy didn't try to trip, embarrass, or harass him in any way.

Finally, Sangwoo burst out, "What're you doing?"

"Huh?" Jaeyoung put on a shocked expression, like he'd just realized he wasn't alone.

"Where are you going?" Sangwoo questioned.

"Uh… Home, I guess?"

"Why are you walking in the direction of my apartment, then?"

"Hey, you're not the only one that lives over this way."

Sangwoo inwardly nodded to himself. It seemed Jaeyoung was simply on his way home, not stalking him.

After a brief silence, Jaeyoung said, "So…you're really good with computers."

"Well, everything I needed just happened to be in that laptop bag."

"I gotta thank you for your help somehow," Jaeyoung continued. It was like the asshole hadn't even heard him.

"Don't worry about it," Sangwoo told him firmly. "I only fixed it because it would have bothered me otherwise."

It wasn't like he'd been looking for a reward. And besides, he didn't want to know what Jaeyoung's idea of "thanking" him was.

"No, no. You should be rewarded for your hard work!"

"It's fine."

There was a long pause. Then, out of nowhere, Jaeyoung asked: "Wanna see a movie?"

Now, Sangwoo wasn't an avid moviegoer, but he was fully aware that two individuals going on an outing to a theater together was usually considered a date. So when he responded, his voice was filled with bewilderment. "Why would I go see a movie with *you*?"

"Hm? No, not *with* me. I meant, I'll buy a ticket for you."

Sangwoo's heart began to pound. He'd misunderstood far too many things in way too short a period of time. "Sure, fine," he muttered.

Thankful that he was almost at his apartment, he started walking even faster. When they finally arrived at the building, Jaeyoung came to a stop at the door.

"Have a good night, Sangwoo," Jaeyoung called out from behind him.

The tone of his voice was incredibly kind, which meant it also felt totally out of place and ridiculous. And yet, to Sangwoo, this goodbye was somehow different than the ones he'd received from Jaeyoung in the past. He wanted to ignore the deadbeat piece of trash, but he couldn't bring himself to do it.

"You too," he uttered, then raced up the stairs, taking them two at a time.

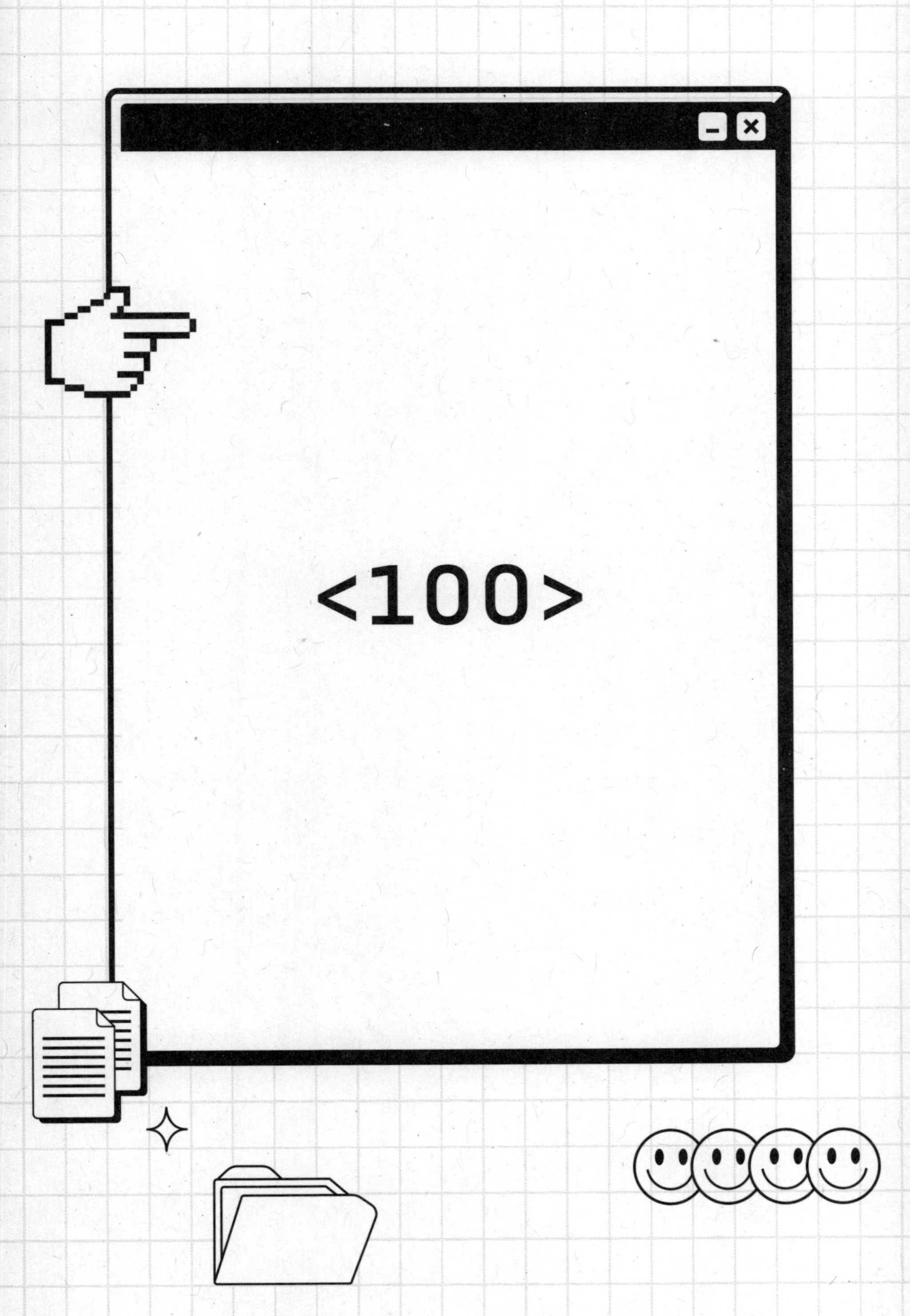
<100>

There was something wrong with Jaeyoung Jang.

In the past, the senior had acted like his life's mission was to pile as much stress as possible onto Sangwoo's shoulders, but the intensity of his harassment had abruptly declined. Now, excluding the low-grade irritation Sangwoo felt from having to sit next to the guy during class or be around him in general, he found his stress level was a solid zero.

The change had first been apparent on the Monday after the laptop incident. They'd been sitting in Intermediate Chinese, practicing some expressions as part of an in-class activity where they'd been instructed to work with a classmate nearby. Shockingly enough, Jaeyoung had actually proved *helpful*.

Originally, Sangwoo had attempted to partner up with the girl to his left, but she'd turned him down in favor of working with her friend. That had been disappointing enough, but he'd been even more depressed to find that he'd wasted so much time talking to her that everyone else around him had already found someone else to work with. In the end, he'd had no other choice but to turn his gaze to Jaeyoung, who'd been leaning back in his chair with a mocking smile on his face.

"*Gongche dao Shou'er zhan duo chang shijian?*" Sangwoo started out, doing his best to ask how long it would take to get to Seoul Station by bus.

Jaeyoung sat there and listened silently, then commented, "Not very good at languages, huh?"

Ignoring him, Sangwoo moved on to the next sample conversation. As long as he got some practice, it'd be fine. The first sentence was: *Do you want to see a movie with me tomorrow?*

"Women mingtian yiqi qu kan dianying ba?"

Jaeyoung stared at him for a moment, then smiled mysteriously. After quickly clearing his throat, he responded, "*Hǎo ā! Nǎ yí bù?*"

"That's not the correct response," Sangwoo said with a frown. According to the textbook, it was supposed to be: *I cannot. I am busy tomorrow.*

Honestly, should he even be surprised? Of course Jaeyoung would try and mess with him—at this point, it felt like being a troll was a part of the asshole's programming.

"Oh, you know what I said? Tell me, then."

"You agreed, then asked what movie we should watch. Now say the right response."

Jaeyoung snickered. "You're good at reading, writing, and listening, but your speaking skills… Whew! I can't believe you made it to Intermediate Chinese."

"I'm imitating what's written in the textbook word for word."

"Okay, but language is all about communication. You've gotta make an effort to learn how native speakers actually talk to one another."

What are you, the professor? Sangwoo thought crankily. Still, as much as he hated to admit it, the memory of receiving that A- in Chinese 101 during the first semester of freshman year haunted him. In a sea of A+'s, it had been the only lower mark. And just like Jaeyoung had pointed out, it'd been his horrible pronunciation that got him there.

Jaeyoung pointed at a sentence and said, "Try reading this."

Sangwoo obediently made his best effort. He thought he'd read the sentence quite accurately, but judging by the way Jaeyoung pressed a hand over his lips to hold back laughter, the other man didn't agree.

"Why are you laughing?" Sangwoo demanded. "I said it correctly."

Seeing the unamused look on Sangwoo's face, Jaeyoung forced his face back into neutral lines. "I wasn't laughing at *you*. I just thought you sounded kinda cu—" He cut himself off, shaking his head. "Anyway, you can keep pronouncing the first syllable that way, but you need to hold it a bit longer."

He gave a demonstration, and Sangwoo repeated it after him.

"Good. For the second syllable, hmm… Imagine a plane traveling up at a diagonal. Like this." Jaeyoung raised his arm at an angle and mimicked a jet taking off as he verbalized the correct sound. When Sangwoo repeated it after him, he erupted: "That's it! You're following along great."

In his excitement, Jaeyoung reached over to pat the back of Sangwoo's head a few times, as if in praise. It took Sangwoo entirely off guard—that spot on his scalp felt tingly and strange.

For a moment, he forgot how to breathe.

In his science classes, Sangwoo had learned that the human body had evolved to protect itself from the many dangers posed by nature. With that in mind, his reaction to Jaeyoung's touch was only natural—his body must have interpreted it as a threat and instinctively tensed up.

Not that the asshole in question had noticed. He wasn't even looking at Sangwoo anymore, his attention fixated on his own hands as he moved them around to aid his demonstration. It was like he had become a professor himself.

"For the third syllable, your pitch has gotta come down, then go back up. Imagine the sound flowing in a scooping motion, almost. Try it."

"*Er…*"

"No, no, you're messing it up again. Let's go back to the second syllable."

"*Ni.*"

"Come on, dude, you were doing so well! Are you malfunctioning now or what? If you can't get this, you're *definitely* not getting a hundred on the skit."

Sangwoo took out the desk divider from his backpack, but not to use it for its original purpose—he needed something to fan his face with. As he cooled himself off, Jaeyoung briefly turned around and rummaged through his bag, then handed a piece of paper full of simplified Chinese characters to Sangwoo.

Examining the text closer, Sangwoo quickly realized exactly what it was: a script involving a Qing dynasty merchant, a customer, and a person being scammed. His eyes widened. Not only was everything neatly organized, but Jaeyoung had included pinyin for every line as well.

Narrowing his eyes, Sangwoo went over the script even more carefully. All the sentences had been adjusted according to context, and any rough transitions had been smoothed out with what appeared to be original lines. It was a stark contrast to their initial draft, which had been laden with example sentences.

Even if I put everything I had into the script, I couldn't have made it this good, Sangwoo realized, turning to look at Jaeyoung. *And it would have taken hours and hours of searching around on the internet to get anywhere close.*

The asshole smiled at him playfully. "What, no compliments?"

"Did you get rid of all the profanities?"

"Of course I did."

Or so he claims. Sangwoo didn't trust him in the slightest. Fortunately, the professor happened to be walking by, and he requested that she look over the revised version. She gave both of them a doubtful glance as she took the script and read it. Then, gradually, a smile crept over her face, growing wider until she burst out into a full-blown laugh.

"What do you think?" Jaeyoung asked, spinning a pen between his fingers.

"You managed to get rid of all the vulgar language. Good job," she said. "I have a feeling this will be a fantastic skit. Maybe I should record it..."

"Sangwoo was the mastermind behind it."

"You keep saying that, but I find it hard to believe he'd know language that foul."

"Foul?! That's a bit harsh, Professor!"

She chuckled and lightly placed her hand on Sangwoo's shoulder. "Well, I'll be looking forward to seeing the finished product next week."

Sangwoo frowned. Something was wrong. He didn't want to admit it—he really, *really* didn't—but he would be an idiot if he kept ignoring it.

Jaeyoung was being...nice.

return 0;

The second the lecture for Algorithms was over, Jaeyoung shot out of his seat and stretched.

"Time to eat!" he announced after a yawn. There was a ridiculously gleeful note to his tone, as if he'd actually paid attention during class instead of sleeping through the whole thing.

Sangwoo had become accustomed to his new routine by now. He and Jaeyoung would walk down the hallway of the engineering building together, descend the staircase side by side, then go to the dining hall and have lunch together. However, contrary to his expectations, it seemed the third step wasn't to be that day.

"Sadly, I promised someone else I'd hang out with them today, Sangwoo," Jaeyoung announced, having stopped right outside the doors of the engineering building. "Sorry."

The turn of events was unexpected, but Sangwoo found Jaeyoung's announcement weirder than anything else. Why was that asshole acting like they'd had plans to eat lunch together? It wasn't like they had any sort of preexisting arrangement.

Deciding there was an urgent need to dispel the misunderstanding, Sangwoo looked straight at Jaeyoung and unenthusiastically cheered, "Yay…" He then clapped five times in applause.

Unfortunately, his sarcasm didn't have the intended effect. Jaeyoung just smirked at him, gave him a can of Black Holic, and studied him like a concerned parent sending their kid off to a summer camp.

"Make sure you eat a proper meal and drink enough water! Also, don't forget that you're supposed to chew everything fully before you swallow. And *no* following people in white vans, okay?"

Was the deadbeat trying to console him or something? Sangwoo's eyes narrowed. "There is something I've been meaning to ask: Have you lost it?"

Jaeyoung smiled at him and gave Sangwoo a pat on the head.

The gears in Sangwoo's head screeched to a halt. By the time he had enough presence of mind to decide the asshole needed a full dressing down, his adversary had already scurried off.

"Are you malfunctioning now or what?" Jaeyoung had asked during Intermediate Chinese.

Malfunctioning, Sangwoo mouthed to himself. During that class, Jaeyoung had criticized his pronunciation and basically placed a curse on him, saying he wouldn't get a hundred on the skit. However, that particular word was what'd stuck with him the most. *Malfunctioning.*

Since when had Jaeyoung started invading his personal space? Sangwoo wasn't sure, but one thing he did know was that the other man was getting way, *way* too close. Casual intimacy, which was something Sangwoo had never had reason to become accustomed to, always made him freeze up like a system with a critical error.

I'll yell at him the next time he tries it, he decided, his breath coming out in short, heated huffs.

He was angry, obviously. What other emotion could he possibly be feeling?

With a pounding heart, Sangwoo stormed across campus.

Unfortunately, he hadn't made it very far when he caught sight of Jaeyoung again. He was standing in front of a bench with two other people—a guy and a girl. Judging by the way the guy was doubled over with laughter and the playful smack the chortling girl gave Jaeyoung's back, he must have just told some sort of joke. As Sangwoo watched, Jaeyoung put the guy in a headlock and they both collapsed to the ground, laughing even harder.

Sangwoo forced himself to look away. *I am in a good mood,* he told himself forcefully. After all, what reason did he have to be in a bad one? Now that Jaeyoung had gone to hang out with his friends, Sangwoo could finally enjoy his lunch at the appropriate time without getting indigestion or being disrupted. He was in a good mood. *Of course* he was.

In the end, lunch proved both peaceful and completely uneventful. Standing up from his table—occupied by only one other student—Sangwoo put away his tray and looked over at the clock. The hands read 12:28 PM. He was right on schedule.

Opening up the can of Black Holic Jaeyoung had presented him, Sangwoo walked out of the dining hall. He couldn't even remember the last time he'd been able to finish lunch on time. Once again, the world around him felt entirely familiar—from the angle of the sun in the sky, the taste of the coffee in his hand, down to even the general atmosphere.

By the time Sangwoo finished walking the loop of his usual walking path, he felt delightfully refreshed. He tossed the empty can of Black Holic in the second trash can in front of the natural science building, then headed to his next destination.

I am in a good mood, he reminded himself. *Really, I am.*

As it turned out, the library was fairly empty that day, which meant he would likely be able to study entirely uninterrupted. Sangwoo requested the books he needed before flipping through some new titles, then checked out a new programming text and took his reserved seat.

Am I really going to be able to read all of these? he wondered, feeling a bit regretful. For some reason, he'd been struggling just to keep up with his classes this semester. Still, his doubts didn't stop him from placing the thick books in his backpack. He pulled out the electrical engineering textbook that he was planning on studying next while he was at it.

The table where he was sitting was completely empty, but Sangwoo found himself staring at the empty chair next to him for a moment before he turned his attention to his studies. *Condensers, capacitors, inductors, direct currents, alternating currents…* His gaze wandered over the words on the page aimlessly. While his mind automatically deciphered the characters, for some reason, he couldn't seem to comprehend the text.

Who cares about stupid currents? he thought to himself, then flinched in surprise. Never in his life had he ever gotten annoyed at an academic text before.

Straightening his back, Sangwoo did his best to reorient himself. But no matter how many times he reread the paragraphs before his eyes, the core concepts continued to elude him.

It was because Jaeyoung had made him fall so far behind that he was having such a difficult time, he decided. It had to be.

return 0;

Unfortunately, despite how crappy Sangwoo felt, time waited for no man. The next day rolled in without an ounce of mercy.

At first, things seemed like they were going to play out just as they always did, but minor differences began to crop up.

For one, though Jaeyoung's usual leather shoulder bag was sitting on the desk next to his as usual, the chair itself remained empty even twenty minutes after class started. Sangwoo could have moved it aside and reclaimed his rightful seat, of course, but the absence of his saboteur was making him feel slightly uneasy.

Finally, at exactly twenty-two minutes into the hour, Jaeyoung stumbled through the back door of the classroom. The professor teaching Embedded Systems gave the asshole a death glare as he slumped on top of his desk, seemingly unconcerned by his extreme tardiness.

From the smell wafting off his nemesis, Sangwoo was pretty sure he'd gotten wasted the night before. *Was it with those people hanging out around him at the bench yesterday?* he wondered for some unknown reason.

But instead of asking that, he whispered, "Why were you late?"

Admittedly, it was kind of a stupid thing to say. The answer was obvious.

Jaeyoung glanced up at Sangwoo, not moving from his slouched position. "Why do you think?" he asked in a rather pointed tone.

"Because you were out late drinking?"

"Bingo," Jaeyoung drawled.

That was when the question that had been bubbling away in the back of Sangwoo's throat finally slipped from between his lips. "Who were you with?"

Though Jaeyoung looked too hungover to even lift his head, his eyes began to sparkle with mirth. "Hmm? Why do you care?"

"I'm curious to know who was stupid enough to drink with you."

The smile on Jaeyoung's face widened. "Aw… You can just say you wanna get hammered with me, you know."

"I would never."

Sangwoo tried to turn his attention back to the lecture, but everything the professor said went right over his head. He wanted to blame it on the distracting asshole next to him, but he could be honest enough with himself to admit he'd lost his focus on the lecture long before Jaeyoung's arrival.

The more likely culprit was the strange emotion that had been haunting him lately. He couldn't quite define it, but it was always accompanied by a sense of vertigo, like his whole world had been turned on its head.

Even as his mind whirled, Sangwoo couldn't keep himself from glancing over at the back of Jaeyoung's head. It was clear that he wouldn't be able to focus anytime soon. He was going to miss out on learning most of the material for the day *again*.

Even after class ended, Jaeyoung didn't stir. He just remained where he was, draped over his desk like washed-up seaweed.

Sangwoo knew he could just abandon Jaeyoung and go to his next class, but he called out anyway. "Hey."

There was no response.

After a short pause, he said again, "Hey, so…"

Without lifting his head, Jaeyoung reached out and snatched hold of Sangwoo's arm with one hand. The move immediately made Sangwoo feel severely uncomfortable, but his unease went entirely unnoticed by Jaeyoung. The hungover man continued to cling to him, even going so far as to grab onto him with his other hand as well.

"Think I'm gonna…hurl," Jaeyoung muttered, barely managing to get to his feet. He placed a can of Black Holic on the desk and slowly staggered out of the room.

Sangwoo picked up the coffee and headed to his next class, where he was greeted with the familiar sight of a backpack sitting on top of his favorite desk. For the very first time, he removed it and hung it over the back of the chair, reclaiming his rightful spot. It might be rude to move an object someone had put down to save a seat, but that point was moot when you knew said person wasn't going to show.

Surprisingly, despite this victory, Sangwoo found he didn't feel particularly satisfied. Worse, he found he couldn't focus on the contents of the Algorithms lecture, either, even though the topics covered that day were relatively easy.

I wonder if he's throwing up in a bathroom somewhere.

Of course, Jaeyoung's current state was his own fault. He was the one who'd decided to drink so much on a school night. But still...Sangwoo had to admit that he felt slightly bad for him, given how much he seemed to be suffering.

Suddenly, a situation from the past popped into his mind. The logical structure was nearly identical: Jaeyoung had done a stupid thing, and had thereafter suffered the consequences. But back then, when the asshole hadn't been able to graduate, Sangwoo hadn't felt an ounce of pity for him. He'd been entirely certain Jaeyoung deserved everything he got.

A wave of confusion swept over Sangwoo. The realization that cracks were beginning to appear in his logic seized him in its grip and refused to let go. Even when class ended and he walked to the dining hall, he found himself haunted by the sensation.

By the time Sangwoo entered the dining hall, his mind had gone entirely blank. He only sat down because there was an empty seat and only ate the soup on his tray because there was a spoon in his hand.

When he saw his bowl was empty, he stood up. Sangwoo's movements were completely mechanical as he scraped the leftover bits of his food into the compost bin and placed the empty tray on the conveyor belt. Then, after situating his reusable spoon and pair of chopsticks in their respective containers to be washed, he blindly headed over to the water fountain and drank a glass of water. There had been no deviations to his normal routine, so he wrapped up just as the clock hit 12:28 PM.

He passed through the next few minutes like a machine on autopilot. It was only once he'd entered the convenience store and stopped in front of the fridge that he came back to himself and realized there were still no cans of Black Holic inside.

"Hi there," the store owner said, noticing him standing there. She walked over and gave Sangwoo an apologetic pat on the shoulder. "Haven't seen you in a while. Don't worry, I made sure to order a new shipment of your coffee. It should be arriving on Monday."

"Okay," Sangwoo responded, pushing her hand away.

"I know you must be craving it," the store owner continued. "I feel bad you have to go without your favorite drink. I mean, you used to have a can every single day..."

The words drifted right through one of Sangwoo's ears and out the other. His eyes were on the fridge—not the fifth shelf, which was empty, but the one above it. On it sat a bottle with a label that read:

Dawn777 – The #1 Hangover Cure
We've got your back, party animals!

He reached out without even thinking about it, then curled his hand into a fist and forced it back to his side. But almost immediately, the same disobedient hand traveled up again, and he was forced to return it to its original position. It was like the appendage had gained a mind of its own—it refused to follow any of his brain's commands.

A brief battle played out, ultimately ending in his brain's defeat. Having fully usurped control, the triumphant hand reached out and opened the fridge.

The store owner watched as his fingers wrapped around the Dawn777. "Oh, did you go out drinking last night?" she asked. "You know what—why don't you just take it? Hopefully it'll make you feel better about not having your coffee."

This left Sangwoo in a bit of a predicament. He'd acquired a free can of hangover cure, but he didn't have any idea what to do with it. He was about to propose a trade—perhaps the store owner would be willing to just give him the drink's value in cash instead?—but the owner had already made his way back behind the checkout counter.

Upon exiting the convenience store, Sangwoo went on his usual walk, sipping on the coffee he'd gotten from Jaeyoung earlier that morning as he strolled along. When he reached the natural sciences building, he tossed his empty can of coffee in the second trash bin, then let his feet take him to the library. There, he requested some new titles and checked some books out before heading to his reserved seat.

When he opened his backpack to grab his study materials, he saw the bottle of Dawn777 resting between two textbooks. First, he extracted the book he needed and placed it on the desk at a perfect angle. Then he pulled out the hangover cure, examining the bottle carefully.

We've got your back, party animals!

Party animal... The moniker immediately reminded him of Jaeyoung, staggering around the classroom like a drunkard. No one else who came to his mind seemed to fit the title.

Trying to erase Jaeyoung from his thoughts, Sangwoo attempted to visualize a party. When that failed, he turned to picturing various animals. But no matter how hard he tried, the asshole wouldn't get out of his head.

For what felt like forever, Sangwoo just sat in his chair, staring straight ahead. Then he sprang up, grabbed the Dawn777, and nearly raced down the library stairs. He strode across the building's lobby with hurried steps.

Problem-solving was something Sangwoo enjoyed. Of course, this particular problem had nothing to do with him, but he could still solve it—at least, if the words printed on the bottle in his hand were true. The drink *did* promise to cure hangovers, after all.

There were holes in this logic, of course. It was possible that Jaeyoung had already ingested a hangover cure. Or the Dawn777 may not work as well as advertised. Not to mention that Jaeyoung might have already gone home.

Doubts formed in Sangwoo's mind one after another, but he continued walking. Since he didn't know where Jaeyoung was, he'd just leave the drink in the drama clubroom. That was the most he could do for the other man—and anyway, he wasn't obligated to do anything else.

Sangwoo was nearing the student center when he saw someone in the distance. His feet slowed to a stop. The figure was so far away that he couldn't even make out the man's facial features, but he could see the vague sight of the man's eyes and nose crinkling in laughter. Even the way the man's hands moved through the air and the slight bend in his legs was familiar. His green coat was sprawled on the ground.

There, before Sangwoo's eyes, was Jaeyoung, splayed out to the point he was taking up an entire bench. A girl with blond bobbed hair was standing in front of him, arms crossed.

Jaeyoung still looked pretty hungover, but he looked much better than he had during class. He rubbed his stomach with an exaggerated expression of pain, and the girl burst out laughing. When Jaeyoung made some comment that Sangwoo couldn't hear, she playfully punched his arm. He laughed, she laughed, they both laughed—

It was too much for Sangwoo. Mind going blank for the second time that day, he spun around and began to walk back the way he'd come, his feet on autopilot. When he finally snapped back to his senses, he was in front of the futsal field. There was a construction worker there, the same one who'd called out to him a while back.

Sangwoo approached the man without hesitation.

The worker blinked at him in surprise. "Whoa, hey there! You're never here around this time!"

"I'm not sure what you're talking about," Sangwoo said, then thrust the drink at him. "This is for you."

"Huh? A hangover cure…? I've actually gone sober—"

"Just take it."

Having successfully discarded the Dawn777, Sangwoo went straight back to the library. He'd never wasted so much time in his life—not even during the past few days when wasting time had started to become a sort of pattern. Just how many seconds, minutes, and hours had he sent swirling down the drain? Overcome with self-recrimination, his heart pounded away in his chest.

It was when he was rummaging around in his backpack for his pencil pouch that it happened—Sangwoo saw his phone screen light up. The device didn't make a sound, as it was on mute, but he'd undeniably received a text. And Sangwoo almost never received texts.

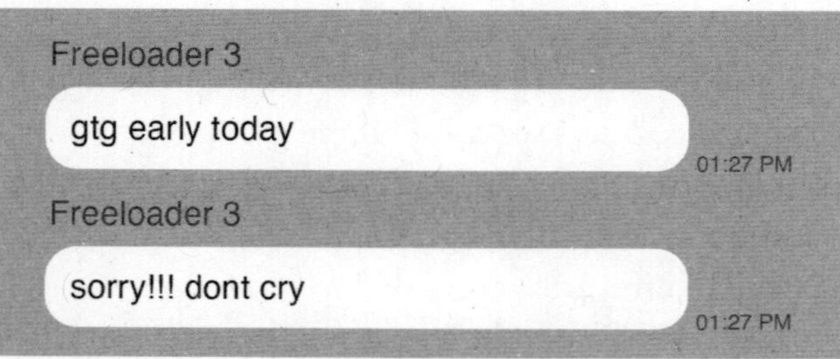

He glared at the screen, reading the short texts over and over again. Finally, he tapped on the reply button, but couldn't decide what to say.

What a relief.
I'm happy to hear that.
Please go home early every day going forward.

None of the drafts felt right, so he erased every single one. In the end, he simply typed "Okay." and threw his phone back in the bag.

Jaeyoung seemed to be suffering under a terrible delusion. It was either that, or the asshole was just messing with him as usual. *Don't cry?* Why in the world would Sangwoo cry about the biggest disruption in his life disappearing from his sight?

`return 0;`

"Morning, Sangchoo," Jihye said, plopping herself down in the chair next to Sangwoo fifteen minutes before their Pop Culture and Cultural Theory class.

He just gave her a nod and turned his gaze back to the thick textbook.

But Jihye was relentless. "Wow, look at you studying hard! I don't think we have a single exam over the next few weeks."

"I'm reading ahead."

"I wish I could, too, but everything's so confusing."

Though Jihye continued a steady stream of dialogue next to him, Sangwoo found his level of distraction was at a record low compared to when Jaeyoung was present—including when Jaeyoung had been asleep. Actually, now that he thought about it, the deadbeat had been disrupting his focus even when he wasn't even there.

"You know, you look super upset right now," Jihye mused.

Sangwoo completely ignored her.

"Here, I have something that'll make you feel better."

Jihye shoved her phone in his face—the screen displayed various pictures of a small white dog, all taken from different angles. Sangwoo stared at them blankly.

"Not a fan? How about this one, then?" She swiped to one side of the screen, revealing a picture of an orange cat.

Sangwoo waited patiently, hoping she would move the phone away soon. But to his dismay, Jihye just kept swiping through different pictures of fluffy animals. Then, out of nowhere, one photo caught his attention.

"Wait," he said. "What was that?"

"Huh?" Jihye went back to the picture that he had pointed out—an image of a keyboard. "Oh… I took a screenshot of this while shopping online. I guess I put it in the wrong folder."

Sangwoo reached out and zoomed in on the keyboard, examining it carefully. It was a black and red TKL model, likely a special edition judging by the LED lights embedded behind each key.

"This is a Filcom AX8990, Honeybee edition."

"What?"

"It'll cost you more, but it should be durable since it has Berry MX switches. The tactile feedback should be pleasant, and it supports simultaneous input, too. Overall, it's a good product. You might want to reconsider because of the LED lights, though. Personally, I find them distracting. What kind of switches are you looking for?"

"Um… Well, I would be working on documents for the most part."

"I would recommend reds, then. They're much less noisy than some of the other switches. If you want something with a decent amount of tactile sensation that's still quiet, try browns. Blues are the switches preferred by gamers."

"Right? That's what I heard!" Jihye exclaimed, nodding enthusiastically. "Should I get the red switches, then?"

After a moment of contemplation, Sangwoo responded, "Just so you know, the market price for this is one hundred and ninety-eight thousand won, but it was released a long time ago. It shouldn't be too hard to find used ones. You could probably find one in good condition for a hundred thousand won."

"Ohhh, okay! Where do you buy used keyboards?"

The rest of the time left until class started was spent explaining to Jihye how to buy used electronics online and giving her helpful tips. Sangwoo would have ended the conversation earlier, but he couldn't find the right time to do so. Jihye was listening too intently—she was even taking notes.

"You're a walking encyclopedia, Sangwoo!"

"I wouldn't say that," he replied, thinking it was a strange comment for her to make.

Just then, the professor walked into the room, and Sangwoo whipped his gaze back to his textbook.

About a minute after class started, Jihye silently placed a torn-out page of her notebook on top of the text he'd been reading. *What am I, her personal trash can?* he thought with deep annoyance—but then he saw something was written on the piece of paper.

Thanks for the info, Sangchoo!! :) Let me know if you have any questions that I can answer in the future. I'd love to help ;)

He wrote "Okay." on the edge of the paper, then gave it back. But even as he did, he wondered what he would ever need to ask Jihye. If he ever had questions about something, he typically turned to books or the internet for answers over other people. Plus, Jihye was only a college student—due to her major, she might understand topics that fell under the humanities umbrella better than him, but how could her knowledge compare to the collective intelligence found on the internet or in an academic text?

Although…there *was* one area where she had decidedly more expertise than him, wasn't there?

Sangwoo mentally put a pin in the question that had surfaced in his head, then turned his attention back to the lecture. He'd ask her about it during the break.

return 0;

"I have something I want to discuss with you," Sangwoo began as soon as the class's short recess started. "It's about…*him*."

Immediately, Jihye turned toward him. Straightening up to her full height, she gave him a serious nod. "Him who?"

"That, uh…Jaeyoung Jang."

"Oh, got it! Go on."

"It looks like he has a girlfriend."

Sangwoo paused. He'd only just started speaking, but he found himself unsure of how to go on. Jihye had offered to answer questions for him—but though the thing he was curious about had felt like a question in his head, once he'd tried to put it into words, it'd become more of a tentative statement instead.

Fortunately, Jihye didn't seem to mind. "Hmm… He doesn't, as far as I'm aware," she responded with a smile. "It's been a year or so since he broke up with his last girlfriend. She was a law student, but she's graduated now. Honestly, I had a bit of a girl crush on her. She was so smart, she was basically a prodigy, suuuper pretty, and her family was absolutely rolling in it."

It was exactly the answer Sangwoo had been looking for. And conveniently, he'd gotten a bunch of extra information on top of it without having to even input another query.

"How do you know all of that stuff?" he asked.

"Mostly from social media, but I've heard rumors."

"What kind of rumors?"

Jihye started chattering once again. A bunch of the information she offered was useless: An entertainment agency had apparently tried to recruit Jaeyoung as an actor when he was twenty years old, he'd briefly worked as a model, his girlfriend from freshman year was now a famous singer…

Realizing that Sangwoo was starting to zone out, Jihye stopped, clearing her throat awkwardly. "I'm not, like, *interested* in him or anything. One of my friends is totally head over heels for the guy, so she keeps telling me a bunch of random stuff."

"Really? Why is she so obsessed with him?"

"Obviously because he's hot."

This was true.

"He's also really fit."

That would make sense, given his talent with a skateboard…

"And he's so nice!"

That, Sangwoo couldn't agree with.

Seeming to read something on his face, Jihye paused. "Isn't he…? I mean, I guess you'd know that better than I do. You guys are friends."

"We are *not* friends."

The only descriptors that came to Sangwoo's mind when he tried to describe Jaeyoung were "insane" and "deadbeat, sadistic piece of trash," accompanied by a single new addition: "randomly, discomfitingly kind human." Given how little Jihye actually knew Jaeyoung, none of them would make any sense to her without extensive explanation.

"Hey, remember when you got all mad at me for talking about Jaeyoung? Now *you're* the one talking about him!"

The comment hit uncomfortably close to home, so Sangwoo pretended he hadn't heard. Thankfully, he was saved from any further conversation by the professor walking back into the room.

return 0;

A short time later, the lecture concluded. As Sangwoo packed up his things, preparing to head to lunch, Jihye piped up again.

"How'd things go with the, you know, desk divider and earplugs?"

"They didn't work." The divider had turned into a fan, the seven cans of Black Holic were sitting in his apartment, unopened, and he had only used the earplugs once.

"Oh… Sorry," she replied sheepishly.

Truthfully, in Sangwoo's mind, she didn't have anything to apologize for. Jaeyoung, as always, was the one to blame. But wait. Hadn't he promised Jihye he would treat her to a meal in return for her assistance?

While it was true that her advice hadn't been particularly helpful, Sangwoo wasn't one to break a promise. He took a meal ticket for the dining hall out of his wallet and put it in front of her.

For a moment, Jihye stared blankly at the piece of paper. "What's this for?"

"I told you I'd treat you to a meal."

"Oh, *come on*! You're supposed to actually take me out somewhere!"

"Just use the ticket."

He put on his backpack and got up, but Jihye reached out and put the meal ticket right back in his pocket.

"No, no. This isn't what you promised. Just treat me whenever you get the chance."

Thinking back to the pasta place she'd taken him to, Sangwoo recalled the sky-high prices of everything on the menu. Maybe Jihye wanted something more expensive than dining hall food?

"Okay. I'll buy you pizza later," he said.

"Really? You mean it? Pizza bagels don't count, okay?"

I didn't realize she was such an untrusting person, Sangwoo mused. *I simply thought she was nice…*

Exiting the building, they began to walk over to the dining hall together. But then, out of nowhere, Sangwoo heard a voice call out from behind him.

"Hey, Sangwoo!"

There was only one person on campus who would call out to him like that. Sangwoo whipped his head around, and there the asshole was—wearing the exact coat Sangwoo had been picturing in his mind.

"Been looking…for you," Jaeyoung gasped, seemingly struggling to catch his breath.

"Why?"

"Because we're supposed to eat lunch together, obviously."

"We are?"

This was news to Sangwoo. Had Jaeyoung mistaken him for someone else? Or maybe he'd misunderstood something somehow?

Whatever the case, it wasn't his problem. Sangwoo turned back around and started walking away without any further ado, but Jaeyoung wasn't done. He swapped targets to Jihye instead.

"Hey. You're a French major, right?"

Jihye blinked in surprise. "Oh, yes… It's good to see you again!"

"Yeah. I forget, have we exchanged names?"

"Not officially. I'm Jihye—Jihye Ryu! And I actually already know yours." She chuckled shyly. "You're kind of a celebrity around here."

Sangwoo did his best to put some distance between the chatting pair and himself, but they kept pace with him. Whether he liked it or not, he was stuck hearing every word they said to one another.

"It seems like you hang out with Sangwoo a lot, Jihye. You were with him when you came to the restaurant I work at, too."

"Actually, that was the first day we met! You see, Sangwoo was nice enough to help me carry some boxes. I happened to put a *ton* of books in this one box—I didn't mean to, of course, and I should have just redistributed all the stuff evenly into other boxes, but anyway… I was trying to carry the books up to the third floor of the library, even though it wasn't like I was going to look at all of them anytime soon…"

It was like Jihye's voice was playing on some never-ending recording. She never even paused for a breath.

The conversation continued in the form of an effortless back-and-forth; Jaeyoung, Jihye, Jaeyoung, Jihye, Jaeyoung…

Is it just me, or is it taking a particularly long time to get into the dining hall today?

"Ha-ha-ha! You're so funny, Jaeyoung! By the way, could I get your signature? Not for me—my friend. She's totally obsessed with you."

"A signature? What am I, a celebrity?"

Jaeyoung's tone had become much more casual at some point, to the degree that a stranger could have mistaken him and Jihye as longtime friends. Sangwoo found listening to their endless chatter a chore and was deeply relieved when the line of people in front of him started to shrink slowly but surely.

Finally, they were all able to grab trays. Sangwoo and Jihye headed to the same station and got in line, while Jaeyoung headed off to another for some *janchi* noodles. Sangwoo tried his best to find a table that only had two empty seats, but failed utterly. To his dismay, the three of them ended up sitting together.

"You have a boyfriend, don't you?" Jaeyoung asked Jihye before he even bothered to touch his food.

"Nope!" she responded with a bright smile.

Jaeyoung hummed under his breath. "That's weird. I thought you would..."

Sangwoo's gaze drifted over to the other man. Jaeyoung was staring at Jihye with an unreadable look on his face.

"Right?" she asked, seemingly oblivious. "I don't think enough guys realize just how great I am."

"Well, I happen to know a bunch of single underclassmen," Jaeyoung said with a grin, crossing his arms and scooching closer to the table. "Want me to set you up on a date? I can already think of a few decent guys. What's your type?"

He took out his phone and started going through his contacts, but Jihye shook her head, laughing.

"No, no. It's okay. I think I'm just gonna focus on my studies this semester. Thanks, though."

"Oh...really?"

Jaeyoung slipped his phone back in his pocket, scanning her face carefully. After a brief silence, he said, "You know, I feel like you and Sangwoo would make a great couple."

Sangwoo spat out the seaweed soup he was eating. Jihye and Jaeyoung both glanced at him in surprise, but he was the most shocked.

Quickly, Jihye grabbed some wet wipes from her bag and handed them to him. "Wow, don't you think that was a bit harsh, Sangchoo? You hated the idea of us being a couple *that* much?"

"Of course I did. Who enjoys being pulled into that kind of conversation for no reason?"

"He was just joking."

"That doesn't mean I have to like it," Sangwoo shot back, drying off his face with one of the wet wipes while simultaneously using the other to vigorously scrub the table clean. The situation had him feeling uneasy and deeply confused, but he knew one thing for sure—he wanted to get the hell away from both of them.

Jaeyoung glanced at him, smirking. "'Sangchoo'? As in, lettuce?"

"Apparently, that was his nickname when he was a kid," Jihye answered for him. "Cute, right?"

"Hmm… You two are using nicknames now? Sounds like you've gotten pretty close with my dear Sangwoo."

My dear…Sangwoo? Even his own mother had never called him that. The food Sangwoo had just eaten churned inside his stomach.

For a long, long time, nobody said another word. Jaeyoung was the one who ultimately broke the silence.

"By the way, Jihye, are you going somewhere nice?"

"Sorry?" she blinked.

"Well, it's just… You seem to have more makeup on than the last time I saw you, that's all."

"Wow, you've got quite the memory, don't you?" Jihye asked with an awkward chuckle. "Um… Last time, I didn't exactly put a lot of effort into my appearance because I knew I'd be hauling stuff around. I usually dress up a bit more."

"I was talking about last Wednesday, actually."

"Oh, uh…" She stuttered, growing audibly more flustered. "I was running late to class because I slept in, so…"

"I see. I assumed you might be meeting someone…important."

It was a meaningless conversation—one that was definitely not helpful for Sangwoo's digestion. Plus, Jihye's face was growing more tense by the minute, probably because Jaeyoung was talking way too much. Sangwoo found that he empathized with her. Honestly, who wouldn't be annoyed if somebody kept talking to them while they were trying to eat?

A while later, as they walked out of the dining hall, Jihye asked something that Sangwoo thought was slightly strange.

"How did you guys become friends, anyway? I mean, you don't seem like you'd have a single thing in common."

Sangwoo immediately spotted an error in her words. "We're not frien—"

"We went through a rough patch in the beginning," Jaeyoung cut in, slinging his arm over Sangwoo's shoulders.

It was just a casual touch that shouldn't have been that big of a deal—but Sangwoo gasped for air, then froze like a deer in front of a pair of blaring headlights. Jaeyoung's arm felt as heavy as a lead beam. Overloaded, Sangwoo forgot to even breathe.

"There were some hard feelings between us...," he heard the asshole continue. "But not anymore, right?"

"I disagree," Sangwoo snapped, shoving Jaeyoung's arm away.

Based on his recent experiences, it seemed Jaeyoung didn't have any qualms with touching other people at all. Regardless of how close he was with someone, it was apparent he thought nothing of slinging his arm over their shoulders, speaking to them casually, touching their face, or playing tricks on them. It felt like he was always trying to get closer to Sangwoo. Too close. And Sangwoo *hated* it.

Sangwoo knew some parents were physically affectionate with their children, but that had never applied to his mother and father. In his world, the only people who could initiate physical contact with him were people of the opposite sex with whom he was romantically involved, and even then, he would expect them to respect his boundaries.

It didn't matter if Jaeyoung didn't mean any offense with his behavior, Sangwoo *was* offended.

"Stop lying to yourself," he snapped at the asshole, the words pouring from his mouth like a flood that had just been unleashed. "Whether you like it or not, those hard feelings are still there. I still despise you. You can pretend to be a nice guy until the end of time, but it changes nothing. We're still in that so-called 'rough patch,' and we're never getting out of it."

"Damn…and I thought we had a good streak going," Jaeyoung muttered impassively while Jihye glanced between them with wide eyes. "You *do* know the skit is tomorrow, right?"

The mocking words diverted Sangwoo's train of thought, cutting off an enraged demand that the asshole never touch him again. Instead, he hissed, "Don't come to class. I can play all three roles by myself."

"Nah, I don't think so," Jaeyoung refused lazily, stretching like a cat. "Sorry, Jihye, but I need to borrow Sangwoo. We have a *really* important presentation tomorrow."

"O-okay, sure," she responded.

Jaeyoung grabbed Sangwoo's wrist and hauled him off before the words had even fully left Jihye's mouth. Sangwoo smacked him away, but the asshole simply slung his arm over his shoulder. The shock of it made Sangwoo completely stop functioning for a moment—nothing remotely like this had ever happened to him before.

Taking advantage of his confusion, Jaeyoung snatched the backpack right off his back and began to race away.

"Hey!" Sangwoo shouted after him. "Wait!"

But Jaeyoung showed no signs of stopping. *What the hell is wrong with him?* Sangwoo thought in disbelief. His next course of action was unfortunately clear—he had no choice but to chase after the asshole. Who knew what Jaeyoung would do to the contents of his backpack? He might throw everything into the sewer, for all Sangwoo knew.

At first, Jaeyoung went at a fast jog. But as Sangwoo began to catch up to him, he began to gradually speed up.

"*Stop!*" Sangwoo roared.

Once again, the crazy asshole ignored him.

By this point, Jaeyoung was full-out sprinting, Sangwoo's backpack slung across his chest. Sangwoo almost caught him by the shoulder once, only for Jaeyoung to put on yet another burst of speed and shoot ahead with infuriating ease. It was distinctly reminiscent of their breakneck race through campus exactly a week ago.

Jaeyoung circled around the engineering building, passing the futsal field, the convenience store, and the student center.

"Damn, that sucked," Jaeyoung heaved, as he finally came to a stop the edge of the spacious grassy field right in front of the school's front gates.

Behind him, Sangwoo screeched to a halt as well. His chest burned as he tried to catch his breath. "Give it…back," he huffed, reaching out limply.

Jaeyoung completely ignored him. And not only that—the asshole unzipped Sangwoo's backpack like it belonged to him and guzzled water straight from his water bottle.

"Have you *actually* lost your mind?"

"Maybe I have."

Jaeyoung tossed the bottle at Sangwoo, and he drank from it too. His heart was still pounding away from the unexpected sprint.

When he finally regained the presence of mind to take in his surroundings, Sangwoo found that he didn't recognize a thing, even after six semesters of attending Hanguk University. Oddly, there also seemed to be a bunch of students lying on the field before him, strung out like laundry left out to dry.

"What're you doing?" Jaeyoung asked, plopping down on the grass himself. "Sit down."

He punctuated the final two words with pats on the ground next to him, but he didn't wait for Sangwoo. Instead, he lay down fully, splaying out his limbs and clasping his hands together comfortably on top of his chest. The stolen backpack found itself co-opted as a pillow.

In that moment, it almost looked like Jaeyoung was sleeping. His eyes had drifted closed, and a gentle smile played on his lips. Sunlight danced over his hair, lightening its color and making it sparkle like dewy spider silk in the light of a new dawn.

"Give me my bag."

"Can't you see I'm using it?" came the nonchalant reply.

"I said, *give me my bag.*"

"Gimme something else I can use as a pillow, then."

Sangwoo crouched down and tugged on the backpack sharply, hoping he'd catch Jaeyoung off guard, but it was useless. His nemesis had looped both his arms through the straps.

"I thought you wanted to prepare for the skit," Sangwoo finally muttered in resignation.

"Yeah. We can do it right here."

"Here? Without any desks or chairs?" he asked in disbelief.

Jaeyoung just shrugged. "Why not? You've memorized the entire script, haven't you?"

Sangwoo nodded, only belatedly realizing that the asshole couldn't see him because he had his eyes closed. Still a bit reluctant, he sat down next to Jaeyoung. *What am I even doing here?* he wondered, breathing in the scent of fresh-cut grass. For some reason, he felt distinctly out of place.

"Let's get started, then," Sangwoo said finally.

"Just give me a ten-minute break."

"That's a waste of ti—"

"Oh, come on," Jaeyoung interrupted. "You can spare ten minutes."

The asshole took another can of Black Holic out of his bag and handed it to Sangwoo, who glanced down at his watch. *It* is *time for my regularly scheduled walk...*

"Fine," Sangwoo muttered. He opened the can.

For a long time, Jaeyoung stayed so silent that it seemed like he might have fallen asleep. But then, when Sangwoo was halfway through drinking his coffee, the asshole called his name.

"Hey, Sangwoo."

"What?"

"What's your type? You know, when it comes to dating."

Sangwoo immediately scowled and glanced over at Jaeyoung, whose eyes remained closed. "Why are you asking me such a personal question?"

"That's what people do when they're not friends. Ask pointless questions as an icebreaker."

"I see," Sangwoo conceded. He began to contemplate how to respond to Jaeyoung's inquiry.

The topic wasn't one he'd ever really dwelled on before, but calculating the answer proved relatively simple—all he needed to do was compile a list of women who had elicited some sort of positive reaction from him in the past.

"I prefer people who maintain a well-groomed, put-together appearance and have levelheaded personalities."

"Nice. So, basically, a kindergarten teacher?"

Ignoring Jaeyoung's comment, Sangwoo took another sip of his coffee. He didn't have to wait long before a second question was shot his way.

"When did you first fall in love?"

"I don't know."

"What do you mean, you don't know?"

"'Love' is a vague concept. You'll need to clarify your definition for an accurate response."

This was enough to make Jaeyoung finally open his eyes, though only very narrowly. He squinted over at Sangwoo, the sun turning his irises light brown.

"Are you asking when I first got into a relationship? Or when I first had intercourse?" Sangwoo elaborated, feeling weirdly defensive. "The question is unclear."

Jaeyoung just continued to stare at him, a confused frown on his face. "So…you've never had a crush on anybody?"

Finally, Sangwoo had a definition to work with. "Oh, so that's how you're defining it. In that case, I first 'fell in love' when I was six. It wasn't with a human being, though."

Jaeyoung immediately let out an incredulous scoff, but his reaction didn't bother Sangwoo one bit—if anyone was delusional here, it was Jaeyoung. The love often depicted in popular media didn't even exist.

What was love, really? In Sangwoo's opinion, it was nothing more than the product of irrational human minds misinterpreting their sexual desires, a lie the government promoted to maintain the social institution of marriage.

The reason behind his disdain was simple: Love was supposed to be an emotion everyone on planet Earth experienced. So why had *he* never even come close to feeling it?

Sangwoo glanced at his watch and sat up. "It's time to start practicing for the skit," he announced. *"Piányi piányi tài piányi… Qǐng mǎi zhè, zài zhè."*

He'd said: "The fruits are cheap. Come and buy a bunch." It was the very first line.

Jaeyoung burst out laughing, the corners of his eyes crinkling. His teeth were neat and white. *"Xīnqíng hǎo,"* he finally said after composing himself.

Sangwoo frowned. "That's not the right line."

"Do you even know what I said?"

"Yes. 'This is nice.'"

"Really? I think so, too."

Sangwoo pressed his lips together in irritation, then sneezed when his nose began to tickle. His stomach felt strange, like a bunch of birds were swooping around in circles inside it. Although, on second thought… maybe those birds were actually butterflies.

`return 0;`

The end of March arrived with an unexpected cold front, which stood in sharp contrast to the mild weather of the previous few weeks.

Sangwoo managed to stay fairly warm by donning a puffer jacket, but he couldn't avoid the freezing wind that whooshed over his face while he pedaled away on his bike. By the time he reached the humanities building, his cheeks had gone red from the biting cold.

After claiming a seat in the Intermediate Chinese classroom, Sangwoo carefully began to read over the skit's script one more time, checking that he had all three roles fully memorized; he still didn't entirely believe Jaeyoung would show up. Once he was satisfied, he headed to the bathroom with his costume and wig. As usual, he entered the left stall instead of the one on the right, which was perpetually marked "OUT OF ORDER."

It took exactly four minutes for Sangwoo to change into his costume. *That should leave me plenty of time to go over the script once more,* he determined. He walked back into the classroom through the back door to do just that, but was immediately confronted by the sight of Jaeyoung sitting in the seat next to his, hunched over and looking at his phone. The asshole was dressed in the shiny yellow costume he had picked out. His wig was slightly crooked, leaving his hair to stick out from under the skin-colored silicone part.

Jaeyoung was the personification of unpredictability and spontaneity. He acted like a totally different person from day to day, and he was so impulsive and inconsistent that Sangwoo couldn't keep track of the lowlife for the life of him. He was a persistent, game-breaking error—but one that Sangwoo had somehow grown used to. In fact, Sangwoo found that he had become accustomed to the deadbeat, sadistic piece of trash.

It was a terrifying and nonsensical notion, but he didn't have time to dwell on it, since Jaeyoung had just glanced back and caught sight of him. The asshole burst out laughing and pointed at Sangwoo with one finger, as if they weren't wearing nearly identical costumes.

"Why are you so early today?" Sangwoo asked nonchalantly.

"I'm the TA for this class, remember?"

It was a slightly ridiculous thing to say, given that Sangwoo had never witnessed Jaeyoung doing anything that a TA would usually do. The only thing he managed in reply was a noncommittal "Right…"

After kicking Jaeyoung's long legs out of the way, Sangwoo claimed his seat. Deciding his memory would benefit from one last review of the script, he sat with one hand on his temple and stared at the paper with the dialogue written out on it.

Jaeyoung took the chance to start snapping several pictures of Sangwoo with his phone.

Scowling, Sangwoo covered his face. "Stop it."

"You know, you should dress like that more often. That outfit was made for you," Jaeyoung said with a big grin. He scrolled through the pictures, then opened the camera app again. "Hey, Sangwoo."

"What?"

"Wanna take a selfie?"

"No."

Unfortunately for Sangwoo, it seemed Jaeyoung didn't particularly care what he thought. Before he knew it, the other man had scooched his chair right up next to his, then lifted his phone up in front of them.

They both looked ridiculous in their queue wigs, but Sangwoo didn't try to move away. *I'll let him do as he pleases this once.*

"C'mon, smile!" Jaeyoung insisted.

Sangwoo ignored the demand—he wasn't in the mood to smile for a stupid photo. Jaeyoung shrugged at the show of defiance, then quickly took three shots: one with a smile, one with his tongue sticking out, and one with his features scrunched up.

"You look the best in this one," Jaeyoung commented as he swiped through them.

In Sangwoo's opinion, they all looked the same—horrible.

There was still some time left before class started, so they decided to use it to go over the script one last time. Jaeyoung was quite attentive in correcting his pronunciation. He listened to each line Sangwoo said very carefully, then forced him to repeat it if it wasn't satisfactory—which meant Sangwoo ended up having to repeat most of the script.

Soon, other students began filing into the classroom. Some of them pointed at Jaeyoung and Sangwoo and giggled loudly, while others even came over to comment on their costumes. The professor arrived slightly early as well, and she burst out laughing when she saw them. Her amusement was obvious even after class started—her lips twitched visibly whenever she glanced over at them.

The day's class was structured so that the professor would only lecture for thirty minutes, with the last twenty minutes reserved for three teams of students to do their skits. The first pair presented themselves as a married Chinese couple who were on a trip in Paris, using phrases such as "What is that?" and "That is the Eiffel Tower." The second team's skit was centered around a Hanguk University student showing a friend from China around the campus—which made Sangwoo suspect that they'd overheard his idea.

Then it was finally Sangwoo and Jaeyoung's turn.

"Jaeyoung and Sangwoo, you're up," the professor said with a smile.

Jaeyoung rose from his seat and stretched like a cat; then shot Sangwoo a confident grin that didn't harbor even a hint of anxiety. He retrieved some grapes, a phone, and a baseball bat from his backpack before walking to the front of the room with Sangwoo following behind him, empty-handed.

Before they could get started, their classmates burst into applause. Seeing the professor begin to film them with her phone, some even snapped pictures of them.

It only took a moment for them to set everything up. Taking a deep breath, Sangwoo faced the audience and announced in Chinese that the fruit was on sale.

Jaeyoung, who had been hiding behind a pillar, approached him with an air of arrogance, fanning himself like some sort of uptight noble. He examined the grapes sitting on the desk and asked Sangwoo how much they cost.

As Sangwoo recited the next line, his eyes met Jaeyoung's. There was something agleam in the other man's gaze—Sangwoo could almost hear him whispering, *See? I told you everything was gonna be fine! Aren't you having a blast?*

Actually...he kind of was. Sangwoo's anxiety melted away, a mild elation taking its place. It was a strange, foreign feeling.

It turned out that Jaeyoung had prepared for the skit much more thoroughly than Sangwoo had expected. Not only had he gathered up a bunch of props, but he'd also made the preparations necessary to play the appropriate sound effects during the phone call scene. When Sangwoo began his short monologue, Jaeyoung quickly ducked behind the podium so he could change into another costume for his second role.

Sangwoo hadn't understood why Jaeyoung was such a renowned

member of the drama club before, but he got it now. In this moment, the classroom was his stage. Sure, he'd ended up altering some of the lines slightly, but Jaeyoung made sure to keep the meaning consistent. The only fault that Sangwoo could find in his performance was the unscripted line Jaeyoung had randomly added in the middle of the skit: "Are you a robot?" Aside from that, however, Sangwoo had to admit that Jaeyoung had done an incredible job.

It would be an understatement to say their skit was well-received. The professor had dropped her pen while filling out the rubric because she was laughing so hard, while the audience had clapped and cheered every time Sangwoo had mechanically recited a line from memory. Several students decided to record the whole thing on their phones, and with all the pictures the rest of the class were taking of the two of them, Sangwoo was starting to feel like a celebrity on the red carpet.

In the end, he had no choice but to admit that Jaeyoung's cocky "I got this" had been nothing but the truth.

After the skit, Jaeyoung reached a hand out to Sangwoo, who returned the high-five without even thinking about it. In that moment, the animosity he'd been carrying in his heart melted away, replaced by something that almost felt like camaraderie.

Later, after the professor had dismissed everyone early, she approached Sangwoo and Jaeyoung.

"That was very, *very* entertaining," she said, giving them a double thumbs-up. "In fact, I would say that was the best skit I've seen in the past ten years." Turning to Sangwoo specifically, she added, "Your pronunciation needs some work, but I'm very impressed that you managed to memorize so many lines."

"Thank you, Professor."

"Of course. Would you be interested in being a TA for this class?"

It was a completely unexpected question. "What?"

"Don't worry, it's really a low-pressure job. All I ask is that, on certain days, you arrive a little bit early for class to print out some materials. Other than that, you just have to collect the exam papers for midterms and finals, as well as the class assignments. You'll get extra credit for the class, and I'll also treat you to a meal at some point."

As the words slowly registered in Sangwoo's brain, his gaze flicked to Jaeyoung, who was watching the professor impassively.

Whatever doubts Sangwoo had about the professor's meaning abruptly evaporated when she clarified, "Jaeyoung recommended you as his replacement."

The two-week period to drop classes was almost up, which meant Jaeyoung was withdrawing from those he had no reason to take. Sangwoo knew this very well—he'd been anxiously awaiting that moment for quite a while now. But it hadn't hit him until this very moment that there were only two days left until Jaeyoung's departure.

"Sure, I'll be your TA," he said with a nod.

The professor smiled at him. "I'm looking forward to working with you." Then, to Jaeyoung, she added: "Thanks for everything, Jaeyoung, including staying until the conclusion of the skit. I'm sure Sangwoo appreciates it."

"Of course, Professor. I'm sorry for dropping out after agreeing to be the TA."

"Don't worry about it. There's nothing wrong with pursuing new opportunities. Can I offer you an early congratulations on your acceptance?"

Jaeyoung let out a bashful laugh. "I did apply again, but I don't know if I'll get accepted."

"Oh, I'm sure they'll take you. They already accepted your application once!"

Although he was packed up and ready to go, Sangwoo stood there blankly, listening to their conversation. The professor went on to ask Jaeyoung about his future plans, to which he responded that he was going to relax for a bit while preparing to study abroad. The conversation then shifted to the school Jaeyoung would be attending to get his graduate degree.

"Talking about this reminds me of my own time studying abroad," the professor commented.

"Feel free to come visit."

"You make it sound like you've already been accepted!"

"*You're* the one who said they'd take me."

It was a friendly, playful conversation, but Sangwoo couldn't bring himself to smile. Something that resembled disappointment was coiling in his chest.

"Let's go," Jaeyoung said, snapping Sangwoo out of his thoughts. He hadn't even noticed that the other man had finished his conversation with the professor.

After bidding her goodbye, the pair of students headed to the bathroom, where they changed out of their costumes. Sangwoo returned the borrowed clothes and wig to Jaeyoung.

When they arrived at their next classroom, the navy backpack was conspicuously missing from its usual spot. Sangwoo blinked in surprise and looked at Jaeyoung, who yanked his phone out of his pocket with a scowl.

Ignoring him, Sangwoo made a beeline for his rightful seat and plopped himself down without an ounce of hesitation. Jaeyoung stared at him with an unreadable look on his face, then looked away to dial someone.

After a few rings, someone picked up. Jaeyoung apparently had the volume to the max, because the voice on the line was loud enough for the entire classroom to hear.

"What's up, Jaeyoung?"

"The hell's wrong with you? Is it really that hard to look after a backpack for two weeks?"

There was a short pause. *"Huh? You didn't give me the backpack yesterday!"*

"I didn't…?"

"No! It wasn't in the locker or practice rooms, so I figured you wanted me to stop."

For a long moment, Jaeyoung stayed silent. Then he slapped a hand over his face in sudden realization. "Damn… I forgot to grab it because I was so wasted two days ago. Someone else must have taken it or something."

"Then do you want me to keep doing it? Hey, I know it might not seem like a big deal, but it takes a lot of effort... Also, I don't get why you're so set on saving that seat! It's not like you ever pay attention in class."

"Shut up. I'm so done with you."

"Awww, c'mon! You're not mad, are you? Also, can you drop by the club-room in the afternoon? Everybody misses you. We can order some takeout."

The person on the other line continued to ramble on in a cheerful voice until Jaeyoung finally hung up on them.

Another overly friendly person... Sangwoo silently mused. He was starting to feel like the entire campus interacted with Jaeyoung that way. It would explain why he didn't hesitate to treat Sangwoo that way as well.

Jaeyoung scoffed incredulously, slipping his phone back into his pocket. "I guess I won't be able to harass you today," he grumbled.

Sangwoo was reminded anew that he was, in fact, being harassed.

Silence fell for a short moment, and then Jaeyoung called his name. When Sangwoo looked over at him, he smiled a bit crookedly.

"If I'm being honest, I don't understand a single thing that's being taught in this class. Also, the professor's glasses look sooo freaking goofy and they make him look like that one cartoon penguin. I have to keep myself from laughing. Anyway... I'll let you enjoy some peace and quiet here from now on."

Not only was he announcing his retreat, but he was explaining exactly why he was doing it. Sangwoo just nodded in reply.

"Are you going to the dining hall later?"

He nodded again.

"You sure you don't wanna go to a restaurant with me...?"

Sangwoo nodded a third time.

"All right, then. Enjoy the school food," Jaeyoung said. He placed a can of Black Holic in front of Sangwoo, then patted him on the back of the head while he wasn't paying attention.

The touch was so light and fleeting that it took Sangwoo a few seconds to process what had happened. By the time he'd angrily opened his mouth to let Jaeyoung have it, the other man was already halfway out of the room.

Sangwoo bristled with dissatisfaction. Every single time Jaeyoung had touched him, his reaction had been so delayed that he hadn't been able to voice an objection. *Next time I see that jerk, I'll tell him just how much I hate it when he does stuff like that. Then he'll never try it again.*

As Sangwoo wrestled with his annoyance—a rather difficult thing to do when one found oneself without a target—the class's professor walked in and began the lecture. Theoretically, he should have been able to focus now that Jaeyoung was gone and he'd reclaimed his rightful seat. But to Sangwoo's dismay, he found he couldn't stop thinking about the professor's glasses and resemblance to a certain cartoon penguin. It made him feel like a total idiot.

Although Engineering Mathematics 2 was supposed to be one of Sangwoo's best subjects, he found he couldn't comprehend anything that was being taught that day. It was the exact same thing he'd experienced during his last Algorithms class.

The lecture flew by, and the room had already filled with the sound of students packing up their belongings before Sangwoo realized that class was over.

He ate lunch by himself, feeling increasingly confused and frustrated. *What's the matter with me?* he asked himself over and over again, but he couldn't come up with an answer.

Forcing his mind to slow down, Sangwoo tried to organize his thoughts. The issue had started when Jaeyoung began his campaign of harassment, sitting next to him in and generally being a huge distraction. But...Jaeyoung wasn't trying to make his life a living hell anymore. The fundamental issue had been solved. So why were his internal functions still so messed up?

Lifting a bite of food to his mouth with one hand, Sangwoo reached out and flipped his phone frontside up with the other. A text notification was waiting for him.

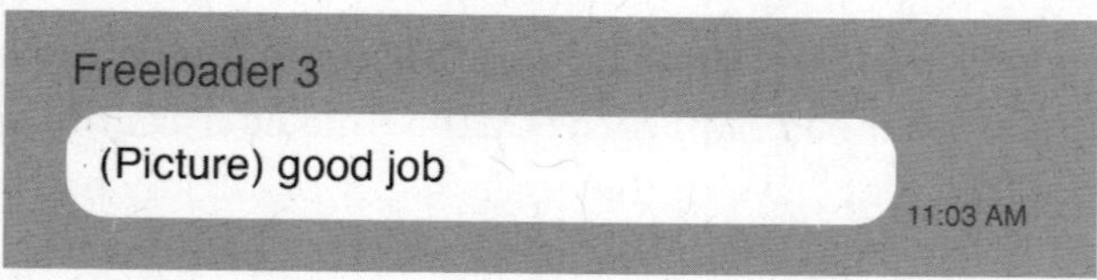

His thumb hovered above the reply button for a moment, but he ended up shoving the phone in his backpack, unable to come up with a suitable response.

Once lunch was over, Sangwoo walked two whole laps around the campus. His mind was a whirlwind of thoughts and emotions that refused to be defined.

Frustration, however, remained a constant. When he arrived at the library, the emotion refused to dissipate. In fact, it grew even more violent, shifting into something he could only guess was anger. But what could he do about it? He'd never experienced anything like this before. He couldn't pinpoint what the strange emotion was directed toward or why it was there, let alone figure out how to resolve it.

"Hey, you're still here!" a voice called out. It belonged to Jaeyoung.

Only seconds before, Sangwoo had been contemplating packing up and heading home early, but as he watched the other man walk closer, the thought vanished without a trace.

Jaeyoung took the seat next to Sangwoo, then pulled the notebook he'd "purchased" from Sangwoo from his bag. Then he reached out and snatched up a pen from Sangwoo's pencil pouch like the thing belonged to him.

He proceeded to doodle in the notebook in his usual position: hunched over with his legs crossed and the notebook atop his knee.

Silence stretched out between them, but as it did, something shifted inside Sangwoo. The emotional turmoil that had been plaguing him subsided in an instant, and when he looked over at his textbook, he found he could finally understand the words inside of it again.

Relief came first, quickly followed by disbelief.

This is bad.

Apparently, Sangwoo's subconscious mind had come to believe that his new default state was being with Jaeyoung. The lowlife's chaos must have warped his brain, changing the variables he'd once used to define normality.

Sangwoo found himself thinking about a common misconception surrounding Chernobyl. Most people thought the land was uninhabitable after the nuclear incident of 1986, but in reality, hawfinches with abnormally high antioxidant levels flourished there. It had become their new normal. Could he have adapted to his own personal disaster just like those birds had?

For once, Jaeyoung didn't actively try to annoy Sangwoo while he was studying. In fact, he stayed completely silent. The only noise that reached Sangwoo's ears was the occasional sound of pen scratching against paper.

For the first time in a very long while, Sangwoo found himself feeling supremely satisfied. He reviewed the topics that he hadn't managed to pay attention to during class with ease, one after another.

When was the last time he'd been able to immerse himself in his studies like this? It certainly hadn't been any time since Jaeyoung had forced his way into his life.

Minutes flew by and turned into hours before Sangwoo finally put his pencil down on his textbook, inwardly giving himself a pat on the back. He glanced over at Jaeyoung, only to find that the senior had been staring at his face again. He'd been drawing another portrait.

When their eyes met, Jaeyoung smiled and whispered, "Your hat's crooked."

Without further ado, he reached out and fixed the offending headwear himself. Sangwoo didn't react, knowing full well that there was nothing for him to get mad at Jaeyoung for—he'd essentially announced what he was going to do in advance, after all.

But then Jaeyoung didn't pull away. His hand remained resting on Sangwoo's head, gradually pressing down with increasing force.

"Hey, Sangwoo… There's something I've been meaning to ask you."

The words felt absurdly loud in the silence of the library, while the hand on his head felt like a lead weight. But for some reason, Sangwoo just couldn't bring himself to tell Jaeyoung to please stop touching him, for heaven's sake. It felt like time itself had screeched to a halt.

Sangwoo's nerves went into overdrive. Suddenly, the very air seemed to be pressing in on him. His eyes roamed around Jaeyoung's face with an inexplicable intensity—he'd drawn so close that Sangwoo could even see his pores.

The lights beaming down from the ceiling reflected off Jaeyoung's brown eyes. His gaze felt unfathomably deep, which was stupid, since

Sangwoo knew the exact structure of the human eye. But that thought evaporated when Jaeyoung blinked very slowly, sending the shadows cast by his eyelashes drifting across his face.

There was a piece of grass stuck to his bangs. He'd probably been rolling around on the lawn again. *I wonder if he was lying there like he was last time.*

Before he'd fully comprehended what he was doing, Sangwoo had reached out and plucked the grass from Jaeyoung's hair.

Jaeyoung flinched visibly, then wetted his lips, the movement strangely sensual. His pink tongue flicked out, slowly swiping over his upper lip from right to left.

The moment seemed to warp and stretch. *The theory of special relativity,* Sangwoo managed to think. It was the only way to explain what he was experiencing.

```
ERROR! ERROR! ERROR!
WARNING! – MALFUNCTION
WARNING! – MALFUNCTION
WARNING! – MALFUNCTION
```

Sangwoo could almost feel his blood racing through his veins. His heart was pounding like a giant drum. His stomach twisted, goose bumps racing all over his skin. *Emergency! Emergency!* his brain was screeching. Overall, it was a reaction that was completely inappropriate for the situation. Confusion and despair rolled over him like a wave.

Desperate to distract himself and quell his body's reaction, Sangwoo turned to reciting the national anthem. *U-until the East Sea's…waves… are dry, and Mt. Baekdu torn awa— No! Worn away…*

Jaeyoung, meanwhile, leaned in even more, his hand still heavy on Sangwoo's head. His lips got closer and closer, and Sangwoo stared at them without even blinking until they'd disappeared from sight. Jaeyoung's ear piercing grazed Sangwoo's cheek, followed by the soft ruffle of his hair. The smell of cigarette smoke assaulted Sangwoo's nostrils.

A hot puff of an exhale drifted over Sangwoo's ear. "Wanna watch a movie with me?" Jaeyoung whispered.

The words traveled to Sangwoo's brain as electric signals, upon which time their message was rapidly decoded. The process was almost instantaneous, its time measurable through his physical reaction to the mental stimuli: a red-hot blush that traveled all the way up his neck to color his face. Even worse, a certain part of his lower body entirely overrode his commands. His autonomic nervous system had seized control instead.

Sangwoo sprang from his seat and bolted out the study room door. It was possible that he knocked over his chair in the process, but he didn't look back to check. He was too busy storming into the men's bathroom like a raging bull.

When he finally came to a stop in front of the mirror, Sangwoo was panting like he'd just run a marathon. His face flushed from top to bottom—he *had* to get it back to normal.

Still breathing heavily, Sangwoo bent over the sink and splashed cold water on his face, hoping that would suppress the heat that was burning inside him.

What in the world is happening to me?

It wasn't that he didn't understand exactly when and why a man's reproductive organ became hard—he just didn't get *why* the phenomenon was occurring at this moment. There was absolutely no reason for him to feel the heat coiling in his lower abdomen or for his penis to react in such a way.

He was malfunctioning. There was no other way to explain it.

The bathroom door swung open just as Sangwoo straightened up. Water dripped from his chin as his eyes met Jaeyoung's in the mirror.

"What the hell…?" Jaeyoung said with a slight frown, taking a step closer.

Sangwoo shivered, an instinctive fear washing over him. He extended one hand as if it would serve as a shield between them.

"No."

"Huh?"

"*No*. I don't want to watch a movie with you."

Sangwoo knew it was a blunt response, but what else was he supposed to say to a *man* who wanted to "watch a movie" with him? The truth was, Jaeyoung's question had knocked over the first in a long line of dominoes that'd been falling into place in Sangwoo's mind, leaving the fortress he'd built within himself in ruins.

Jaeyoung glared at him, narrowing his eyes. "Is it because you don't wanna go with *me*, or is it because you don't wanna go with *a guy*?"

"Both," Sangwoo replied curtly.

"I was only trying to repay you for fixing my laptop. I don't see why you had to run out of the room like I was threatening you with a knife or something."

It'd been a few days since Jaeyoung had come at him with such aggression. Perhaps that was why Sangwoo parted his lips and shot back a rebuttal without a second thought.

"How in the world would hanging out with *you* work as a repayment? Are you actually a moron?"

"Hey, watch your mouth."

Jaeyoung scowled, shifting his weight back on one foot like he was ready to fight. The heavy tension in the air reminded Sangwoo of the day they'd first met. Back then, he hadn't felt an ounce of fear, even when Jaeyoung had cussed at him and acted like a thug.

But this time was different. Though Jaeyoung hadn't raised his voice, a strange, abnormal terror was taking form inside Sangwoo's mind. *Don't touch me! Just stay away,* he wanted to say. *My whole life is falling apart because of you.*

Jaeyoung stayed silent for what felt like forever, staring at Sangwoo. Then he spat, "I'll pay you for your *services*, then. How much?"

"Ten million won."

"Oh, you've gotta be… Why do you always act like such an asshole even when I'm trying so hard to be nice?" Contrary to his words, Jaeyoung's smile was tinged with malice rather than kindness. The sight of it triggered something in Sangwoo, turning the fear racing through his veins into defiance.

"I told you, I don't require any compensation. Stop acting so weird. Go ahead and bully me like you used to."

"'Weird'? What the hell did I do that was so *weird*?"

This time, Sangwoo couldn't keep his voice from rising. "You whispered right in my ear!"

"Yeah, because we're in the library!"

Sangwoo shoved his way past Jaeyoung and ran back out into the reading room. The librarian looked at him with wide eyes, as if she was trying to decide if she should try to stop him or not.

Ignoring her, Sangwoo shoved his belongings into his backpack, and then marched out of the room with the backpack's straps clutched in his hand, not even bothering to zip it up. With each step, the next one came faster and faster, until he was sprinting across campus.

But nobody followed him.

```
ERROR! ERROR! ERROR! ERROR! ERROR! ERROR! ERROR!
ERROR! ERROR! ERROR! ERROR! ERROR! ERROR! ERROR!
ERROR! ERROR! ERROR! ERROR! ERROR! ERROR! ERROR!
ERROR! ERROR! ERROR! ERROR! ERROR! ERROR! ERROR!
ERROR! ERROR! ERROR! ERROR! ERROR! ERROR! ERROR!
ERROR! ERROR! ERROR! ERROR! ERROR! ERROR! ERROR!
ERROR! ERROR! ERROR! ERROR! ERROR! ERROR! ERROR!
ERROR! ERROR! ERROR! ERROR! ERROR! ERROR! ERROR!
ERROR! ERROR! ERROR! ERROR! ERROR! ERROR! ERROR!
ERROR! ERROR! ERROR! ERROR! ERROR! ERROR! ERROR!
ERROR! ERROR! ERROR! ERROR! ERROR! ERROR! ERROR!
ERROR! ERROR! ERROR! ERROR! ERROR! ERROR! ERROR!
ERROR! ERROR! ERROR! ERROR! ERROR! ERROR! ERROR!
ERROR! ERROR! ERROR! ERROR! ERROR! ERROR! ERROR!
ERROR! ERROR! ERROR! ERROR! ERROR! ERROR! ERROR!
```

Sangwoo's mind was flooded with a red light, and a loud alarm was blaring. Something was wrong—something deep and fundamental. Something he might need to visit a hospital to fix. He ran a quick diagnostic.

```
Blood pressure - Abnormally high compared to level of physical activity
Temperature - Abnormally high
Hands - Trembling
```

```
Mouth - Abnormally dry
Reproductive organs - ...Fuck!
```

When he finally stumbled into his apartment, Sangwoo's head was spinning. Without bothering to change, he threw himself on top of his bed and pulled the comforter over his head.

The events from twenty minutes ago were by far the most shocking he'd ever experienced. Something similar had happened back when he was a second-year in middle school, but that was the only thing he could think of that even came close.

It had been many years ago. On the road to his school, a woman had brushed past him wearing a white short-sleeve top with the scent of a pleasant perfume wafting around her. For a moment, his mind had flickered to what lay hidden underneath her shirt, then to a bikini ad that he'd seen at a bus stop not long ago. His heart had started beating faster, and his penis had hardened.

Even then, Sangwoo hadn't been completely clueless—he'd known exactly what had happened to his body. He'd only been shocked because he'd never expected it to happen to *him*, of all people. Feeling a crushing sense of guilt and self-loathing, he'd turned right around and gone straight home.

When he'd relayed what had happened to his mother after she got home from work later that evening, she'd told him that what he'd experienced was completely natural, to his immense relief.

"Do you know what's inside your testicles?" she'd asked.

"Between two hundred and five hundred million sperm cells that are ready for reproduction."

"Correct. They're released through the penis via sexual stimuli, but otherwise, they stay in the testicles. You're too young to have sexual intercourse, so you'll have to induce ejaculation by stimulating your penis with your hand until you can find a legal, consenting partner. Don't do it in public or when you're with somebody else. That's considered taboo. Also, try not to get anything on the floor, and wash your hands before you begin and after."

"Okay," he'd responded. *"Will it make me sick?"*

"What an unscientific thing to ask. Don't worry. Most healthy males begin the practice around age eleven and continue for the majority of their lifespan."

Since hearing his mother's explanation, Sangwoo had managed to retain his composure whenever something similar had happened. Fortunately, his reproductive system was very responsive to logic, and he was often able to prevent an incident from progressing further than the early stages. In fact, even when his body refused to obey him, he'd always been able to suppress his reactions relatively quickly.

Which was why this current situation was inappropriate in every way.

In Sangwoo's mind, developing an erection in response to a particular person meant that he wanted to impregnate them and produce viable offspring. So why was his body responding to *Jaeyoung*, a man who definitely didn't have a uterus?

It seemed that the error that was Jaeyoung wasn't content with upending Sangwoo's routine for the past two weeks—now he was wreaking havoc on his body, too.

```
SANGWOO CHOO - OUT OF ORDER
i.e. Just like the toilet in the second stall of the fourth-floor bathroom in the humanities building.
```

For the rest of that day, Sangwoo didn't do a single thing. He simply stayed in bed, not bothering to eat or drink.

The shock of his physical functions slipping so beyond his control was too much. Suddenly, taking a gap semester didn't seem so crazy an idea.

Sangwoo valued his academics, of course, but he couldn't shake the feeling that something terrible would happen if he didn't put a stop to… whatever was happening with him—something even worse than not getting to graduate on time.

Going to class tomorrow was simply not an option. He knew that Jaeyoung would try to sling an arm over his shoulders, pat him on the head, or lean in to whisper in his ear. And with all the errors he was experiencing, it was entirely possible that his body would malfunction like it had earlier that day.

Sangwoo turned off all his alarms and went to bed late.

```
return 0;
```

Funnily enough, Sangwoo woke up at the exact same time as always. Remembering that he wouldn't be able to attend any of his classes that day, his stomach twisted painfully. But this was necessary if he wanted to prevent himself from suffering even further, so he stubbornly stayed in bed, letting time drift by meaninglessly. As he played a game on his phone, the clock ticked closer and closer to 9:30 AM—the starting time for Embedded Systems.

But Sangwoo didn't move, and class began without him.

10:00 AM

I wonder what the Embedded Systems professor thinks of me now? Sangwoo thought idly.

From the teacher's point of view, Sangwoo was the type of student who fell asleep on his desk the very first day of the semester—with a mustache drawn on his face, at that. Now, he was skipping class without prior notice.

He probably thinks I'm a failure and a delinquent, Sangwoo concluded. *But that's fine. I'm going to take the semester off anyway.*

10:10 AM

A quick online search revealed that applying for a gap semester was much easier than Sangwoo had thought. He decided to get it done before the end of the day.

The only issue was that the website didn't specify what would happen to his full-ride scholarship if he applied in the middle of a semester.

I'll have to inquire with the school.

10:20 AM

My plans will definitely have to change now that I'm taking the semester off, Sangwoo mused.

Initially, he'd been planning to graduate shortly after he turned twenty-six, then start his career at an international game company a few months later.

Actually, maybe it won't affect things that much? It's only going to be for six months.

The biggest problem was that Sangwoo wouldn't be able to make and release his game in the timeframe he'd planned. He'd intended to use it as an integral part of his portfolio when he applied for his future job... But maybe it wasn't too late yet? As long as he got a designer, he could work on the game during his time off.

10:30 AM

Sangwoo logged in to his school's campus forum. After scrolling through quite a number of posts, he finally found the one he'd made a while back—the one where he'd put out a call for a designer.

rless: If you would like to apply, please contact me first instead of Sangwoo. Jaeyoung Jang: Visual Design ***-***-****

PekingDuck: Shot you a text!

Sujin Choi: I texted you, Jaeyoung! :)

mingee03: A bit late but still texted you!!

Scap-jjangS: Are you still looking for someone??

Hyeonjeong Yu: Are you a part of the project?? Just sent you a text

It was a full thirty pages of posts in, which pretty much told Sangwoo no one was paying attention to it anymore. However, there *were* about a dozen comments.

Sangwoo pursed his lips in irritation. Obviously, he wasn't the one they had texted, since he'd never received a single message.

After copying the body text and making a new post, he promptly deleted the old one. Jaeyoung had ruined it anyway. It was also a possibility that Jaeyoung had turned all the visual design majors against him, but that was fine—he could just hire a freelancer.

10:36 AM

Bang! Bang! Bang!

A long second passed before realization hit—someone was pounding on Sangwoo's door. Trying to remember if he had ordered any packages, he stumbled out of bed.

Bang! Bang! Bang! Bang! Bang! Bang!

The sound grew even louder. Whoever it was, it had to be someone incredibly rude and impatient. Sangwoo crept closer to the door, planning on taking a peek outside, but he jumped when somebody yelled so loudly that the metal barrier itself vibrated.

"Sangwoo Choo!"

He halted mid-step, still a few feet away from his destination.

"I know you're in there! Open up!"

Naturally, he stayed silent.

"Oh, you're *ignoring* me now?"

At this point, Sangwoo was scared to make even the slightest noise. He stayed frozen like a statue, his eyes wide in surprise.

"Answer me, you damn asshole!"

The cursing snapped Sangwoo out of his daze. It wasn't too hard to figure out what had happened. He'd skipped class, and Jaeyoung knew where he lived since he'd followed him all the way to his apartment before. Moreover, his bike was still tied to the rack, which meant he was at home. And his unit number was written on the rack.

He scowled, even though he knew Jaeyoung couldn't see him through the thick metal of the door.

"Get lost before I report you to the police for harassment."

Bang!

The sound was so loud that Sangwoo briefly wondered if he'd left a dent in the door.

"Open the door."

"No."

"*Open the damn door!*"

"I said, *no*! This is my apartment!"

A heavy silence lingered in the air as Jaeyoung quieted for a moment. Sangwoo glared at the door, unwilling to be the first one to speak.

Suddenly, Jaeyoung exploded. "Are you serious? You skipped class just because I asked you to watch a *movie* with me?! I know damn well you're trying to avoid me!"

Sangwoo could hear Jaeyoung panting through the door, and he realized that his own breathing was turning ragged as well.

"You'd try to get your stupid seat back even if the whole goddamn planet was going to explode in five minutes! Don't try to tell me that you skipped for no reason."

"I'm not trying to tell you *anything*," Sangwoo retorted.

Thump.

Judging by the soft sound, Jaeyoung had just leaned his back against Sangwoo's door. He muttered, seemingly to himself, "Come on, it's only a movie... What are you gonna do now, take the semester off?" After a short pause, he scoffed and continued, "Here, I've got something you can write down on your permissions form: 'I can't come to school anymore because a pervert with a *dick* tried to ask me out to a movie!'"

"Shut up!"

"It's not like I was gonna, I don't know...kidnap and torture you. What do you think I am, an organ trafficker?"

Finally, Sangwoo snapped, "Who would want to go to a movie with another man? That's...*weird*!"

"You're such a stick-in-the-mud, you know that? I watched a movie with *another man* just yesterday."

"Call me a stick-in-the-mud or whatever else you want—I only watch movies with women I'm planning on courting for marriage! Now, stop being so disruptive and get lost!"

He heard Jaeyoung drop several expletives, followed by a long sigh. "Shit... Thanks for making me feel like an idiot. You have any idea how much time and effort I put into this? Huh?"

Time and effort? "All I know is that you suddenly appeared and started harassing me."

"Yeah, yeah, I harassed you for *two* whole days! And I acted like your obedient little servant for a week after that! Shit, I haven't felt so stupid since I was in the army. Thanks *sooo* much for giving me the chance to feel like an *absolute dumbass*!"

There was something severely wrong with this man. "Why are you yelling at me?" Sangwoo asked in disbelief. "Are you having a mental breakdown or something?"

"Whatever. I'm wasting my time here," Jaeyoung muttered. His voice was much quieter, likely because he'd used up all his energy throwing his little fit.

After another brief moment of silence, a piece of paper slid under Sangwoo's door. It was a movie ticket.

"Just... Just take this and get out of my life."

"You could make that happen right now if you just got the hell out of here," Sangwoo snapped.

"No, *you* get lost, you damn weirdo! Don't ever let me see your face again!"

How am I supposed to "get lost" in my own apartment? It was like a candle telling the wind to go away.

After a short moment, he heard Jaeyoung stomping away. The footsteps faded until, eventually, Sangwoo couldn't hear them anymore.

That worked out for the better.

The thought of taking a six-month break had completely vanished from Sangwoo's mind—it'd gotten drowned out under the rage a certain asshole had triggered in him. Without bothering to take a shower, he quickly slipped into his outside clothes. Hopefully he wouldn't be late for his next class.

The cluttered disaster that had been Sangwoo's mind before Jaeyoung's arrival was now a distant memory. He couldn't even remember what had gotten him so out of whack. All he knew was that things had changed, and he was completely determined to finish the semester strong. That'd be the ultimate way to spit in Jaeyoung's face.

"Don't ever let me see your face again!"

It wasn't the first time the asshole had thrown those words at him. But, just like back at the internet café, Sangwoo found himself feeling both irritated and welcoming of the declaration.

It only took him seven minutes to get changed, sling his backpack on, and rush out of his apartment. He pedaled to school with such vigor that he heard his bike's gears creak. In the end, he managed to arrive just as his first class was coming to an end.

Panting, Sangwoo ran to the engineering building. He felt sure that everything was going to fall back into place now that Jaeyoung had agreed to extract himself from his life. All Sangwoo had to do was rebuild after the tornado.

There were still students from the previous class in room 303, so Sangwoo waited in front of the door until the space was finally empty. There were no irritating obstacles in his path, such as a bag on his favorite seat, and he didn't have any issues getting absorbed in his textbook.

He could still feel the adrenaline pumping through his veins, however.

As it turned out, anger toward Jaeyoung served as a great motivator. Sangwoo made such intense eye contact with his professor that, after a while, the man avoided looking in his direction. He put so much pressure on his pen that he ripped straight through the paper as he took notes, but it didn't matter—every single word of the lecture crystallized in his memory effortlessly. He wasn't fazed when the professor wrote a problem on the board. All he had to do was glare at it for a few seconds, and the knowledge of exactly how to solve it just came to him.

Sangwoo's heart pounded in his ears. He felt like a video game character that had just received a hell of a power boost.

Determined not to let a deadbeat like Jaeyoung ruin his daily routine, Sangwoo powered through the weekend with the determination of a man who knew his time was up. Not only did he study at his desk for hours without even getting up to stretch, but he spent any free time he had while working at the internet café on solving problem sets. He glared at every single letter and number like it was a matter of life and death, not leaving a single question unanswered.

When he came back home Sunday night, he collapsed on his bed like a log. His power boost had lasted for a total of three days, but it was starting to run out.

A sudden wave of exhaustion and slight somberness washed over him. In its wake came a rush of encroaching thoughts, impossible to keep out. Bits and pieces of various memories flashed through his mind: a hand that always touched him out of nowhere, a voice that spat out cuss words at louder and louder decibels when its owner was enraged, a name he used to call out to Sangwoo like an old friend, a pink tongue that darted excruciatingly slowly over its owner's lips…

In the end, they all traced back to one person. There was a virus inside his head called Jaeyoung Jang, and it was corrupting his mind further and further, even as he lay limply on his bed.

Sangwoo turned off the lights, hoping that would extinguish his thoughts as well, but to no avail.

It was an unpleasant night, to say the least.

return 0;

By the time Sangwoo reached the third week of the school year, he'd finally debugged his schedule back to perfection.

```
8:30 AM - Wake up, exercise, shower, eat breakfast
9:16 AM - Bike to campus
9:24 AM - Arrive at campus
9:30 AM - Arrive at first classroom, read over materials for the day's class, review materials from past classes
10:00 AM - First class begins
10:50 AM - Go to second classroom
```

```
11:00 AM - Second class begins
12:00 PM - Go to campus dining hall, eat lunch
12:28 PM - Go to convenience store, purchase cof-
fee, take a walk
12:45 PM - Go to the library, look over new releases,
check out books, work on assignments
6:00 PM - Go to campus dining hall, eat dinner
6:28 PM - Go back home, brush teeth, change, rest
7:00 PM - Gaming time
9:00 PM - Study game trends, community interactions
10:00 PM - Programming study session
12:00 AM - Reserve seat at the library, rest
12:30 AM - Sleep
```

Just like before, he went to school at the exact same time and sat in the exact same seat—with the exact same posture—every single day.

The content in Embedded Systems felt so new that if you'd told Sangwoo he'd never attended the class before that day, he'd have believed you. The fault for that, rather obviously, lay at the feet of a certain someone who'd been distracting him during the lectures like it was his job.

Sangwoo spent the entirety of the class marking down topics he'd have to review later on.

Shortly after the lecture ended, the professor called out to Sangwoo: "Can I talk to you for a minute?"

Sangwoo paused while packing his things. "Of course."

It sounded like he was due for a scolding. Such a thing would've devastated him in the past, but Sangwoo's face remained completely impassive as he resumed placing his books in his backpack. He'd become so numb to stress that facing a professor felt like a walk in the park.

He headed up to the podium, slipping his arms through the straps of his backpack as he went. "Yes, Professor?" he asked gloomily.

The professor, who was in the process of packing up a small microphone, glanced at him. "Why were you absent last class?"

I decided to take the semester off because a pervert with a dick tried to ask me out to a movie, Sangwoo thought. But he could never say that out loud, obviously.

He bowed deeply. "All I can say is I'm sorry, Professor."

"What about the student who always sits next to you and naps during class? Where is he?"

"I believe he dropped the class."

The professor handed his mic over to the TA, then focused his eyes on Sangwoo. Most people would say the man's gaze was intimidating, but Sangwoo didn't feel particularly scared. Honestly, he didn't feel much of anything.

The professor finally said, "I've got high expectations for you, Sangwoo."

"You know my name...?"

"Of course. Every professor in the department knows you." The professor smiled, but the expression was so faint that Sangwoo nearly missed it. "I must admit, I was a bit disappointed at first, but you still have time to redeem yourself. I have faith in your abilities."

"Yes, Professor."

Sangwoo bowed a second time, then left the classroom and headed to the dining hall. At this point, he'd developed a habit of glancing around as he ate, in case somebody decided to sit down next to him. Not a single soul was remotely interested in doing so, however, and Sangwoo walked out of the dining hall right on schedule.

The convenience store manager spotted him as soon as he stepped into the building. "I just got a new coffee shipment!" she said cheerfully.

"Oh... I see."

"Feel free to take your pick."

Without even thinking, Sangwoo drifted over to the third fridge. He watched, feeling detached, as his hand opened the door and grabbed a can of Black Holic from the fifth shelf.

I have seven of these back home, he thought blankly as he made his purchase.

He opened the can as he walked out of the store and took a sip. Strangely enough, it didn't taste as good as it used to. But that didn't make any sense—it was mass-produced, so it should taste the same as before.

As Sangwoo mulled over the bitter taste of the coffee, he realized that not everything had returned to normal.

`return 0;`

The rest of the week passed without anything out of the ordinary happening. Everything strictly adhered to Sangwoo's routine. However, he couldn't shake the sense that *something* was different.

For one, there was a sort of dark cloud hanging over him, which he'd never experienced before. Despite trying his best to immerse himself in his studies, Sangwoo's life just kept falling apart around him, piece by piece, like a poorly greased machine.

His attention span had become significantly shorter, and it took him an infuriatingly long time to comprehend what others were saying. Games were no longer entertaining—in fact, *everything* felt like a chore. And throughout the day, whether he was brushing his teeth, reading a book, or even just walking, he'd sometimes randomly freeze up like a lagging computer. When that happened, returning to whatever task he'd been doing required conscious effort.

All in all, it was extremely annoying.

In addition, Sangwoo also found himself dragging his feet whenever he walked by certain places, such as the lecture hall, the engineering building, the stairs of the humanities building, the dining hall, and the library. At first, he figured it was just a knee-jerk reaction, considering how he'd been trying to avoid Jaeyoung for what felt like ages. But even though he knew there was a 0 percent chance that the asshole would pop up again, he found he couldn't shake the habit.

Soon enough, Sangwoo found that he was plagued by all sorts of other, smaller errors. He'd grab three chopsticks and no spoon at the dining hall, or put his shirt on backward, or wear mismatching socks, or just sit, frozen, zoning out for ten straight minutes.

They persisted and persisted, until one day, he saw Jaeyoung again.

Sangwoo was walking past the school's front gates when he spotted him, but this time, the asshole wasn't wearing a red puffer or even a green coat. Instead, he had on a varsity jacket and a pair of glasses—an outfit Sangwoo had never seen before. There were two other guys with him, doing various tricks on their skateboards and laughing.

Honestly, Sangwoo didn't know how he'd managed to spot Jaeyoung when he was mixed up in a crowd far in the distance. Maybe it was the asshole's lopsided stance, or the way he towered above most people, or his slender build, or maybe even that pretty smile on his face…

The thoughts felt too foreign in Sangwoo's head. He quickly rushed past the group, but he could already feel color seeping back into his world just from that simple encounter. He felt a brief rush of adrenaline, washing away the gloom that had been hanging over him before.

For the first time in days, he felt like himself again…and then an error message flashed in his brain.

```
ERROR! ERROR!
SANGWOO CHOO - OUT OF ORDER
```

Suddenly feeling exhausted, Sangwoo staggered into his apartment, his shoulders slumped. After washing his hands, he plopped himself down at his desk and glanced at his phone—he'd gotten a text.

Sangwoo's heart fell. He scrambled to unlock the screen, only to press his lips together in disappointment.

Unknown Sender

Hi! Saw your post about the game ur developonng :)) I'm a jinor & desing major!! id be super intesrsted in the projct if u still llooking for seomone

04:52 PM

Sangwoo had been waiting for a text like that for ages, but now that it had actually arrived, he found he didn't feel particularly excited. Although, the seven whole typos might have had something to do with that.

Quickly typing out a reply, he gave the unknown sender his email address and asked for their portfolio. But instead of locking his screen when he was done, his finger drifted over and opened up a text that someone else had sent a while ago.

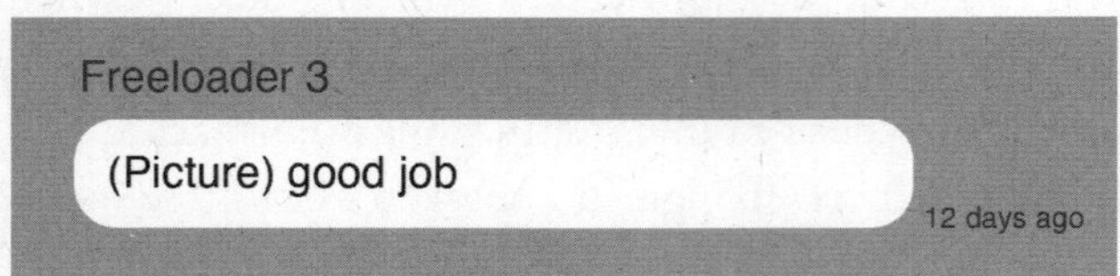

He tapped on the thumbnail image without thinking, and the picture popped open to fill the entire screen. Jaeyoung was cheerfully sticking out his tongue while Sangwoo stared stiffly at the camera next to him. The rubber of the wigs they were wearing reflected the fluorescent light from the ceiling.

Sangwoo's fingers zoomed the photo in once, then again and again, only stopping when Jaeyoung's face was all that was visible on the screen. But the image was of terrible quality—the pixelation irritated him.

Jihye said he's on social media, right?

Putting his phone aside, Sangwoo scrambled to turn his PC on. It took mere seconds to boot up thanks to the modifications he'd made, but he still found himself feeling impatient.

As soon as the desktop screen came up, he opened his web browser and logged into his social media account. He'd abandoned it long ago, nearly immediately after creating it. Unsurprisingly, he only had two followers. Still, he did have some DMs from middle school and high school friends that had been sent a few years ago.

—Sangchoooooo wtf pick up ur phone!!
—SangSangChooChoo when u gettnng discharged?

Ignoring them, Sangwoo searched Jaeyoung's name. A long list of people popped up, but it wasn't too hard to find the right one—the accounts with the most followers were at the very top.

* * *

Jaeyoung Jang (Jae. J)
Graphic Designer / Graffiti Artist / Skateboarder

The bio was short and sweet, and there was a link to his portfolio right underneath. Sangwoo glanced at the number of posts—only twenty-two. The most recent one was the picture they'd taken together on the day of the Chinese class skit.

The caption read:

w/ a cute underclassman

Jaeyoung must have uploaded the post right before they'd ripped into each other in the library. It had hundreds of likes from people Sangwoo had never met.

Before he knew it, Sangwoo had zoomed in to the picture as much as he could without cutting off the caption and then saved it onto his desktop. It felt like he'd just taken a step into Jaeyoung's stalkerish shoes.

Sangwoo scrolled down to the very first post Jaeyoung had made, which turned out to be a selfie from early last year. Under the caption—*nice 2 meet u*—there were dozens of comments, most of them consisting of heart-eye or crying emojis.

Zooming into the picture, Sangwoo's attention immediately caught on to the spiky-looking cone piercings in Jaeyoung's earlobes. His bleached hair was frizzy and a light orange, while his face was totally expressionless.

What a delinquent. I hate it, Sangwoo thought. He leaned forward so much that his forehead nearly touched the screen, then saved the picture to his computer.

Jaeyoung's second post was tagged at Olive Tree, the Italian restaurant where he worked. It looked like he'd gotten a job there through knowing the owner. The picture showed the two of them in front of the establishment; the caption listed his work schedule.

That's the fakest smile I've ever seen.

Saved.

The next post was another promotional post. Sangwoo scrolled past it and found himself greeted by the sight of Jaeyoung in a black beanie and glasses, a laptop sitting in front of him. His hair was still bleached, and it was completely dark outside, suggesting that he was pulling an all-nighter.

For someone who's supposedly going without sleep, he looks plenty rested. It's so staged.

Saved.

His cursor moved frantically as he scrolled, clicked, scrolled, clicked. In one of the posts, Jaeyoung and his friends were striking bizarre poses in fancy suits.

He sure loves attention...

Saved.

There was a short video in which Jaeyoung was practicing a move on his skateboard, wearing a helmet and protective gear. The video ended by zooming in on his face as he sat sprawled on the ground, laughing.

What an idiot.

Saved.

Sangwoo moved on to the next picture. Jaeyoung was standing in front of a huge wall, holding a spray can as if to highlight the graffiti: strange neon letters and a black tongue.

Weird... Just like him.

Saved.

In another picture, Jaeyoung stood in front of a black background with his eyes closed. His face was accentuated by dramatic stage makeup.

For the longest time, Sangwoo stared at the image silently.

Saved.

Everything about Jaeyoung was chaotic, starting with his entrancing smile, those eyes that always sparkled with interest, the mischievous curve of his lips, his sarcastic smirk, and his wicked laughter...

Suddenly, Sangwoo was reminded of his first time seeing a miniature excavator model. He'd been six years old and had subsequently begged his parents to buy it for him for fifteen days straight until his father had finally caved and bought it without his mother knowing. Even now, in his mid-twenties, Sangwoo's heart still beat a bit faster whenever he saw an excavator...just like it did when he saw Jaeyoung.

Over the next few hours, Sangwoo scoured Jaeyoung's profile on a certain social media platform and saved every single one of the drama club advertisements and skateboarding and graffiti videos. He also looked up Jaeyoung's username to deduce his interests and even found his playlist, which mainly consisted of EDM.

Sangwoo dug so deep that he even found a few comments Jaeyoung had left on forums and his product reviews.

—whoaaaa he's AMAZING he's on a total roll this season!!!
—Nah dont buy, it doesnt rly work and you keep spraying all over the place
—wtf it looks so nice but idk if it's gonna last long

Next, he drifted over to Jaeyoung's portfolio page, where he carefully studied his senior project, award-winning works, websites he had worked on as a freelancer, concert posters, banners for indie artists, and magazine illustrations, along with the graffiti and other artwork he did in his free time.

Once he was done, Sangwoo moved to combing through the school forum to read all of his posts about recruiting for the drama club, promoting various plays, and exhibition announcements.

(5 mins from campus) Looking for a male roommate, all furnished, super easy move-in

He blinked as he found himself dissecting every single word in a post Jaeyoung had made six years ago. When he glanced at the clock, he saw that it was well past midnight.

What am I doing?

Somehow, he'd ended up with a new folder on his desktop named "Jaeyoung Jang," which contained exactly thirty-six pictures and nine videos organized in chronological order. Even as Sangwoo questioned his own sanity, he mechanically opened file after file and began studying the contents like he'd never even laid eyes on them before. Despite their rather turbulent relationship, flipping through the pictures gave Sangwoo the odd feeling that he knew Jaeyoung like an old friend.

What have you done to me, Jaeyoung Jang? he asked silently, the last word slipping into his thoughts without being filtered.

It hadn't been that long since he'd run into Jaeyoung at the internet café for the first time, where he'd proceeded to curse Sangwoo out before telling him he never wanted to see his face again. Back then, the asshole had only been a measly format error, easily resolved. But somehow, Sangwoo's system was still malfunctioning. There was something going wrong inside him, something that refused to disappear—like the seven cans of Black Holic that still sat in his fridge.

Maybe, in trying to get rid of the error, he'd deleted code that was vital to his core processing.

Twelve days had passed since Sangwoo's last fight with Jaeyoung. Coffee tasted flavorless, his favorite video games had lost their spark, and his mind was weighed down by depression. Sangwoo had always prioritized reason over feelings, but he couldn't deny that he'd been at the mercy of his own emotions over the past three weeks.

```
i) Annoyance (MAX), Anxiety (MAX), Resentment - Duration: 2 days
ii) Annoyance (Low), Anxiety (Low), Suspicion - Duration: 3 days
iii) Confusion, Anger, Disorientation - Duration: 6 days
iv) Depression, Anger - Duration: 12 days
```

Issues one, two, and three had been resolved as soon as Jaeyoung had disappeared from Sangwoo's life, since the asshole's existence itself had been the problem. But issue four was the result of Jaeyoung's absence.

For the past ten days, Sangwoo had tried his best to ignore that fact, even as his system crumbled piece by piece. However, he knew he had to take a different approach now. Pretending the problem didn't exist hadn't solved anything, so he'd have to delve deeper until he uncovered what was at its core.

Sangwoo carefully examined the different aspects that fed into the problem at hand. What benefits had he and Jaeyoung taken away from their relationship? How had their circumstances affected those benefits?

Often, the most complex issues had the simplest solutions. Brushing aside the irrational factors—the strange emotions he'd been feeling, how his body had been refusing to cooperate with his brain, etc.—he analyzed the facts of the situation.

Multiple paths aligned in his mind like gears clicking together, and among them, the optimal solution rose to the surface. His dissatisfaction stemmed from Jaeyoung's absence. To rid himself of it, he just had to find a reason for the asshole to come back and stick around.

It was the only solution Sangwoo could think of. And he'd never been one to shy away from taking the most efficient route.

return 0;

It wasn't long before Sangwoo put his plan into motion. His Pop Culture and Cultural Theory class had just ended, and he was eating lunch with Jihye in the dining hall when he said abruptly, "Hey."

She glanced up curiously from her bowl of stew.

"Do you remember how I promised to take you out for a meal?"

"Yeah?"

"How about today?"

Jihye's previously impassive face brightened with a smile. Taken aback by the expression, Sangwoo couldn't help but wonder if she was running low on cash to pay for her meals.

"If you wish to accept my offer, then come to Olive Tree at six," Sangwoo explained flatly.

"Olive Tree? That's where we first ate together! I didn't think you'd remember! But…that place is super pricey," she added hesitantly.

"I know. Are you going to come or not?"

"Yes, yes! I'll be there!"

Is a free meal from an expensive restaurant really something to get so excited over? Sangwoo mused. Nevertheless, he proceeded to get her number so they wouldn't struggle to find each other. She stuttered as she recited it to him.

"What was your last name again?"

"Ryu."

He saved her as "French Major Jihye Ryu," then slipped his phone back into his bag.

"Hold on. Do you know what my name is?" Jihye asked suspiciously.

"Jihye."

"Whoa… Nice. I didn't think you'd remember."

Sangwoo briefly wondered why she seemed so eager to test his memory.

Just past six o'clock, Sangwoo and Jihye were standing in line for a table at Olive Tree. Never in his life had he wasted so much time waiting to eat, but this time, he was willing to make an exception.

"Looks like we're finally up! Let's go in."

A small bell jingled as an employee held the door open for them. Sangwoo stepped inside, his eyes sweeping across the spacious interior. Between the tables—which were all occupied—three servers in black aprons moved about with practiced ease.

Across the hall, Jaeyoung was busy taking orders from one of those tables, jotting something down on a notepad.

His handwriting's probably even worse than a doctor's, Sangwoo mused. *No doubt he's the only one who can read it.*

Soon after, Jaeyoung slipped his notepad into his apron and turned around. Sangwoo was certain their eyes met, but then Jaeyoung sped off toward the kitchen. Had he been mistaken?

For some reason, Sangwoo had gotten it into his head that Jaeyoung would be the server who came over and took their order like last time. Instead, some other random member of the waitstaff was assigned to them—Jihye ordered a *spaghetti alle vongole*, and Sangwoo mindlessly pointed at something at the very top of the page.

"Are you a fan of seafood, Sangwoo?" Jihye asked with a laugh as the server briskly walked away. "I remember you had lobster last time."

"Huh?"

"You got *impepata di cozze*! Only *real* foodies order that stuff. I'm impressed!"

Sangwoo had absolutely no idea what she was talking about. And, unfortunately for Jihye, he was too preoccupied with trying to locate Jaeyoung to respond to her.

He narrowed his eyes when he spotted his target exiting the kitchen and heading toward the exit—Jaeyoung was still wearing his apron, so it was unlikely he'd clocked out.

Did something urgent come up? Sangwoo wondered. *Or…is he trying to avoid me?*

Just as Sangwoo was being swallowed by a sinkhole of his own pointless questions, the server came back with their food. Jihye's dish looked fairly simple and familiar, but the monstrosity they placed in front of Sangwoo was a chaotic mixture of some thick red sauce and mussels.

Sangwoo wasn't exactly a picky eater, but he still found the task of prying mussels out of their shells irritating. With a sigh, he gingerly began to deconstruct them with a spoon and fork.

"Do you like it?" Jihye asked hopefully.

"No."

"Oh…sorry."

His gaze kept flickering to the door, but even after he'd mechanically worked his way through nearly half the imposing pile of mussels, Jaeyoung was still nowhere to be seen. Unable to bear the suspense any longer, Sangwoo shot up out of his seat.

Jihye blinked at him in surprise. "Where're you going?"

"Outside. I'll be a few minutes," he responded half-heartedly.

"Hey, hold on!" she yelped. "You better not ditch me again!"

"I'll leave my wallet with you, then."

She's a nice girl, but a little too suspicious for her own good, Sangwoo mused as he followed through on his words. Then, leaving Jihye behind with her new hostage, he hurried out of the restaurant.

His steps grew more frantic as he burst through the glass doors and raced down the stairs, but he abruptly paused at the bottom.

Shrouded in shadow as he was, Sangwoo couldn't mistake the unique lines that made up Jaeyoung's face. Cigarette tucked in his fingers, the older man was leaning against the side of the building as he talked into his cellphone.

Sangwoo's heart began to pound. The villain before him—the one who had so meticulously dismantled his entire carefully constructed routine—had now caused an error in every aspect of his system.

After what felt like forever, Jaeyoung's eyes shifted in Sangwoo's direction. His irises were stained pitch-black by the darkness. It was like the two of them had been catapulted into a neo-noir video game.

Jaeyoung frowned at the sight of him, then continued to talk to the person on the other side of his call. "Yeah, for the time being… I'm taking a break right now."

For a brief moment, Sangwoo thought Jaeyoung would end the call and talk to him instead. There was just something in his eyes.

But in the end, Jaeyoung simply looked away and took another puff of his cigarette.

"No, you're fine. I'm not doing anything," he said, then placed his phone between his shoulder and neck so he could peer at his watch.

Without thinking, Sangwoo blurted out, "Hey."

Jaeyoung glared at the wall for a long moment, then slowly turned his gaze to Sangwoo.

Sangwoo met the other man's gaze and declared, "Tell them you're busy and hang up. I have something important to say."

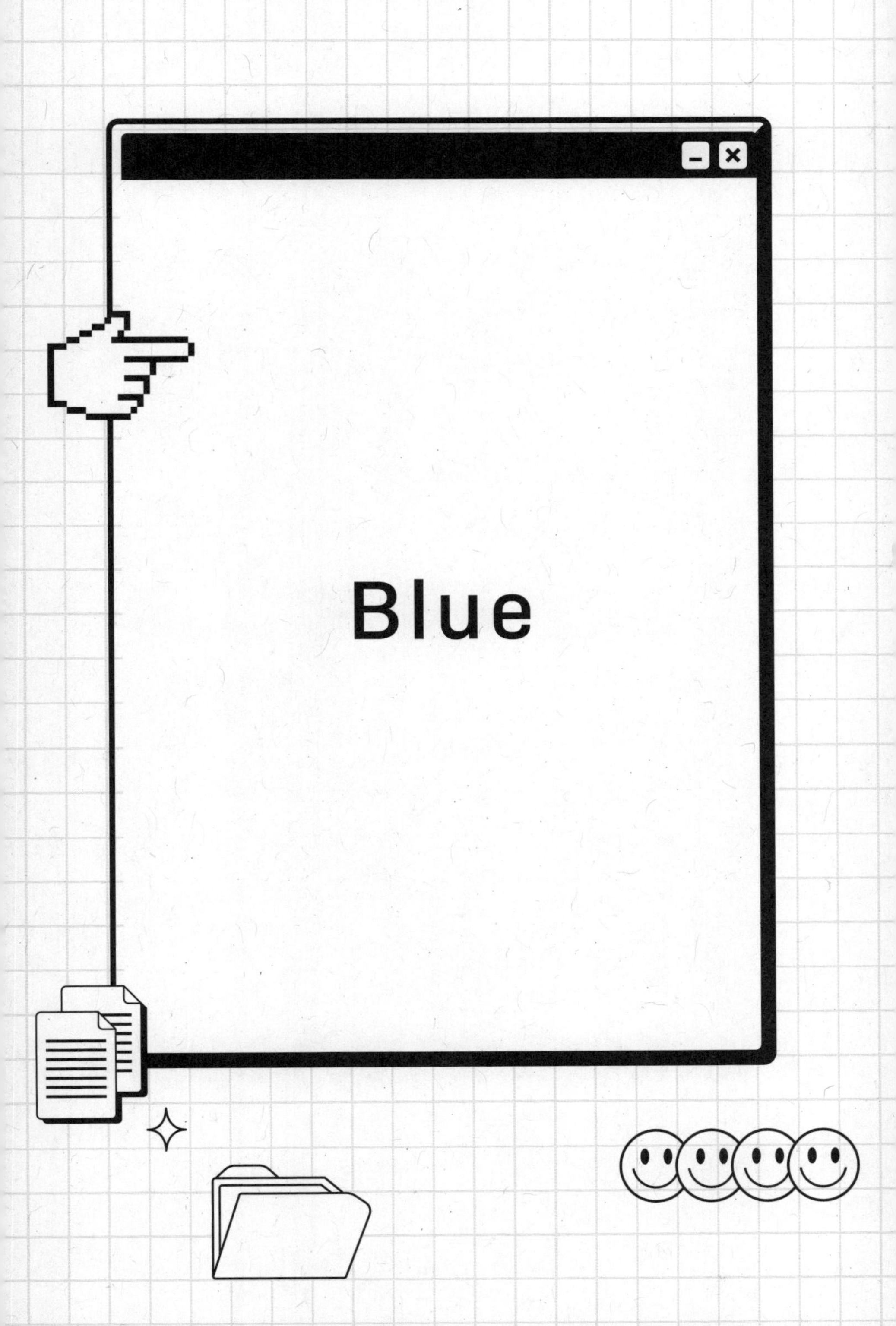

Blue

Judging from the piles of evidence Jaeyoung had from past experience, the loyalty of an underclassman could easily be bought with the right amount of kindness and the occasional meal.

There was only one person he knew who was an exception to this rule: a certain weirdo who ate food like it was simply fuel that would pass through his digestive system. He'd chew up pizza with complete apathy, like it might as well have been made of dirt. Risotto was no different—he'd shovel it into his mouth like it was the most bland thing he'd ever had the misfortune of eating. And in Jaeyoung's opinion, the risotto in question had been pretty damn decent. It should've blown the weirdo's mind after exclusively eating at the dining hall, which didn't exactly provide a five-star dining experience.

At this point, Jaeyoung had been in college for five years. He was more or less an expert at making underclassmen like him—he'd even started specializing his approach based on his target's gender.

Guys were easy enough: order them some takeout and do a few skateboard tricks, and they were usually sold. Girls, on the other hand, were different. You had to get them food as well, but you also had to interact with them with relative frequency. To talk with them and make an effort to smile as they spoke.

In that sense, Sangwoo didn't really match his previous experiences of either gender.

Jaeyoung had tried literally everything he could think of to win that weirdo over. Admittedly, he hadn't quite been able to suppress his desire to mess with the guy on a certain number of occasions, but he'd truly done his best not to provoke him.

He'd limited his vocabulary to words that wouldn't set the weirdo off, presented him with his favorite coffee every single day to help him maintain his precious routine, and basically carried their entire Intermediate Chinese skit on his back. He'd even drawn a caricature of the guy—although it'd had the opposite effect than the one he'd intended—and escorted him all the way home on his skateboard, which was basically his finisher move.

There was literally nothing more he could've done. And yet…

"I hope you have a nightmare."

…shockingly enough, none of it had worked.

Initially, Jaeyoung had been so frustrated that he'd almost given up on the jerk entirely, but then he'd remembered the effort he'd already poured into winning the weirdo over. Determined, he'd come at the challenge with renewed vigor.

If he's gonna keep acting like a robot, I'll just have to approach him like one.

The idea came to Jaeyoung one Sunday as he was watching soccer on his garbage spare laptop, which was slower than a snail. Sure, taking apart his own laptop in order to have a reason to talk to Sangwoo could be seen as being obsessive, but he refused to give up on something once he'd started. Besides, if he straight-out asked the weirdo to format his computer, Jaeyoung knew the guy would turn him down right away. If he came up with another plausible issue, on the other hand…

He'd grabbed all the necessary materials and headed off to the enemy's base: the internet café.

Just as Jaeyoung had expected, the weirdo's eyes had started to sparkle as soon as he began working on the laptop—an expression in stark contrast to the disinterest he treated his fellow humans with.

It was kind of sexy, seeing him in his element. *I guess this is why people are attracted to competence.*

Jaeyoung had leaned against the counter and watched Sangwoo work for a long time, his interest piqued. When the weirdo announced that he'd formatted and optimized the system—without Jaeyoung even asking him to do it—he'd found the guy kind of...cute, was the word that came to mind.

It was impossible to explain, honestly. Some people had the same sort of adorableness about them as a puppy, kitten, or even a rabbit, but not Sangwoo. Even so...*something* about him struck Jaeyoung as cute.

Being impulsive and free-spirited was something Jaeyoung took pride in, which meant he and the weirdo were polar opposites. The guy acted like he had his whole life already planned out, and even worse, he refused to ever deviate from his annoying schedule. Honestly, Jaeyoung would bet money that if Sangwoo woke up one day and realized that everybody else in the world had disappeared, the weirdo would still wait for the light to turn green before he crossed the road.

In the past, Jaeyoung would have ignored someone like Sangwoo. When he'd first started getting to know him, he'd found the guy's little habits and mannerisms ridiculous. Somewhere along the way, however, he'd started to appreciate them as something that made the weirdo unique.

The way Sangwoo always answered his questions, even though he acted like it was the last thing he wanted to do; the way he tried so hard to complete his little tasks; even the way his Chinese pronunciation was horrendous despite his impeccable spelling and grammar... Jaeyoung found it all cute.

Even the guy's appearance was fascinating—his pale skin was such a sharp contrast to his all-black outfits and the way he was such a stickler for rules.

In Jaeyoung's imagination, Sangwoo was like a cuddly little fawn that had mutated to have shadowy black attributes and could now use a computer keyboard—maybe in a cyberpunk-style world set after the apocalypse. And despite everything, he didn't think anything was wrong.

Honestly, it was only natural that Jaeyoung was attracted to the weirdo. He was an artist, after all—how could he not be drawn to a creature of contrasts that looked entirely different every time one of its layers was peeled away?

But then things had started spiraling. An unsettled feeling had crept over him.

Sure, it was totally fine for an upperclassman to find an underclassman cute, but where was he supposed to draw the line? Obviously, thinking the weirdo was adorable for scribbling on his nose with a marker during class was fine. But what was he supposed to do with this craving to sink his teeth into the pale skin at the guy's nape?

Jaeyoung had always wanted to see what Sangwoo looked like without the hat that had seemed to be glued to his head. But when that desire had been fulfilled, he'd been overcome by a ravenous need for *more.* He'd wanted to strip the weirdo of his jacket, shirt, shoes, and socks in order to find the answers to a variety of questions: Were his shoulders as skinny as the rest of his body? What did his toes look like? How much body hair did he have? What color were his nipples?

You're completely right, Sangwoo. I am *the scum of the earth.*

It was a good thing that Sangwoo wasn't a mind reader—if he'd gotten a glimpse of Jaeyoung's perverted thoughts, he would've reached for his phone immediately and called the police on him.

Jaeyoung had polished his "nice upperclassman" act even as his thoughts had spun further and further out of control. Fortunately, maintaining the facade was as easy as breathing. He just had to use a low, gentle voice, keep a smile pasted on his face, and lighten his intonation at the ends of his sentences. Seriously—that was all it took to make most people think he was the nicest guy in the world.

Sangwoo had been no exception. His struggle to hate the green coat version of Jaeyoung as much as he did the red puffer jacket version had been palpable.

Jaeyoung had to admit, though, it had been pretty childish of him to snap at the girl who hung out with the weirdo.

"Well, it's just… You seem to have more makeup on than the last time I saw you, that's all."

A part of him hated himself for hurling that line at her. It was such a cliché, mean girl thing to say. But at the same time, another part of him had thought: *That's what you get for acting like you're his girlfriend.* It was only later that he'd realized she was six whole years younger than him, which meant he'd been one-sidedly feuding with a girl who'd been a little kid while he was in high school.

The entire thing with Sangwoo had started as a stupid joke, but somehow, without Jaeyoung realizing it, it seemed to have spiraled into something much more bizarre and meaningful.

Around that time, Jaeyoung had started contemplating whether he was romantically attracted to Sangwoo. Sure, the guy was a weirdo, but Jaeyoung had always been attracted to people who piqued his curiosity. The only problem was...well, there were too many problems.

For one, Jaeyoung wasn't going to be around for very long. He'd applied to the same grad school that had already accepted him last semester, and judging by the tone of their emails, it seemed like a done deal in his favor.

The biggest issue was that Sangwoo was a man. The weirdo's gender itself wasn't the problem—once, a few years back, Jaeyoung had slept with a cute, petite man on a whim when he'd been traveling in Europe. It was just that he'd never felt the desire to go on a date or get into a relationship with one. And while he wasn't *against* the idea...with Sangwoo Choo? The robotic weirdo who malfunctioned at the mere thought of two guys going to a movie together?

No matter how much Jaeyoung thought about it, he always came to the same conclusion: It wasn't going to work out. Funnily enough, that had actually inspired him to throw caution to the wind—why not, when they were never going to develop into anything anyway? And so, despite knowing it was being ill-received, he'd kept poking and prodding at Sangwoo under the guise of a nice upperclassman.

Initially, he'd only planned to mess with the weirdo for a few days. But before he'd known it, those days had turned into a week, then two weeks. As the time to drop his unnecessary classes had neared, Jaeyoung had even found himself feeling slightly disappointed—time really *did* fly by when you were having fun.

Although he'd once hoped for more, it'd still been pretty gratifying to see his and the weirdo's relationship coalesce into something closer to a friendship. Maybe that was why he'd poured so much effort into the stupid skit for Intermediate Chinese. He'd not only come up with the scenario and put together the costumes and props, he'd done all the script translation and edits, too, along with printing out the documents and even helping Sangwoo with his pronunciation. Considering the project was for an elective course, putting in that kind of elbow grease had been kind of unprecedented for Jaeyoung. But even after all that, he hadn't realized how screwed he was until the day of the skit.

Jaeyoung had set ten alarms the night before, just in case he didn't wake up, so he'd successfully headed over to campus on time with a bundle of costumes and props.

That was when he'd seen Sangwoo come walking down the hallway. The weirdo had marched forward like he was being graded on his posture, even though there had been no one around but Jaeyoung to see.

Jaeyoung's heart had skipped a beat. His eyes had devoured Sangwoo's outfit, completely entranced—the old, collared navy shirt, the pair of black pants with the tiny fold at the ankles, the black baseball cap that Jaeyoung had an immense desire to send up in flames…

Nothing about the man should've been attractive, and yet the sight of him had managed to send butterflies fluttering through Jaeyoung's stomach.

And so, he'd just stood there, utterly dumbfounded—wearing a queue wig, of all things!—feeling distinctly like his life just turned into some cheesy romcom.

The rupture had occurred after the skit.

Foolishly enough, Jaeyoung had thought Sangwoo might open up to him a bit more. But when the weirdo had taken his offer to watch a movie together and had thrown it right back in his face, he'd realized just how wrong he was.

Did the idiot think he was trying to harass or kidnap him or something? It was the furthest thing from the truth—Jaeyoung had simply wanted was to see how Sangwoo's expressionless face looked in the dark, staring at a movie screen.

After everything he'd done for that jerk, couldn't he have just said yes?

Although, if Jaeyoung was being honest with himself…Sangwoo wasn't in the wrong. Infuriating as it was, he rarely ever erred. *Was* there really a reason for two guys to go to the movies together, especially when one of them found being around the other a chore?

Until that point, Jaeyoung had handled the weirdo's rejections with a playful smile—but something had been different about that one. Faced with the unfortunate realization that everything he'd done had been for absolutely nothing, Jaeyoung had completely flown off the handle.

Why exactly was it so hard for him to put on a mask around Sangwoo? Jaeyoung didn't get it—especially considering his acting was so good he could convince most people that he was some kind of saint. But whatever the case, the consequence of letting it slip had been the disintegration of every bit of the relationship he and the weirdo had managed to build—not that there'd been much of one in the first place.

Once he'd gotten back to his apartment, Jaeyoung had contemplated the situation—but he hadn't been able to stop arguing with himself.

Part of him had just wanted to blow the whole thing off and say: *Whatever. If he hates my guts so much, I guess I'll get lost.* But another part just kept shaking its head and insisting they at least end things on good terms.

In the end, the thought that emerged victorious was some Frankenstein combination of both, fueled by his selfish desire to see Sangwoo again.

If this ends, it'll be on my *terms.*

The following day, Jaeyoung had gone to class as usual.

His plan had been to walk up to Sangwoo before Embedded Systems, nonchalantly shove a movie ticket into his hand, and swagger away. That way, he'd be able to salvage some of his pride, though most of the damage had already been done.

But the weirdo had never shown up.

Realizing Sangwoo was planning on skipping class, Jaeyoung had been overwhelmed by a sense of betrayal. He *knew* how obsessed that jerk was with maintaining a pristine attendance record. It wasn't like he'd asked to hold his hand—he'd only wanted to watch a damn movie with him! Unable to contain his injured pride, Jaeyoung had raced over to Sangwoo's apartment and started making a scene.

Once upon a time, he'd wanted the weirdo to see him as a respectable upperclassman, but that ship sailed far, far away the moment he started banging on Sangwoo's door. All he'd been able to do to hide his disappointment and mangled pride was to declare he never wanted to see the dipshit again—just like he had after their first confrontation in the internet café.

After that incident, Jaeyoung had only gone to campus on Wednesdays for his godforsaken Ethics class. And while he was there, he made a concerted effort to stay the hell out of Sangwoo's path.

He'd filled the rest of his time with drinking, playing pool, bowling, clubbing, gaming, and going to the movies with semi-flings—and before he knew it, two Wednesdays had passed. He'd managed to forget all about that weirdo! Although, he *had* looked at the selfie he'd taken of the two of them about fifteen separate times…

But then, out of nowhere, Sangwoo had appeared at Olive Tree during his shift. The weirdo must've been out of his mind to show up here after Jaeyoung had told him he never wanted to see his face again. It was too much—he saw red.

Overcome with frustration and rage, Jaeyoung had ducked into the kitchen and stood with his back against the wall for a few minutes. Eventually, he'd finally cooled off.

Think about this logically, he'd told himself. It was highly likely that Sangwoo didn't mean anything by popping up at his place of work. He didn't keep any data deemed useless in his precise system, after all. There was no way he still remembered that Jaeyoung worked at some Italian restaurant.

Plus, Jihye had been there, too. It was obvious the two of them were on a cute little date. Jaeyoung could see it now: The next time they walked into the restaurant, they'd be holding hands. At some point, they'd wind up sleeping together, and then the wedding invitations would start showing up in the mail. Before long, Jihye would be giggling about their baby.

Jaeyoung had told the owner of the restaurant he needed a break.

Stepping outside, he'd leaned against the side of the building and pulled out a cigarette. One of his friends called him, but none of their words registered. He knew he must sound distracted, but found he didn't really care.

The cigarette tasted particularly bitter.

Then Jaeyoung glanced up, and realization hit him—Sangwoo had followed him out of the restaurant. The weirdo had an incredibly determined look on his face for some reason, like he was about to toss down a glove and challenge Jaeyoung to a duel.

"Hey."

The gears turned slowly in Jaeyoung's head, creaking and groaning. He couldn't remember the last time Sangwoo had actually approached him first.

"Tell them you're busy and hang up. I have something important to say."

The weirdo's stern tone left no room for argument. Feeling like a new recruit to the military, Jaeyoung quickly promised his friend he'd call him back and hung up. He had no idea what Sangwoo had to say—maybe the guy had come to inform him he'd be suing for emotional damage? Honestly, Jaeyoung wouldn't have been surprised.

There was a moment of silence. Then he asked the weirdo, "What is it?"

"I want to talk to you, Jaeyoung."

"What…?"

He had to be hallucinating. How else could he explain Sangwoo Choo addressing him in a civil manner? All the cold rejections Sangwoo had previously tossed in his face flashed through his mind.

"I can when they're an asshole."

"I only have a sister."

"I'll pass. Also, stop acting so chummy with me."

Even now, Sangwoo's voice was impassive as he said, "Let's develop the game together. I need a skilled designer."

Jaeyoung nearly scoffed in disbelief. It was clear the weirdo didn't think his offer would be rejected. Did he seriously expect Jaeyoung to just toss everything aside and throw himself into the project with sudden vigor, shouting something like "Yes! Let's *do* this!"? Although, actually…

Jaeyoung was struck by a sudden realization. Sangwoo literally didn't understand what usually happened in a relationship after two people had an argument, nor did he know how difficult it was for those involved to reconcile.

"I'm confident in my abilities to develop the game. Working with me will also fund your study-abroad experience, not to mention provide you with an excellent addition to your portfolio. I can work with any concepts or designs you've been wanting to try. I promise you won't be disappointed."

When the hell did this asshole become a door-to-door salesman? Jaeyoung blinked in disbelief, then glared at the weirdo, who was standing there with his fists clenched dramatically at his sides for some reason, like a comic book hero ready to face down a supervillain.

"Just…hold up," Jaeyoung said, raising one hand to stop Sangwoo from continuing. He needed to backtrack for a moment. "*What* did you just say?"

"I said I needed a skilled designer."

Jaeyoung shook his head. "No, no, before that."

"What?"

"You called me by my name, and nicely at that."

Sangwoo immediately fell silent and ducked his head slightly. The rim of his black cap covered his face. Then, he said, "It was a slip of the tongue."

They both fell silent.

Jaeyoung's mind was reeling. Why had that weirdo decided to play nice all of a sudden after obsessively refusing to for so long? And that wasn't even the most confusing thing the guy had said—what the hell had driven him to try and recruit Jaeyoung for a project after treating him like radioactive waste?

Abruptly, Sangwoo looked up at him, his eyes gleaming rebelliously. "Is there any reason I *can't* be so familiar with you? Everyone else is."

Forcing himself to remain nonchalant, Jaeyoung dropped his cigarette on the ground and put it out with the heel of his shoe. His palms were positively dripping with sweat, his heart about to pound through his ribcage.

"Yeah, well, you're an exception."

Because I can't have you giving me a full-on heart attack.

"Fine, then."

Yet another awkward silence stretched between them. Sangwoo glared at the wall, pouting.

There's something seriously wrong with me, Jaeyoung thought. How could he, even now, think the weirdo looked adorable?

Forcing himself to look down at the ground, he focused instead on trying to figure out why Sangwoo had sought him out so randomly. But the answer was really pretty simple: Sangwoo needed him.

Sangwoo was programmed to do things with maximum efficiency. Their big, ugly fight was probably only a minor obstacle—one that was basically nonexistent—compared with his need to secure a competent collaborator.

In a way, the guy's inability to hold a grudge was admirable. But Jaeyoung was a *human*, not a robot. So what if Sangwoo was confident in his programming abilities? The one Jaeyoung wasn't confident in was himself—who knew if he'd be able to keep it together, working with that weirdo?

His pride had already been ripped to shreds and flushed down the toilet. Sangwoo could act like he hadn't treated Jaeyoung like shit if he wanted, but it was too late for Jaeyoung. The critical blow had already been dealt.

Furthermore, Jaeyoung had already spent two weeks trying to suppress his feelings and perverted desires for Sangwoo, and he wasn't interested in prolonging his suffering. So he'd take the weirdo's offer and throw it right back in his fa—

"You really think you can finish it before the semester ends?"

He should've turned him down. Really, Jaeyoung *knew* that. But... Sangwoo had never asked him for a favor before.

I basically rolled over as soon as that jerk threw me a bone, Jaeyoung thought, feeling more stupid and spineless than he ever had in his life. He'd essentially wiped the slate clean between the two of them, even after all the disappointment and embarrassment Sangwoo had put him through. *I'm a complete idiot.*

On the other hand, maybe he was on the verge of something great? What else would have driven a robot who went into attack mode anytime Jaeyoung spoke to suddenly try and make a deal with him?

I feel like I deserve the Nobel Peace Prize for this.

"I know you're planning to study abroad," Sangwoo continued. "So I'm asking for four months, including the time we're on break. I promise I can finish it."

"That's nowhere near enough time. You have classes, too, in case you've forgotten."

"I'm not taking many classes this semester. And I'll reduce the amount of hard coding I have to do by relying more on game engines," Sangwoo declared.

It was as if he *knew* everything would work out. Where had this drive, confidence, and determination come from? It left Jaeyoung speechless.

And, much as he hated to admit it, it made Sangwoo's clumsy proposal just convincing enough to work on him.

He liked being a helpful upperclassman. Plus, the game *would* be a useful addition to his portfolio, and Sangwoo *was* a skilled developer. But if Jaeyoung was being honest, the real reason he decided to agree was that, deep down, he wanted to spend more time with the enigma that was Sangwoo.

"Fine… I'll do it," Jaeyoung said, then immediately wished he could take his words back. *Why the hell did I say that?*

Immediately, Sangwoo nodded. Although it was fleeting, Jaeyoung could've sworn he saw the weirdo smile.

"I'll be in touch, Jaeyoung," Sangwoo said, sounding incredibly sure of himself. It was like he'd morphed into some movie protagonist.

Jaeyoung stood rooted to the spot, watching him walk away. Goose bumps ran down his arms.

It was a good thing that it was fairly dark outside—he didn't even

want to think about how Sangwoo would have reacted if they'd been standing in broad daylight. Surely, even a robot like that weirdo would have the ability to recognize what the bulge in Jaeyoung's apron meant.

Did I seriously get hard just because of how he called my name?

The world spun, fractured, then snapped back into place.

...Shit...

Just like when he tried to force his garbage laptop to run graphic design programs, he felt like his system was stuck on a blue screen.

JAEYOUNG JANG - OUT OF ORDER

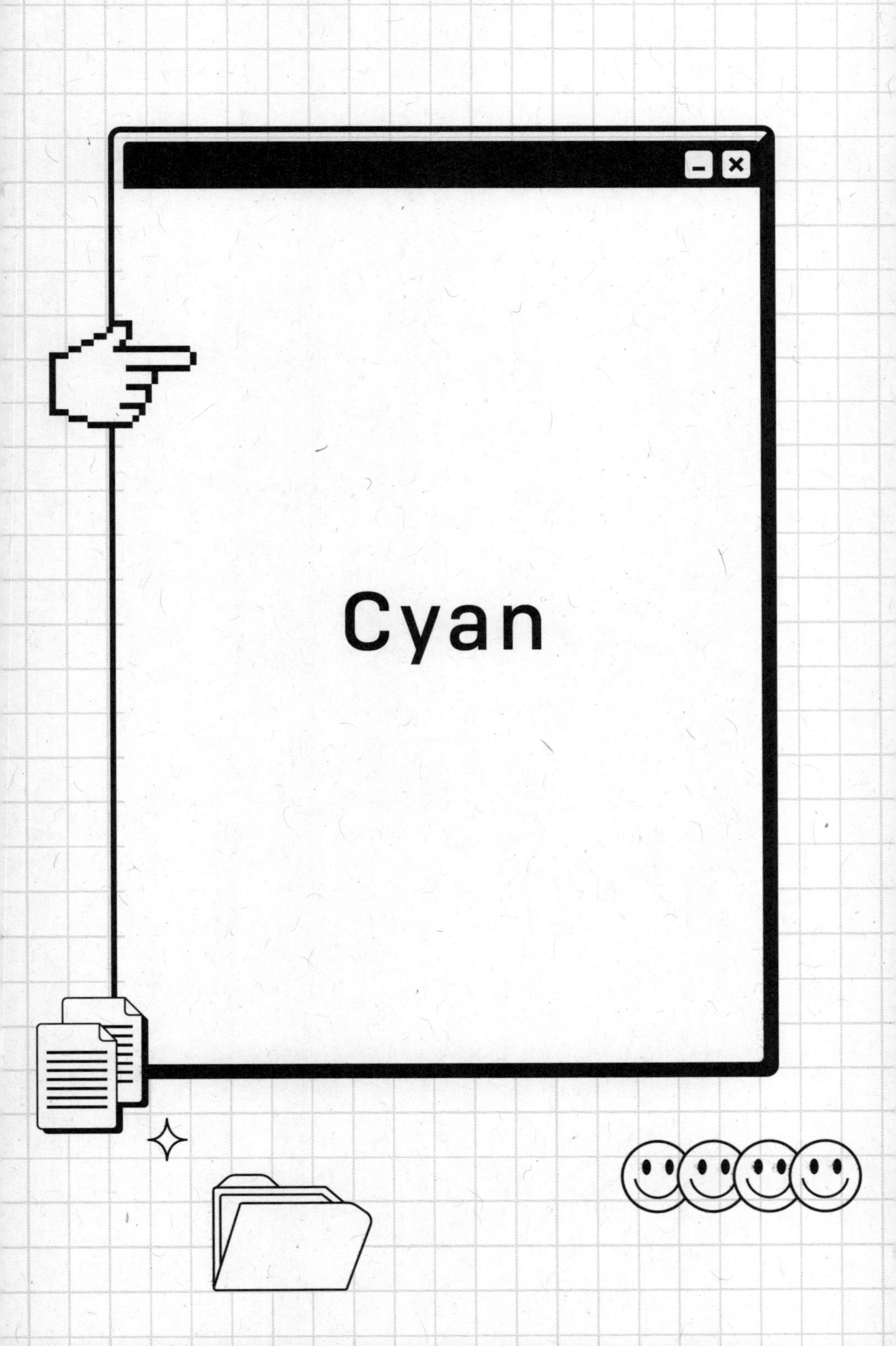

Cyan

When Jaeyoung arrived at the meeting room, he found Sangwoo waiting for him inside, dressed in a loose navy plaid shirt and a pair of dark jeans. Making sure to sit as far away from the weirdo as possible, Jaeyoung stubbornly stared at the rim of his hat instead of making eye contact.

"This is an improvement," Sangwoo observed with a mocking smirk. "You were only late by twelve minutes this time."

Jaeyoung stayed silent, barely managing an uncomfortable smile. The truth was, he'd gotten to campus an entire hour before their scheduled meeting. However, he'd wasted the bulk of that time contemplating whether he should meet up with Sangwoo in his current state, pondering where their relationship was headed, and wondering if it wasn't too late to back out of their agreement.

"I got these for you," Sangwoo continued. "Help yourself."

Jaeyoung scanned the assortment of snacks and drinks the weirdo had placed on the table. *Did his latest software update include a hospitality module or something?* he wondered. But then his brain finally processed what was on offer: fermented rice drinks, sweet potato chips, honey twists, traditional sweets like *yakgwa*… How old did Sangwoo think he was, seventy?

Jaeyoung popped a sweet potato chip into his mouth anyway, figuring it'd be rude to leave the snacks untouched. "Thanks, I guess…," he mumbled as he munched away.

When he discreetly stole a glance at the weirdo, the guy had a cold, indifferent look on his face. Judging by his expression, you would have thought Jaeyoung was some stranger who'd randomly decided to barge into the room. It left him feeling slightly disconcerted—after all, if it wasn't for Sangwoo's coaxing, he wouldn't have agreed to help in the first place!

Back in the alley, the weirdo's eyes had *sparkled* as he'd spoken to Jaeyoung. It'd seemed like, for once, the guy had found his presence tolerable. But the way he was acting now, Jaeyoung found himself seriously contemplating whether it had been a hallucination.

"There are two rules that you must follow when it comes to this partnership," Sangwoo said without any preamble. "One: You must adhere to deadlines and show up to meetings on time."

"Fine."

"Two: You must have complete and utter dedication to the project."

Jaeyoung stayed silent.

"If either of those conditions is too much for you, leave now."

It took a tremendous amount of effort for Jaeyoung to keep his face from crumpling. Of course, the logical part of him knew that Sangwoo had come to find him at the restaurant because the weirdo needed a skilled designer—nothing more, nothing less. But his stupid emotions had gotten in the way. How could they not, when Sangwoo was so much more than just a "skilled developer" to him?

Maybe I really did imagine the spark between us yesterday, Jaeyoung mused as he sat there in silence. But…it had felt so special. In its wake, he'd been left flushed and aroused.

"No complaints," Sangwoo said with a nod, despite the fact that Jaeyoung hadn't said a word. "Noted." He pulled out a printout and handed it over.

Jaeyoung was struck speechless. If he was being honest, he'd scoffed inwardly when Sangwoo had laid out his grand plan to develop an amazing game in merely four months. Sangwoo was a computer science prodigy, sure, but he was also a student, not a professional. Plus, with a timeframe as limited as that, it would be basically impossible for two people to develop a game by themselves, *period.*

But, apparently, Sangwoo had meant every single word of what he'd said. The flowchart laid out before Jaeyoung's eyes broke down everything to the last detail—from the initial planning stage to the post-development QA process.

After a pause, Jaeyoung said, "Y'know, I think the schedule is a bit tight...especially your part."

The planning and design stages were definitely nothing to scoff at, but the development stage was on a whole other level. Despite their short production period, it seemed Sangwoo was aiming to launch their app simultaneously on both iOS and Android.

The list of tasks for the last month was particularly brutal: server integration; network, security, and performance testing; device-specific optimization... Jaeyoung might not know much about game development, but even he could tell those tasks would be incredibly time-consuming.

Sangwoo sounded totally nonchalant as he said, "I'll be fine. Do you have any complaints about the design schedule?"

Jaeyoung frowned. Since the outline hadn't been fully finalized, his workload wasn't as heavy as Sangwoo's—but the early stages were going to be a problem. To keep up, he'd have to complete multiple character, item, and map designs every single day. That might've been possible for a machine, but he was flesh and blood!

"No complaints. Noted," Sangwoo said once again. He straightened in his chair, then crossed his arms and gazed across the table.

Jaeyoung nearly flinched when he met Sangwoo's eyes. In that moment, the guy looked almost frighteningly robotic.

"The revenue split will be eighty-twenty. I get eighty, and you get twenty."

Jaeyoung honestly didn't care how the money would be split. Who knew if they would even manage to finish the project at all? Besides, he'd only agreed to work on the game in the first place because it provided an excuse to see Sangwoo again—he wasn't afraid to admit it.

What Jaeyoung *did* have a problem with, however, was that it seemed like the weirdo was bulldozing his way into taking complete control of the project. Which meant Jaeyoung needed to establish his own position before things went any further.

"Wow, what a rip-off," he said snarkily.

"I believe I'm being quite generous, actually. The planning is already complete, so your only job is to doodle a few lines. You seemed to have plenty of time in your schedule to harass me, so I assume you can devote an equal amount of time to your work."

"Oh, you did *not* just say that."

For all the value Sangwoo had just placed on his work, Jaeyoung might as well've been some scam artist who traced every one of his sketches. The words were a clear provocation—whether the younger man had intended them to be or not—and Jaeyoung had no intention of letting sleeping dogs lie. He crossed his arms, mirroring Sangwoo's posture, and leaned back in his chair.

"Honestly, I don't get why we're talking about the revenue split when we haven't even started the damn project! Who knows? It might be a total flop. Keep it up, and I might just ditch your stupid schedule entirely."

"What would you like me to do, then?" Sangwoo asked calmly, seemingly completely unaffected by Jaeyoung's cranky tone.

"Why are you asking me? Fix the damn schedule! You're the one who made it!"

"How would *you* change it?"

Jaeyoung scoffed. "By scrapping it, obviously. There's no way it's gonna work."

"All right," Sangwoo agreed stoically, giving him a nod. "I suppose it would be difficult to finish revisions today, so I'll give you until our next meeting. Your assistance will make you an active participant in the planning process, so I'll change the revenue split to fifty-fifty."

"What…?"

Realization hit—he'd fallen right into the weirdo's trap. He'd never intended to plan out everything by himself.

Jaeyoung's mouth fell open indignantly, but before he could get a word out, Sangwoo had already shoved a document outlining the game's initial concept in his face. It was the same one he'd seen before.

"You said this sucked the last time I showed it to you. Find a way to make it more entertaining by our next meeting, or I'm keeping it. Revisions are due by midnight the day before the meeting. You can send them to the email address on the paper here."

Jaeyoung reflexively glanced at the schedule and scoffed in disbelief. The "next meeting" was tomorrow, which meant the revisions were due in seven hours.

"You're kidding, right?"

"We're running on a tight schedule. We don't have time to waste on planning," Sangwoo responded coolly as he gathered all the documents and slipped them into his backpack. When he stood up, he didn't even look in Jaeyoung's direction.

Jaeyoung had figured the meeting wouldn't go exactly as he'd envisioned, but Sangwoo acting like some cutthroat businessman hadn't been on his bingo card, either. Where was the special connection he'd felt between them the night before? It seemed to have vanished without a trace.

Without thinking, Jaeyoung asked, "Leaving already?"

"I can't stay with you for long."

"How come?"

"I'd prefer to keep my reasons to myself," the weirdo responded cryptically.

Jaeyoung raised an eyebrow. In his opinion, he was pretty good at picking up on subtle cues, but he couldn't begin to guess why Sangwoo was rushing out of the room like it was on fire. He was struck speechless as the door opened.

You know what? he muttered inwardly. *Maybe this is a good thing. Better to keep business and pleasure separate…*

But he still couldn't stave off a pang of disappointment.

"Oh, I almost forgot," Sangwoo said.

Jaeyoung's head shot up, his gaze colliding with Sangwoo's. The rim of the guy's black hat cast a dark shadow over his unreadable eyes.

"Moving forward, don't touch me without warning. It makes me incredibly uncomfortable."

Could Sangwoo see through him, to the filthy desire coiled in his mind? Jaeyoung didn't think so, but he felt exposed all the same. A blush crept across his face as his pride crumpled beneath the weirdo's blow.

But Sangwoo wasn't done. "And if you could take care not to touch the top of my head, grab my forearm, or whisper directly in my ear," he continued relentlessly.

"Yeah, yeah, whatever."

"I'll see you at our next meeting, then."

"Dude, just say you'll see me tomorrow. It's not like the meeting's in a few days."

"My wording is up to my own discretion."

With that, Sangwoo turned and left, leaving Jaeyoung to try and make sense of what'd just happened. He felt as if a hurricane had swept through the room, leaving him disoriented, confused, and surrounded by snacks and drinks he'd never asked for.

What the hell…?

Mobile game development wasn't one of Jaeyoung's areas of interest, nor had it ever been. He certainly wasn't desperate enough to sacrifice the next few months of his life grinding away on some insane schedule. And yet, he'd agreed to do just that—for one reason and one reason only. The way Sangwoo had said his damn name.

However, when he'd stepped into the meeting room, he'd been greeted by a workaholic maniac, not the cute underclassman he'd been hoping for.

Well, this is lame…

Jaeyoung started gathering up the food in front of him. It took him so long that he was late to meet up with a friend.

⌘W

"You're developing a game in *four* months, *during* school? With just one other person?"

Jaeyoung's friend frowned incredulously as he leaned on the pool table with his arm, lined up his cue, and took a shot. His form was flashy enough that he looked like he was recording a shot for a movie, but he missed spectacularly.

"You don't think it's gonna work?" Jaeyoung asked as he walked around the table.

"I mean…depends on what sort of game you're aiming to make and how high a quality you want it to be. Technically, you could make a simple fixed shooter in a day if you really wanted to."

"The guy I'm working with is supposed to be some kind of coding genius. I think he's hoping for, like, tens of millions of won in profits."

Jaeyoung's friend scoffed. "Yeah, no way in hell! He's scamming you, dude."

"You think so?"

Jaeyoung chuckled as he gripped his cue, bent over the table, and slid the long pole back and forth under his index finger a few times. Unfortunately, his careful adjustments went up in smoke when he got a text notification and his concentration shattered into a million pieces. When another beep followed, he begrudgingly set the cue down to check his phone.

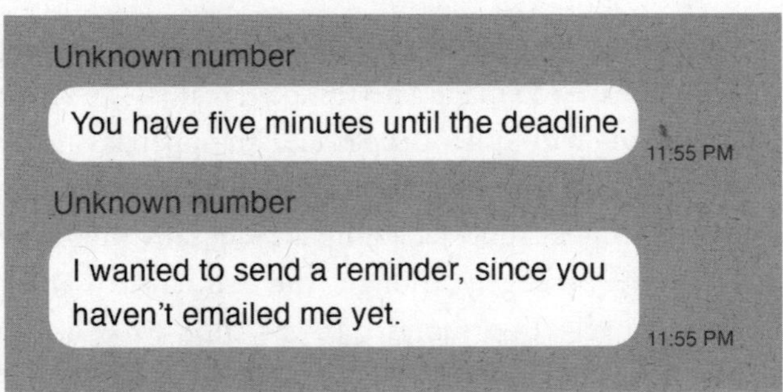

Scowling in annoyance, Jaeyoung shoved his phone back into his pocket. The texts were an unwelcome reminder of the apathetic gaze Sangwoo had turned on him, as if nothing had happened between them. Although, if he asked the weirdo himself, the jerk would probably deny that anything had.

Jaeyoung's grip on his cue tightened until his knuckles were white. Pursing his lips, he reassumed his position and struck the white ball hard, putting a spin on it. It slid across the table and hit the red ball, sending it into one of the corner pockets.

"What kinda magic was that?" his friend exclaimed in surprise.

"Please, that was pure skill."

Jaeyoung stepped aside, and his friend made a big show of bending over the table and carefully aiming the cue with all the grandeur of a professional player. He took another shot.

"You said the guy's the same major as me, right? What's his name?"

"Sangwoo Choo."

"Hmm… Nope, doesn't ring a bell. Guess I'm getting too old to remember young'uns like him…"

"He's only two years below you," Jaeyoung said with a snort. "You probably know of him. He's the freshman who made a scene during the welcome party when we were juniors. Y'know, Mr. 'I *can* drink, but I do not wish to at this particular moment.'"

"Oh, *that* weirdo? Yeah, yeah, I remember him. I bet he's a absolute genius when it comes to code, but when it comes to working in a team…" He trailed off, shrugging.

Tell me about it, Jaeyoung thought, but he stayed silent as he aimed his cue again. He and the weirdo made a perfect pair, really—an underclassman who sucked at working with other people, and an upperclassman who got a boner simply because said underclassman called his name a certain way.

When he took his next shot, Jaeyoung accidentally put way too much force behind the cue. Strangely, though, the ball curved, and it made it into the pocket by a very thin margin. It was almost like…he really *was* performing magic.

His friend gave a low whistle. "You're on a roll, dude."

Jaeyoung's phone went off just as he was about to reply. Frowning, he grabbed it and checked the screen, only to see an incoming call from the same unknown number as before.

Jaeyoung declined it. It was probably just *a certain someone* trying to hound him now that his precious deadline had passed.

The next few minutes passed in relative silence as Jaeyoung and his friend traded turns hunching over the pool table, focusing on lining up their shots. Though his friend wasn't half bad, it looked like Jaeyoung was going to win the game by a landslide.

He was taking a break to stretch his back when his phone rang again with a call from an unknown number. His first assumption was it was Sangwoo calling to nag him, but this time, the number was from a landline.

The gears in Jaeyoung's head spun into furious motion. His grandfather had been known to call him from random hotels in the past, since he didn't have a phone. Plus, there was no way Sangwoo had a landline in that tiny apartment.

In the end, Jaeyoung picked up. "Hello?"

"This is Sangwoo Choo."

Jaeyoung held his breath, unsure of what to say.

"I decided to call because you still haven't emailed me. Is something prohibiting you from meeting the deadline we agreed upon?"

Sangwoo's voice was drier than tree bark.

It was the perfect chance for Jaeyoung to say he didn't want to work on the project anymore. After all, free will *was* a thing. But somehow, knowing that Sangwoo was on the other end of that call…he couldn't do it. He couldn't bring himself to say the words.

"I'm pretty busy, actually," he finally managed to mutter.

"You say that, but…"

"But what?"

"I can hear billiard balls."

There wasn't any judgment in Sangwoo's calm, impassive voice, but Jaeyoung suddenly felt like a kid being scolded by his parents.

"I'll have everything together by tomorrow's meeting."

"Please make an effort to be more punctual next time."

Sangwoo fell silent for a moment, and Jaeyoung heard a baby crying in the background. Apparently, the weirdo was borrowing his neighbor's phone just so he could yell at Jaeyoung.

"I'm hanging up."

"Okay."

Jaeyoung sighed as he slipped his phone back into his pocket. He didn't feel motivated to work on the stupid project in the slightest, but he couldn't back out of it, either. When he glanced at the pool table, he didn't even feel like playing anymore.

"I'll pay for the table," he said to his friend. "I gotta go. See ya."

"Seriously? Come on, dude!"

His friend threw up his hands in annoyance, but Jaeyoung headed back to his apartment without saying another word.

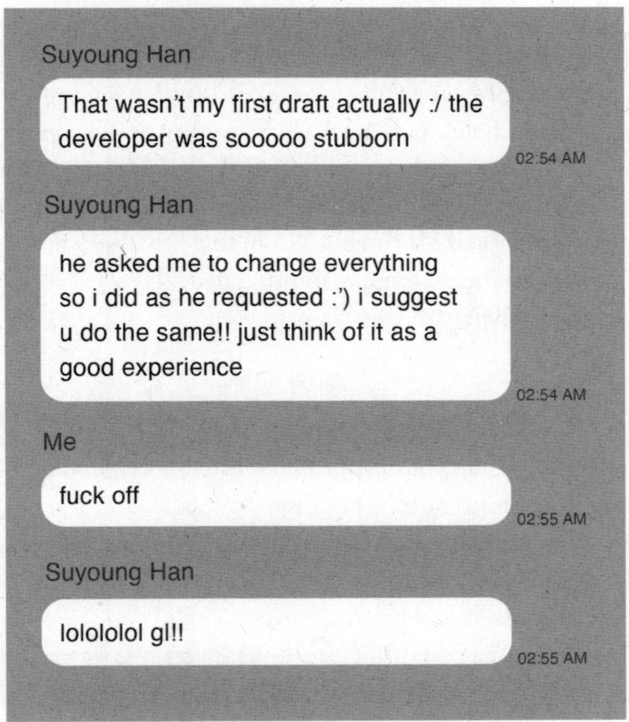

The initial draft for *Veggie Man* was so terrible that it left Jaeyoung totally stumped. He went through draft after draft, then felt a surge of rage when he realized he was 90 percent of the way through an all-nighter. The fact that he was starting to see Sangwoo as a romantic interest was problematic enough on its own, but now he *also* had to put up with being stuck on a project that was basically doomed from the beginning? It was absolutely ridiculous.

At this point, the game's success had become a matter of Jaeyoung's pride—if his name was going to be attached to it, he had to ensure it was *at least* of decent quality. However, coming up with an entirely new game concept wasn't something he could pump out in a couple of hours. And to make matters worse, he was severely lacking in the motivation department. Unsurprisingly, it was kinda hard to summon the urge to put in any effort for a guy who treated you like radioactive waste.

Once again, Jaeyoung found his thoughts had circled back to Sangwoo. He heaved a sigh. How could he have developed such a massive crush on a machine? Not to mention one merciless enough to try and bully him into coming up with a bunch of quality designs in a single day.

I wish I could never see that stupid weirdo again…but I also miss him.

He was stuck between a rock and a hard place. Jaeyoung's pen spun faster and faster between his fingers. No matter what he wanted to do, he couldn't show up to the meeting empty-handed.

He uncapped the pen and got back to work.

⌘W

"Given how much pride you seem to take in your originality, I had high expectations. But I must admit, I'm disappointed."

Even though Jaeyoung had braced himself for this very outcome, he was barely able to hold back a scowl at Sangwoo's words. Crossing his arms, he forced himself to remain calm.

"The name and basic outline are unchanged," Sangwoo continued. "The only thing that's different is the character design… And do you actually believe these align with our game concept?"

Sangwoo placed the three pieces of paper with the character designs on the desk, but Jaeyoung's attention was drawn to the fingers that had held them instead. Objectively, they were pretty damn far from pretty or delicate—the knuckles were pronounced, like many men's were. But for some reason, Jaeyoung still found himself overcome with an inexplicable desire to place each digit in his mouth and curl his tongue around them one by one. His eyes followed the weirdo's hand as it pulled the rim of his hat down slightly, then tucked itself beneath the meeting room table alongside the other.

"As I've told you already, this game is for children," Sangwoo said, abruptly breaking Jaeyoung out of his trance. "That means our customer base will be young parents. I highly doubt they'll let their children play a game like *this*."

Jaeyoung glared across the table at Sangwoo, but his gaze was partially blocked by the weirdo's hat. "Care to explain why not?"

Sangwoo's lips, previously in a straight line, twisted unhappily. A single digit emerged from beneath the desk to point at the first of the three characters.

Once again, Jaeyoung found his gaze drawn to that finger. The nail at the end of it was a little too short, suggesting it had been trimmed recently. Still, there was enough left of the pale crescent at the end to keep him spellbound.

"One: This eggplant looks like a thug suffering from kidney disease. I wasn't aware that we were developing a horror game."

Sangwoo pushed the paper aside and pointed at the second character.

"Two: It's impossible to tell if this is supposed to be lettuce or celery. I expect something better for an educational game."

With the first two characters having been ruthlessly rejected, Jaeyoung readied himself for another round of verbal beatdown.

"Three: It doesn't make sense for a potato to walk around on its sprouts. It looks scary, too. Can't you come up with a better mode of transportation for this character?"

Jaeyoung could only manage a scoff of disbelief. If he was being honest, seeing the absurd plan Sangwoo had come up with had made him completely lose faith in the weirdo, but now it seemed like he actually *did* have some standards. He couldn't exactly brush off the guy's criticism when he'd made a couple of valid points.

Jaeyoung took a long look at the character designs, starting to see them in a new light. The eggplant *was* admittedly a bit monstrous, mainly due to his personal art preferences. And it was true that he'd struggled to find a way to give the potato legs, botching his original design by giving up and making the sprouts longer. Even he had to admit that it looked pretty odd. As for the lettuce, well...he'd needed something to fill the page.

Still, none of that meant Jaeyoung was gonna lie down and let Sangwoo smack him around.

"What the hell did you expect?!" he erupted, banging a fist on the meeting room table. "You only gave me one day to work on this shit!"

To be clear, despite this outburst, Jaeyoung hadn't even dedicated a full hour to creating his designs—in fact, they'd taken him all of...seven minutes? Still, confidence was everything, and forcing a designer to complete work with such a short turnaround was a sign of inexperience in the field.

And yet, when Sangwoo responded, he didn't seem to be feeling an ounce of shame.

"I wouldn't have such high expectations if I was working with someone else. But I'm working with *you*."

Jaeyoung's mouth dropped open. If the weirdo had criticized him further, he could've easily summoned a retort. But when he said things like that…

All the fight drained from Jaeyoung's limbs, and his chest tightened painfully. Sure, he could *try* to tell Sangwoo that he'd barely put in effort with those designs, but there was no way the jerk would actually believe him.

"We'll go with the original draft," Sangwoo announced.

"No," Jaeyoung countered immediately.

"Do you have a backup plan in mind?"

Subjected to the icy coldness of Sangwoo's gaze, Jaeyoung found himself grateful to the weirdo's stupid black hat for once. At least it had the decency to shield him from half of the jerk's intense stare.

"I'll redo the entire thing," he said.

"We don't have the time."

"I'll get it done by our next meeting! When is it, anyway…? Monday?"

Jaeyoung scowled. Now that he was taking a closer look at the schedule, it seemed Sangwoo had scheduled them to have one of these stupid meetings every single day except for Saturday and Sunday, when the weirdo was supposed to be at work. It was almost obsessive.

Given how much Sangwoo had gone on about how busy they were going to be, Jaeyoung had thought most of their communication would be over email. But it seemed like the weirdo had so little trust in him that he'd made arrangements to monitor him nearly twenty-four seven.

Jaeyoung glanced at Sangwoo's lips, which were pressed together in a thin line. Maybe, if he actually produced something that met the guy's lofty standards, he could get a compliment for once.

"I'll be in touch, Jaeyoung."

The voice sounded much warmer in Jaeyoung's mind than it had in reality, he was sure. Even though that was the only time Sangwoo had treated him like a human being over the course of their entire relationship, it had been enough to completely throw Jaeyoung out of order. He shook his head violently, trying to stop the memory from taking over his mind.

"In that case, I'll give you the whole weekend to work on it," Sangwoo said in a generous tone, although he was only giving Jaeyoung a couple more days. "Please email me the finished product by midnight on Sunda—"

"Nope. And don't call me and nag about it, either."

"Why?"

"That's not how I work, okay? Sometimes I spend the whole day being unproductive, but I still get things done a few hours before the deadline."

Sangwoo's eyes narrowed. He didn't look very happy. "Basically, you're a ticking time bomb."

"A *proper* leader can manage people well regardless of how they work. Plus, trust me—I've never missed an important deadline."

"Do you consider this project to be important?"

"Hmm… Kinda, I guess. Depends on how important you make it for me."

"Very ambiguous."

Sangwoo's face remained totally impassive as he began to pack up his things, signaling yet another early end to their meeting. The weirdo didn't even spare Jaeyoung another glance—simply carefully zipped up his backpack, slung it across his shoulder, and walked over to the door. But after he'd pushed it halfway open, he turned his head to face Jaeyoung.

"I'll see you at the next meeting."

"Leaving already?"

"Yes."

"Aaand lemme guess. You still won't tell me why you're leaving so early."

"Correct."

The weirdo stepped through the door, and it clicked shut behind him.

For a long moment, Jaeyoung just stared at the space where Sangwoo had been sitting. It was no surprise they weren't getting along—they were polar opposites. They were bound to clash, no matter the topic of conversation, which meant the rift between them would only grow wider over time. And if Jaeyoung ever tried to get chummy, Sangwoo would push him away by snapping at him like some kind of overbearing, micromanaging boss instead of responding in kind.

And yet, despite knowing all of this, Jaeyoung had walked right into Sangwoo's trap, baited by the possibility that he'd be able to pursue his personal interests. Now, the logical part of his brain was screaming at him, reminding him he didn't have to endure Sangwoo's verbal abuse and that he would benefit much more in the long run if he just quit the project.

But unfortunately, Jaeyoung wasn't willing to take such a large blow to his pride.

Just you wait and see.

He imagined Sangwoo gaping at the sight of his new character design, his eyes sparkling as he clasped his hands together in delight. "Oh my gosh, you're the absolute freaking best, Jaeyoung!" he gushed in a completely uncharacteristic manner.

Jaeyoung scoffed bitterly, scooping up his rejected designs before carelessly folding them in half. He'd finally found the motivation needed to work on the project.

⌘W

Despite his initial determination, Jaeyoung found himself struggling to come up with designs that would satisfy his robot of an employer. Though he sat at his desk, materials at the ready, any bit of concentration he managed to gather was scattered to the wind whenever he thought of Sangwoo's infuriatingly impassive face. No matter what he came up with, he could practically hear the weirdo's voice echoing in the back of his mind: "How disappointing. I was wrong to have so much faith in your abilities. Let's go with the original designs."

The words unsurprisingly came easily to his imaginary Sangwoo's lips—after all, in his world, art basically amounted to doodling a few lines.

Jaeyoung came up with a few character designs on Friday, then tossed them in the garbage and went out to drink with his friends. They flocked to a K-BBQ place near campus for some soju and pork belly, then sat down at a bar in Yeonseok-dong for cocktails. After dancing at a club for a couple hours and chugging a few cans of beer, there was no way his fingers could even hold a pen.

Half of Saturday was spent nursing his hangover. A steaming bowl of hangover soup brought him back to life later in the evening, after which he watched two movies back-to-back.

Finally, on Sunday—after sleeping in until early afternoon—Jaeyoung sat back down at his desk. Fortunately, inspiration came to him right away, and his first quick doodle ended up looking pretty decent. The character was gender-neutral, with frizzy red hair tied up in a ponytail and a laser gun in each hand. The genre, he decided, would be survival with action/adventure elements and a weapon system based on character evolution. The setting could be in a steampunk dystopia.

After sketching a scene of the character attached to a parachute, floating downward as a building exploded in the background, Jaeyoung turned his focus to creating two separate sketches of their evolutions. The first involved the character growing a set of wings, while the second showed them evolving into a jaguar form.

When he was finished, Jaeyoung was certain that nobody in their right mind would compare his work to Suyoung's sad little carrot man—not even Sangwoo. He grabbed a sticky note, scribbled down a few lines about the game's concept and storyline, and stuck it on the design.

Now he was more than ready for tomorrow's meeting.

Totally satisfied, Jaeyoung went out for dinner. One of his friends from high school had just opened a webfoot octopus restaurant, and he'd invited Jaeyoung to come and check it out.

After dinner, Jaeyoung headed to a small auditorium to watch an indie artist perform live.

All in all, it was a good day.

⌘W

"It could work…*if* we were developing this game for PC users."

Damn it! Jaeyoung groaned inwardly. The second rejection stung even more than the first.

Sangwoo rummaged in his folder a bit before producing a thick packet of paper. "Here is an analysis of the top hundred games that are currently on the Android and iOS app stores," he began mechanically. "Sixty-eight percent are simple arcade, action, or puzzle games. While RPGs make up about eleven percent of the list, all of them were developed by large companies. This strongly suggests that your plan cannot be implemented as a mobile game by two people in four months."

"*You're* the one who said you'd work with whatever idea I wanted to try out," Jaeyoung grumbled back.

"Yes, within reason."

Sangwoo pushed Jaeyoung's character designs aside, his face as flat and emotionless as ever. The cold, swift rejection left Jaeyoung dumbfounded, and he sat there silently for a long moment.

"I understand why you made the mistake, since you've never played mobile games before," Sangwoo continued. "But now I'd like you to focus on the original draft instead of wasting any more of our time."

The words snapped Jaeyoung out of his daze. "No."

"What is it now?"

Although Sangwoo's voice remained monotonous, Jaeyoung could detect a hint of irritation in his words. But instead of responding right away, he took a moment to contemplate. Why, exactly, was he cowering like he'd screwed everything up when Sangwoo was being a jerk and trying to enforce an insane schedule? He was acting like some rookie designer—which he absolutely wasn't.

Springing to his feet, Jaeyoung slammed both his hands on the meeting room table. "I promise your precious time won't be wasted," he declared as Sangwoo slowly looked up at him. "Give me one more day."

It wasn't actually a request—Jaeyoung fully planned on giving himself another day whether Sangwoo allowed it or not. However, what happened next completely upset his expectations.

The younger man glanced away slightly and sighed. "Fine."

Huh…? Did he actually say that? Jaeyoung stared at Sangwoo intently, fighting the urge to demand, "Who are you and what have you done with Sangwoo Choo?"

Clearing his throat, Sangwoo began to gather the documents on the table into a neat stack. Yet again, Jaeyoung found himself studying Sangwoo's side profile, angular fingers, and bony wrists. Then Jaeyoung snapped back to his senses and quickly walked over to the door. But right as he took a step out of the meeting room, he heard Sangwoo's low voice behind him.

"You're a hard person to work with."

"Yeah, well, you're certainly one to talk," Jaeyoung grumbled back. He didn't even ask when their next meeting would be before he resumed walking. "See you tomorrow."

"I will."

It was a little past five o'clock. Jaeyoung's original plan had been to grab dinner with a friend and then go clubbing, but instead, he headed straight to the on-campus art studio.

The underclassman who'd been assigned the desk next to his blinked in surprise when Jaeyoung appeared, which was understandable—seeing him in the studio had become as rare as a bigfoot sighting. Though he'd requested a spot, he hadn't had any reason to use it lately since he didn't have any projects to work on.

Jaeyoung turned on the PC on his desk—which appeared to have sat there, untouched for the entire time he'd been absent—slid into his seat, and cracked his knuckles.

"What are you doing here, Jaeyoung?" his neighbor asked reverently.

"Got something to do. Where's Yuna?"

"Um…not sure. She was here just a few minutes ago…"

As he waited for the PC to boot up, Jaeyoung went on his phone and looked at which games had the top rankings on the app store. The list was full of intriguing action games; there was no way a children's game would survive in that kind of market. But, more importantly, the stupid *Veggie Man* game concept didn't mesh with him as a designer.

When the home screen of the PC finally popped up, Jaeyoung pulled up an empty document and typed: "Design Proposal." He didn't usually see the point in adhering to dull formalities, but since Sangwoo was so obsessed with them, he figured he'd play along for once.

Section 1 - Market Research and Popular Game Analysis
Section 2 - Genre Change Proposal

Section 3 – Title Change Proposal
Section 4 - Concept and Storyline
Section 5 - Characters, Weapons, Monster Designs, and Setting

Jaeyoung's fingers flew across the keyboard as his eyes darted between his phone and the computer screen, analyzing the existing data while simultaneously crafting a new proposal. As for his crumpled pride, it was shoved into a distant corner, where it shouted futile protests.

He finished the market analysis in no time, then decided their game would be a side-scrolling shooter. After a brief moment of contemplation, he added a few lines of text describing it as a "retro game with platform-jumping action," and left the title blank. It felt like his head was a boiling pot overflowing with ideas, the fire underneath fueled by his anger.

Imaginary brushstrokes painted a picture in his mind: a sprawling farm, contaminated with cosmic materials after being struck by a meteorite. Only the mutated vegetables, enhanced by the meteorite's mysterious power, were capable of subduing the animals that had been transformed into grotesque monsters. The plot revolved around a scientist who was obsessed with winning a Nobel Prize in biology—he would try to approach the center of the farm for "research purposes."

Jaeyoung grabbed the first piece of paper within reach and quickly sketched an image of the mad scientist swinging a carrot like a sword. As always, the hardest part was getting started—once that design was complete, more flooded out of him one after another. The radish became a club, the corn turned into a rifle, the seeds became bullets, the pumpkin turned into dynamite, the potatoes became grenades, and the lettuce became booby traps.

His pen moved fervently, like his life depended on it. The intensity of his focus was so extreme, he didn't even realize his phone was ringing until Seongjin—the underclassman with the desk next to him—tapped on his shoulder.

Without even looking, Jaeyoung said, "It's probably Yuna. Just tell her I can't make it."

"Got it! Hello? It's me, Seongjin. Yeah, Jaeyoung said he can't make it… Not sure. I think he's working on something super important… No, I have no idea what it is. Uh, I don't think he's *totally* lost it yet… Here, she wants to talk to you."

"Tell her I'm not going."

"Yuna, Jaeyoung said he's definitely not going. No clue. I'm just the messenger, you know… I swear I have no idea what he's doing. I'm hanging up, okay? Yeah…" Seongjin quickly ended the call and handed the phone back to Jaeyoung. "She said she's gonna murder you."

Ignoring his comment, Jaeyoung snatched the phone back and checked the app store to see if there were any other games that followed a concept similar to his. He smirked proudly after a moment—of course, no one had. He was the only one who could possibly come up with such a unique idea.

Giving himself an invisible pat on the back, Jaeyoung went back to the character designs. Curious, Seongjin snuck closer, glancing at the paper.

"Whoa, that looks so good!" he exclaimed in wonder. "What's this for?"

"My study-abroad funds," Jaeyoung responded, then chuckled under his breath.

How was it that he'd gotten so immersed in this stupid project that he'd flaked on a friend at the last minute? It was unbelievable. He had to give it to Sangwoo—the jerk had actually convinced him to get his lazy ass off the couch.

This time, he would *definitely* extract a compliment from Sangwoo's lips instead of a biting remark. He was sure of it.

Gritting his teeth, Jaeyoung gripped his pen tighter.

⌘W

When the time for their next meeting arrived, Jaeyoung showed up fully prepared. He had three different drafts in his arsenal: the first one, which he'd poured his heart and soul into, and two filler drafts he'd brought just in case. The perfectly written proposal he'd brought two copies of, their corners stapled neatly. He'd even paid special attention to his outfit, not that Sangwoo would ever notice.

"Hmm..." Sangwoo rumbled as he flipped through the proposal.

Jaeyoung fidgeted nervously, wishing he knew what was going through the weirdo's computer of a brain. His face was as emotionless as usual, but Jaeyoung could detect the slightest of smiles on his lips...or at least, he *thought* he could.

Forcing himself to appear nonchalant, Jaeyoung made a show of leaning back in his chair. Assuming an air of arrogance, he looked down his nose at Sangwoo.

When at last the weirdo spoke, it was to ask, "Are you fluent in English?"

The question was probably about the title Jaeyoung had suggested: *Veggie Venturer*. Even though he doubted he'd see the project through to the end, the name "*Veggie Man*" was simply too tragic. *Veggie Venturer* was easier to shorten, too—they could go with *VeVen* or *VV*.

"I'm decent," Jaeyoung responded.

"How surprising. You have many talents."

"That's rich coming from you. I know you're bilingual, too."

Sangwoo contemplated this for a moment. "That's correct. I can speak Korean and Chinese."

"I was talking about Korean and code, actually. You're fluent in both, right?"

For a moment, Sangwoo stared blankly at Jaeyoung, his face filled with incomprehension. A beat later, he narrowed his eyes. "Please try to sound less uneducated in the future. Do you have any idea how many programming languages exist? You essentially just insinuated I was fluent in six languages."

The weirdo stiffly turned his gaze back to the proposal. His fingers flipped the page once, then twice, but he didn't make any comments suggesting anything needed to be changed. Jaeyoung's hawklike gaze even caught a tiny nod.

Strangely enough, Jaeyoung found himself feeling even more anxious than he'd been while waiting for the results of a competition he'd dedicated six months of his life to.

Then, just a moment later, Sangwoo's face began to shift. The change was minuscule, and Jaeyoung would've missed it if he hadn't been looking for it—the faintest hint of a smile tugged at Sangwoo's emotionless lips, and his icy eyes curved into two crescent moons. In all honesty, the sight almost took Jaeyoung's breath away.

"This character looks like you," Sangwoo said.

"How?" he barely managed to respond.

"It just does."

Jaeyoung quickly reviewed the three character designs he'd come up with in his head: a mad scientist, a weird-looking skeleton, and cartoonish people with heads as big as their bodies. None of them made a flattering comparison.

But Sangwoo seemed oblivious to Jaeyoung's inner turmoil. He silently placed the proposal on the desk, then looked at him across the table. When their gazes met, Jaeyoung witnessed something special he'd never seen before. Sangwoo's eyes had widened slightly and were abuzz with excitement.

"Good job."

The words were simple and brief, but they provided the affirmation Jaeyoung had been longing so desperately for. His chest swelled with pride. To think—he'd gotten a compliment out of the most meticulous, robotic developer in the world.

Alas, the hint of emotion slipped away from Sangwoo's face just as quickly as it had appeared. He regarded Jaeyoung calmly as he announced, "We'll go with the third character design."

"Huh?"

The moment shattered. Jaeyoung snatched up the proposal and flipped through the pages, searching for the first character, the one he had spent the most time and effort on—the mad scientist with frizzy silver hair, spiral glasses, and abnormally large hands and feet. He had made sure to show the man's bulging muscles through the rips in his lab coat. Just the coloring process alone had taken over an hour.

He flipped through two more pages and landed on the third character design, which was a clumsily drawn pair of characters—one male, one female—that he'd come up with in five minutes as filler. The male character was modeled after Sangwoo, with pale skin, sharp eyes, thin limbs, and loose clothes. The only thing missing was his hat.

"That's supposed to be you, correct?" Sangwoo asked, pointing right at the female character.

A scowl formed on Jaeyoung's face as he tried to determine if the weirdo was trying to screw with him or not. He *had* to be insulting him, right? The character had short orange hair and large eyes that took up nearly half of her face—she looked absolutely nothing like him.

Quickly shaking off his shock, Jaeyoung said, "Personally, I really like the first design."

"I prefer the third one."

Jaeyoung shook his head sternly. It may be hard to tell from his personal life, but he happened to be pretty damn good at advocating for himself as a designer. It was a skill he'd acquired after having to cater to too many clients who preferred designs that were "simple yet decorative" or "monotone yet colorful." And so, for the next two minutes, he passionately explained why the first character design was a perfect fit for their overall concept.

Sangwoo nodded at the end of his speech. "Thank you for sharing your thoughts. We'll go with the third character design."

"The mad scientist gives the adventure a sense of purpose! What do this young man and woman have to do with the plot? Huh?"

"You have a valid point. However, I'm going with the third character design."

Jaeyoung threw his hands up in frustration. "*But why?*"

"It's a conclusion I've come to after considering every possible factor available to me," Sangwoo replied, sounding uncharacteristically vague.

There was only one conclusion Jaeyoung could come to: something about those stupid characters with enormous heads had captivated the weirdo.

"Come on, let's just do the first one…"

"No."

It was obvious that Sangwoo wasn't going to yield in the slightest.

"Fine! Whatever," Jaeyoung said with a sigh.

There was no point in arguing about it, anyway—now that he'd achieved his goal, he could abandon the project with his pride intact.

Sangwoo carefully slipped the proposal into his folder and looked at

Jaeyoung. "When you digitize the characters, please separate them into parts. Keep in mind that you'll need to add animation later. You can keep the original files, but please send them to me in PNG format with the correct dimensions. I'll email you the guidelines later, along with the specifications and size charts. Please make sure to adhere to them. As for the file names..."

Jaeyoung stared blankly at Sangwoo with his chin propped up on one hand, watching the weirdo's lips move. Everything else seemed to fade away, and Sangwoo's words turned to gibberish in his ears—he might as well have been listening to birdsong or the barking of a neighborhood dog. It was only when Sangwoo finally stopped talking that his senses snapped back into place.

"Are you all right?" Sangwoo asked flatly.

"No."

"Perhaps you're feeling tired after putting so much work into the proposal. Keep it up. Again, make sure to read the materials I email you and adhere to them."

"Right..."

"Keep it up"...? The words sounded foreign coming from Sangwoo's mouth. It was like some motivational speaker had temporarily taken over the weirdo's vocal cords. But strangely enough, a part of Jaeyoung felt... satisfied. Maybe he'd been wrong to think that Sangwoo was a robot-brained jerk who hadn't been socialized properly when he was a kid—maybe he only complimented people when he really meant it.

"Also, come over here," Sangwoo added abruptly.

Jaeyoung glanced up in surprise. "Huh? Why?"

"I'm going to praise you by patting you on the head. Consider yourself forewarned."

The weirdo rose to his feet and reached out hesitantly. Jaeyoung couldn't do anything but watch, frozen, as his fingers came closer.

Sangwoo's hand hovered near Jaeyoung's forehead for a moment, then lifted up and came back down on top of his head in a distinctly mechanical movement once, twice, three times before quickly withdrawing.

Reflexively, Jaeyoung squeezed his eyes shut. He couldn't remember the last time someone had patted him on the head. It had to have been when he was a child. Face burning, head spinning, he pressed one hand to his lips.

The door to the meeting room clicked shut.

Jaeyoung's eyes shot open, but a quick glance around the room revealed Sangwoo had left. A heavy exhale escaped his lungs, followed by another.

"What the hell was that...?"

⌘W

Jaeyoung staggered out of the meeting room, dazed. He suddenly understood why all those sailors in Greek myths had swum toward the sirens singing to them on the rocks. His name spoken oh so sweetly had yanked him into the ring by the lapels, but it was the headpats that'd hit him like a blow to the face. He felt tingly, like his entire body wanted to sneeze.

When Jaeyoung walked out of the library, he stared up at the sky, feeling a sudden urge to spread his arms and spin. The sky was an unbelievably vivid shade of cyan. His body was throbbing with exhaustion, but his heart was pounding and a smile was tugging at his lips. The blue screen that his mind had been stuck on, torturing him, suddenly turned into the turquoise hue of the clear sky.

At that moment, he knew he could never quit the project.

Even as Jaeyoung smiled to himself like an idiot, the gears in his head were starting to turn rapidly. Something was off about what'd just happened. Sure, it was possible the robot had finally learned how to give compliments—but the way he'd gone about it was so uncharacteristic for him that it was almost bizarre.

As soon as Jaeyoung accounted for how Sangwoo Choo functioned as a program, though, the situation became comprehensible. When he'd patted the weirdo on the head in the past, the action must have gotten mapped to his internal controller. Then he'd hit the button and returned the behavior as praise, likely assuming Jaeyoung liked headpats himself.

Despite the logical explanation, Jaeyoung found he was slightly uneasy about the whole thing. A mixture of feelings swirled in his gut—a nagging knowledge that he'd missed something important, a persistent anxiety over the precariousness of the peace he was enjoying now, and an uncontrollable excitement.

He blindly walked into the on-campus studio, only to find Yuna and Seongjin had already taken up residence. The moment Yuna saw him, she started ranting about how he'd "totally stood her up" the previous night. Jaeyoung nodded absently, letting the words drift in one ear and out the other.

"...and it got *so* crazy after midnight. I even got her to sign my back after the performance!" Yuna raved.

"Good to hear you had fun."

"Yeah, you missed out! What the hell were you doing, anyway?"

"A high-priority task," he said, borrowing Sangwoo's way of speaking. "That's what I'm gonna do right now, actually. Stop talking to me."

As Yuna stared at him like he had just sprouted a second head, he realized Seongjin was packing up his PC.

"And what are you doing?"

"I enlisted."

"Huh?"

Seongjin morosely informed them he was taking a gap year to enlist because his crush had rejected him and he'd lost all will to live. The underclassman's story finally stopped Yuna from growling at Jaeyoung long enough to offer him a solemn word of comfort. Jaeyoung also promised to treat him to dinner.

Seongjin was so touched he began tearfully spill his heart out to the two older students, but Jaeyoung's attention span rapidly ran out. He only managed to listen for about five minutes before he turned around and booted up his PC.

Strangely, he couldn't shake the sense Sangwoo was rubbing off on him. He felt as if he was starting to morph into a workaholic, which was beyond strange to think about. Part of him felt like he'd walked right into the weirdo's trap, but even if he had, it wasn't like he could just ditch the project now.

Jaeyoung scanned his character designs, uploaded them onto the PC, and began to digitize them with his design software.

⌘W

"All right, I'm heading home!" Yuna announced, then glanced at Jaeyoung. "Hellooo? Are you gonna keep working?"

"What time is it?"

"Almost midnight."

Jaeyoung blinked blearily and glanced at his watch. Yuna was right. Sighing, he tried to recall what he'd done for the past few hours. It'd been around seven when he got back to the studio after treating Seongjin to dinner, and then…he'd been working nonstop ever since.

He stretched, a wave of exhaustion suddenly washing over him. Yuna peeked over his shoulder curiously.

"What are you so obsessed with? Something profitable, maybe? Hmm?"

How am I supposed to explain this?

After a brief moment of contemplation, Jaeyoung said simply, "It's a mobile game."

"Well, it sure looks like you're having fun with it."

He nodded silently. It wasn't like he could say "Thanks! I'm working extra hard so I can get headpats from the developer!"

Leaning back in his chair, Jaeyoung decided he'd grab a cup of coffee and head home. But before he could act on it, he got a text.

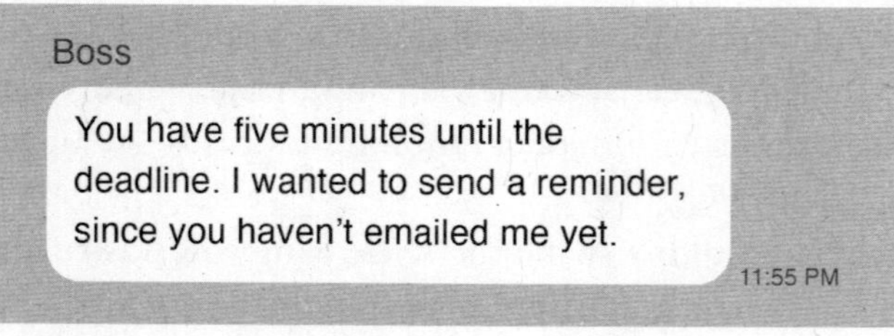

It was the exact same businesslike text that the weirdo had sent him last time, but Jaeyoung was so blinded by his attraction to Sangwoo that receiving it made him feel giddy. Not to mention, he had more than enough stuff to send the guy, since he'd worked through the night. He immediately opened up his email and began to attach the image files… then paused as an idea popped into his mind.

Smirking, Jaeyoung leaned back in his chair and waited instead of shooting off the email. Three minutes passed as he stared at his phone, bouncing his leg.

The phone rang precisely at midnight. He waited six seconds before picking up, taking the time to clear his throat and make his voice as gravelly as possible.

"Hey, Sangwoo."

"H-hello…?"

"Why'd you call?"

"Oh… I didn't get an email from you, and it's past the deadline, so… I wanted to remind you."

"My bad. Totally slipped my mind. Thanks for calling, okay? I'll send them over right away."

Silence ensued from Sangwoo's end.

"Did you have dinner?"

"Yes."

"What'd you have?"

"I went to the dining hall. Why?"

"Nice! What were they serving today?"

"Rice, soybean paste soup with greens, kimchi, stir-fried sausage and vegetables, stir-fried anchovies, and a yogurt drink. But what does that matter to you?"

"Just wanted to hear your voice."

Another looong beat of silence ensued from Sangwoo's end.

"I like listening to people speak, you see."

"What a bizarre hobby. Goodbye."

Sangwoo hung up without giving him the chance to respond.

Jaeyoung tilted his head thoughtfully—it seemed the results of his test had come back negative. If Sangwoo had feelings for him, he wouldn't have given such a cold response and hung up on him, right?

Maybe I was mistaken. Honestly, that would be for the best.

Behind him, Yuna muttered, "Oh my God. What the hell was that?"

"What?"

"Please don't *ever* talk like that around me again."

"Wasn't talking to you anyway."

Sangwoo's feelings might be unclear, but Jaeyoung had a much better understanding of his own now. These feelings he was experiencing were the early signs of love—which meant it was time for him to bask in all the butterflies he wanted, free of the weighty responsibilities that came with a deeper romance.

This was Jaeyoung's favorite stage in a relationship—as long as he maintained his boundaries, things wouldn't get complicated, messy, or even risky. He was confident he could handle it. He'd never once lost himself to his emotions.

But then…why was he polishing the forbidden fruit that was Sangwoo if he wasn't going to take a bite?

Jaeyoung smiled bitterly as he looked at his folder full of character designs. That weirdo had definitely played some kind of trick on him. There was no other way to explain why he was scurrying around at the guy's beck and call.

Jaeyoung opened his email again and attached the work he'd toiled so hard to scrape together.

Sent. Mission complete.

⌘W

When Jaeyoung met with Sangwoo the next day, the weirdo was—as always—as stiff as a rusted robot.

"I looked over the files you sent," he pronounced. "Overall, they're fine, but I want to go over a few things."

Without sparing the other man a glance, Sangwoo opened his laptop and pulled up the files Jaeyoung had sent him the night before, then zoomed in on one of the images and pointed at the corner.

"As you can see, there is some pixelation here. Please fix it."

"How the hell is anybody gonna notice that on their phone?"

"Even minutiae are important. Please be more careful moving forward."

Next, Sangwoo pulled up two of the weapon designs.

"These should have the same color code. Please fix it."

Jaeyoung had to give it to the guy—he really did have a good eye for detail. Although the "errors" were pretty insignificant, Sangwoo technically wasn't wrong.

After pointing out a few more things that needed fixing, Sangwoo sorted the folder by file name.

"I specified in the guideline to rename the files before you send them over. They should all go: category, underscore, subcategory, underscore, with two-digit numbers at the end."

Jaeyoung pursed his lips silently.

"You are missing an underscore here, and all of the numbers are single digits. Please add a zero in front moving forward. Also, don't mix uppercase and lowercase letters. Only use lowercase. I thought you'd worked on web projects before. Was I mistaken? I fixed your mistakes this time, but please be more mindful in the future."

The thing was, Jaeyoung *had* been mindful. How the hell was everything supposed to be perfect when he'd created dozens of files in one night while working under an insanely tight deadline? Given that he usually named files something like final_final11_frfrfinal_1_final.ai, a mistake or two was to be expected.

"I bet you even *bleed* code," Jaeyoung snarked.

Sangwoo ignored him and packed up his laptop.

Although Jaeyoung didn't wanna admit it, a part of him was waiting for the weirdo to say something like "Good job" again. However, there was only a cold silence.

After all that work, this is what I get? he thought bitterly. Clearly, he was fooling himself, believing that Sangwoo was actually interested in him.

Sangwoo finished packing up his things, then quietly stood up from his chair.

Without thinking, Jaeyoung called out, "Hey!"

"What?"

There was a beat of silence. "How…are your classes going?"

It was the type of question a distant uncle would pose at a family gathering, but Jaeyoung couldn't think of anything else to ask.

With a slightly bewildered—maybe even irritated—look on his face, Sangwoo replied, "They're going well. I have already studied the material for tomorrow's classes."

"Well, aren't you an overachiever?"

"I have been feeling good lately. It's much easier to focus in class these days."

"Yeah, yeah, it's probably because I'm not bothering you in class anymore. You're welcome."

Jaeyoung knew exactly what would happen next. Sangwoo would scowl at him like he was some kind of sewer rat and say, "Are you done?" However, the weirdo simply glanced up, avoided his eyes, and fixed his glare on a random corner of the ceiling.

"Not exactly," he finally said.

"What do you mean?"

"I'd prefer to keep my reasons—"

"To yourself. Right. What, is that your new catchphrase or something?"

This was Sangwoo's cue to commence his escape from the meeting room. He began to walk toward the door.

Unconsciously, Jaeyoung reached out to grab his arm. But, remembering that the weirdo treated physical contact like the plague, he changed course just in time to grab Sangwoo's backpack strap instead.

"Hey, do I look like I've lost weight?"

"No. Let go of me."

Jaeyoung had bought himself about a second with his rambling—he had approximately three more left before Sangwoo was gone entirely. The gears in his head spun frantically into motion. In the back of his mind, a nearly flawless idea began to form.

"You know I have to make a ton of edits now, right?" he pointed out. "Some of the stuff you want me to do seem kinda confusing, so it'd be nice if you could, y'know, help me look over things."

"You're really having trouble comprehending those simple directions?"

"Hey, better safe than sorry, right? Plus, I bet you've never been inside the art building. Come on, I'll show you around my studio. You said you're done studying, so what's the problem?"

"Your…studio?"

Jaeyoung had no earthly idea what the weirdo was thinking. His robotic voice, paired with the damn hat that was covering his eyes, made even guessing impossible.

He gave Sangwoo's backpack strap a light tug. "Come on, it's not like you have anything better to do."

"I do, in fact, have many better things to do," the weirdo said stonily, crossing his arms. "But I would like to inspect your working environment. I doubt it's ideal. It'd be best for both of us if we maximized your productivity, since you have so much to do."

"Yes, exactly!"

Jaeyoung had been draped over the meeting room desk like a hunk of seaweed, but Sangwoo's words sent him springing to his feet. The weirdo's eyes widened at the sight.

"What, *right now*?"

"Yeah, obviously."

"I'm not…ready yet."

"What is there to be ready for? It'll only take a moment. It's not a big deal. Follow me."

Jaeyoung marched forward, Sangwoo's backpack strap in hand. The weirdo obediently let himself be hauled along, not saying a single word.

It was the beginning of April, with clear skies up above and a pleasant breeze blowing down below. In terms of weather, it was probably Jaeyoung's favorite time of year. He whistled cheerfully as he strolled along, making sure to give brief tugs on the strap if he began to lag behind. Before long, they'd reached the College of Arts and Design.

Jaeyoung only released Sangwoo's backpack once they reached the door to the studio. "This workspace is limited to four people each. You have to put in a request every semester to be able to use it."

"Does that mean there might be other people here as well?"

"There'll be two at most, but one of them recently started his military service. The other one does her own thing, so don't worry."

"Is she my upperclassman?"

"She's the same year as you, but she's my age. You can say hi if you want."

Sangwoo's face tensed, as if the information made him nervous. Normally, he would've addressed her politely since she was older than him, but the fact that she was a junior, too, meant that the level of social nicety he owed her wasn't as clear-cut. Jaeyoung could tell the situation was throwing Sangwoo for a loop.

Jaeyoung gave the door to the studio a push, revealing a space with four large desks. "Go right ahead," he told Sangwoo.

The weirdo shuffled awkwardly into the studio.

Jaeyoung suddenly found himself feeling strangely embarrassed. The colorful posters covering the studio walls looked messy to his eyes, and the floor was conspicuously littered with empty boxes, crumpled bits of paper, empty bags of chips, a broken speaker, a hair straightener, a leg massager, and a single slipper. The sound of Yuna's heavy metal music filled the space, sounding several times louder than it actually was.

Watching his studiomate's bleach-blond hair whip back and forth as she engaged in some enthusiastically violent headbanging, Jaeyoung started to wonder if he'd been too optimistic in thinking she and the weirdo would get along.

"Hey, Yuna!" he called out. "Look over here."

"Why?" she demanded, not even glancing his way.

Jaeyoung looked over at Sangwoo, who looked like he'd seen a ghost strolling around in broad daylight. Jaeyoung shook his head. He must have been out of his mind, thinking these two could be friends. Maybe if Yuna hadn't been wearing a bright-red leather jacket and a black choker that day, there would have been a chance, but…

"Whatever. Ignore her. You can sit over there," he said, pointing Sangwoo at Seongjin's empty seat.

The weirdo stiffly walked over, then hung his backpack on the back of the chair. This was the moment Yuna finally decided to turn around and gasp dramatically.

"Who's that?!"

"An underclassman who's working on a project with me. Go back to whatever you were doing."

"Whoa, you mean that game? What's his name? Is he a visual arts guy, too?"

"Sangwoo Choo. Computer science. I know he looks mad, but ignore it. That's his happy face."

"Sangwoo Choo? Sangchoo Choo?! That's a hilarious name!" Yuna burst out laughing, clapping her hands like a seal.

A part of Jaeyoung thought Sangwoo might simply get up and leave, but he remained in his seat, looking on like an incredibly disapproving statue.

Grabbing one of the assortment of individually wrapped crackers lying around Seongjin's desk, Jaeyoung handed one to the weirdo. "Go ahead and make yourself comfortable," he ordered.

"How could I possibly do that in such an unsettling environment?"

"Good point."

Jaeyoung reached out to boot up the PC on his desk, but Sangwoo swiftly raised a hand and stopped him.

"Clean up the garbage first."

The desk was strewn with things like crumbs, soda cans, empty cigarette cases, and crumpled toilet paper. Jaeyoung obediently gathered up the trash and threw everything in the garbage can. The stuff on the floor was carelessly shoved into a corner.

As soon as he sat down, he received his next order.

"Get rid of the socks."

Jaeyoung grabbed the socks he had put behind the monitor and stuffed them in his backpack.

"Ventilate the room."

He trudged over to the windows and opened them.

"Organize your books."

With a sigh, he neatly stacked the few books he had lying around.

"Now, turn on the PC."

Jaeyoung silently followed the weirdo's order and leaned back in his chair, staring at the ceiling.

"Clean up your desktop before you start working."

"Seriously? This is my private workspace, you know..."

"It bothers me. Just do it."

The continuous orders were starting to become slightly annoying, but Jaeyoung went ahead and deleted the files he didn't need, rearranging the rest into their correct folders.

"You should really try to be tidier," Sangwoo remarked.

"Hey, you're the one who's invading my territory here," Jaeyoung responded playfully, but there was still a sharp edge to his voice. "Lay off."

"That is incredibly ironic, coming from you."

"Ha! I didn't realize you knew how to crack jokes."

A smile played on Jaeyoung's lips. His first instinct was to put Sangwoo in a headlock or ruffle his hair, but he knew both those things were strictly forbidden.

For a while, Sangwoo sat silently in place, arms crossed and eyes glaring disapprovingly at the ceiling. Then he spun his chair around and looked directly at Yuna. "Excuse me. This is a shared space. Your music is too loud."

Looking slightly baffled, she glanced between Sangwoo and Jaeyoung.

"I see that you have a nice set of headphones there. Use them."

Yuna wasn't exactly the meek or submissive type, but it seemed the weirdo had struck her completely speechless. As she sat there with her mouth agape, Jaeyoung went over and forced the headphones onto her head. When he turned them on, the music completely disappeared, much to Sangwoo's visible relief.

"Now, pull up your software."

It was time for Jaeyoung to shine. He quickly sat back down, flexed his fingers, then placed his left hand on the keyboard and his right on the mouse.

"Get started," the weirdo ordered curtly, then turned his attention to the open book he'd placed on the now clean desk.

A part of Jaeyoung had expected Sangwoo to act like a micromanaging boss, but once the weirdo was done examining his working environment, he left him alone for the most part. He was so silent, in fact, that Jaeyoung almost forgot he was there.

Other than Yuna's occasional humming, the sounds of his keyboard and mouse clicking were now the only things Jaeyoung could hear. The studio was practically distraction-free. His heart sped up just a bit, and a thin layer of sweat spread over his palms. It was a pleasant feeling.

Diligently, he turned his attention to creating one of the level maps for the game. Time flew by—maybe several hours. When he glanced to the side, he saw that Sangwoo was no longer looking at his computer science textbook. Instead, the younger man had his elbows propped up on the desk, his eyes fixated on Jaeyoung's computer screen.

Immediately, Jaeyoung's gaze was drawn to Sangwoo's long, straight neck. The black long-sleeve tee he was wearing was slightly stretched out around his nape, revealing a mole that stood out strikingly against his pale skin.

If he could just rip that T-shirt off and sink his teeth into that pale shoulder…

Nope. Stop.

Jaeyoung hurriedly scrubbed the mental image of himself leaving red marks all over Sangwoo's snowy skin from his mind, forcing his eyes back to his computer screen. *Phew, that was a close one,* he thought. If he'd decided to make his fantasies a reality, he would've definitely shown up on the news tomorrow—and not for a good reason.

[BREAKING] College Student Takes Upperclassman to Court for Biting His Shoulder

"Yes, it hurt a lot. I've gotten tested for rabies, and I'm waiting for the results. No, I'm not planning on withdrawing the lawsuit. I can only hope he gets the maximum sentence for his crime…"

Jaeyoung's cursor paused for a long moment on the screen as he imagined the weirdo giving an interview in his typical robotic tone. Noticing his distraction, Sangwoo gave him a questioning look.

"Can I help you?" Jaeyoung demanded abruptly, feeling a sudden need to defend himself.

"I was thinking that I picked a fantastic designer."

Jaeyoung blinked.

"Your lifestyle leaves much to be desired," the weirdo continued nonchalantly, "but your skills are undeniable."

It was nothing Jaeyoung hadn't heard before, but Sangwoo had a way of leaving him completely dumbfounded. Somehow, the words sounded infinitely more special when they came from his mouth.

Jaeyoung's hands darted across the keyboard, his fingers dancing even faster on the keys. It was yet another day on the grind—the only difference was that his desk was clean, the studio was much quieter, there was a fresh breeze, and someone was studying right next to him.

So why did he feel as refreshed as if he'd gone on a picnic?

That first day, Sangwoo studied for exactly one hour, then left. He rushed out of the studio so fast that Jaeyoung hadn't even had the chance to call out his name.

But everything changed on the second day.

After eating dinner, Sangwoo showed up, laptop in hand, and proceeded to neatly organize the resources Jaeyoung had prepared and incorporate them into his code. Jaeyoung, meanwhile, had unhurriedly continued working on completing the game's various level maps. With the designs for the characters, weapons, and effects completed, he'd figured he could relax slightly.

But every time he slacked off even a bit, Sangwoo was there, cracking the metaphorical whip. It seemed like the weirdo had decided that if Jaeyoung wasn't going to put his own nose to the grindstone, Sangwoo would do it for him.

"You have to match my pace if we're going to collaborate."

"That kind of mindset is completely inappropriate. You should know better—I thought you were basically a professional."

"Stop bouncing your leg."

"Sit up straight."

"Was that a yawn? With the pitiful amount of work you've gotten done, the word 'tired' shouldn't even be in your vocabulary."

"You had plenty of time to think over whether or not you should take on this project. If you want to jump ship now, too bad—that chance sailed long ago."

For all intents and purposes, Sangwoo seemed to hate everything about Jaeyoung aside from his skills as a designer. But after enduring three days of constant nagging and criticism, Jaeyoung found he'd reached a point of transcendence where nothing the weirdo said fazed him anymore.

"Of course, Mr. Choo. Whateeever you want."

"You got it, Your Majesty! I forgot for a sec that I'm but a lowly peasant."

"What are you, a damn loan shark? If you're not, then there's still time to change your profession."

"Hold up, I gotta find the phone number for the Department of Labor. I need to report you."

"Dude, if you keep pushing me like this…I might be compelled to smash this PC."

"Give me a break already…"

Really, it was inevitable that the two of them would clash often—despite the staggering workload required to follow the absurd schedule Sangwoo had created, the younger man was still determined to follow it. And despite Jaeyoung's insistent promises that he would finish everything when he got a burst of energy, Sangwoo didn't believe him.

Yuna usually ended up getting so annoyed with their bickering that she willingly put on her headphones the moment they started going at it.

As for Jaeyoung, though he grumbled and complained, he didn't regret bringing Sangwoo to the studio the tiniest bit.

He was having the time of his life.

"I need a fifteen-minute break, Mr. Choo!" Jaeyoung exclaimed, pushing his mouse aside and stretching.

It was currently Monday. Over the past weekend, he'd had not one but two sets of plans: First, he'd agreed to play some basketball with a few of his friends, and after that, he'd promised to hit up some places for drinks with another group of his buddies. In actuality, however, he'd ditched drinks altogether with the excuse that he was "busy"—prompting a barrage of angry texts—and left the basketball game after-party early. The latter had unfortunately earned him the nickname "Cinderella."

So, why exactly had he made all these sacrifices? Truthfully, he'd just wanted to go to the studio and finish up the five level maps he'd been working on for the game, making every single correction Sangwoo requested. And so he had—in fact, they'd turned out pretty damn good.

Despite that, the idea of Jaeyoung taking fifteen minutes off seemed to displease the weirdo. He glared at Jaeyoung before finally saying, "Fine."

Of course, Jaeyoung knew that the moment his time was up, Sangwoo would come order him to get back to work. Not wasting even a second, he got up and walked over to the cot in the corner of the studio, brushed Yuna's clothes to the floor, and plopped himself down.

Sangwoo, meanwhile, remained seated. His back was ramrod straight as he typed into his code editor. At this point, Jaeyoung was accustomed to seeing him in the studio late in the evening.

"You should probably take a break, too," he called out.

"I have a lot of work to do."

"Yeah, yeah, I know. But you still need a break."

"I can't while I still have tasks to complete."

At this, Jaeyoung shrugged. "Maybe I'll just keep distracting you, then. Make it so you have no other choice."

"In England in the 1850s, when trees began to darken because of pollution, light-colored peppered moths decreased while dark-colored peppered moths thrived."

"Um...how is that relevant to this discussion, exactly?"

"I'm illustrating that living creatures instinctively adapt to external threats."

"Oh, I see. So I'm pollution, and you're the poor moth? Have fun changing your wing colors, then. I'll be rooting for you!"

"If you wish to help, it'd be best if you simply refrained from speaking."

As always, Sangwoo was acting like some vending machine that gave you facts at the push of a button. Aware that there was no way to win the argument, Jaeyoung turned his attention to his phone instead.

After replying to a few texts, he began to play a music video from his favorite band. Back when Yuna and Seongjin were the only other occupants of the studio, he'd blasted music as he liked when he was working. But now, he couldn't remember the last time he'd played a song so the whole room could hear—just that it had been before Sangwoo unofficially joined the studio.

Yuna had protested the new "rule" at first, but now she put on her headphones with a big sigh whenever Sangwoo arrived. She had no other choice, since he'd read her the riot act a couple of times already. Today, though, she'd headed out early enough to avoid having to endure the unjust weight upon her ears.

Even as Jaeyoung closed his eyes and enjoyed the music, he was waiting for Sangwoo's rebuke. The band's synthesizer gave the song a dreamy feel, as did the low, deep hum of the bass and the singer's languidly smooth vocals. The drumbeats stirred up Jaeyoung's spirit, while the electric guitar pulled at something deep in his heart.

He cracked one eye open. Sangwoo was still typing away, back straight as a board.

"So you like this song, huh?" Jaeyoung said slyly.

"Not particularly."

"This band is called Psyche—"

"Yes, Psychedel. I know them."

"The title is 'Mag—'"

"'Magnetic Field.' It's the eighth track on their fifth album, *Electricity*. Now, be quiet."

His response shocked Jaeyoung so much that he dropped his phone. Psychedel, his favorite artist, wasn't exactly well-known in South Korea. The fact that Sangwoo knew the name of the album *and* the track number meant the weirdo had to be an avid listener despite his denial.

As Jaeyoung struggled to come up with something to say, the playlist automatically advanced to the next song. It was a South Korean indie band that people rarely recognized.

"Trumpeter's second album, *Bullshit*, track number twelve. 'Gonna Overthrow the Boss and Take Over the Company.'"

For an entire minute, Jaeyoung stared at Sangwoo's black hat. *Do we have the same taste in music?* What were the odds, really? Suddenly feeling elated, Jaeyoung played the next song.

"Jochiwon Band's first album, *Red and Black*. Track number seven, 'The Red Giant.'"

"Holy shit!" Jaeyoung exclaimed. "This is crazy. Our musical preferences are basically identical!"

"No, it's not," Sangwoo responded petulantly. "Please refrain from making such claims in the future."

But Jaeyoung wasn't going to let himself be fooled this time. If Sangwoo knew the exact track number of each of the songs, that meant he'd probably listened to the albums countless times.

Still riding the high of this realization, Jaeyoung flipped through the rest of his playlist— Sangwoo recognized every single one of the songs, regardless of the genre and whether the artists were international or South Korean. That song-recognition phone app—Shazoo, was it...?—was nothing in comparison.

Jaeyoung went to hit the next button again, but his finger slipped. Instead of one of his songs, a popular K-pop track started blasting from his phone. This time, there was radio silence from Sangwoo, even though he'd identified the other songs within ten seconds.

"Don't know this one, huh?" he asked curiously.

"How am I supposed to know what it is?"

The thing was, most people would have no trouble identifying this particular song since it was everywhere these days. *Kinda weird...* Jaeyoung gave his head a confused scratch.

"Look at this. The tip of the reinforced grenade is missing the outline. Please fix it. Once you're done, take a look at the corn as well. Also, it's been fifteen minutes. Back to work."

That little...

Jaeyoung stubbornly stayed reclined on the cot for about five seconds, then trudged back to his chair. Sangwoo glanced at him, then immediately turned back to his laptop.

How can someone be so adorable but also not at the same time?

He reached out toward the weirdo, fully intending on delivering a hard pinch to his cheek, then remembered that physical contact was forbidden—but Sangwoo was already glaring at him with his brow furrowed. Thinking fast, Jaeyoung performed a complex maneuver with his hand and ended it with a loud clap.

"Would you look at that? A mosquito!"

"There are no mosquitoes around. It's April."

"Well, I saw one right there."

"Let me see your palm, then."

Jaeyoung made a show of checking his hands. "Oops, looks like it escaped!"

Frowning even more, Sangwoo began to type on his laptop again. The screen was filled with all sorts of gibberish that Jaeyoung wasn't interested in even trying to understand, which made Sangwoo look like some omnipotent deity as he worked.

For the longest time, Jaeyoung stared at Sangwoo with his chin propped on his hands. Then, without thinking, he asked, "Why are you developing this game, anyway?"

Belatedly, he realized the question had probably come to his mind a few weeks too late. He had no idea why Sangwoo was so obsessed with developing *Veggie Venturer*. The guy didn't understand anything about making game content, creating graphics, or crafting sounds—his only talent lay in programming. Not to mention, it seemed off-brand for him to do anything that required collaboration with an outsider, like a designer or project manager, when he was the furthest thing from being a team player.

"Because I enjoy games."

The response caught Jaeyoung off guard. In his head, Sangwoo had always been a weirdo who had no hobbies or things he particularly enjoyed.

"There's a game development company that I'm interested in working for. I played one of their games for the first time when I was fifteen years old. It was so entertaining that I stayed up all night, something I'd never done before in my life. It was a turning point for me. I've been studying English and game development ever since because I want to develop a game of my own just like it." Sangwoo glanced at Jaeyoung. "I know. You didn't ask," he said, and turned his eyes back to the screen.

Chuckling under his breath, Jaeyoung shook his head. "No, no. That was actually kinda cool to hear. Well, what was the game?"

"*Starkraft 1.*"

Jaeyoung made a mental note to never play *Starkraft* against Sangwoo if they ever went to an internet café together.

"What was your dream before you decided to become a game developer?"

"An excavator operator."

Jaeyoung was struck speechless for a moment, but then his mind began turning, reviewing the new facts he'd learned. Apparently, Sangwoo *wasn't* a machine programmed to do nothing but schoolwork—he knew how to enjoy music, and he even had a dream. Remembering how the weirdo's eyes had blazed with passion, Jaeyoung was shell-shocked once more.

"I'm planning on joining the company in the latter half of next year," Sangwoo added. "The success of *Veggie Venturer* will help me get there."

"Y'know, you said this project would help me with *my* portfolio, but it sounds like you're mostly worried about yours."

"It's a mutually beneficial arrangement."

Veggie Venturer was still a work in progress, with only two people grinding away on an insane schedule to get it done. It was crazy for Sangwoo to act like the game taking off was a foregone conclusion—Jaeyoung knew that. But listening to the weirdo lay out the path he had planned to achieve his dream job, he somehow sounded more cool and confident than foolish.

It wouldn't be easy for Sangwoo to actually achieve his goals, of course. But…Jaeyoung found himself feeling like they could definitely do it in the end. A wave of pride and affection surged through him, followed by a desire to do a certain forbidden activity.

"Hey."

"Yes?"

"Exactly one minute from now, can I pat you on the head?"

Sangwoo stayed silent for a long moment, but he didn't shoot Jaeyoung down outright, which was definitely a new development.

The clock ticked away without a response.

"You don't have to say yes if it bothers you too much," Jaeyoung added.

Sangwoo scratched his neck awkwardly. "No…it doesn't bother me terribly. You just have to warn me in advance."

It was an incredibly generous response compared to where they'd started. Jaeyoung fought the urge to reach out toward the weirdo's black hat, asking instead, "You need a moment to prepare yourself?"

"Yes, I do. I don't like it when something unexpected happens."

"Well, what would you do if your grandma called you in the middle of class and said she was at your apartment because she missed you so much?"

"I don't check my phone when I'm in class, and both my grandmothers are deceased."

"Oh… My bad. Let me think of a different example, then." Jaeyoung thought for a moment. "What would you do if you were making instant ramen, but the package didn't come with a soup packet?"

"I would never end up in that situation in the first place. I always make sure I have all the ingredients in a recipe before I start cooking."

"Now that I think of it, you *are* pretty good at making instant ramen…"

"How could anybody be bad at making instant ramen? It only requires two functional hands and enough intelligence to comprehend the instructions."

"You'd think that, wouldn't you? But tons of people manage to screw it— Oh, it's time."

Without hesitation, Jaeyoung reached out and gave Sangwoo several pats on the head. Satisfaction washed over him now that he'd achieved his goal, and it tasted extra sweet knowing he'd taken the correct path to get there. Part of him wanted to sling his arm across the weirdo's shoulder, too, but he didn't want to push his luck.

"I'll do my best to help you reach your goal," Jaeyoung whispered, his voice much more hoarse than he'd intended. It seemed his emotions were getting to him a little bit. "I'm a lot more invested now."

Sangwoo blinked at him. Then, exactly two seconds later, he shook off Jaeyoung's hand. With a sudden, curt, "That's enough," he closed his laptop and began to pack up his things.

For the past three minutes, Jaeyoung had only been allowed to see the weirdo's side profile. Resigning himself to the fact that he wouldn't get to see Sangwoo from any other angle, he glanced at the clock. It was only nine thirty.

He stayed for thirty more minutes yesterday…

After packing his backpack, Sangwoo sprang to his feet and walked over to the door without acknowledging Jaeyoung. It was like he wasn't even in the room. But then the weirdo paused for a moment, staring straight at the door.

"I'm off. I'll see you at the next meeting."

Why can't he just say "I'll see you tomorrow" like a normal person?

"Sure. See you," Jaeyoung muttered at the back of his head.

A moment later, the door loudly clicked shut.

Running a hand down his face, Jaeyoung turned his eyes to the ceiling. Thoughts swirled through his mind—maybe he should have held back, especially knowing how much Sangwoo despised physical contact. But there'd been something strange about Sangwoo's reaction. It hadn't exactly signaled discomfort or irritation…

"I need a smoke."

Something was off about the whole situation, but Jaeyoung couldn't figure out what. Unease filled his mind like a thick fog. He would need to observe Sangwoo's behavior *very* closely.

⌘W

A collection of incidents from the Sangwoo Choo Observation Journal:

(1)

April 9th, Tuesday – Five days since Sangwoo entered the studio

Checked into the studio: 6:31 PM

Checked out of the studio: 10:00 PM

*Excerpt of key scene: "Yuna vs. Sangwoo"

"Yo, Sangchoo Choo!"

"Please refer to me by my actual name."

"You always complain about my music, but you don't say anything when Jaeyoung listens to his. Why is that, huh?"

Yuna launched a powerful attack, but Sangwoo retaliated swiftly!

"On average, Jaeyoung only plays music for about nine minutes, and that is during his break. I choose not to say anything because quality rest is valuable. On the other hand, you keep your music on twenty-four seven. I recommend that you go home in silence, at the very least. I pity your headphones."

Yuna had no comeback!

Sangwoo: Destroyed opponent with defensive maneuvers

Yuna: KO

*Notable observations of subject: Spoke in Jaeyoung's defense, used his name when referring to him

*Conclusion: No abnormalities

(2)

April 10th, Wednesday – Six days since Sangwoo entered the studio

Checked into the studio: 6:31 PM

Checked out of the studio: 10:00 PM

*Excerpt of key scene: "Sangwoo's Angriest Moments"

"You need to relax, all right?" Jaeyoung said with a sigh. "If you keep beating me to the ground with work, I might be tempted to toss my PC out the window."

"You should seek treatment for your anger management issues."

If there was one thing that Sangwoo absolutely *sucked* at, it was identifying a joke.

"Tell me your top three angriest moments," Jaeyoung said, knowing his break was coming to an end, but *also* knowing full well that Sangwoo always answered his questions.

Just as he'd thought, the weirdo glanced up at the ceiling thoughtfully. "Hmm…" After a moment, he answered, "First place: When you asked me to watch a movie with you."

"Huh? *That's* the angriest you've ever been? Seriously?"

Has this jerk's life just been exceptionally chill, or did I really shock him that *bad?*

"Yes. As for second place… It was when I was in the bathroom during the first lecture for Embedded Systems, washing off the mustache you drew on my face."

Sounds like I've been given the honor of first and *second place.* But knowing he only had himself to blame, Jaeyoung stayed silent.

"My third angriest moment was in sixth grade, during the pi memorization contest."

"Why? 'Cause you didn't get first place?"

"What? Of course I got first place."

"Why were you mad, then?"

"I hated myself for only being able to memorize six hundred and twenty-two digits. I put in more effort and memorized one thousand and twenty-four digits later on, but I stopped after that since it felt like a waste of time."

"You're really something else, aren't you…?"

*Notable observations of subject: Confirmed—once again—that Jaeyoung had made a terrible impression on subject

*Conclusion: No abnormalities

(3)

April 11th, Thursday – Seven days since Sangwoo entered the studio

Checked into the studio: 6:31 PM

Checked out of the studio: 8:25 PM

*Excerpt of key scene: "Platinum and Diamond"

The designs for the characters, items, and effects were already done, as were the level maps and the UI. There were still countless things left to work on, but Jaeyoung was itching to take a break now that he'd reached a major checkpoint.

"Let's go and do some market research." he declared, not wanting Sangwoo to think he'd take a no for an answer.

"Please elaborate."

"I think we should experience what it's like to play successful, established games from other companies firsthand. Then we can analyze their strengths and weaknesses and discuss them. Not only can we gain artistic inspiration and reflect on how they became so successful, we can also strengthen our bond as a team and blow off some steam."

Sangwoo didn't respond for a long time—it was like Jaeyoung had spoken to him in a foreign language. Finally, he said, "In other words, you want to play a game?"

He was catching on faster and faster.

"Just for two hours. I swear I'll finish everything I have piled up tomorrow."

"Will you actually?"

"Of course! C'mon, don't be so skeptical."

Somehow, Jaeyoung's persistence paid off, and he managed to convince Sangwoo that "market research" really was necessary. Of course, he had ulterior motives. His skills were far above average in most games, so he was used to carrying whoever he played with. It meant practically all his friends wanted to be on his team, which might have inflated his ego a little bit. Maybe more than a little.

Jaeyoung's grand plan was to show off and gain the weirdo's respect through his gaming skills, since his attempt to do that with skateboarding had already failed.

Ultimately, the two of them decided to go to the same internet café where Sangwoo worked. The owner greeted them warmly and gave them free drinks—apparently, it was the first time Sangwoo had ever visited the place as a customer.

"What do you wanna play?" Jaeyoung cheerfully asked.

"You can choose. I'm adept at most multiplayer games."

"Let's see, what's popular nowadays... *Wargrounds*? *Underwatch*? *League of Champions*? What are you most confident in?"

"I'm decent at *Wargrounds* and *Underwatch*. I'm not very good at *LoC*, though. It's been some time since I played."

"Let's start with that, then."

Jaeyoung had meant it as a joke, but Sangwoo seemed take his suggestion seriously. He agreed and opened the game.

Jaeyoung picked an assassin who utilized flashy, effective combo attacks and dealt significant damage. The character Sangwoo picked was an ugly utility tanker.

As they waited for the game to start, Sangwoo went on the game's wiki and carefully looked over the skills and item builds of the newly released characters. Jaeyoung, who had been filling the time by scrolling through some comic on his phone, gaped in shock the moment his game began to load.

What the hell?! He's got a diamond border! I thought he wasn't very good at League!

Basically, the weirdo was an elite player who'd ranked in the top 1 or 2 percent in the previous season. Jaeyoung's own rank—which he loved to brag to his friends about—was platinum, which was two rungs lower.

Jaeyoung started to feel slightly nervous. And unfortunately, the weirdo immediately proved he'd been right to be. Jaeyoung based his gaming strategy around following his instincts and leaning into the strengths of his chosen character, but Sangwoo was another beast entirely. He carefully paved his way to victory by calculating the enemy's movements and taking advantage of their cooldown times.

"Can't you calculate skill damage?"

"Are you not taking your opponent's cooldown time into account?"

"You knew I was about to gank. You should have engaged the enemy and pinned them to the spot."

"What's up with your CS? We're already nearing the midpoint of the game."

"If you're not fully confident you can get a kill, just try to stay back."

The weirdo spent the entirety of the next two hours calmly tearing Jaeyoung to shreds. Strangely enough, the older man's best plays started to look like rash decisions, and his instinctive choices looked more like clumsy mistakes.

Jaeyoung had initially asked Sangwoo to go to the internet café for a breath of fresh air, but their dynamic ended up being exactly the same as when they were working in the studio.

He made a mental note—*In the future, don't challenge Sangwoo to a game of* Wargrounds, Underwatch, *or* Starkraft. *What the hell am I supposed to play with him, then?* Marzio Kart*?*

*Notable observations of subject: Is a gaming prodigy

*Conclusion: No abnormalities

* * *

(4)

April 12th, Friday – Eight days since Sangwoo entered the studio

Checked into the studio: 6:31 PM

Checked out of the studio: 10:02 PM

*Excerpt of key scene: "X's and O's"

At around nine thirty at night, Jaeyoung was completely exhausted after finishing the stats tab, inventory, and skills pages. He collapsed on the cot, muttering that he needed a fifteen-minute break, but ended up dozing off.

"I'm going home," The sound of Sangwoo's voice immediately woke Jaeyoung up, but the drowsy older man didn't move a muscle. He felt so languid that even managing a word of goodbye was too much effort.

A moment later, he heard the rustling of Sangwoo packing up his things over at the desk.

"Get up. You said you would finish the designs for the gacha and title screens by the end of the day."

The weirdo's robotic yet pleasant voice registered distantly in Jaeyoung's brain, as if coming from the end of a long tunnel.

"Are you asleep?"

Jaeyoung still didn't respond.

"Hey, are you asleep?"

It was the exact same question, but Sangwoo's voice was slightly closer.

"Are you…*really* asleep?"

Now it sounded like Sangwoo was standing right next to the dozing man. Wondering if the weirdo was planning on drawing a moustache on his face or something, Jaeyoung committed to fooling Sangwoo into thinking he wasn't awake. Then, when Sangwoo started doing whatever he'd cooked up in his head, Jaeyoung would spring up and scare the shit out of—

"You're actually asleep, right, Jaeyoung?"

That's the same way he said my name last time…

The mischievousness drained out of Jaeyoung. It was like he was in a game and had just gotten struck with a whole pile of status effects all at once—he was rendered mute, paralyzed, stunned, frozen, petrified, and confused. The world moved in slow-mo.

Even with his eyes closed, Jaeyoung could sense Sangwoo crouching down to examine his face up close.

"You really are asleep, right…?"

Sangwoo was now so close that Jaeyoung could feel a warm breath tickling his eyelids. Then, fingertips brushed against his forehead as Sangwoo…began toying with his hair?

Jaeyoung's breath quickened in bewilderment, but he kept his eyes shut, calling on all his acting skills to keep his cool.

Each passing second felt like an hour. Jaeyoung's face was so tense that his cheek muscles were starting to twitch. Finally, he decided to turn over in his "sleep."

That was when it happened. Something soft pressed against Jaeyoung's lips.

It took every ounce of self-restraint he had to keep his eyes closed and maintain his composure. The pressure disappeared as quickly as it'd come.

By the time Jaeyoung opened his eyes, Sangwoo was already walking out of the room.

*Notable observations of subject: aslfhnasljfhoqkwuhfoq WTF???

*Conclusion: SIGNIFICANT ABNORMALITY DETECTED

⌘W

"Anything in particular you're craving?"

"No."

"I'll take the *okonomiyaki*, the fish cake set, and two bottles of soju." Jaeyoung closed the menu and handed it to the waitress, who took their order and left behind the folding screen.

It was Saturday night, and Jaeyoung had snatched up Sangwoo once he'd gotten off work. Now, they were sitting in the corner of a quiet *izakaya* where they could talk in private. Jaeyoung had been distracted all day because of the incident from the night before. Unless he'd been dreaming, Sangwoo had snuck a kiss and run away, but why he'd done it was still a total mystery.

For one, Sangwoo was the most rigid, antiquated person to ever exist. Jaeyoung would've found it far less shocking if he'd turned out to be asexual than gay. Not to mention, the weirdo's gaze was completely apathetic when it met Jaeyoung's across the table. There was not a trace of love or affection in his eyes.

It was starting to feel much more plausible that Jaeyoung had been so tired he'd hallucinated the whole thing.

"Why did you bring me here?" Sangwoo asked flatly.

"I figured we should go out for drinks, since we've already been working together for two weeks."

"I suppose...that's all right, then."

A long, suffocating silence followed.

In stark contrast to how he'd used to feel, Jaeyoung was no longer confident in his ability to maintain his composure around Sangwoo. Whether it had been done intentionally or not, the weirdo had hit him where it hurt one too many times over the past two weeks. The walls he'd once used to shield himself had crumbled to nothing, and the moat he'd dug around them was filled with dirt.

That's why he'd essentially forced Sangwoo to sit down at this pub with him—he knew he had to follow the uneasy feeling in his chest wherever it was leading him.

Downtempo electronica—one of Jaeyoung's favorite music genres—poured from the restaurant's speakers, filling the room with a gentle ambiance. Across the table from him, Sangwoo had his head craned back, looking up at the ceiling. Jaeyoung's eyes fell on Sangwoo's neck again for one second, two, and then he forced himself to look away.

A few minutes later, their waitress reappeared with their alcohol and some simple side dishes. A part of Jaeyoung had assumed the weirdo had probably never sat down with anybody for drinks before, but Sangwoo surprised him by reaching out and shaking the soju bottle with practiced ease before opening it.

Feeling his nerves vibrating like violin strings, Jaeyoung allowed

Sangwoo to pour him a drink first. His form was impeccable, and he followed the etiquette to a tee—he poured with his right hand, his left hand supporting the opposite wrist. Most people didn't really care about the trivial, made-up rule that you should cover the label of a bottle with one palm while pouring, but the weirdo perfectly managed that as well.

"Who did you learn that from?"

"My mother. She taught it to me as soon as I came of age, saying it would be important in the future."

It was Jaeyoung's turn to pour now. Sangwoo held out his glass, still supporting his wrist with his opposite hand in a show of deference.

Part of Jaeyoung thought it was slightly ridiculous that the weirdo was being so formal when the two of them were just college students, but he didn't say anything—he knew how important it was to Sangwoo to follow the rules, no matter what situation he found himself in. So he just poured the clear liquid into Sangwoo's glass, filling it almost to the brim. They clinked their glasses together, then downed their shots at the same time.

After nibbling on a few pieces of edamame, Jaeyoung turned his gaze back to Sangwoo, who remained totally nonchalant. Unable to think of anything to say, he filled their glasses again. They drank.

"You can handle your liquor pretty well."

"Yes. My aldehyde dehydrogenase enzymes tend to be very active."

"I thought you avoided the stuff like the plague."

"Why?"

"Remember your freshman welcome party? You refused to take a single sip."

Sangwoo blinked in confusion as he refilled Jaeyoung's glass. Returning the favor, Jaeyoung continued, "I was there, too."

"Oh. I remember something very irritating happening… You saw everything?"

"Obviously. I'm the one who threw your phone."

"The corner of my phone cracked that day. I was planning on reporting the asshole who did it for property damage, but I gave up because I couldn't identify him."

Jaeyoung chuckled softly and ate a few more pieces of edamame. "Y'know, you only managed to escape because I stopped the computer science rep."

"What is it that you want me to say? 'Thank you'?"

This jerk never changes, huh? Jaeyoung mused. *Wonder if he'll stay like this forever.*

From the very beginning, Sangwoo's words had never failed to piss him off. But things were different now.

"Aren't you supposed to be smart? Like, some kind of computer science genius...? Although, I guess your specialty is reading machines, not people..."

It was the same insult he'd hurled at Sangwoo before. The weirdo's eyes curved into twin crescents as a smile spread across his face.

He's so fricking cute.

Closing his eyes, Jaeyoung knocked back another glass of soju.

"You know, I've run into you a few times in the past," he said.

"When?"

"For one, we were in the same class a few years ago."

"Really?"

"Yeah, for real! You tried to steal my money in front of the convenience store once...and you made me look like an idiot when I tried to interview you during the festival."

There was no recognition in Sangwoo's face. He downed a glass of soju as the waitress brought over a large pot filled with stew and fish cake skewers, accompanied by *okonomiyaki* heaped with dried bonito flakes.

"The point is, I've known you for a long time, though it took you *forever* to recognize me and remember my name."

"It did?"

"You called me Youngjae Kim the first time you came to the restaurant, remember? Man, that was unbelievable..."

Grumbling, Jaeyoung picked up a skewer and bit into one of the fish cakes. Sangwoo sat frozen for a moment, then grabbed a skewer for himself. A few minutes passed as they ate the food and drank the two bottles of soju in silence. They ordered some more when they were done.

Finally, the weirdo said, "I had a senior in the military named Youngjae Kim, and he was just as annoying as you. That must be why I made the mistake."

The words felt like a fist to Jaeyoung's gut, but they gave him an opportunity to move on to a topic he'd been curious about.

"Where'd you serve?"

"Goyang-si. I was in the artillery unit."

"Oh, the Cheonma Artillery Brigade? I heard they're extremely tough on you."

"It was fine."

Jaeyoung was slightly surprised to hear Sangwoo discussing his military years so casually—for some reason, he'd assumed the weirdo had been placed under special observation or something after being unable to fit into his cohort.

"How'd you like the military, anyway? Was this Youngjae Kim the only one who bullied you?"

"Yes. He was transferred to another unit while I was serving as a private. From that point on, nobody else bothered me."

"Why'd he get transferred?"

"I didn't say anything when he kept dumping chores on me and waking me up at night, but then he started smacking me on the head on a regular basis. I put a note into the complaints box and talked to the company commander, but nothing happened. So I reported him to the military police."

Whoa… Did he really?

Clearing his throat awkwardly, Jaeyoung asked, "Did you get along well with the others?"

"When I had to. It's not like a military base is a place for socializing. I only talked to them when it was necessary."

"Gotcha. Did you get sick of it or anything?"

"Not at all. I got to study a good deal in my free time. I was recognized for being a perfect shot and possessing excellent combat ability. I also became a model special forces soldier, which I got an award for. My father said I was born to be in the military."

Damn, Sangwoo…

It made sense that Sangwoo had been so good at enduring physical suffering and the monotony of the military. Jaeyoung, on the contrary, had *hated* every second he spent there. Waking up at ass o'clock, wiping down the damn guns every single day, not being able to do anything interesting with your hair or outfits, being confined to the barracks, the disgusting food, the endless combat practice, the long marches, the duty stations… All those things had made Jaeyoung endlessly miserable—and that wasn't even getting into the mental stuff. Military culture had made him sick, but he'd been forced to yell at the younger soldiers and try to discipline them because of his MOS.

"I was the drill instructor," Jaeyoung said.

"Hmm… Interesting. I'm surprised you were qualified to train anybody else."

"Yeah, agreed. They arbitrarily picked me because I'm tall."

"I'm sure the new soldiers didn't take you seriously."

Jaeyoung scoffed. "As if! They called me Sergeant Deathstalker. You know, like the scorpion?"

"You're lying," Sangwoo responded impassively.

"I swear, you're the only one who thinks I'm some kind of loser."

For a moment, Sangwoo stayed silent. Then he said, "You're not *that* much of a loser."

They both fell into silence again as they downed glass after glass of soju. In the blink of an eye, they'd finished four bottles. Feeling tipsy, Jaeyoung blinked slowly as he watched Sangwoo pick up his glass, turn his head to the side, then whip back and empty the whole thing. If Jaeyoung didn't know any better, he would've said the weirdo was drinking water, not alcohol.

He has no right to be so damn sexy, Jaeyoung thought, then immediately tried to remind himself that Sangwoo was a man. He scrubbed his eyes with his fists, but nothing changed—there was still a slight blush on Sangwoo's cheeks, and a cherry-red gleam to his lips.

Hungrily latching onto every single detail, Jaeyoung's eyes traveled down Sangwoo's long neck and lingered on his plaid shirt for a moment.

But when the weirdo opened a fresh bottle of soju, his gaze quickly danced over to take in the newly defined muscles along his forearms.

Bless rolled-up sleeves, Jaeyoung thought reverently as Sangwoo twisted the cap off, veins slightly prominent beneath his pale skin. *At this rate, I wouldn't be surprised if I got a nosebleed...*

Exhaling sharply, Jaeyoung brushed a hand over his face—his skin radiated heat under his fingers. And much as he didn't like to admit it, that couldn't entirely be blamed on the alcohol.

"Recommended games... 'Open Up Your Heart,'" Sangwoo muttered.

Jaeyoung snapped his head up to see that the weirdo was pointing at the wall behind him. Raising an eyebrow, he turned around to look as well. There was a large poster on the wall, listing "The Best Drinking Games to Spice Up Your Night." A short description accompanied each of the games—"Kings," "Never Have I Ever," "First Impressions," and "Open Up Your Heart," which was a game where underclassmen and upperclassmen would switch places in the social hierarchy. Slowly, Jaeyoung turned back around to face Sangwoo, whose eyes were gleaming with uncharacteristic interest.

"You wanna play?" Jaeyoung asked.

The answer came immediately.

"Yes."

"Geez... Sounds like someone's holding a grudge or two."

Sangwoo just stared at him intently. Fortunately, Jaeyoung wasn't the type to get offended if an underclassman spoke to him rudely or way too casually for a few minutes. "Go for it, then," he said.

Immediately, Sangwoo began the game. "Hey, Jaeyoung Jang."

Maybe Jaeyoung was imagining it, but he could see a determined glint in Sangwoo's eyes. His heart began to pound. Hamming it up, he scooted closer to the table and respectfully clasped his hands together.

"Yes, sir! What can I do for you?"

There was a short pause, wherein Sangwoo cleared his throat a few times. He looked away briefly before redirecting his gaze to Jaeyoung.

"You need to start taking my criticism more seriously, understand?"

"Whatever do you mean, sir? I'm already taking it seriously!"

"Why do you keep repeating the same mistakes, then?"

"I'll be more careful in the future."

"Is your underscore key broken or what? I know you're good at English, so you have no reason to be making so many typos. It's not that hard. Try to be more mindful, all right?"

Leave it to this asshole to bring up work while we're out grabbing drinks...

Jaeyoung picked up a fish cake skewer and shoved it in Sangwoo's mouth. "Here, allow me."

Sangwoo diligently chewed on the fish cake and swallowed. Then he continued, "Also, we're falling behind schedule because you're missing deadlines. Don't pretend it's not an issue."

"Please understand, I'm trying my best. I promise I'll get everything done."

"That's an empty promise."

"Not at all! I was grinding away earlier today, actually."

That was a bold-faced lie. He'd achieved absolutely nothing because he'd been too busy thinking about Sangwoo the entire day. But he was confident that, despite procrastinating, he'd be able to cobble something decent together at the last minute.

Jaeyoung smirked playfully. "My, my, sir. It looks like you picked this game because you wanted to give me a scolding."

A frown started to form on Sangwoo's face, but Jaeyoung disrupted it by scooping up some *okonomiyaki* and force-feeding it to him. Unlike before, Sangwoo was starting to look a bit tipsy, too—his eyes were slightly unfocused, and his robotic demeanor was nowhere to be found. He didn't even bother to fight back when Jaeyoung pushed the bite of food into his mouth.

After a moment, Sangwoo muttered, "I just wanted to hear you talk to me politely... You dumb brat."

"I see... Have another drink."

Jaeyoung grabbed Sangwoo's glass and held it up to the weirdo's lips, and he promptly drank from it like a baby bird. After swallowing, he pointed at Jaeyoung accusingly.

"You. Jaeyoung Jang."

"Yes?"

"You know...that you're completely out of your mind, right...?"

"Oh, of course I do."

Scoffing, Sangwoo crossed his arms over his chest and leaned back in his chair. "You're suuuuch an asshole. I still remember how you doodled on my face..."

"Right, right. I don't know how I'll ever atone for my sins."

"Then you bought all my coffee... That's called stockpiling. It's not... allowed."

"Of course it's not. You should've reported me to the Consumer Union, really. I mean, I'm a terrible, terrible person."

"You're...garbage. Sewer garbage..."

"Oh no, I'm *radioactive waste.* But I can kneel at your feet and beg for forgiveness, if you want."

Abruptly, Sangwoo leaned forward across the table. It almost felt like some unseen force had reached out and tugged him in Jaeyoung's direction. But then he placed his arms on the table and crossed them, resting his chin on top. One of his elbows shoved the *okonomiyaki* to the side, and Jaeyoung barely managed to grab it before it fell to the floor.

At that point, Jaeyoung was sitting pretty damn close to the table, too. Somehow, they had ended up so close together that the rim of Sangwoo's hat had almost brushed Jaeyoung's forehead.

Jaeyoung lowered himself to the table just like Sangwoo, until he could finally see his eyes. His heart began to race even faster. He watched, mesmerized, as Sangwoo's dense eyelashes fluttered as he blinked. As his lips moved to form a mumbled string of words.

"You're lucky that you're so...decent-looking, you know."

"That's true. Nobody would want anything to do with me if I didn't at least look decent."

"At least you're self-aware."

It was clear that Sangwoo was feeling the alcohol; the weirdo's eyes were slightly unfocused as he studied Jaeyoung's face. There was a strange intensity to that gaze—it left heat lingering on Jaeyoung's skin wherever it touched, though perhaps that was his imagination.

Sangwoo's focus lingered on Jaeyoung's forehead, then moved to his nose, neck, chin, and finally his lips. Sangwoo's eyes narrowed slightly, and he seemed to mouth something to himself.

At last, Jaeyoung broke the silence between them. "Is there something on my face?"

Sangwoo's eyes turned into such thin slits that a bystander might've thought he was falling asleep, but then he turned his gaze to the side and poured Jaeyoung another glass of soju.

Jaeyoung downed the alcohol right away, then asked yet another question. "Do you think I'm hot?"

It was like Sangwoo hadn't heard him. The weirdo just refilled his glass yet again instead of responding.

Jaeyoung emptied it in one gulp. "Do you…think I'm…hot, Sangwoo?" he repeated slowly, staring directly into Sangwoo's dark eyes. Their usual sharpness was nowhere to be found.

What are you thinking? If my guess is correct…you probably want me.

After a moment, the younger man answered in a small voice, "Yes."

Jaeyoung blinked slowly, momentarily struck speechless. The butterflies in his stomach were starting to spread throughout his entire body, swarming around his heart. Maybe it was the alcohol, but he found his mind dominated by a single thought. Acting on it might jeopardize their entire relationship, but he found he didn't care about that anymore.

Placing both his hands on the table, Jaeyoung sprang to his feet, stumbling slightly before managing to regain his balance. He found himself getting irritated at the piece of furniture taking up the space between them—he pushed it roughly aside and took a step toward Sangwoo, who craned his head back to look at him.

Thanks to this, Jaeyoung got a good view of the other man's entire face.

"Hey, Sangwoo."

"Yes?"

"Can I take it off you?"

His face turning crimson, Sangwoo fell silent. But that flush wasn't from tipsiness this time—Jaeyoung could just feel it.

"I was talking about your hat, dummy. Unless…you thought I was referring to something else."

Without bothering to ask for permission, Jaeyoung reached out and lifted the black cap off the weirdo's head. A strange sense of satisfaction surged in him as Sangwoo froze, visibly flustered.

There was nothing special about the guy, really—he wasn't like one of those fictional characters who turned into complete hunks whenever they took off their glasses. He was just a regular guy with hat hair.

That is, if one was being logical. Alas, Jaeyoung had long turned off that part of his brain.

In that moment, all he could think about was how striking the sharp contrast was between Sangwoo's dark eyes and pale skin. How he looked curiously put together and yet disheveled at the same time, his usual mask of calmness discarded entirely.

Sure, maybe it was a mirage conjured by a combination of alcohol and his own emotions, but the weirdo loomed before Jaeyoung's eyes like some sort of temptress. R-rated fantasies flooded into his mind one after another, unstoppable.

"Not gonna yell at me this time?" Jaeyoung asked, his voice coming out huskier than usual. There was something about Sangwoo that stripped him of all self-control—whether that was over his voice, face, or his stupid dick.

"Give it back," Sangwoo said, sending him an indignant glare as he fidgeted awkwardly with his bangs.

Jaeyoung's heart skipped a beat. *Not a chance.*

"I *said*, give it back."

"Sorry, I don't wanna."

"Give it back now!"

"Ooh, is someone mad?"

"Enough is *enough*!"

Sangwoo sprang to his feet angrily. His height was average—not too tall or too short—and Jaeyoung loved it. He liked how the weirdo had to tip his head back to meet his eyes, and it was oddly satisfying to look down at his angry face.

Jaeyoung's breath hitched with excitement. He waited patiently until Sangwoo reached for his hat, then grabbed his wrist tightly and tugged hard, bringing the weirdo's disoriented face only inches from his.

Their eyes made contact for a brief, intense moment. Then Sangwoo directed his glare at the floor instead.

"Shit..." The word sounded foreign coming from Sangwoo. His voice was rough and low, just like Jaeyoung's.

"Sorry, what was that?"

"I wasn't talking to you, Jaeyoung," Sangwoo said, then glowered at him with renewed determination.

But Jaeyoung just stood frozen in place, his breath coming out in heated huffs. His hands itched to grab, touch, or simply brush against Sangwoo. At this point, he would take anything.

"Hey, Sangwoo."

"Yes?"

In a painstakingly slow movement, Jaeyoung raised his right hand and gently placed it on Sangwoo's cheek. Faint tremors radiated under his thumb as he stroked it across the flushed cheek.

"I'm giving you fair warning—stop calling my name like that."

"Okay..."

"I can't promise what I'll do if you—"

"...Jaeyoung."

Jaeyoung's hand tensed, but Sangwoo just stared unwaveringly into his eyes.

"You're so damn hot, Jaeyoung."

Jaeyoung felt something plummet—probably his heart. Biting his lip, he slowly slid his hand down to Sangwoo's neck, feeling like he was invading forbidden territory. The skin he found there was hot, almost feverish. Curling his fingers behind Sangwoo's nape, he pulled him in slightly until their foreheads were nearly touching.

Sangwoo's flushed face was *right there*. His dark eyes didn't leave Jaeyoung's for a second. They were so, so close...but though the string tethering Jaeyoung's rationality was starting to fray, he still managed to remember what the rules were.

"Advance notice: I'm going to kiss you in exactly one minute." His words were almost businesslike, betraying the emotions burning in his throat. "So, if you're gonna run...this is your last chance."

Jaeyoung's breath turned ragged as a low, desperate hum resounded between his ears. His skin was on fire, but he couldn't tell if the heat came from Sangwoo or himself. In his head, he pictured his body engulfed in a raging inferno.

Sangwoo's eyelashes fluttered as he blinked, briefly shadowing his eyes and breaking their unwavering eye contact. But then, as Jaeyoung stared on dazedly, Sangwoo reached out with his free hand to grab the fabric of Jaeyoung's shirt and pull him closer.

There are forty-eight seconds left, Jaeyoung thought absently as he watched Sangwoo's eyes slip shut. But then the weirdo's lips pressed against his, as they had the previous day.

Something finally snapped inside Jaeyoung, and he roughly pulled Sangwoo even closer, tilting his head to get a better angle. He jolted slightly when Sangwoo's tongue suddenly slipped between his lips, but he recovered instantly and returned the favor.

The world faded away after that. The only sensations he was aware of were those of their lips melting together, their tongues tangling, and their breath becoming one.

The heat growing inside Jaeyoung was primal and wild. His overwhelming thirst grew faster than it could be sated, turning into a throbbing pain. He was burning up, and he welcomed it.

Their kiss was far from romantic, having gone from zero to a hundred with no in-between, and they jerked back from each other with the same urgency with which they'd collided. As Sangwoo wiped his lips with his sleeve, panting frantically, Jaeyoung leaned against the wall and tried to catch his breath.

Shit... He practically ate me alive.

His heart raced a million miles an hour, threatening to burst.

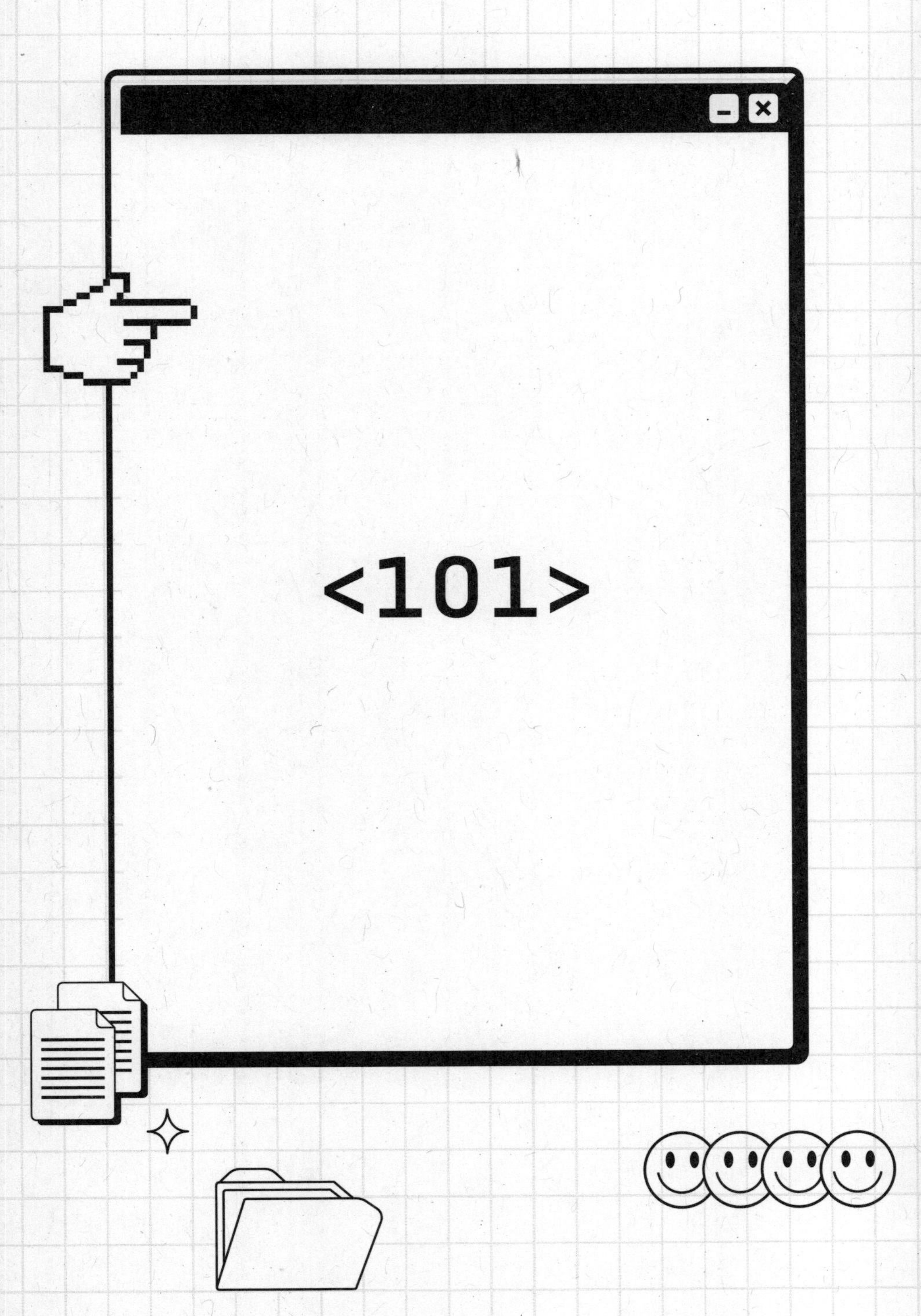
<101>

"Let's develop the game together. I need a skilled designer."

"Fine. I'll do it."

Simply put, Sangwoo's plan had been a success.

He'd hit two birds with one stone, as one would say. Not only had he recruited the most talented designer on campus to work alongside him, but he'd also managed to incorporate Jaeyoung back into his daily routine. It was the best solution he could've come up with—this way, he figured he'd be able to rid his brain of the strange abnormalities that had been cropping up while developing his game at the same time.

This prediction had turned out to be mostly correct. The minor issues that'd plagued him since the deadbeat had vanished from his life had started to fade since Sangwoo had begun meeting with Jaeyoung regularly. Finally, he found himself able to focus in class and study for hours in his usual library seat again. And so, in the days that followed, he dedicated himself to academics until 4 PM, after which he'd throw himself into game development.

Overall, he thought things had been going well. The mere thought of his afternoon meetings with Jaeyoung energized him in the morning, keeping his mood slightly elevated for the majority of the day. The only issue he could pinpoint was that his mental state began to deteriorate as the meeting approached. Starting around thirty minutes beforehand, his palms would start to sweat and his heart would begin to race.

He'd put in a lot of effort for their very first meeting. Sangwoo had neatly compiled the most recent information about the mobile app market, printed it, and even gone so far as to buy a variety of snacks from the convenience store before arranging them carefully on the meeting room table.

Ultimately, though, he'd been left disappointed. He could have perhaps persuaded himself to overlook Jaeyoung's tardiness—the asshole had arrived a whole twelve minutes late—but it was his demeanor that Sangwoo found the most problematic. Jaeyoung hadn't been cooperative in the slightest. The only silver lining was that he hadn't tried to act as friendly and clingy as before.

Later, as the midnight deadline had approached, Sangwoo had waited for Jaeyoung to send over the materials, continuously refreshing his email to no avail. When he'd finally managed to reach Jaeyoung by making a call from his neighbor's landline phone, it had been immediately obvious that the asshole was out playing pool somewhere. Even worse, the concept artwork he'd brought to their meeting the next day was clearly the result of minimal effort, which had plunged Sangwoo's mood yet further into the abyss.

"Give me one more day," Jaeyoung had asked.

Strangely enough, Sangwoo had found himself unable to turn down the asshole's request. It was nonsensical—he'd had no time to waste, especially after the entire weekend had gone down the drain because of Jaeyoung's prior redo request. The project *had* to proceed according to schedule… And yet, Sangwoo had caved and let Jaeyoung rework the designs one more time simply because the asshole had looked into his eyes and pleaded.

To Sangwoo's surprise, Jaeyoung had shown up to their meeting on Tuesday with something incredible—a side-scrolling shooter game that revolved around platforming. The plot was familiar yet unique, and the artwork was so polished that it could've been pulled straight from a game already on the market. Finally, every single element of the game was explained neatly in a document, which also contained a new tentative title:

Working title: *Veggie Venturer*

* * *

Needless to say, Sangwoo had been quite pleased. But it was the third of the three character designs that really caught his eye. With its flashy hair and pretty face, one of the cartoony characters immediately reminded him of the man sitting across the table from him. It'd been fairly obvious that Jaeyoung wanted to use another character, but Sangwoo had stubbornly refused. After all, who wouldn't love playing a game with such a cute, adorable protagonist?

After that, everything had gone smoothly and according to plan. While Jaeyoung *had* kept missing things here and there, which made Sangwoo slightly concerned, it was impossible to deny that the designer was incredibly skilled.

When a big problem finally arose, it'd had nothing to do with the project.

"I bet you've never been inside the art building. Come on, I'll show you my studio and make you a cup of tea."

In hindsight, things had gone wrong the moment he'd stepped foot inside Jaeyoung's disgusting cave. He should've left after their short, five-minute meeting, where anything abnormal was unlikely to happen. But instead, he'd given in to his curiosity and ended up following Jaeyoung to his studio so he could see it. He'd prepared himself for the worst, but what he saw when the door swung open was a literal hell on earth.

Simply put, the studio was a complete mess. Things were scattered all over the room, and even the objects that seemed to be in their proper places were random items with no discernible purpose.

In one corner of this hellhole sat a person dressed in an extremely concerning outfit. Sangwoo stared at the dog collar around her neck as she headbanged to the music she was blaring.

He felt a sudden, overwhelming desire to crumple up the whole room like a sheet of paper and slam it into the nearest trash can. How did Jaeyoung get anything done in such a dump? Sangwoo couldn't begin to understand.

It had already been established that Jaeyoung was a two-faced jerk—as well as a deadbeat, attention-seeking, sadistic piece of trash—but now it was becoming obvious that he was absolutely disgusting as well. The only things Sangwoo liked about the guy were his design and illustration skills—he wouldn't have gone *near* Jaeyoung if he wasn't already malfunctioning. But even as he'd grumbled to himself inwardly, he helped Jaeyoung clean up the studio.

The room became semi-presentable once the clutter was gone, and Sangwoo suddenly realized there were posters plastered all over the walls. The ones Jaeyoung had worked on looked like they'd been printed in the most vivid, dramatic colors the senior could find, especially in comparison to the others, which frankly could've been black and white for all Sangwoo cared. Maybe it was because he had looked at Jaeyoung's portfolio so often during his "research," but he could actually pinpoint exactly which year each one had been produced.

Before Jaeyoung had started working, he'd been sitting at his desk like a total deadbeat, his eyes unfocused behind glasses that slipped down his nose as he yawned lazily. But once he'd booted up his PC, it was like a switch flipped inside him; each of his hands controlled separate inputs, moving with the goal of maximum efficiency. His eyes—usually so expressive—became sharp and calm as he worked, carefully scrutinizing each step of his process.

There was no trace of his usual carefree smile on his now motionless, serious lips. That's when it had hit Sangwoo: He was sitting in the studio of a skilled professional.

At some point, Sangwoo had realized the five-minute meetings were far too short. They soon stretched to an hour, then three and a half hours. The downsides of letting such a thing happen were clear: He was heightening his risk of experiencing another abnormal reaction. Beyond that, he was now stuck working daily in an art studio that remained perpetually dirty—no matter how many times he cleaned it—alongside the weirdest female he'd ever met, and Jaeyoung, who he always ended up bickering with. And yet, he'd found himself coming back again and again and again.

Sangwoo's database on the older man had gained a good deal of new information during the two weeks they'd worked together in the studio. Jaeyoung had a younger twin brother; he was very close with his maternal grandfather; he was not only fluent in Korean, Mandarin, and English, but also Cantonese and French; he didn't like messing around in water, whether that be waterparks or the beach; he frequently changed his computer background, which was always of some female celebrity; he preferred comic books over novels and movies over comic books; he absolutely despised mediocre or bad food; he was a cat person; he loved anything cyberpunk; he was a terrible gamer… The list went on.

After taking over the desk belonging to the student who was currently serving in the military, Sangwoo had found himself quickly becoming accustomed to Jaeyoung's presence. His brain had greedily absorbed anything related to the other man, while his ears had recorded the sound of his voice—which his brain inevitably started replaying as he was preparing to go to bed. Every single day, he'd stolen glances at Jaeyoung's face—directly and indirectly, for brief moments and long ones—to the degree that he grew confident in his ability to recreate it on paper, despite having no talent for art.

Jaeyoung had been slowly seeping into Sangwoo's very being, and looking back, he knew exactly when he'd reached the point of no return. Exactly sixteen days after joining Jaeyoung in his studio for the first time, on one unforgettable Friday, Sangwoo had become completely corrupted.

That day, Sangwoo had finished a variety of small tasks, including planning the difficulty level and rewards for each stage of *Veggie Venturer*, the level-up bonuses the player would receive, and the HP and attack stats of each monster. As for Jaeyoung, he'd finished designing several major UI elements after hours of grinding away at his desk. Exhausted, he'd stumbled over to the small studio cot and collapsed.

Usually, Jaeyoung would spend his break making dumb jokes, messing around on his phone, or shuffling through his playlist. But this time, his eyes had closed tiredly. By the time the fifteen-minute break concluded and Sangwoo turned around to call his name, he had fallen fast asleep.

He should have woken Jaeyoung up—they'd agreed on exactly fifteen minutes. But for some reason, Sangwoo had turned back to his PC without saying anything. Time had flown by until it was 10 PM—it was time for him to leave.

"I'm going home."

The only reply Sangwoo got was silence, indicating that Jaeyoung was knocked out. Sangwoo was ready to go, his backpack slung over his shoulders, but for some inexplicable reason, he found himself drawn to the bed.

"Hey, are you asleep? Are you…really asleep?"

With each careful confirmation, Sangwoo moved closer to Jaeyoung—one step, then another. When he finally reached the cot, he silently looked down at Jaeyoung's sleeping face. His bangs were slightly ruffled, covering his eyes.

Slowly, Sangwoo bent down and crouched next to the bed. His heart beat faster and faster as he drew closer to Jaeyoung's face—it felt as though someone was squeezing his heart in a fist, much like the sensation he got when he was carsick.

Belatedly realizing his hands were clenched into fists, Sangwoo uncurled his fingers and gently brushed Jaeyoung's bangs aside. He carefully swept them up onto Jaeyoung's forehead.

How pretty. The words, simple and sudden, slipped into Sangwoo's mind. He could've sat there, staring at Jaeyoung, all day long. A strange possessiveness seized him by the throat, and longing filled him. He wanted to *touch* Jaeyoung, to run his fingers over his closed eyelids, the tip of his nose, his mouth…

Sangwoo's gaze drifted to Jaeyoung's slightly parted lips. Realization hit; he'd been mistaken. A mere sweep of his fingertips wouldn't be enough to satisfy his desire—what he wanted was something else, something he would never even dream of doing if Jaeyoung were awake.

The opportunity hung right there before his eyes, fleeting yet tempting. Why not just act on it? Nobody would know unless he confessed.

He was malfunctioning, glitching out. Seriously. That was the only reason he pressed his lips against Jaeyoung's, then ran off like some petty thief.

Sangwoo raced out of the studio and into the hallway, but didn't get far before he slumped against the wall and slid to the floor, boneless. For the past twenty-five years, his logic, morals, self-restraint, composure, judgment, and sense of humanity had never wavered, as steady as a block of concrete. But in one moment of foolishness, they had all turned to rubble.

Nobody knows what happened. It's fine, he muttered inwardly as he dragged himself home, feeling like some murderer in a crime novel.

By the time he collapsed in bed, he'd convinced himself that nothing abnormal had occurred—his pounding heart, however, didn't seem to have gotten the memo.

Unfortunately, this was only the beginning of Sangwoo's suffering. Unbeknownst to him, something was going to happen the very next day that would drive the final nail into his coffin, triggering a wave of internal destruction that would leave him in complete and utter ruin.

"There you are! Come on, I wanna take you somewhere."

When Jaeyoung had grabbed him in front of the internet café, smiling like a sly fox, Sangwoo's heart had dropped to his feet. Looking back, that moment had been his last chance to realize something was wrong and make a run for it. However, his judgment had long been severely impaired—as was obvious from all the other bad decisions he'd been making lately.

```
printf("No, thank you. I am very busy and in no mood to be around you. Goodbye.")
```

That was the command Sangwoo had entered into his system, but the output had been completely different.

"Okay. Where are we going?"

As for the consequences...they'd been severe. There was no recovering from what he'd done at the restaurant, and Sangwoo knew it.

So instead, he shoved his hat back on his head, walked around the folding screen, paid half the bill at the register, and then sprinted back home, where he brushed his teeth, washed his face, changed, and slipped into bed. But naturally, none of those actions purged his memory of what'd happened.

Sangwoo practically writhed in embarrassment under his sheets, kicking at them until they ghosted up into the air and fell over his face. He trembled as he lay there in the darkness, completely mortified.

Am I only a slave to my desires?

Do I have *to graduate from Hanguk University?*

Is my life still worth living?

Tormented by this barrage of yes/no questions, Sangwoo didn't get a wink of sleep until the early morning.

Adolescence was typically a time when individuals experienced an intense sexual desire toward another person—Sangwoo knew that much. For instance, he remembered experiencing an acceleration of his heartbeat when he'd passed a group of female students on the bus who emanated a pleasant scent. And back in high school, he'd discreetly admired a teacher's beauty, and engaged in a romantic relationship with a member of the opposite sex when he'd reached an appropriate age.

Losing control of his desires to the point where he'd molested a sleeping individual—and in their own studio, no less!—was entirely new, however. And that wasn't even the biggest issue. Jaeyoung was, in every sense of the word, a man.

Sangwoo had never felt any kind of attraction toward a male before, despite being surrounded by people of the same sex in middle school, high school, college, and the military. To him, it was a complete aberration. He'd gone his entire life thinking that he would become physically affectionate with a woman, fornicate, and get married. His entire extended family had done that, after all. But now? Now there was an unexpected bug in his code that had crept its way in and disrupted the natural order of things.

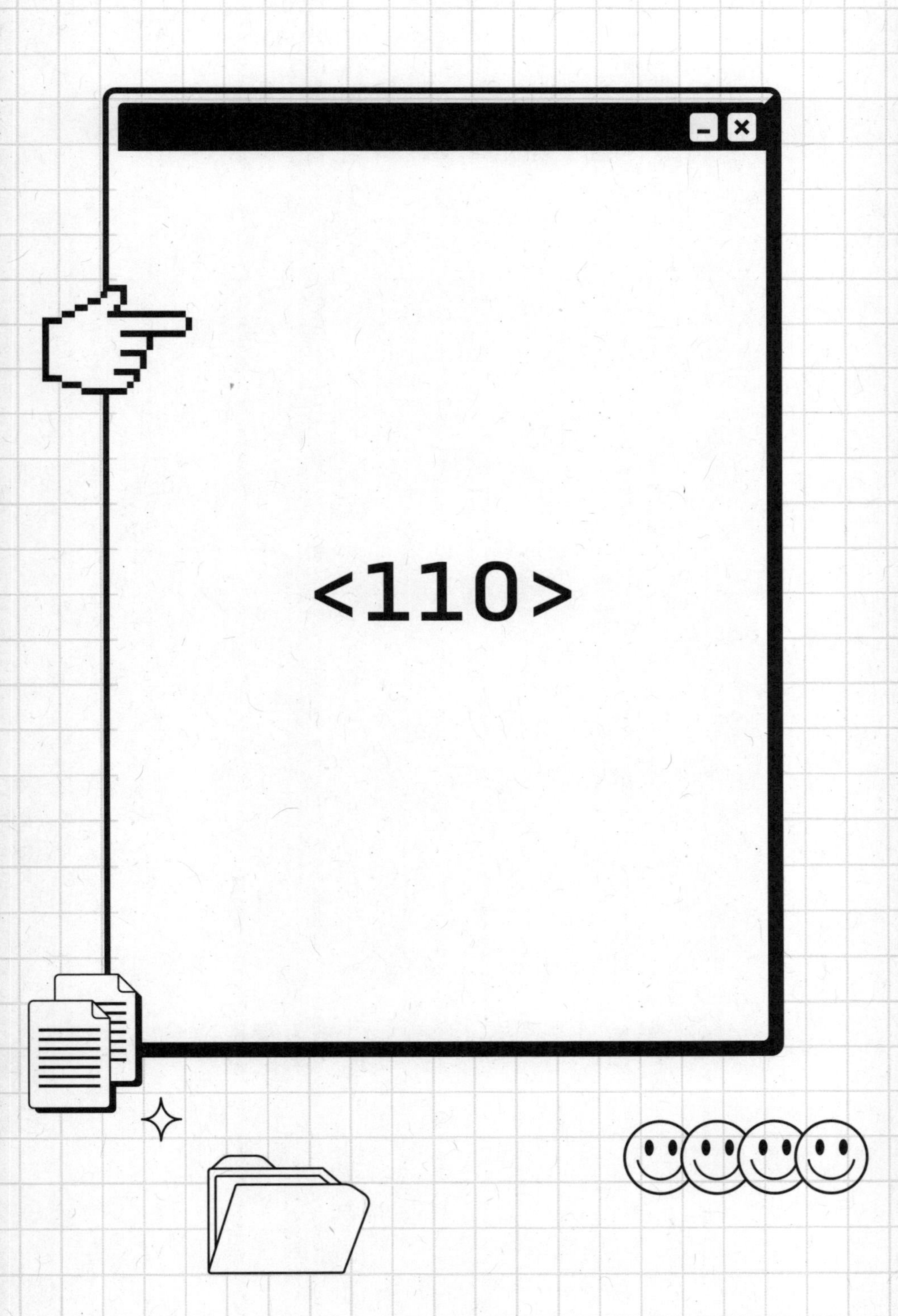
<110>

It was Sunday, and Sangwoo was heading home from work. To say he was in a terrible mood after the events of the previous day would be an understatement—his feet dragged under the weight of his own exhaustion and irritation.

Turning into the alley right in front of his apartment, he relished the idea of falling into bed the moment he walked through his front door. But then he was jolted back to the present at the sight of a figure sitting at the base of the stairs leading to the entryway to his building.

Dressed in gray sweatpants and a yellow jacket, with his hood pulled low over his head and gum in his mouth, Jaeyoung looked like some loafer who'd spent most of his week wasting his life away in an arcade. He blew a big bubble, watching it expand until it popped.

It was hard to believe that Sangwoo had voluntarily made contact with that deadbeat's lips, not once, but twice. Regardless, he wasn't in the mood to talk. He quickly strode toward the entrance.

He didn't make it far. Jaeyoung suddenly sprang into motion, swinging his leg forward to block Sangwoo's path. When Sangwoo stubbornly tried to move it out of the way, Jaeyoung hooked his fingers into the back pocket of Sangwoo's jeans and yanked hard, causing him to stumble backward.

This is sexual harassment, he wanted to snap. Jaeyoung's hand had touched his butt, after all. But unfortunately, he knew he had no right to make that accusation.

"What the hell? Were you gonna walk past me?"

Jaeyoung leapt to his feet and blocked the entrance with his entire body, scowling like a thug about to demand Sangwoo hand over his lunch money. Eerily calm, Sangwoo began calculating an escape route. He could probably rush past if he really wanted to, but Jaeyoung would definitely catch him before he managed to enter his code into the door's keypad.

"This is absolutely insane," Jaeyoung continued. "I mean, you've already kissed me twice. Don't you think you owe me an explanation? That was basically sexual assault!"

Sangwoo's thoughts came to a screeching halt. He'd confirmed that Jaeyoung was asleep multiple times, but maybe he'd been mistaken…?

After a moment's hesitation, he ventured, "As for the first incident, I have no excuses. I apologize. However, the second incident occurred due to mutual negligence. Forget it ever happened."

"Mutual negligence?"

"Yes. You're the one who touched my face and said those…things. The point is, we were both drunk, and we made a mistake. I assure you, I'm usually much more careful."

Jaeyoung didn't respond, staring at Sangwoo with cold, gleaming eyes. His usual smile was nowhere to be found, leaving his face eerily emotionless.

Sangwoo found himself shifting uncomfortably.

Finally, Jaeyoung spat, "What, am I supposed to say sorry, too, now?"

"Yes. It'd be best to exchange apologies and ensure the incident doesn't repeat itself."

Jaeyoung's lips twisted into a mocking smile. "Well, guess what? I'm *not* sorry, and I can't promise it won't happen again," he snapped.

Sangwoo found himself caught off guard. For some reason, he'd assumed that Jaeyoung would also want to pretend like the incident had never happened. It took him a moment of hesitation to find the words to speak again.

"I don't understand. What happened between us isn't anything to be proud of."

"But why should I sweep it under the rug?" Jaeyoung retorted. "It wasn't a mistake, and I know you felt the same way I did."

"And what way was that? All I felt was an abnormal sexual desire, nothing more."

Jaeyoung paused for a moment, his eyes darting to the side as if he was trying to process what he'd heard. "'An…abnormal sexual desire'?"

"Yes. Through evolution, humans have developed complex biological mechanisms that trigger them to feel sexual desire for members of the opposite sex for the purpose of reproduction. While it's not that efficient, humanity has survived and thrived by pairing up and going through the complicated stages of pregnancy. Therefore, feeling sexual attraction to someone of the same sex is nothing but a meaningless illusion that does not contribute to humankind's survival or evolution."

For the longest time, Jaeyoung was rooted to the spot, repeatedly blowing up bubbles with his gum until they popped. His face was so impassive that Sangwoo couldn't get a read on it.

Finally, he picked his ear with one finger and tilted his head. It was likely he hadn't been paying attention to anything Sangwoo had said.

"Okay, and…?" he snarked. "I don't recall signing up for a bio lecture. Whatever. I have one question for you: Did you get hard yesterday?"

"Get hard? In what respect?"

"What do you think? I'm talking about your external reproductive organ, idiot."

Sangwoo hadn't been expecting Jaeyoung to ask such a personal, prying question, but this was one he could tolerate answering. The desire for reproduction was ingrained deep within his DNA, after all. Sure, it had been triggered in error, but that was nothing to be ashamed about.

"I do become erect quite often when I'm with you," he said without hesitation. "I'm not going to deny the presence of my sexual desires."

"That's a real fancy way to say yes."

Sangwoo ignored the mocking comment. "But that doesn't change anything. It's scientifically impossible for your Y chromosome to turn into an X chromosome."

The two of them were like a pair of magnets polarized in the same direction—they would never be able to be together.

Heaving a sigh, Sangwoo continued, "Let me be fully transparent.

This has been happening for a while, but I'm certain I will recover soon enough. Unfortunately, I'm currently unable to control my impulses. Something seems to be malfunctioning…so I might need some time. The issue might be that we've been around each other too much. But I also don't want to give up on *Veggie Venturer…*"

Jaeyoung scoffed loudly. "Oh, I see! So you want me to stay the hell away from you, but you still want my designs?"

"I don't want to give up on this project. We can work remotely if necessary," Sangwoo said stubbornly. "Please don't abandon the game."

Reaching into his hood to brush his hair back, Jaeyoung stretched his neck with a look of disbelief. When he took a step forward, Sangwoo took one in the opposite direction.

"Y'know, I don't get you sometimes. Did you ever consider that this situation might be making *me* uncomfortable?"

"Is it?"

Another step forward, another step back.

"You really think I'm worried about the game right now? Honestly, you're the most self-centered asshole I've ever met! How come you never even *try* to consider my perspective?"

"What is your perspective?"

Jaeyoung's face screwed up in anger and he began to advance faster. Sangwoo stumbled back just as quickly.

"Are you trying to piss me off?"

"I swear it was a genuine question."

Finally coming to a stop, Jaeyoung tilted his head back and massaged his neck. A deep sigh escaped his lips. "C'mon. You can't expect me to keep working like nothing happened. There's no way I'm gonna be able to focus on the damn game when you're around."

"You could try to suppress your desires and think more logica—"

"Sorry, but I don't *work* like that."

"Calm down. Besides, as you can see, I'm a man," Sangwoo declared. But once the words left his mouth, he abruptly felt like an idiot.

Jaeyoung let out another scoff. *Even that expression looks handsome on him,* pointed out the more primal part of Sangwoo's brain. The logical part couldn't believe that was what he was focused on.

"I don't give a shit about evolution and chromosomes. Unlike you, I don't put labels on myself. I still don't know what I'm gonna do with my life, but that's fine, because what matters most to me is what I feel right *here* and *now.*"

Jaeyoung put his hand over his heart, then surged yet another step forward toward Sangwoo. With the streetlight shining on him from behind, his shoulders looked much broader than usual. A sudden tendril of fear unfurled within Sangwoo.

"Call it abnormal if you want, but I'm not like you," Jaeyoung said angrily. "If I catch feelings for someone, I just go for it. The only reason I've been holding back is because you're a dude, and because I know it would break a pile of your stupid rules! Not because I'm some kind of gentleman, all right? But you can't even return that favor! You're acting like my opinion doesn't even matter in this situation!"

Sangwoo took another step back, but this time, his back bumped into a wall. He was trapped—cornered. His mind went blank as he scrambled to think of any self-defense techniques he could use against someone bigger than him.

When did he get so close?! Sangwoo thought, a wave of panic rushing over him as Jaeyoung continued to advance. At this point, their lips were about two steps apart. Sangwoo flinched in horror at the realization of how close the events of the previous day were to repeating themselves.

"You're the one who started this," Jaeyoung was saying. "Don't you dare tell me to...give up. You have no right—"

This is my chance! Seizing the opening, Sangwoo shoved his elbow into Jaeyoung's side as hard as he could, then took off running.

"Are you serious?! Get your ass back here! I'm not done with you yet!"

Ignoring Jaeyoung's enraged shouting, Sangwoo raced straight for his apartment building. Unfortunately, he didn't have the room to gain enough momentum, and Jaeyoung caught him just as he reached the dirty glass doors.

Tightening his grip into a headlock, Jaeyoung grabbed one of Sangwoo's arms and tried to twist it behind his back. Realizing what was happening, Sangwoo tensed, jerking his arm and shaking his head wildly in a desperate attempt to break free. He quickly drove an elbow toward Jaeyoung's stomach again with his free arm—but to Sangwoo's dismay, Jaeyoung blocked it effortlessly with his other arm.

For what felt like an eternity, the two of them grappled fiercely outside the apartment building.

"Let...go of me!" Sangwoo gasped.

He tried to trip Jaeyoung with one leg, but the bigger man had already used his physical advantage to completely trap Sangwoo in his arms. Naturally, when he went tumbling to the ground, he took his prey with him.

Jaeyoung's back collided with the asphalt first, and he grunted in pain. Hoping to take advantage of the opening and regain his footing, Sangwoo drove a punch into the asshole's chin, but Jaeyoung immediately wrapped his legs around Sangwoo's waist and flipped them both around.

Damn it. If only there was something to whack him with...

Jaeyoung wasn't that much bigger than him but large enough to keep Sangwoo from overpowering him. Before he knew it, Sangwoo was on his back with Jaeyoung on top of him.

Trapping Sangwoo's thighs between his knees, Jaeyoung firmly pinned his wrists to the asphalt. It was clear the asshole had gained the upper hand—Sangwoo had no chance of shaking him off from where he lay on the ground.

The position sent the memories of their tussle from literal seconds ago up in smoke, and Sangwoo squeezed his eyes shut. "What do you think you're doing?" he barely managed to say.

Jaeyoung's fingers tightened around Sangwoo's wrists. "*You're* the one who ran away in the middle of an important conversation. Feel like acting like a grown-up now?"

"I have nothing more to say," Sangwoo said stubbornly.

"Open your eyes."

He did not.

"If you don't, I'm gonna kiss you."

Sangwoo's eyes snapped open, his heartbeat jolting into a gallop in his chest. Whether it was because so much of their bodies was pressed together, or because Jaeyoung's face was so close to his, he couldn't tell. Even worse, it was impossible to hide his physical malfunction—his chest was rising and falling rapidly.

Grasping at straws, Sangwoo began to recite the national anthem in his head. But Jaeyoung appeared oblivious to his struggles.

"Listen *very* closely," the asshole said in a serious tone. "I don't care that you're a man. So you have two choices now: Let's see where this goes, or I'm dumping the damn game and we can go our separate ways. Those are your only options."

"See where what goes?"

"What the hell do you think?" Jaeyoung asked. The streetlight cast warmth onto his cheeks, and his eyes seemed a shade lighter under the orange glow.

Jaeyoung's words felt like they were in a code to which Sangwoo only had half a key. He had a good guess as to why the other man was so angry and to what he was proposing, but he needed to be sure.

"Basically, you're suggesting that we keep doing...those things," Sangwoo said. His words came out even more flatly than Jaeyoung's, and it didn't help that his voice was so hoarse.

"'Those things'? Care to elaborate?"

"You want the two of us to act like we're in a relationship even though we're both men for the sake of relieving our sexual desires. You want us to hold hands, kiss, and...fornicate."

"'*Act like* we're in a relationship'? Sangwoo, I swear..."

His brow furrowing in irritation, Jaeyoung squeezed Sangwoo's wrists even tighter. A shadow fell across Sangwoo's eyes when he leaned closer.

"Let me ask you something. What's your definition of a relationship?"

"A relationship is when a man and woman engage in a romantic courtship with the goal of eventually getting married. By doing this, you're basically utilizing a trial version of the existing official software."

"And two guys can't do that?"

"I would think the answer to that is obvious."

Without warning, Jaeyoung released Sangwoo's wrists and took a few steps back before sinking down on the ground, blinking in disbelief. The streetlight bathed his skin in a glowing sea of orange.

"Wait there. I need to think," he muttered. "And don't you *dare* try running off again."

After tossing his gum into a nearby trash can, Jaeyoung pulled a pack of cigarettes from his pocket and slipped one between his lips. A small spark flared in the darkness as he lit it, and a thin trail of smoke rose into the sky.

As Jaeyoung's cheeks puffed out, then deflated, Sangwoo sat up and put some distance between himself and the other man. Settling himself onto the ground as well, he bent his knees partway to his chest.

Jaeyoung didn't say a word the entire time he smoked his cigarette. Once he finished it, he stubbed it out with his heel and ran both his hands over his face.

Sangwoo waited patiently, unsure how much time had passed—he had no way of telling without checking his watch, but it felt like it had been a while.

And then, finally, their eyes met.

"Maybe it's easier this way," Jaeyoung muttered coldly, seemingly to himself. "Sure, let's call it sexual desire if that's the only way you can understand it." He motioned for Sangwoo to come closer.

Sangwoo tensed, slightly unsettled by the emotionless mask that had settled over Jaeyoung's face.

"Get over here, or you'll really piss me off."

Inch by inch, Sangwoo crawled toward Jaeyoung on his knees. The psycho simply stared at him impassively, beckoning him closer again and again. Forward, forward, forward…

Sangwoo continued until they were about a desk's width apart, then stopped. "What?"

The word had barely left his mouth when Jaeyoung raised himself to his knees and scooted closer, snatching Sangwoo's hand off the ground and lacing their fingers together. It happened so fast that there was no avoiding him—Sangwoo simply froze into a statue.

"We're holding hands now...," Jaeyoung muttered, reaching out his other hand to cup Sangwoo's cheek. His thumb slowly brushed over Sangwoo's lips. "And we've already kissed."

Shuddering instinctively, Sangwoo tried to lean back, but Jaeyoung quickly pulled him closer to his chest by the neck.

"Now...we just have to fornicate, right?" Jaeyoung whispered in Sangwoo's ear.

Goose bumps immediately ran down the younger man's arms.

Jaeyoung leaned in even closer until his forehead made contact with Sangwoo's hat. Slowly, the rim was pushed up and back until the piece of headwear came loose and fell to the ground.

As Jaeyoung's light brown eyes gazed into his, Sangwoo struggled to decipher some kind of thought, intent, or emotion in them...but it was impossible. He couldn't tell if Jaeyoung was being sarcastic or genuine. To make things even worse, he couldn't process anything that was happening—not with his heart threatening to burst through his chest and his skin's temperature regulation system malfunctioning.

Struggling to compose himself, Sangwoo managed to say, "I have two questions."

Jaeyoung jerked his chin up slightly, signaling him he was allowed to continue.

"First question: Given that men cannot engage in fornication, I'm not quite sure how you plan for us to relieve our sexual desi—"

"They can."

"S-sorry? How... I mean, where... What...?"

"Don't worry about it. I'll take care of it once we get there."

"How can you be so confident without even try—"

"I have prior experience," Jaeyoung interrupted, finally breaking his intense stare to awkwardly scratch at his neck. "Next question."

Sangwoo hadn't really gotten a solid answer to his first inquiry, but he quietly filed away the new information and planned to do additional research on how things worked at a later date.

"Second question: What is the benefit of forming such an irrational relationship?"

"All right. Imagine yourself as a general in the Qing dynasty," Jaeyoung whispered in a low voice, squeezing Sangwoo's hand even harder. "The enemy is besieging your castle. Soon, they're gonna shoot arrows over the walls, cut off your water supply, and all that jazz… At that point, you have two options." He extended his index finger. "One: Just ignore them and wait until they leave…"

Sangwoo stayed silent—he had a good idea of what Jaeyoung was trying to say.

Jaeyoung held up another finger. "Two: Ditch the castle and go beat the shit out of them. Which one sounds better to you?"

Still, Sangwoo didn't say anything.

"Think about it. The most efficient way to solve a problem is by eliminating the root cause. At least, I figured you might relate to that…"

Nodding wordlessly, Sangwoo recalled a memory from his time as a corporal—his unit's living space had been infested with bees, so he'd had to suit up in CBRN safety gear and remove the beehive himself.

Jaeyoung poked him right above the heart with a single finger. "See? That's the only way to curb your 'abnormal' desires. Don't try to run from them or ignore them. How about we see how things feel and where we end up? Who knows? Maybe that'll get rid of these annoying emotions."

It was a convincing argument. And this way, Sangwoo would be able to continue *Veggie Venturer* as well. That being said, he honestly didn't get how he'd wound up agreeing with Jaeyoung—after all, the suggestions didn't align with his values at all. The vast majority of people online seemed to agree that having friends with benefits for the sole purpose of satisfying one's sexual desires was unethical. Rejecting the offer would be the right thing to do as a civilized human being, no matter how much he wanted to engage in sexual activity…but Jaeyoung had a good point.

Sweat beaded on Sangwoo's palm where his skin pressed against Jaeyoung's. An irrational urge was building inside him to not let the hand go. Rather, he wanted to see, touch, kiss…and maybe take things further.

No matter how much Sangwoo tried to push the thoughts away, desire clung to his mind. But was indulging himself really the only way to rid himself of these impulses? Unfortunately, he lacked the resources to reach a proper conclusion, as he'd never even considered the question before.

Finally, Sangwoo spoke. "To begin with, let go of me."

Pushing Jaeyoung back with one hand as he reclaimed the other, Sangwoo scooted backward. The psycho's proposal was a tempting one, to be sure, but he wasn't the type to make important decisions on a whim.

Picking up his hat and putting it back on, he added, "I need some time to review your offer."

"How much time?"

"Two weeks."

"Seriously? I'm on a tight schedule here."

"I'm aware. In fact, if you take a look at what we have planned for the next two weeks, you'll see we don't have any meetings scheduled due to midterms. I'll use that period to think things over. In the meantime, please proceed with the tasks outlined in the schedule. All files should be uploaded to the cloud drive by Friday, April 26th."

"Seriously? You're doing this now?"

Ignoring the comment, Sangwoo rose to his feet. He could still feel his hand throbbing from Jaeyoung's tight grip. As he brushed past Jaeyoung, he heard the other man call his name.

"Sangwoo Choo."

"What?"

"Why do you always have to make things so hard, huh?"

"I have no clue what you're talking about. I'll see you at the next meeting."

"Meeting, my ass…"

As Sangwoo finally walked into his apartment building, he could feel an excessive amount of adrenaline coursing through his veins.

`return 0;`

Exams rarely prompted Sangwoo to change up his routine—his study sessions became slightly longer, but that was about it. He felt no need to cram at the very last minute, since he reviewed lecture materials every single day. To be fair, he was going to have to put in a bit more effort this particular time, since he'd missed the majority of his lectures at the beginning of the semester. But even that wasn't going to give him much trouble, since he'd been diligent about catching up after Jaeyoung had dropped out at the two-week mark. In fact, Sangwoo had so much free time on his hands that he'd even been able to test out his completed resources in *Veggie Venturer*'s game engine occasionally. The only difference was that he didn't have his meetings with Jaeyoung.

On Wednesday, Jihye had suggested that they meet up over the weekend to study for Pop Culture and Cultural Theory together. Sangwoo had taken her up on the offer, hoping that Jihye's presence would turn out to be useful—the class *was* one of his weakest links, after all.

He didn't work during midterms, so they'd met that Saturday at a café Jihye had picked out. The meeting had turned out to be very productive, to Sangwoo's satisfaction. They'd traded explanations back and forth on various theories, and then quizzed each other on them, making sure to review topics they were shaky on.

When exam week had arrived, it flew by. Most of Sangwoo's exams were written, but he'd had to do an oral exam for Intermediate Chinese, and some of his professors assigned projects instead. Thankfully, he didn't have much trouble with any of them. He'd always been at the top of his class, even when he was taking seven or eight lectures in the same semester—five was a piece of cake.

"That was pretty hard," Jihye said with a loud sigh as they walked out of the Pop Culture and Cultural Theory classroom after the exam. "Question fifteen really killed me! How are we supposed to know the cities where every single one of the theories originated? That's insanely hyperspecific! It's like the professor was trying to screw us over."

"I thought question twenty-two was difficult."

"Really? That was the short answer where you had to criticize postmodernism from Adorno's perspective, right? Hmm… That's weird. You had both those theories down when we were studying together."

They continued to thoroughly review the exam questions together as they ate in the dining hall. It turned out that Jihye cared a great deal about performing well on her exams, which made sense, considering how hard she worked in school.

"Honestly, it kinda sounds like you did much better on the exam than I did. You might've gotten all the questions right aside from number twenty-two."

"Perhaps."

"This is *sooo* unfair. I'm the one who explained those theories to you!"

"It's unreasonable to expect me to perform poorly on purpose simply because you helped me."

Jihye pouted silently. Her frustration and disappointment were valid—it probably stung to know she had performed worse than someone who didn't understand the subject as well as she did. Sangwoo figured it might improve her mood to say something kind to her for once—humans were emotional creatures, as a certain *someone* kept reminding him.

"Memorization has always been my strong suit," he said, "but I don't think I would have managed to understand the concepts if you hadn't helped out."

"Really? You mean that?"

Why is she trying to extract the same compliment from me twice? Sangwoo wondered. Ignoring her, he silently finished his food.

Once he was done eating, Sangwoo put his tray away and headed to the convenience store, planning on grabbing some coffee. Jihye followed him, unasked, as per usual. She snatched the Black Holic from him and paid for it before he could say anything.

"So, I think I can ask for a favor. I helped you ace the exam, and now I even got you coffee!"

"That was a trap, then?"

"I guess…? Anyway, come on, please? You owe me!"

The words might've sounded threatening from anyone else, but Jihye's bright smile took the teeth out of them. Sangwoo tried to guess what she might want from him, but his imagination only produced generic hypotheses like a nice meal or helping her carry heavy things. Though honestly, if either one of those options was the case, he wouldn't mind complying with her wishes.

"Tell me what the favor is first."

"Do you have any plans for the school festival?"

Sangwoo frowned, caught off guard. The word "festival" failed to elicit any kind of positive emotion within him. For one, he'd never participated in one before. Since classes were usually canceled during the festival week, he typically took advantage of the free time to do something *actually* productive.

"I'll be working."

"Oh...I see. Well, you can take a day off, right? I went out of my way to help you study, you know..."

"But why do you want me to do that?"

"Because I want you to hang out at the festival with me! Would Monday work?"

"But why do you want me to—"

"I don't have any friends to enjoy the festival with!"

"Why do you need a friend for that?"

Jihye rolled her eyes. "Cut it out. That's what I'm asking for, so please say yes."

Turning her down didn't seem to be an option. It *was* true that Jihye had been very helpful to him, and he'd look like a complete jerk if he hypothetically slammed the door in her face after giving her a rare compliment.

"Fine," he said sullenly.

Jihye beamed and made him promise to meet her at the campus front gates at eleven on Monday.

return 0;

The end of exam week had finally arrived. The results had already come out, and they were exactly what Sangwoo had anticipated—the only anomaly being that his grade in Pop Culture and Cultural Theory would be much higher than he'd thought it would be.

After eating lunch at the dining hall, Sangwoo bought a can of coffee and took a walk along his usual path. His steps were brisk with excitement. The past two weeks had been hectic, but the absence of a particular individual had been painfully noticeable. In the past, he'd made tons of stupid mistakes and lost his ability to concentrate due to the asshole's absence. This time, though, he'd found it much more bearable, probably because he knew exactly when he would see him again. The folder on his desktop, simply named "Jaeyoung Jang," had helped as well.

"Don't try to run from them or ignore them. How about we see how things feel and where we end up? Who knows? Maybe that'll get rid of these annoying emotions."

Sangwoo had been running an experiment during the exam period to test two different solutions to the problem at hand. If the desire he felt in Jaeyoung's presence was only a temporary malfunction, then it should have fizzled out over the past two weeks. If it resurfaced when he saw Jaeyoung next, he'd have no choice but to confront the issue head-on and eliminate the root cause.

For as long as he could remember, Sangwoo had avoided uncertainty like the plague, but as Jaeyoung had pointed out, there was no running from it this time. All he could do was wait and see what would emerge from all the uncertainty and confusion.

Now that the exam period had wrapped, so had Sangwoo's experiment. Over the past two weeks, he had carefully observed his own state with the objectivity of a scientist, making sure to keep his emotions from influencing his rational side. The results were irrefutable—the enemies outside his castle had only grown in number and become more aggressive upon being ignored. He found himself longing for everything related to Jaeyoung, even if he'd hated it in the beginning. His face, voice, little gestures, facial expressions, his crude speech, the way he smelled… An intense craving burned through Sangwoo, one that couldn't be satisfied even by looking at Jaeyoung's pictures and videos every day or listening to a playlist filled with Jaeyoung's favorite songs before bed. The desire inside him had multiplied like a virus left unchecked, infecting his mind from the inside out.

Now, he only had one option remaining of the two Jaeyoung had offered him. It was easy enough to make up his mind, despite there being a couple of days left until their agreed-upon deadline.

Sangwoo headed into the studio like a general going to war. There, he only found the design major who was in his year despite being two years older.

"Uh… Jaeyoung isn't here," she said.

To Sangwoo's eyes, the woman's obnoxious fur jacket made her look like a poacher. When he glanced over at her, she flinched visibly and turned down her music. Her speaker was surrounded by a pile of tangled cords—after a few seconds, Sangwoo could identify a keyboard, mouse, monitor, and external drive hookup along with chargers for a tablet and a phone mixed with two different USB jacks and a four-way power strip. Sangwoo felt a part of him dying inside at the sight.

The poacher tried to press some buttons on the speaker but ended up knocking it over. "I don't know why they make the cords on these things so short nowadays," she muttered sheepishly.

Sangwoo blinked at her. This was the first time he'd been so completely flabbergasted that he genuinely couldn't think of anything to say.

Deciding it would be better not to engage further, he claimed his typical empty seat and waited. Eyes drifting over to Jaeyoung's perpetually messy desk, he silently began to gather up all the trash and throw it away. When he was done, he then put a pack of cigarettes, lip balm, an umbrella cover, earphones, and a lighter in the desk drawer.

There was also a notebook with a familiar cover inside, which brought Sangwoo to a stop before he slid the drawer shut. It was the one Jaeyoung had forcibly "bought" from him a while ago—the same kind Sangwoo had been buying over and over again for the past few years. On that day, Jaeyoung had drawn a picture of him, and Sangwoo had ripped it into small pieces.

That had been during the first week of the semester—six whole weeks ago. At the time, Jaeyoung had been following Sangwoo around like a stalker, harassing him like it was his job to do so.

Sangwoo began to flip through the notebook, a strange sense of nostalgia stirring inside him. The last time he'd seen these pages, they'd been blank, but now they were filled with doodles. A few of them depicted cars and guns, but the rest were of humanoid figures. In fact, they seemed to be drawings of the same person—a guy with slanted eyes, absurdly deep dark circles, and a black baseball cap. The figure's face was nearly twice the size of its thin, twig-like body.

A few more turns of the page revealed a series of comic strips titled *How to Kill S.W.C. When did he draw this garbage?* Sangwoo wondered, flipping through episode after episode. In each one, a crude, bobble-headed replica of Sangwoo himself died in some grotesque way—getting cut in two, ground into powder, filled up with air until he popped like an overfilled balloon, or—strangely—shriveling up and wasting away after getting his hat stolen.

Despite the subject matter, Jaeyoung had somehow managed to make it look so comical that Sangwoo found himself snickering. He paused when he reached the very last page, where the art style underwent a sudden shift. The sketch was a side profile of a man wearing a black hat.

Is that supposed to be me?

The man depicted on the page was so incredibly handsome—well, maybe *pretty* was the right word—that he could probably be a celebrity if he wanted to. His lashes were long and full, complementing his straight nose bridge and soft smile. It also seemed a lot of energy had been put into drawing his neck; beyond the incredibly detailed shading, Jaeyoung had made sure to include protruding tendons, the muscles that swept from neck to shoulder, and even a mole near his neckline.

Sangwoo quickly glanced down at his shoulder, realizing for the first time in his life that he did, in fact, have a mole there.

"Hey! Does Jaeyoung even know you're here? Why don't you try calling him instead of sitting around?" the poacher suggested loudly.

Suddenly feeling like a thief, Sangwoo shoved the notebook back in Jaeyoung's drawer and closed it. "I can afford to wait a bit longer. I don't have anything else scheduled for today."

"Okay, but what if he never shows up…? You know what? *I'll* call him for you. Trust me, I'm doing this for my sake, not yours."

"If that's what you want, I have no objections."

Exhaling loudly, the poacher grabbed her phone, tapped on the screen, and put the call on speaker. The dial tone rang loudly in the silence of the room.

Riiing... Riiing... Riiing...

The tension grew every time the tone repeated itself, but Jaeyoung never picked up. Immediately, the poacher called him again, but the call only went to voicemail.

"That asshole!" the poacher snarled. "Seriously? He better pick up!"

She called Jaeyoung a few more times in rapid succession, but she never got past the voicemail prompt.

"Okay, he's definitely being a lazy ass and ignoring my calls. Let me try calling with yours."

Nodding, Sangwoo dialed Jaeyoung's number and handed his cell over to the poacher, who put the call on speaker again.

Riiing... Riiing... Riii—

"Hello?"

"What the hell? Why didn't you pick up when I phoned you?" the poacher snapped.

"Are you with Sangwoo?"

The poacher glared at the phone. "Where are you?"

"Home. Are you with Sangwoo?"

"Look, this guy has been sitting in the studio for ages, staring around with this super judgmental look on his face. Come fetch him before I throw myself out the window, okay? Drive, don't walk!"

Sangwoo heard Jaeyoung's low sigh.

"Fine."

Then he hung up.

"I swear to God, he never takes me seriously," the poacher grumbled. "Now I know he's always ignoring my calls on purpose."

She seethed for a few more seconds, then handed Sangwoo his phone back. After slipping it into his backpack, he took out his textbook.

There was a brief, awkward silence. "Um... Hey, Sangchoo Choo."

"Please make an effort to say my name correctly," he replied flatly. It was the tenth time he'd made the request since meeting the poacher.

Sangwoo scoured his mind for the woman's name, but it seemed it had never been recorded in his memory. Thankfully, he was saved by the gold necklace around her neck, which spelled out "Yuna Choi."

"How would you feel if I called you 'Yuchoi Choi'?"

"I wouldn't care, honestly."

"All right, then. From now on, I'll refer to you as such."

This time, the poacher didn't respond, giving Sangwoo an uncomfortable glance instead. Sangwoo understood the sentiment—after all, he'd only ever bickered with her since he'd started regularly visiting the studio. And anyway, he didn't exactly feel the need to be friends with someone who seemed so wild and stubborn…

Suddenly, the poacher asked, "Did you two have a fight or something? You haven't been here in a while, and Jaeyoung's been acting *weird…*"

"There's no need to break the silence with pointless chatter, you know. Pretend I'm not here and get to work, Yuchoi Choi."

"I'm just curious, that's all! I bet you had an argument. What was it about?"

"There was no argument," Sangwoo shot back. "And even if there was, it would be none of your business, Yuchoi Choi."

There was no reason for him to elaborate. After all, he wouldn't exactly benefit from telling the poacher that he and Jaeyoung—a pair of men—had gone out for drinks, kissed, and then ended up disagreeing on where to take their relationship next.

His gaze drifted back to the poacher's desk and her pile of hopelessly tangled cords. He felt a flare of irritation—somehow, the sight seemed to be a reflection of his own life. Rising to his feet, he marched over to her desk with a sense of purpose. The poacher looked up at him in confusion.

"Go and take a break if you're not planning on doing any work," he said, waving her away.

Once she'd hesitantly stood from her seat, he quickly saved all twelve of the programs that had been running on her computer and turned off the desktop, speaker, and monitor. He also found the power button on a strange machine that appeared to be some sort of heated tongs, turned it off, and did the same to a second large, mysterious machine underneath her desk. Then he got to work on the cords.

First, Sangwoo unplugged the external hard drive, folded its cord at regular intervals, and put it into its case. As for the connectors for the tongs-like machine and the tablet and phone chargers, he carefully coiled the cords and placed them in the desk's drawer. Then he unplugged the mouse, keyboard, and speaker, pushed them to the side for the time being, and untangled the cords belonging to the monitor and PC tower so he could plug them back in neatly. The four-socket power strip went behind the monitor.

Once he'd organized all of the other devices so their cords wouldn't be tangled, the desk looked much tidier. Sangwoo smiled in satisfaction as he grabbed a rubber band from the desk and tied the cords together neatly. The connector for the speaker was not, in fact, as short as the poacher had intimated—in this case, the fault lay with the user. In Sangwoo's opinion, humans mistreated machines way too frequently.

The poacher whistled under her breath. "Dang… You should apply to be in one of those TV programs for people with weird talents."

"Try to keep the cords organized," he said, ignoring her comment. "Your desk was only cluttered because you kept so many machines plugged in despite not using them."

"But…I *do* use them."

"Feel free to maintain your dismal lifestyle, then."

The door suddenly opened in the middle of this exchange, and Jaeyoung strode into the room, kicking the door shut behind him. He wore a white sweatshirt with the logo of a baseball team embroidered on the chest and a pair of black pants. Without acknowledging Sangwoo, he brushed past him and plopped down in his chair.

"There you are. The Incarnation of Desire," he said to Sangwoo mockingly.

The poacher burst out laughing. "What the heck is that supposed to mean?" she asked.

"Dunno. Ask him yourself," Jaeyoung responded without even looking at her, staring at his phone instead.

Sangwoo gazed at him silently, but the psycho's eyes remained fixated on the screen. His side profile was cold and emotionless.

After a moment, the poacher chuckled awkwardly. "Hey… We're all friends here. Let's apologize and move on, yeah?"

"Don't worry, we didn't have an argument. It's a lot more complicated than that," Jaeyoung said, crossing his legs and peering at his nails. "Why are you here, anyway?" he added, addressing Sangwoo now. "If you want the final products, you're shit outta luck. I've been slacking off this whole time. What should I do now? Want me to beg for forgiveness?"

"No," Sangwoo responded. "I said I would consider your proposal and present my decision the day after tomorrow, if you recall."

"Yeah."

"Well, I would like to move the deadline to today."

Jaeyoung narrowed his eyes, then glanced at the back of the poacher's head. "Hey. Almost time for your smoke break, isn't it?"

She turned to him in surprise. "Huh? Are you kicking me out?"

"Ten minutes."

"It's not like you own the freaking place," she muttered.

For a moment, Sangwoo thought she would vehemently protest Jaeyoung's unjust order, but she quickly gathered up her phone and wallet even as she grumbled under her breath.

"I'll be back in ten, okay? You two better have made up by then. I'm tired of tiptoeing around you."

With that, she walked backward out of the room, pointing an accusing finger at them the whole time.

The door slammed shut, leaving Sangwoo and Jaeyoung alone in the studio. For a long moment, neither one of them spoke. Jaeyoung slipped his phone back into his pocket and stared at Sangwoo unblinkingly, his eyes devoid of their usual playfulness. Sangwoo, meanwhile, was silently taking note of the inevitable hormonal reaction happening within his body as a result of seeing Jaeyoung for the first time in two whole weeks.

Finally, Sangwoo said impassively, "I accept your proposal. It seems to be based on rational reasoning, and it would be preferable to go into such a venture with someone who is experienced like you. We can start next Monday."

It was Sangwoo's way of declaring war on the pure, unadulterated sexual desire that only seemed to serve as a distraction to his daily life. He would hunt it down with a spear like some kind of barbarian hunting for sustenance.

Jaeyoung's face remained completely emotionless as he listened. Then he said, "I want to review exactly what my proposal consisted of."

"As I understood it, the two of us will give each other the privilege to perform actions that are typically only acceptable to those within the bounds of a relationship."

"To relieve our sexual desires, right?"

"Correct."

"So we'd be…friends with benefits?"

"Correct."

Jaeyoung scoffed in disbelief. "You've gotta be kidding me…"

Though his reasoning was difficult for Sangwoo to comprehend, Jaeyoung seemed to be acting like it was Sangwoo who was at fault for their current situation. But it was Jaeyoung who'd made the immoral proposal in the first place.

The psycho heaved a long sigh. "If I'm being honest, I was preparing myself for a rejection. Like, I don't even know what to say," he muttered. "Looking forward to it, I guess…?"

"Yes. I'll be in touch," Sangwoo said with a nod. He began to rise to his feet, but froze when Jaeyoung called out to him.

"Wait."

When Sangwoo glanced over, he found Jaeyoung staring at him with a face like a statue—completely impassive. When he spoke again, his tone was flat and dry.

"Why start Monday? You gotta prepare yourself or something?"

"That's right. I also need to do some research."

"What research?"

"I would rather keep that to myself."

Jaeyoung's mouth fell open slightly as an unreadable look flashed across his face. Finally, he said, "Yeah, got it. So, we'll grab a room at a motel on Monday, then…?"

"Yes. That's what we agreed to."

Drawing in such a deep breath that his cheeks puffed up, Jaeyoung tilted his head back and let out a long sigh. He ran a hand roughly over his face. "Fine. You sure you don't wanna *do* anything today? I'm sure you're pent up after two whole weeks of no contact."

Sangwoo stiffened. "Of course we can't…do *it* today. I haven't had the chance to prepare."

"That's not what I'm talking about," Jaeyoung said, pressing on.

The other man had a habit of beating around the bush whenever he broached a topic, which meant Sangwoo ended up having to spend much more energy than was necessary on processing the given information. Thankfully, it didn't take him long to decipher what Jaeyoung was getting at.

"We already did that at the bar the Saturday before last."

"So? Doing it again wouldn't hurt, right?"

He has a point. After a brief pause, Sangwoo extended a knee and hooked the tip of his shoe under one of the wheeled legs of Jaeyoung's office chair. After a subtle tug, it rolled closer, colliding with Sangwoo's own chair like they were playing a game of bumper cars.

Jaeyoung's chair tilted back slightly from the impact, but Sangwoo quickly steadied it and looked up into Jaeyoung's face. Right in front of him, mere inches away, the senior stared at him with dilated eyes.

Desire surged through Sangwoo's stomach, hot and wild. "I'm going to kiss you now," he announced. "Would you like me to lock the door beforehand?"

"Go for it."

Sangwoo immediately rose to his feet and walked over to the door, locking it with a click. When he turned back around, he found Jaeyoung standing only inches away from him.

"When did you—"

But he never got the chance to finish his sentence. Jaeyoung's hands shot up to cup his cheeks, and their lips pressed together. The world seemed to spin. Sangwoo let his eyes slip shut, savoring the taste of vanilla on Jaeyoung's lips. How could someone's saliva taste so sweet?

All semblance of logical thought slipped from Sangwoo's mind, swept away by a raging hurricane. As lightning crashed and thunder boomed, he was left in total disarray—but his tongue moved of its own accord, exploring Jaeyoung's mouth with an intensity that mirrored the overwhelming surge of emotion flooding him.

It was as if Jaeyoung had placed some kind of spell on him, throwing his feelings completely off course. The only thing in his mind was the urge to devour the man he was kissing, to stake his claim on him. Whether this strange desire was something he wanted to preserve was not something Sangwoo could decide in this particular moment. He just felt the heat of it rushing through him, setting every nerve alight.

After what felt like forever, Sangwoo shoved Jaeyoung away with both hands, his lungs screaming for air. He hunched over slightly like he had run a marathon, panting and wiping his lips with the back of his hand.

Jaeyoung stared at him, his brow furrowed slightly. "Damn," he said, his voice a low, husky whisper. "I didn't take you for such a wild kisser."

Sangwoo immediately felt another surge of desire, followed by crushing regret. His condition hadn't improved in the slightest—in fact, it had worsened even further. He stood there, his breathing coming out in ragged gasps, grappling with how he was supposed to quell the fire raging inside him.

Wait until Monday, he told himself. *After that, I won't have to deal with this anymore.*

For a moment, they stood there in silence, Jaeyoung studying Sangwoo's face with a quiet, intense focus.

"Sometimes, I can't tell if you're an idiot or a genius," the psycho said abruptly.

"I have no idea what you're talking about," Sangwoo responded curtly. "Bye."

Rushing back to his seat, he slung his backpack across his shoulders and left the studio without another word, afraid he'd do something completely rash if he stayed for any longer.

`return 0;`

Sangwoo had witnessed the madhouse his campus became during its annual festival in the past, so he was prepared for what he saw: a jumble of tacky events, ugly banners fluttering in the wind, tents in every color, and students wearing monstrous costumes. Loud shouting, accompanied by music, blared throughout the space. Basically, it was a house of horrors made entirely for Sangwoo's five senses.

"This is sooo cool, right?!"

Sangwoo's assessment of Jihye was usually positive. After all, she had proven herself to be an incredibly logical student with a flexible way of thinking. However, she wasn't acting like herself as she walked through the festival. Instead, her eyes were wide with joy and wonder as she exclaimed things like "That looks delicious!" or "Whoaaa, awesome!"

The two of them had met at exactly 11:00 AM as she'd requested and watched a performance put on by the magic club where the members had tried to convince the audience they could escape the laws of physics. At 12:02 PM, Jihye had dragged him over to a tarot café where he'd eaten a sandwich while trying to tune out the ramblings of students trying to derive meaning from illustrations.

Next had been the school band's obnoxiously loud performance at 12:42 PM, to which he sorely regretted not bringing a set of earplugs. Then they'd sat at the comic club's booth and flipped through grimy, used comic books while sipping on drinks from 01:13 PM to 03:43 PM. By the time they left the booth, Jihye's eyes were swollen and red from crying.

"I can't believe Aran died from leukemia," she said tearfully. "That's so depressing! Also, isn't it *crazy* that she turned out to be half-siblings with Huihyeol?"

"Why are you crying over a fictional character?"

"Because it's *sad*! Which one did you read?"

"*Seonhee and Jaeyoung*."

"Oh, nice. Did you like it?"

"No."

It had been the most boring plot that he'd ever had to suffer through. The only reason he'd flipped through it was because a particular name had repeatedly appeared in the speech bubbles.

Jihye insisted on getting a picture of the two of them together as they took a brief stroll through campus. Apparently, she kept a photo journal to help with her terrible memory. Sangwoo obediently stood beside her as she snapped a selfie.

Once they continued walking, he noticed a colorful poster on the wall and came to a stop.

Join the Arcade Game Competition! Hosted by the Retro Gamers' Club!!!

The word "game" had jumped out at him first, but he found his interest further piqued as he scanned the rest of the poster—one of the prizes was a discontinued game console that he'd unsuccessfully tried to purchase in the past.

Jihye gasped. "Wanna try it? Look, you can win that mechanical keyboard! I think that's the same one I was thinking about buying!"

"That's true."

Quickly, Sangwoo weighed the benefits of entering the competition. If they participated and won, they'd both get something they wanted. It seemed like a rewarding activity, unlike the dull, pointless ones Jihye had dragged him to over the past few hours.

He nodded, and they made their way to the engineering building, where the competition was being held. A large crowd had already gathered in the area. It seemed the participants could choose to compete in either *Tetrus*, *Bubble Bubble*, *Tekkin Tag*, or *Metal Snail*. Before entering the competition, Sangwoo and Jihye quickly discussed their strategies.

"You're trying to win the SMES-CX, right?" she said.

"Yes, the prize you get from winning *Tetrus*."

She brushed back her hair in an odd way and smiled confidently. "I'll get you that console. Don't you worry."

According to Jihye, she'd been pretty good at *Tetrus* back when she was a kid. She'd been the undisputed champion in her elementary school, and her skills had achieved near godly status after beating adults left and right. Sangwoo had to admit he didn't find the tale entirely trustworthy, but he agreed to her proposal because he wasn't confident in his own *Tetrus* skills.

"Let's see… The keyboard is the prize for *Tekkin Tag*," Jihye said thoughtfully. "Have you played that game before? I haven't."

"Sure, I can enter that one."

It had been a long time since he'd last played *Tekkin Tag*, but Sangwoo knew he could do well—he'd spent countless hours playing the game in neighborhood arcades when he was a kid. The mechanics of fighting games were fairly simple, and besides, the competition was small in scale. If he picked a character and memorized their combos ahead of time, he figured he could probably wipe the floor with the other students.

Sangwoo and Jihye glanced at each other, sharing a brief moment of camaraderie.

"I win the console, you win the keyboard, and we exchange prizes!" she declared, eyes blazing with determination.

"Sounds good!"

After submitting their registration forms, Sangwoo and Jihye sat on the staircase by the venue for a few minutes, waiting for an open spot. There were around fifty students participating, and most of them were playing *Tekkin Tag*. A spot opened up in the *Tetrus* section first, and Jihye sprang to her feet, cracking her neck with the air of a winner. She looked at Sangwoo with a cocky smile.

"I'll be back with your console."

Her heels clicked against the ground as she walked over and settled into a low folding chair. For *Tetrus*, the goal seemed to be aiming to get the highest overall score instead of going head-to-head with anyone.

Jihye picked the hardest difficulty, so more than half her screen was already filled with obstacles when she started, and the blocks started falling at lightning speed. A catchy rhythm started blaring from the machine as Sangwoo watched her hands fly across the controls.

It quickly became obvious that Jihye's hand-eye coordination, judgment, and controller skills were simply exceptional. Every single block fell in the perfect spot near instantly, and she was incredibly precise in how she moved and rotated them. Sangwoo felt a rush of satisfaction deep within his heart every time a long, straight piece cleared four lines of tightly stacked blocks.

Jihye finally threw in the towel after lasting a solid fourteen minutes, when the blocks started raining down so fast that Sangwoo couldn't see them. When she walked back to him, she was beaming.

"Told you I'd win!"

There was no question that she had crushed her competitors, scoring one hundred thousand more points than the student in second place. The console would definitely fall into her hands.

"Good work!" Sangwoo said with a nod. He bestowed her with a crisp high five when she reached out.

Jihye's face lit up with a proud smile as she sat down beside him, her cheeks still flushed from the excitement. Sangwoo was still waiting for his turn, so he turned his focus to looking up two characters from *Tekkin Tag* and memorizing their combos. Finally, a seat opened up.

"Good luck!"

"I'll try my very best."

Sangwoo walked over to the *Tekkin Tag* section. Two arcade machines were set up facing each other, one for each dueling competitor. A large crowd of onlookers had gathered around them, and—unlike any of the other stations—two commentators were offering live commentary.

"All right, who's up next? Let me check the registration sheet… Another computer science major!"

"Since when did this turn into a computer science meet-up…?"

"I mean, to be fair…we're computer science majors, too."

Sangwoo examined the guy standing at the machine across from him. He was wearing a baseball cap and plaid shirt and looked to be a couple years older and in good physical shape.

"Our new challenger has picked…Ade! Did he seriously choose the worst character in the history of *Tekkin Tag* as his first pick? Maybe his hand slipped!"

"Ade and…Tristan, huh? Quite the pair, really. If there's one thing they have in common, it's that they're both unorthodox characters. If you can't use them properly, they're totally useless! All right, here we go, looks like they're starting!"

Ten seconds.

That was all the time Sangwoo needed to lay low and observe how skilled his opponent was. The guy may have already beaten five other competitors, but Sangwoo could tell that his gameplay was full of unnecessary movements, and his reaction time was noticeably slow.

"Ade goes for the low sweep!" one of the commentators roared. "He shuts down his opponent's combo and goes for a drop kick! That's a perfect wave dash…and there's the bread and butter!"

"Amazing play! This guy might be the best player we've had so far! I'm willing to bet five hundred won that his parents own an arcade!"

Beating his first opponent had been so easy that Sangwoo was tempted to yawn. After the guy stood up, scratching his head awkwardly after his defeat, another student quickly took his place—this one wore a hat as well but looked a fair bit younger than the previous challenger. Sangwoo picked the same two characters for his next match.

"Ade and Tristan again? Ooh, maybe he's trying to send a message. Like, 'I don't even need to change up my strategy to beat garbage like you.'"

"It's also possible he doesn't know how to play any other character… Oh, there it is! He parried our newcomer's attack!"

"That's it, Ade's got him! Our new challenger is looking a bit flustered! Infinite comboooo! And…he's finished! Unbelievable!"

After easily defeating his seventh opponent, Sangwoo waved at Jihye, who was cheering for him from the sidelines. The next two challengers were a total joke as well—their best strategy seemed to be pressing the buttons at random instead of coming up with a single decent combo. Eight, nine, ten… Before he knew it, he'd gone through fourteen opponents.

One of the commentators whistled. "Impressive! Looks like we've got our champion… Just ten more minutes, and he gets the prize! There's only one challenger left. Let's see if Ade and Tristan can defend the throne!"

"The final challenger has taken his seat! Hm, that's an interesting outfit… Maybe he came straight from the cosplay club? Oh, who would've guessed? This one's *not* a computer science major!"

Slightly curious, Sangwoo took a peek at his last opponent.

It was like the guy had been teleported to the festival straight from medieval Europe—he wore a red vest, a white shirt with ruffles, black dress pants, dark shoes, and had a high-collared cape draped over his shoulders. His face, however, was covered by the mask of a traditional Korean imp.

What a weirdo, Sangwoo thought absently as he selected Ade and Tristan again.

"You got this, Sangchoo!" Jihye shouted, and Sangwoo pumped his fist in the air confidently.

Suddenly, his opponent's character dashed forward and struck Sangwoo's character with a mid-range attack. Sangwoo quickly dodged to stop his character from being flung into the air, but his HP still took a huge hit.

This one might be difficult...

"Holy shit, that strike was lightning fast! Looks like our last challenger has a pretty good grip on playing Rossie!"

"Rossie is definitely one of the best characters in the game. Do you think our defending champion can win with a trash character like Ade? Let's wait and see!"

The opponent's character darted back and forth constantly, landing quick jabs on Sangwoo's. At first glance, it looked like he was shifting around too much, but he never fell into any of Sangwoo's traps. There was a quiet precision in his approach, almost as if he had a natural talent at measuring the distance between his character and his opponent's.

"Ooh, that could've been a wall splat! A good call on the defender's part!"

"The challenger just screwed up Rossie's combo! So close... He could've won the entire thing!"

"He might've messed up, but he's still crazy fast! High, high, low... Dang, his moves are totally unpredictable!"

The challenger's constant barrage of attacks made it impossible for Sangwoo to execute his combos. Realizing Ade wasn't the best character for the opponent's complex gameplay, he quickly switched to Tristan, who he could use to KO his opponent as long as he managed to get the character in the air. *The second I launch him upward, it's game over.*

"And now we have Tristaaaaan! Oh, he's immediately looking for an opening! RP4, RP4, RP4! He's really going for it… Oh, there it is! The double uppercut! He's in the air!"

"Aerial combo! Three hits, four hits… He just keeps going! Holy shit, what year is he in? Is he our underclassman?"

"Who cares? From now on, I bow to him! Oh, the challenger is flabbergasted! He's done! KO! KO!"

As soon as Rossie was taken down, Sangwoo's opponent's backup character appeared on screen. Unfortunately, Sangwoo let his guard down, his opponent unleashed a combo out of nowhere.

"Oh my, would you look at that? Looks like our challenger is really pissed now!"

"A low fake, then…bread and butter! This changes everything! Who will seize victory?"

Sangwoo's character took a heavy beating and died after taking another 30 percent of the opponent's HP. Gritting his teeth, he called on Ade again. It was time for a deathmatch.

"Our challenger is playing some impressive mind games here."

"Yes, but our defender is also flawless and precise! It's like he's hooked into the game system itself! Will he become the final champion, or will the fifteenth challenger take him down?"

Sangwoo and his opponent exchanged a few jabs and low strikes. His opponent tried to land a left uppercut combo, but Sangwoo shut it down immediately. Unfortunately, his counterattack was blocked as well. Sweat started to pool in his palms, and his nerves pulled tight as he leaned closer to the screen, every fiber of his being focused on the game.

Then, out of the corner of his eye, Sangwoo noticed his opponent bouncing his leg. There was something oddly familiar about the movement, and his gaze shifted to the knee jutting out from beneath the arcade machine.

The brief distraction nearly cost Sangwoo the match. His opponent's next move almost launched his character into the air.

A bead of cold sweat rolled down Sangwoo's back. He *knew* that leg. The way it was bouncing brought a certain someone to mind—intensely.

Suddenly, he heard a low voice. "Done with your research, huh?"

Sangwoo felt a chill race down his spine. After quickly shifting his character to the corner of the screen, out of his opponent's reach, he craned his neck to the side to peer around the machines. Despite his opponent's bizarre mask, Sangwoo could sense it—the asshole's gaze had met his.

The voice continued, "I sure hope you're prepared for Monday."

"Jae...young?" Sangwoo whispered in disbelief. "What are you... doing here?"

Tearing his gaze away, he grabbed the controller again, but his composure was shattered.

"Or does your 'research' involve gaming at a festival, hm?"

Ade was crumbling under Lilith's relentless attacks.

"I'm guessing..."

Sangwoo watched his opponent's low-hitting rage drive unfold in slow motion. It was going to be fatal—and it was far too late to dodge.

"...you're pretty damn confident in your *technique*, Sangwoo."

A mid-level kick struck Ade right in the face, reducing his HP bar by more than half.

"I'm looking forward to seeing you in action."

Lilith landed a deadly combo, and Ade collapsed to the ground.

Amid the loud roar from the spectators, the commentators shouted something, but Sangwoo could only sit there, dazed.

return 0;

"No, no, it's okay! You can have it."

"Keep it. I don't deserve it."

Sangwoo trudged along, his shoulders slumped in defeat. He was empty-handed, unlike Jihye, who held the SMES-CX. The shame was crushing—they had promised to do an exchange after winning the prizes, but he had failed dismally.

"I really don't mind," Jihye said sympathetically. "Like, I don't even know how to use this thing. It's so old."

"You can sell it on the marketplace I showed you last time."

"Why don't I sell it to you, then?"

Sangwoo perked up immediately, impressed by the novel solution—the second one she'd come up with in one day. His mind raced, quickly piecing together the optimal course of action.

"You can create a listing later this evening," he said excitedly. "I'll find it and reach out to you on the app. Make sure not to sell it to anybody else—"

"Geez, you're so silly sometimes."

Jihye burst out laughing, grabbing his shoulder for support, but he turned away slightly, letting her hand fall back to her side.

After chuckling for about a minute, she handed him the paper bag that held the console. "Here you go. Transaction complete."

"What...?"

"Take me to dinner tonight, your treat. That can be your payment."

He hesitated. "But...this console is worth more than one hundred thousand won."

"If you don't like the terms, feel free to give it back," she said, extending her hand sternly.

Sangwoo's mind began to race. His stomach turned as he recalled the text he had received the previous night.

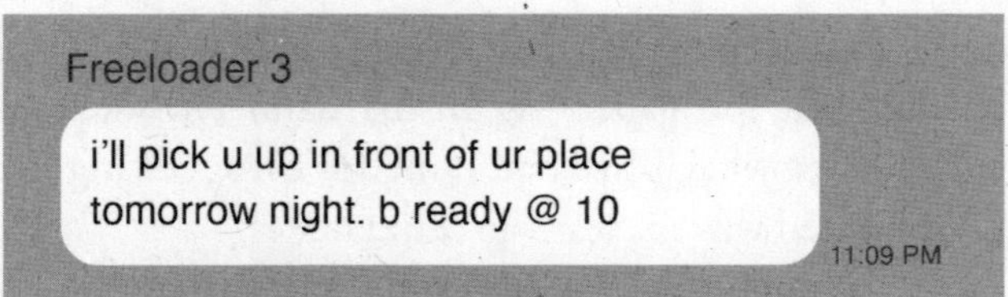

His original plan had been to leave the festival in a few minutes and head back home so he could prepare himself. But his confidence had plummeted rapidly since Friday, when he'd first learned how men were supposed to have intercourse.

Frankly, he didn't think he could do it. He'd been planning on apologizing to Jaeyoung and calling off their arrangement anyway, so...

Clutching the console to his chest, he said, "No, it's fine. We can go to dinner."

"Great!" Jihye covered her lips with one hand and chuckled mirthfully for a while, and Sangwoo shot her a strange look.

The sun had dipped well below the horizon, and the path to the humanities building was illuminated by lights in various shades as Jihye pulled Sangwoo along. Colorful ribbons decorated the area—a sight he found slightly grating—and booths lined the path, each set up by a different club: an a cappella karaoke bar, an aquarium-themed restaurant, a dog café, and even a board game stall.

Jihye, who had been walking silently, suddenly perked up like an excited puppy. "Ooh, let's go to that one!" she exclaimed, pointing to one with a long line stretching away from it.

"The Haunted Tavern," the sign read. A grim reaper and a female ghost, dressed in a traditional white Korean *hanbok* with long black hair, stood by the entrance, playfully scaring customers as they entered.

When Sangwoo and Jihye walked up to the hostess, who was dressed as an ogre from Korean folklore. She kept apologetically repeating the same line, "I'm sorry, but we're full. You'll have to wait for an hour and a half even if you put your name on the waitlist."

"Oh… That's a shame. It looks super interesting," Jihye said, frowning in disappointment.

Personally, Sangwoo wasn't particularly interested in ghosts or haunted taverns, but the paper bag in his hand felt like a weight on his conscience. After what Jihye had done for him, getting her into the restaurant she wanted was the least he could do.

"Wait here," he said, quickly pushing his way through the crowd. He slipped into the tent.

The dark, cave-like interior was filled with all sorts of creepy decorations. There were ten tables, each of them occupied. Servers darted around the tent with plates full of food, occasionally slipping into their roles to entertain the customers. Sangwoo spotted a zombie, a magician, a shaman, an angel, a demon, a vampire, and even a version of Frankenstein's monster. His eyes drifted to the vampire, who stood leaning on one leg with his arms crossed. The figure seemed strangely familiar.

Wait, could that be…? The last challenger who'd defeated him in the arcade game competition had been dressed in the exact same outfit.

Sangwoo squinted at the vampire, trying to get a better look, but then the creature suddenly spun around. Their gazes locked.

It felt like someone had whacked him in the head with a hammer. His mind whirling, Sangwoo staggered backward and ended up running into the hostess. "I'm sorry, but we're full," she said, as if reciting a prerecorded message.

"Okay. I'm leaving now," he replied quickly, turning to leave. To his dismay, he heard the vampire speak up from behind him.

"Hey, can we set up another table?"

"Huh? There's literally no more space, Jaeyoung!"

"Kick out the ones who are done eating, then."

Sangwoo rushed out of the tent and found Jihye in the crowd. "They don't have any more tables," he explained frantically. "We'll have to go somewhere else."

She gave him a dejected nod. They'd just started to walk away when the hostess ran out of the tent, glancing around until her eyes found Sangwoo.

"Excuse me! Guy with the hat!" she shouted. "You can come on in. A table opened up!"

"It's fine," he said immediately. "I saw that it was completely full. We're leaving now."

"I'd come and sit down, if I were you," the hostess said in a suddenly flat voice that made Sangwoo pause.

In that brief moment of hesitation, the Frankenstein's monster and zombie servers emerged from the tent and grabbed him by his arms. He couldn't fight back as they were too strong. They had to be student athletes of some kind.

"Right this way, sir!" Frankenstein's monster said cheerfully.

"Let me go! This is kidnapping!"

As Sangwoo flailed around, trying to free himself, Jihye stepped aside to talk with the hostess. "Wow, we got super lucky, Sangwoo!" she said with a delighted laugh.

She slipped into the tent, leaving Sangwoo with no reinforcements. He barely managed to smack Frankenstein's monster away, but his efforts were rendered useless when the zombie pushed him forward. Unfortunately, the two servers were much stronger than he was, and he was dragged helplessly into the tent.

The vampire stood there, staring at Sangwoo and Jihye with an irritated scowl. "Welcome in," he bit out. His hair was slicked back with wax, revealing his flawless forehead. Dark eyeliner accentuated his eyes, and his face was covered with a layer of pale foundation. Fake blood dripped from his lips.

Despite the creepy makeup, Jaeyoung somehow still managed to look incredible, standing out like a swan among crows compared to the other costumed servers. Even as he stood in front of Sangwoo, students lingered nearby, waiting to take a picture with him.

"Good to see you, Jaeyoung!" Jihye exclaimed.

Jaeyoung smiled. "Long time no see, Jihye. I'll have to throw in some dishes on the house for you."

"Really? Thank you so much! By the way, your costume and makeup look *amazing*! You could've stepped off the set of *Dracula*!"

Her comment was met with a careless nod. "I see you two are…on a date?" Jaeyoung said, the last word rising in question.

"Oh, no! No way!" Jihye chuckled awkwardly. "Sangchoo is treating me to dinner because he owes me something."

"I see. I hope you two have a good time."

Jaeyoung walked away without another word.

Despite not having eaten anything in the past few hours, Sangwoo felt like he was about to throw up. In contrast, Jihye seemed to be in a pretty good mood.

"Wow, these decorations are amazing! The drama club always goes all out. I love it," she said, snapping pictures of the pumpkin and bat decorations hanging from the ceiling. Then she slipped her phone back in her pocket and said in a hushed voice, "You know…I wouldn't have come in here if I'd known this was the drama club's booth."

"Why?"

At this, she glanced around like a spy, making sure nobody was listening. Then she whispered, "I don't think Jaeyoung likes me very much."

"Why?"

"Just a gut feeling, I guess."

"But…I don't see why he would dislike you."

"I know," Jihye said with a sigh. "It was really bothering me…but maybe I was imagining it, based on how he was talking to me just now. So I feel much better."

Sangwoo decided to refrain from commenting, though he was still frowning in incomprehension.

"By the way…" Jihye said in a low voice, "I need to tell you something."

She leaned over the table as if she was about to discuss something highly confidential. Sangwoo followed suit, but only because he couldn't hear her very well.

The orange glow of the candlelight cast a shimmering reflection on Jihye's dark irises. Suddenly, he realized he'd never taken such a close look at her face before. There were faint dimples on her cheeks, and—

"Abracadabra!"

A student dressed as a wizard with a lightning mark drawn on his forehead ran up to their table and interrupted the conversation by thrusting a menu between them, effectively severing their eye contact. Sangwoo returned to his original position, maintaining a straight back as he examined said menu.

The items—which included a horrifried rolled-egg omelet, a serving of primordial fish roe rice, and a bowl of spine-chilling fish cake stew—were admittedly a bit pricey, but the cost was nothing compared to the value of the console Jihye had won for him.

"You can order whatever you want, as long as it's within one hundred and thirty thousand won."

"Okay!"

Jihye pored over the menu for a bit, then settled on the rancid tempura udon. Sangwoo ordered a bowl of maddening kimchi stew along with lint ball rice.

The wizard disappeared after taking their orders, and Sangwoo turned his attention back to Jihye, only to realize she looked slightly irritated.

"What were you about to say?"

"Oh…nothing. I'll tell you later."

"All right."

Silence settled over the table. Though Sangwoo sat motionless, he was on high alert, paying close attention to everything happening in the tent. More specifically, he wanted to know what Jaeyoung was doing, who he was talking to, and what he was talking about.

Jaeyoung seemed to be roaming around, his voice popping up everywhere. One minute, he was laughing and joking with people Sangwoo didn't recognize—the next, he was taking orders and serving food. As he listened closely, Sangwoo's heart began to beat slightly faster.

Jihye's voice snapped him back to reality. "Hey, want me to tell you a funny story?"

"What…? Okay, go ahead."

"A tuna *kimbap* was walking along the street with a cheese *kimbap*, and then they ran into pickled radish, who—"

"Graaaaaaah!"

The server dressed as Frankenstein's monster shoved his head right in front of Jihye, and she shrieked, jumping a foot into the air.

"Aaaaah! Oh my God!"

She seethed for a moment after the server walked away, but didn't complain—she probably knew that eating at a haunted tavern came with some playful jumpscares. Finally, she grumbled, "The servers are a bit mean, don't you think?"

"You're the one who wanted to eat here."

"Yeah… That's true, I guess."

Their conversation fizzled out once again. For a while, Jihye sat there, fiddling with her fingers. Then, she said abruptly, "Sangwoo. I've been meaning to ask… Do you have a girlfriend?"

"No," he responded curtly. But internally, he was thinking: *What kind of question is that?*

She perked up visibly. "Really? Well, if you ever found the right person…would you consider getting into a relationship?"

No. I'm too busy with school, he was about to say. But he was rudely interrupted by a demon, who raced up to them and shouted something in a strange language, presumably some kind of curse—though Sangwoo's money was on the moment being completely improvised. The demon disappeared as quickly as she had come.

"What was that about?" Sangwoo muttered under his breath.

For a while, Jihye stayed silent. Then she said, "Let's just eat and leave."

"Sure. Whatever you want."

"Okay… It's so loud in here that I can barely hear myself think."

At first, Sangwoo thought she was overreacting a bit. As the night progressed, though, he began to empathize with her more and more. The servers seemed to deliver their dishes whenever Jihye tried to say something, and once they actually started talking, a drama club member jumped in and ruined the flow of the conversation. He figured it was a coincidence, but Jihye was right—the Haunted Tavern was not an ideal location for any conversation.

But maybe it didn't even matter. Even as Jihye tried to talk to him, his attention was on a certain someone who'd never approached their table throughout the entire dinner, not even giving Sangwoo a chance to take another look at his costume.

Meanwhile, he's letting everyone else take pictures with him, he thought petulantly. *I guess I'm nothing but a friend with benefits.*

Of course, even that label would disappear soon enough.

Sighing, he slouched against his chair. The more he tried to imagine having sexual intercourse with Jaeyoung, the more he despaired. How was he supposed to insert his penis into Jaeyoung's anus? And even aside from that, the mere idea of seeing Jaeyoung in pain like the men in the audiovisual materials he'd referenced made him balk.

As it turned out, Jaeyoung kept his word about providing dishes on the house—their table had already received three bottles of soju, a serving of dried squid, a bowl of fruit, and a rolled-egg omelet that they'd never ordered. Even Jihye, who'd been adamant about leaving the tent as soon as possible, crumbled at the enticing sight of free food and drinks.

"You handle your liquor pretty well," she remarked. The amount of soju Sangwoo was drinking was probably three times what Jihye was pouring for herself—the copious amount of stress he'd felt over the weekend was making him want to drink more than usual.

Sangwoo's mind was like a compiler with about a hundred red error codes flashing on the screen. There were so many unsettling, ambiguous emotions simmering inside him that he couldn't even begin to untangle them: a strange mix of hurt, fear, disappointment, resistance to the idea of having sexual intercourse, overwhelming anxiety, an ever-present desire, and even a feeling of defeat after losing the keyboard… If alcohol could wash the feelings away, he would drown himself in it.

The Frankenstein's monster server lumbered back to their table. "Grrrr… Soju and side dishes. Grrrrrr…"

"More? Thank you! You sure it's okay for us accept so much?"

"Grr… Foolish humans…"

"Hold on, let me take the buttered corn," Jihye said. "I don't want you to drop it." Her initial wariness of the server seemed to have vanished now that she'd gotten used to his pranks and jumpscares.

Once again, they silently helped themselves to the free food and alcohol. After a couple more glasses, Jihye's face had become visibly flushed, and she began to giggle and hum under her breath, as she swayed from side to side. Sangwoo blinked slowly, his eyelids feeling bizarrely heavy. He, too, was incredibly tipsy.

"Sangwoo, remember what I said…about needing to tell you something?"

"Yes. You can say it now."

But Jihye shook her head. She clumsily reached up to brush her hair back, scooted her chair closer to the table, and looked at him very solemnly. "No. I'll tell you next time. I'm worried I'll say something that I don't mean because I'm a bit drunk."

"Next time? When?"

"I'm sure I'll get another chance. Just remember all the fun stuff we did today...like reading comic books, playing arcade games, and...drinking. Okay?"

Jihye smiled, extending her hand. Sangwoo recognized the gesture from before, when she'd won the gaming console—she was asking for a high five. The memory brought a small chuckle to his lips as he raised his right hand, bringing it closer to hers...

But his hand ended up pressed against the vampire's palm instead, the monster's five long fingers holding him captive.

"Hate to ruin the moment, kids, but it's closing time," Jaeyoung said, tossing Sangwoo's hand back into his lap. When Jihye stared at him with a look of disbelief, still holding out her hand, he flashed her a bright smile. "Have you told your parents you're gonna be late?"

"I'll be fine," she managed to say. "I don't have a curfew, and my parents are pretty easygoing."

"That doesn't mean you should stay out late. They'll be worried! If you rush, you should be able to catch the last train, wherever your neighborhood is."

Deciding their conversation didn't have much meaning to him, Sangwoo let his eyes slip shut. He was suddenly feeling very sleepy. It was strange—now that he could hear Jaeyoung talking right above him, his inner turmoil had dissipated, replaced by a pleasant buzz. He knew nothing had been resolved, but...

It had to be the alcohol.

"I'll get going, then. Thank you for your concern," Jihye responded stiffly, and an awkward silence settled. "Come on, Sangchoo."

"Don't worry about him," Jaeyoung cut in. "I'll make sure he gets home safe."

"Sorry...?"

"I can't have him walking home when it's so dark outside. It's a dangerous world, you know."

Jihye stared at him, dumbfounded.

"Take care, Jihye."

Sangwoo's consciousness faded for a moment, then slowly drifted back. When he finally managed to reopen his eyes, he saw Jihye briskly walking out of the tent. Though he knew he should head home, he couldn't find the strength to do it.

The tent was bustling with students darting around, picking up silverware and plates from tables. Jaeyoung was there, too, saying something to a student he couldn't see...

The older man glanced over at him, their eyes meeting. Sangwoo's lips moved of their own accord, spreading into a beaming smile.

Damn it... I probably look like an idiot.

He turned his face away with a self-deprecating scowl. His chest was a whirlwind of soaring excitement and overwhelming anxiety. Then, all of a sudden, his vision went dark—it took him a moment to realize a large hand had covered his eyes. His heart skipped a beat, and his lips parted involuntarily.

"Hey, Hyungjin. You know where my car is, right?"

"Yeah."

"Would you mind putting him in the passenger seat?"

"Sure thing. I'll take your keys, then. What about you? Aren't you going home?"

"Not before I change and get this makeup off."

"Oh, that's a good point. Anyway... Thanks for helping out today even though you're so busy. We got an amazing turnout because of you."

"No problem. I had fun, too."

"It's crazy that you stayed until close when you were only supposed to pop in for a bit near opening time. Seriously, thank you so, so much."

"It was only a few hours. No biggie."

Jaeyoung's hand finally lifted, and light seeped back into Sangwoo's world. When he opened his eyes, the psycho was already walking away from him.

"Hey, excuse me!" Someone shook Sangwoo roughly by the shoulder. "You need to wake up. Jaeyoung asked me to take you to his car."

It was Frankenstein's monster, pulling on Sangwoo's arm as if he was playing a one-sided game of tug of war.

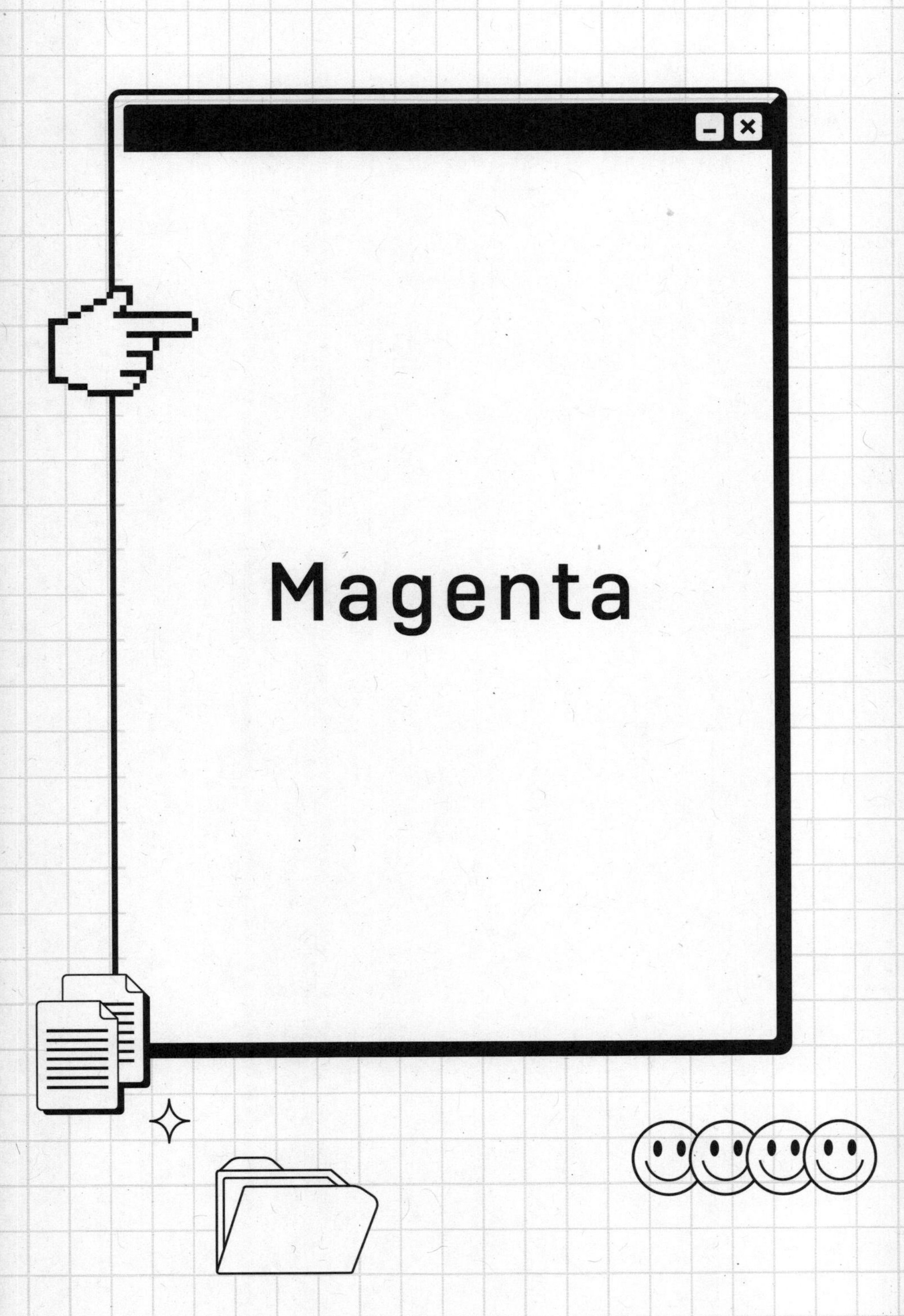
Magenta

Jaeyoung splashed water onto his face, scrubbing every inch of his skin before finally looking up at the mirror. His reflection stared back at him with an unreadable look simmering in its eyes, water dripping down its chin.

With a sigh, he ran his palm over his face. All day, he'd been plagued by a whirlwind of emotions—excitement, shock, rage, self-deprecation, jealousy—each one mixing into the next, leaving him feeling lost. Honestly, it was shocking he'd felt such a large range of emotions in a span of twenty-four hours.

Jaeyoung patted his face dry with a towel, the cacophony inside him settling slightly. "Shit… What am I even doing?" he muttered bitterly, grabbing the paper bag that held his costume and heading out of the humanities building.

When he stepped outside, a warm breeze brushed past, but Jaeyoung barely even noticed; his mind was elsewhere. Sangwoo didn't consider him relationship material—that much was obvious. The weirdo was only willing to be in a "normal" relationship, and Jaeyoung was nothing but a way for him to relieve his "abnormal sexual desires."

For a moment, he'd actually considered the idea of being friends with benefits with *Sangwoo Choo*, of all people. It had been a bizarre thought, as off-putting as a steamy comic drawn in the style of a children's cartoon. But maybe it was for the best. He knew himself well enough—his attention was fickle and fleeting, and his interest in Sangwoo would likely fizzle out after the first time they slept together. That was far preferable to a messier scenario where the two of them tried to be in a relationship and things wound up as dramatic as a soap opera.

When he'd first spotted Sangwoo at the festival, Jaeyoung had been wandering around campus dressed like a medieval vampire with a sign advertising the drama club's tent. The sight of the weirdo taking a selfie with Jihye in front of a flowering tree had emptied any semblance of rational thought from his mind.

Oh, I get it. So you want to sleep *with me, but* dating *is for Jihye?*

There that asshole was, on a cute little outing with Jihye, after everything he'd done with Jaeyoung. Calling his name in that manner, convincing him to develop *VV* together, flirting with him in the studio, patting him on the head, sneaking a kiss, leaving him dumbfounded after that passionate kiss at the bar… And yet, he'd shot down the idea of them being in a relationship without a second thought.

And he thinks I'm *a scumbag? What an absolute hypocrite.*

Jaeyoung's heart pounded angrily in his chest. Sangwoo had given him so much shit for having someone answer roll call for him, but that was nothing compared to what the asshole was doing now—it was like a sewage treatment plant calling a small bag of garbage "trash."

Before he registered what he was doing, Jaeyoung snatched a mask from one of the underclassmen in the drama club and chased after Sangwoo and Jihye with the sole intent of ruining their date.

Later, when Jaeyoung had been making his way back to the Haunted Tavern with the mechanical keyboard he'd won, he'd suddenly found himself confused. Try as he might, he couldn't think of any way to justify his anger. He and Sangwoo had agreed to be friends with benefits, after all—the only point of their relationship was to "relieve their sexual desires," as Sangwoo would put it. What did it matter that Sangwoo had suddenly decided to become the personification of a sewage treatment plant? He could ignore the weirdo, and everything would be fine.

This ends tonight. We do it once, and this desire will be gone… I don't need more than that.

Needless to say, his plan had gone right out the window the moment

Sangwoo walked into the drama club tent. Jaeyoung couldn't explain why he'd forced the underclassmen to set up a table for him and Jihye or had them load it with complimentary dishes to make sure the two of them would stay. He didn't have any good answers for why he'd stayed at the booth the entire day when he'd only been supposed to help out with advertising during the opening, either.

Even worse, over the course of his observation of Sangwoo and Jihye's candlelit dinner, Jaeyoung had been forced to admit that the two of them looked *good* together. Sangwoo's introverted, stoic, and diligent personality paired surprisingly well with that of the extroverted, bubbly, and friendly Jihye.

If he was being honest, it was obvious Sangwoo didn't have an inkling of romantic interest in Jihye. Despite that, Jaeyoung found himself nearly sick with jealousy. He could practically hear the weirdo rambling on in his head.

"Through evolution, humans have developed complex biological mechanisms that trigger them to feel sexual desire for members of the opposite sex for the purpose of reproduction. While it's not that efficient, humanity has survived and thrived by pairing up and going through the complicated stages of pregnancy. Therefore, feeling sexual attraction to someone of the same sex is nothing but a meaningless illusion that does not contribute to humankind's survival or evolution."

If nobody interfered, Sangwoo's life would probably follow an entirely predictable, nicely paved path—he'd fall for some girl, date her, and get married… The thought of himself being the only anomaly in that equation, prohibiting Sangwoo from living a "normal" life, made Jaeyoung's stomach turn.

To make things even worse, it seemed like Jihye was determined to finagle her way into becoming the weirdo's girlfriend. She'd been putting more and more effort into her makeup and outfits over time—tonight, as she sat across from Sangwoo, she wore a green dress with pleats at the waist, patent leather shoes, and a headband studded with cute gemstones.

Just so you know, this isn't Kansas.

Jaeyoung wanted to get all snarky and laugh to himself about how overboard she'd gone with the outfit, but…the reality was, she looked bubbly and adorable. Every time he saw Sangwoo cast a glance in her direction, another wave of irritation rushed through him.

In the end, he resorted to pettiness.

"Seonghyeok, don't forget to give table three their menu."

"Oh, right! I'll do that now!"

"Hyungjin. Is it just me, or do the kiddos over at table three look a bit bored?"

"We can't have that. I'll go and entertain them."

"Dayun, give table three some complimentary dishes."

"Got it!"

"Seohyeon, table three…"

"You got it!"

"Hyungjin—"

"Going now!"

It got to the point where the underclassmen started delivering food and drinks to Sangwoo's table without Jaeyoung even saying anything. The whole situation was a mess—as was his hair, which was currently smothered in hair wax.

When Jaeyoung was done washing up, he went to pack up his things and pose in a couple of group pictures. Then he headed to his car, giving the underclassmen a wave as they thanked him profusely.

Honestly, I could do so much better…, he mused as he stood at the edge of the parking lot for a smoke. One cigarette turned to two, then three.

What was so special about Sangwoo, anyway? What had driven him to follow the weirdo around and pull his metaphorical pigtails like a stupid kid with a crush, disassemble his own laptop simply to get his attention, grind day and night for his damn game, stalk him, and finally compete in some game tournament he himself couldn't give a damn about?

Jaeyoung could pinpoint the exact moment when it had started. *That day when I came to school in a red puffer jacket, red jersey, red beanie, and red boxers… I should've known that I was in for something bad. Hindsight really is twenty-twenty…*

In the beginning, he'd been bummed that Sangwoo didn't know his name or remember him at all. Then he'd gotten depressed at the thought that the weirdo didn't seem to recognize that he was a genuinely decent human being. And now...he was hurt that Sangwoo didn't consider him to be relationship material.

The cigarette tasted bitter in Jaeyoung's mouth. He looked up at the night sky, a heavy sigh slipping from his lips. Frankly, he was in no position to enter a new relationship. So why was he so hung up on Sangwoo? It was a complete waste of his time and energy. Seriously, why?!

He couldn't come up with an answer.

After putting out the half-burned cigarette under his heel, Jaeyoung opened the door to his car and slipped inside. His heart almost stopped the moment he glanced over at the passenger's seat, his breath catching in his throat.

Sangwoo was asleep with his head turned toward the door, which meant his long, white neck was completely exposed—Jaeyoung's biggest weakness. That stupid body part was the root of all his misfortune.

Jaeyoung's hands curled into fists, and he felt his breath quicken. In that moment, there were countless things he wished he could do—things that would probably earn him a lawsuit from Sangwoo—but he forced himself to close his eyes and take a deep breath. Sure, he was desperate and horny, but he had enough sense not to force himself on someone who was drunk and asleep.

Snap out of it.

Thankfully, he felt much calmer by the time he opened his eyes. Pulling another deep breath into his lungs, Jaeyoung turned his eyes to Sangwoo again and slowly reached over.

I'm only putting on his seat belt for him, that's all. Safety first.

Stretching out his arm, he grabbed the seat belt, then pulled it over to the fastener. Sangwoo's hand was right there, lying limply on the seat right next to the red button. His nails were neat and short, as if he'd clipped them the day before, and each finger bore a prominent, well-defined knuckle.

Click.

The seat belt snapped into place. As Jaeyoung righted himself, he purposefully turned his face toward Sangwoo's and saw that the weirdo's slightly parted lips were a mere ten centimeters away. His head spun. The scent of Sangwoo's breath stirred something in his lower abdomen. *Since when is the reek of alcohol a turn-on?*

Very slowly, Jaeyoung returned to his seat, but his eyes continued to greedily drink in the sight of Sangwoo's pale nape. Putting on the weirdo's seat belt was such a simple task, but it had taken most of his self-restraint.

After taking some deep breaths, Jaeyoung started the car. His cock was straining against the fabric of his pants—but in all honesty, he'd been hard since he got in the car. *What the hell's the matter with me?* he wondered. *It's like I have a spring installed in my dick...*

Mentally, it seemed as if he'd gone back in time to middle school, when he'd just discovered what sex was for the first time. Everything around him felt like it had the potential to be sensual or arousing.

Jaeyoung stepped on the gas, forcing himself not to look to his right, and turned his car in the direction of Sangwoo's apartment. Not only was it much closer than his own place, but he wasn't sure how the situation would play out yet.

It turned out there weren't any parking spaces in front of Sangwoo's apartment building, but Jaeyoung managed to squeeze his car into a spot anyway and thumbed off the ignition.

"Wake up, Sangwoo," he said loudly. *It's time to fornicate, you asshole,* he added inwardly.

For a few seconds, he sat silently, forcing himself to calm down. Then he unbuckled his seat belt, took a deep breath, and turned to face Sangwoo.

That damn neck... It had no right being so long and pretty. Narrowing his eyes, he shook the weirdo by the shoulder to wake him up, but Sangwoo didn't stir.

"Here...let me unbuckle your seat belt," he muttered, feeling like some kind of creep.

Sangwoo didn't respond, of course. Jaeyoung draped his right arm over the backrest and reached out with his left to grab the door handle, leaning forward despite not needing to. Any closer, and his nose would brush against Sangwoo's cheek.

In the darkness, the younger man's pale skin seemed to reflect the moonlight. It was like he'd suddenly slipped into a black-and-white movie. Overtaken by a sudden desire to see Sangwoo's face, Jaeyoung grabbed the hat off his head and tossed it into the back seat.

The monochrome scene before him was striking. His heart began to pound loudly. There was something about the shadows cast by Sangwoo's nose, his lashes, his lips, paired with the dark pattern on his cheek formed by a stain on the window...

In that moment, Sangwoo was the main character of their film. He looked so much more innocent in his sleep, and Jaeyoung felt a pang of guilt even as his arousal grew.

What am I to do with him? Hell, why do I want him so badly? It makes no sense!

Sangwoo had nothing in common with anyone Jaeyoung had been attracted to in the past. There was nothing special about him that would catch someone's attention, and he was quiet. Some people might call him a stick-in-the-mud. And sure, he was pretty damn good at certain things, but he was a complete rookie when it came to dating.

At this point, Jaeyoung was something of a relationship expert, which meant he knew better than to pursue someone who wasn't interested. There were plenty of fish in the sea, and all that. There was no point in being obsessed with someone over a skin-deep desire that would fizzle away after a brief moment of ecstasy.

So, given that...why couldn't he be logical when it came to Sangwoo Choo?

Suddenly, the younger man's eyes fluttered open. He blinked a few times, still looking sleepy, before staring at Jaeyoung with wide eyes.

"I didn't do anything, I swear!" Jaeyoung said frantically.

It wasn't very convincing, considering he looked like he was seconds away from kissing Sangwoo. As he watched, the weirdo's chest began to rise and fall rapidly. Jaeyoung raised both his hands up in surrender, as though he'd just been caught raiding a bank and was showing he was unarmed.

"This is a total misunderstanding. Now…stay still." Jaeyoung lowered his arm very slowly. "See? *This* is what I was about to do." He pressed on the red button to unbuckle the weirdo's seat belt, and it loosened with a soft swish.

Sangwoo stared down at his lap, breathing heavily. It was time for Jaeyoung to return to his seat, but he found himself frozen, unable to move.

"I have…something to say," Sangwoo muttered.

It felt like the inside of the car had turned into a sauna—the windows were fogging up, and Jaeyoung's breath felt hot and heavy in his lungs.

"I've been meaning to tell you… Ah, fuck…"

So he starts cussing when he's drunk. It was the second time Sangwoo had lost his verbal filter in front of him.

"You see, I…" With a low groan, Sangwoo scowled and covered his eyes with one hand. A long moment passed before he lowered it again, revealing a gaze that looked strangely tired. "Damn it, this is hard…"

How the hell is he so damn sexy? A moment ago, Jaeyoung had assumed Sangwoo was a dewy-eyed innocent when it came to dating, but the man before him now looked as if he could easily be in the starring role of a porno. The shift between two extremes left him reeling, and he gulped.

"I—I was… I was doing some research…"

To be honest, Jaeyoung wasn't interested in hearing what Sangwoo had to say. He could see that the weirdo's lips were moving, but the only thought in his head was: *Even his lips are sexy.*

"I made sure to take a completely legal route, of course… Blah blah-blah purchased… Blah-blah blah downloaded…"

What in the world is he talking about?

"I just can't bring myself to… Blah-blah blah blah-blah violent… Blah-blah blah the anus…"

A violent rush of desire overtook Jaeyoung, drowning out the rest of whatever Sangwoo was saying. It was like he was watching a video without any sound. Something snapped in his head, and he rushed forward blindly.

"Aah!"

The noise was somewhere between a shout and a moan, but it was quickly muffled by Jaeyoung's lips. For a moment, he felt Sangwoo hesitate, but then his tongue pushed its way into Jaeyoung's mouth with the force of a charging bull. There wasn't any technique or gentleness.

It's like I'm kissing a vacuum, Jaeyoung thought. And yet something about the forcefulness drew him in, left him wanting more.

Without thinking, Jaeyoung returned the favor, tangling his tongue with Sangwoo's and sucking relentlessly at his lips. Their movements only grew more passionate, like they both felt they were running out of time.

As Jaeyoung bit at Sangwoo's lips, the weirdo's fingers dug into the hair at the back of his head and tightened into fists, grabbing hold of whatever purchase he could find. His other arm traveled around Jaeyoung's torso and pulled him in closer.

Jaeyoung didn't even try to resist as his left knee was pulled onto Sangwoo's thigh. He was practically in the passenger's seat now, sitting on Sangwoo's lap as he kissed him passionately. He had to hunch over deeply for the angle to work, but in that moment, he didn't care.

After what felt like an eternity, Sangwoo pushed Jaeyoung's face away with one hand. He was panting as though he'd sprinted a mile—as was Jaeyoung. A sudden wave of shame washed over the older man; they were acting like dogs in heat. But any lingering sense of self-restraint vanished when he saw the raw desire gleaming in Sangwoo's eyes.

Looking was nowhere near enough. An invisible force pulled them back together before they could even catch their breath.

Jaeyoung's entire mind was aflame with the desire to consume Sangwoo whole. To mark his skin and make sure everyone knew he was his. There was no longer any point in trying to distinguish whether he was acting like Sangwoo's special friend with benefits or trying to build a relationship.

Crouched over Sangwoo's lap, Jaeyoung reached under the seat with his left hand and pulled the lever, causing them to sharply recline. With a start, Sangwoo yelped, his short, dark hair scattering over the backrest. There was nothing sexual about the way the weirdo was staring up at him in surprise, but the fact that he was lying between Jaeyoung's legs made it seem like he was trying to be seductive.

They were only apart for a few seconds, but Jaeyoung couldn't stand

it any longer. He leaned forward, pressing his chest flush against Sangwoo's. When he glanced up, he saw that the Sangwoo's expression was twisted slightly, as if he was scared. With something like tenderness, Jaeyoung ran his hand along Sangwoo's cheek, then traced a line with his finger from his shoulder to his neck. Then, at last, he did what he'd been longing to do—he dug his teeth into Sangwoo's nape.

Sangwoo's fingers clenched tightly around his shoulders. "Have you lost your mind?" he squeaked.

Without bothering to respond, Jaeyoung pressed his lips against the spot where he'd just bitten. Sangwoo's dark mole stood out starkly against his pale skin, and he turned his attention to that next, causing the weirdo to flinch slightly under him.

For a moment, Jaeyoung stayed in place, content with lapping lightly at Sangwoo's skin and occasionally diving in for another nibble. How could he taste so sweet? What made him so special?

Jaeyoung licked a trail from Sangwoo's neck to his chin, then pressed a few kisses to one cheek before tracing his tongue around the little grooves of his ear. A low groan slipped from Sangwoo's lips as Jaeyoung nibbled on his earlobe.

Satisfied for the moment, he kissed Sangwoo again, savoring the feeling as he snaked his right hand around the weirdo's waist, which was currently hidden under his navy plaid shirt. Sangwoo's torso felt exactly as he'd imagined—lean, but muscular.

A feeling that could only be described as ecstasy swept over Jaeyoung as he ran both hands over Sangwoo's back. His fingers hungrily roamed over the younger man's flat stomach, then traveled to his chest and played with his nipples before they settled again at his neck.

Their lips finally broke apart. Sangwoo was panting heavily, his brow furrowed. Jaeyoung knew Sangwoo would recover faster if he breathed through his nose instead, but he was feeling too impatient to stop and give that piece of advice. His fingers kept slipping as he tried to unbutton Sangwoo's shirt, though he was usually pretty good with his hands.

It was the damn plaid shirt's fault—it had way too many buttons. Jaeyoung only managed to make it through three before he accidentally ended up ripping through the rest, sending miniature white circles bouncing off the car's seat to vanish into the shadows.

He waited for Sangwoo to snap at him, but strangely, he didn't seem to mind in the slightest. Instead, he reached out to grab Jaeyoung's wrist.

"Hey… Did you hear what I said?"

"Yeah."

"I'm very…intoxicated. I don't know what I'm doing…"

"Got it… But damn, your chest…"

Jaeyoung felt lightheaded and dizzy, like the alcohol Sangwoo had chugged was hitting him instead. He couldn't hold himself back any further—he pressed his lips against Sangwoo's bare torso, sucking on the skin and lapping at the enticing dip of his collarbone.

Sangwoo's thighs bucked under him. Jaeyoung felt the weirdo's grip tighten on his arms, then flex as he tried to push him away. But Jaeyoung refused to let him go, pressing Sangwoo down firmly against the seat and continuing his exploration of his torso.

"Nngh… Why…aren't you listening to me?"

Apparently, Jaeyoung's brain had lost the ability to process language, because he couldn't understand a word Sangwoo was saying. The only thing he registered was that Sangwoo was struggling relentlessly against him, but there was no real strength behind his limbs—likely because he was drunk and aroused.

"No need to waste your breath," Jaeyoung rasped. "Let your body do the talking."

His mouth traveled down to Sangwoo's nipples, and he pulled one between his lips, teasing the other with his fingers. Sangwoo twitched and twisted every time Jaeyoung's tongue made contact, his fingers tightening in his hair.

Taking this to be a good sign, Jaeyoung tightened his grip around Sangwoo's waist, holding on to him like he'd slip away if he wasn't careful. The curve of the younger man's spine was damp with sweat.

Belatedly, Jaeyoung realized Sangwoo had tugged his shirt up around his neck. Without hesitation, he slipped off his jacket and short-sleeved tee in quick succession, tossing them into the backseat. His glasses slipped off his face, and his vision blurred, but he didn't care—his attention was solely on Sangwoo, who was lying there and staring at him intently. He could almost feel the heat of Sangwoo's gaze on his skin.

"Hey, Sangwoo."

"Yes?"

Jaeyoung almost laughed. Even in his disheveled state, with arousal burning in his eyes, Sangwoo had responded to him as diligently as if they were having a regular conversation.

His gaze drifted down to the prominent bulge in Sangwoo's jeans. Excitement filled him at the thought of pulling away yet another layer of Sangwoo's defenses—gone now were the boring black clothes, the modest attitude… Beyond leagues of pale skin, what else would he find hidden within?

"Who would've known you were hiding such a wild side?" Jaeyoung said with a smirk.

"What the hell are you talking about, you… You pervert!"

Grinning, Jaeyoung unbuckled Sangwoo's belt, relieving the pressure on his erection, and immediately began to unbutton his jeans.

"Wait," Sangwoo said frantically, grabbing Jaeyoung's hand.

"What? I'm in the middle of something, you know."

"I have something important to say."

"Okay. Say it."

"But you're not giving me a chance to speak!"

"Don't say it, then."

Jaeyoung swooped down and pressed his lips against Sangwoo's, effectively blocking off whatever he was about to say next. His hands worked diligently, unzipping Sangwoo's jeans and pulling them down. Even with his eyes closed, Jaeyoung could feel the cotton of the boxers. And then, at last, his fingers brushed against Sangwoo's cock. As he mapped out uncharted territory, Sangwoo bit down on Jaeyoung's lip, hard.

Until that point, Jaeyoung had simply assumed that Sangwoo was just as hard as he was—it was a reasonable conclusion, based on the visible arousal on Sangwoo's face, his unfocused gaze, trembling voice, and passionate kisses. But now, Jaeyoung could actually feel the truth of it in his hand.

Any semblance of coherent thought disappeared from his mind, and he gripped Sangwoo's dick through the damp fabric of his underwear, not bothering to engage in any gentle foreplay. Sangwoo's body tensed, and he groaned under his breath.

"You feel that, Sangwoo?" Jaeyoung asked pointedly. "What's going on here?"

"As the result of local stimulation… Blah blah-blah the corpora cavernosa of the penis… Blah-blah blah-blah an increase in blood flow…"

Why'd I even ask? Jaeyoung sighed inwardly.

Up to this point, Sangwoo had been mostly cooperative, but it was like a switch had flipped in him when Jaeyoung touched his genitals. The younger man desperately slapped his hands away, and whenever Jaeyoung's hands ventured back toward the apparently forbidden area, he put up a vigorous defense. They soon found themselves locked in a standoff.

"Nngh… No…"

"What do you mean, *no*?" Jaeyoung growled.

He was already suppressing the desire to pin Sangwoo under him and fuck him senseless—the only thing stopping him was the fact that Sangwoo would probably get hurt in the cramped car.

Breathing heavily, Jaeyoung gripped Sangwoo's wrists and forced him to meet his gaze. Sangwoo's eyes were half-focused, filled with a mixture of torment and arousal. Jaeyoung felt the exact same way.

Shit… At this rate, my dick will explode.

His lower abdomen had been throbbing for the past few minutes, an unfortunate side effect of neglecting his erection for so long. He quickly unbuttoned his pants and pulled them down roughly. His boxer briefs were nearly glued to his skin and dripping wet from all the precum.

Tugging both of their boxers down at the same time, Jaeyoung pressed his entire body against Sangwoo's. When he grabbed their both of their cocks in one hand, Sangwoo twitched and desperately reached out to stop him.

"I—I…I can do that myself…at home."

"You sure you wanna pass up the chance to cum while looking at my face?"

"I do that anyway."

"What the hell is *that* supposed to mean?"

"I don't want to tell you… Ungh!"

Jaeyoung's fingers could barely wrap around both their shafts, but he squeezed them together and began to stroke roughly. The stimulation was way too intense, and he ended up collapsing breathless against the headrest despite wanting to continue looking at Sangwoo's face.

"Shit…!"

Burying his face in Sangwoo's nape, Jaeyoung began to move his hand again. Even with his eyes closed, the sensations were overwhelming—Sangwoo's breath brushing against his earlobe, his nails digging into his back… The scent of skin and sweat tickled Jaeyoung's nose, and the smoldering heat of Sangwoo's skin made him nearly lose his self-restraint.

"Damn it, Sangwoo…"

His hand began to move faster and faster. Though he knew exactly how to stimulate his own body, he'd never handled two dicks at the same time before.

"Sangwoo Choo, do you know…what you're doing to me? Huh?"

Whether he answered or not didn't even matter. Jaeyoung's cock was so sensitive that even the clumsiest touch was enough to send a wave of pleasure through him. Their shafts rubbed against each other, precum dripping down and pooling in Jaeyoung's palm. His arm was starting to ache, but he simply sped up instead of taking a break.

Sangwoo was bucking wildly, his ass lifting off the seat, but he was almost completely silent. Wanting to hear his voice, Jaeyoung kept talking to him.

"What are *we* doing to each other? A-ah… Nngh!"

The pleasure became overwhelming, and Jaeyoung slumped over Sangwoo's torso. As he struggled to catch his breath, he stroked their shafts faster and faster. Sangwoo's arm slipped around his neck and held him tightly, while his other hand overlapped Jaeyoung's, pressing their cocks together even more firmly. Twisting his head, Jaeyoung pressed his lips against Sangwoo's neck.

"Say…my name."

His vision was turning white. He barely managed to right himself and lean his chin against Sangwoo's chest. When he glanced up, he saw that Sangwoo was clenching his jaw shut so tightly that the muscles in his face were pulled taut.

With the hand that wasn't stroking them both to completion, Jaeyoung reached up and pried Sangwoo's lips open.

"Hrgh! Haah… Ah!"

The moans that burst forth were so damn hot that Jaeyoung nearly came right then and there. Barely managing to restrain himself, he pushed his fingers between Sangwoo's teeth so that he wouldn't be able to bite on his lip.

"Nngh… Aah… Hnngh…" Sangwoo moaned, his voice buckling almost into a sob.

Almost there…!

"I sure hope you won't cry…once we actually go all the way," Jaeyoung muttered, stroking as fast as he could.

The simple knowledge that he had Sangwoo pinned under him, moaning and gasping, was enough to bring him closer and closer to his climax. The pleasure was so blinding that he couldn't feel the pain of Sangwoo biting on his fingers.

"Sangwoo… Say it."

"Shut…up."

"Watch your language… Ungh… Now…spit it out."

"Nngh! Fuck… J-Jae…young!"

Jaeyoung.

It was just his name, really, but when the sound of it combined with the sight of Sangwoo beneath him, it overloaded Jaeyoung's mind. His hands clenched, and his eyes shut tight.

He felt like a train with a broken brake, racing downhill only to fly weightlessly into the air when his track abruptly came to an end. The pleasure that had been growing relentlessly inside him finally burst, and he saw red—the color of desire. Sangwoo, who had been biting on Jaeyoung's fingers like they were his lifeline, shuddered violently and groaned.

They came at the same time into Jaeyoung's palm. Jaeyoung went limp against Sangwoo's body, breathing heavily as the strength drained from him. Shivers from the climax relentlessly sparked through his body, as if this was the first time he'd experienced such ecstasy in his entire life. It was like he'd been struck by lightning—everything was sensitive and throbbing.

"Haah... Haah..."

The overwhelming pleasure ebbed, soon giving way to a gentle, relaxing lull. Feeling Sangwoo's shoulders quivering underneath him, Jaeyoung tried to wrap his arm around him but froze when he realized his hand was still covered in cum.

"Damn... I had no idea you were such a horndog...," Jaeyoung whispered slyly.

"You're...one to talk."

Finally managing to push himself off Sangwoo, Jaeyoung reached out and cupped the weirdo's cheek with one hand, no longer caring that his palm was dirty. He wiped away a tear from Sangwoo's eye with the back of his hand, then pulled him into a kiss.

There was only silence as the two of them panted against each other's lips, their chests pressed together. However, it was obvious that neither of them were fully satisfied yet, judging by the hardness Jaeyoung could feel pressing against him.

Suddenly, the car felt way too cramped for the two of them. Jaeyoung sat up slowly, feeling the stickiness of their cum on his chest. Sangwoo stayed right where he was, covering his face with one arm and pursing his lips like he'd committed some unspeakable crime.

"I feel gross now," Jaeyoung said, pulling up his boxer briefs.

Sangwoo remained silent.

"I guess we'll have to shower at your place."

After a long moment, Sangwoo finally said, "Are you suggesting that we have intercourse in my apartment?"

He was starting to catch on much faster nowadays.

"What, you don't wanna?"

To be fair, Sangwoo had been acting slightly off for the past few minutes.

It was understandable if he felt repulsed by what'd happened, but it looked like there was something else going on. Unfortunately for him, Jaeyoung was thinking with his dick, and he didn't have any room to be considerate—even now, after that insane climax, he still had a raging erection.

"First, get off me. I have something to say, but...I can't do it like this," Sangwoo mumbled.

Instead of responding, Jaeyoung took in the other man's disheveled state. Sangwoo's shirt was spread wide open, his hair was drenched with sweat, there was cum on his cheek, and his cock was still hard. Jaeyoung felt another stir of arousal, but he forced it down and returned to the driver's seat. After zipping his pants back up, he grabbed a condom from the glove box—one he'd left there specifically for such an occasion—and shoved it into his pocket. He didn't bother to put his shirt back on, figuring it'd come off again soon enough anyway.

When he looked back at the passenger's seat, he saw that Sangwoo had already exited the car and was now quickly making his way over to his apartment building. There was a hurriedness to his stride that almost made it seem like he was trying to escape, and Jaeyoung immediately chased after him.

It didn't take him long to realize that Sangwoo *was*, in fact, trying to run away—that Sangwoo was taking the stairs two at a time, his plaid shirt flapping wildly behind him, proved to be plenty of evidence.

Jaeyoung caught up to Sangwoo on the third floor, nearly tackling him as he wrapped his arms around the weirdo's waist from behind. Sangwoo spun around like he'd been struck.

"Why are you running away?" Jaeyoung demanded.

The stairwell was poorly lit, the only light coming from a streetlight. Its glow streamed in through the window, casting a reflection in Sangwoo's dark eyes.

The first time they'd met, those same eyes had regarded Jaeyoung with utter indifference. Over time, they'd filled with hatred and irritation, which had then slowly transformed into a hesitant sense of solidarity. Now, they held something fiery and bright, but there was still a flicker of discomfort behind it.

Jaeyoung couldn't understand it. Why was he acting like this when they could simply be enjoying the moment? Maybe it was because he'd shut Sangwoo down before he could say whatever he needed to, but, frankly, Jaeyoung wasn't interested in hearing him out right now. His arms tightened around Sangwoo's waist.

Why waste time on talking when there's a much better way to get our feelings across?

Jaeyoung himself was more than ready to express the emotion burning in his heart and pumping through his veins like lava—physically, at least. Pulling Sangwoo in closer, he closed his eyes and pressed his lips against Sangwoo's neck. His hands roamed around Sangwoo's lean, muscular back as he kissed his shoulder.

Sangwoo's skin was burning hot under Jaeyoung's curious fingers. He let them slowly move down the smaller man's body to his waist, then walked them up his ribcage, brushed them over his armpits, and explored the muscles of his arms. Finally, he laced his fingers together with Sangwoo's, then let his eyes drift back open.

Sangwoo immediately shoved him away, sending him stumbling backward until his spine collided with the cold wall. But Sangwoo wasn't trying to escape this time—instead, he moved in close, an oddly pained scowl on his face.

"Just…let me say something."

If I lean in a little bit, our lips would meet, pointed out Jaeyoung's runaway mind. The guy had to be releasing some sort of pheromone or something—what other explanation was there for the heat pooling in his gut?

"You have to stop…seducing me. I… I can't handle it," Sangwoo muttered. Tipping his head forward until their foreheads met, he placed one hand over Jaeyoung's eyes.

Suddenly surrounded by darkness, Jaeyoung could only hear his heart pounding. A moment passed, then he felt Sangwoo's lips press against his neck. He sank his teeth in next, as if he felt obligated to return exactly what Jaeyoung had done for him.

Sangwoo's tongue, hot and wet, teased at Jaeyoung's collarbone. It was a clumsy attempt at best, but Jaeyoung felt his head spin regardless.

In the silence of the staircase, he could only hear the sound of Sangwoo lapping at his skin.

What little patience he had left frayed almost instantly, and he pulled Sangwoo into a tight embrace before pushing him up the stairs. When they stumbled onto the narrow landing, barely a meter wide, he pressed Sangwoo against the wall. But Sangwoo flipped things on him and gripped his wrists instead, turning him around and backing him into the corner.

"My turn now," he whispered, then resumed his exploration of Jaeyoung's skin with his tongue. His hands remained where they were, trapping Jaeyoung against the wall, as if he was worried his prey would try to slip away.

Jaeyoung stood still and let Sangwoo do what he wanted, but he found it more and more difficult to contain himself—he was dying to strip Sangwoo of his clothes, toss him on the closest flat surface, and finally do the deed proper. A shiver ran down his back as he imagined how tight Sangwoo would be, how enthusiastic he'd be in bed, and how his moans would sound.

Finally, he couldn't take it anymore. "Let's go inside," he declared, reaching down and removing Sangwoo's venturing hand from the back of his pants.

They walked up the staircase and reached the door to Sangwoo's apartment in seconds, but to Jaeyoung, the time felt like an eternity. Granted, he'd been busy groping Sangwoo's chest and nibbling on his ears from behind the whole time, so their ascent hadn't been as fast as it could have.

It took Sangwoo three tries to enter his code into the keypad, but his door eventually swung open.

The moment they found themselves in the privacy of the weirdo's dark apartment, Jaeyoung pounced on him and began walking forward, sending Sangwoo stumbling back toward the faint outline of his bed. Pushing him onto the mattress, Jaeyoung immediately straddled Sangwoo's hips and tried to kiss him. But to his mild irritation, Sangwoo turned away and tried to push him off.

"I need some time to…prepare myself," he gasped.

Brushing Sangwoo's concerns aside, Jaeyoung grabbed the other man's chin and turned his face back toward his. But when he pressed their lips together, Sangwoo pushed him away again, flailing in earnest this time.

"I said I have to prepare myself… Wait, please…"

Still ignoring him, Jaeyoung unbuckled the weirdo's pants and pulled them down swiftly, and—

Sangwoo lost it. Surging abruptly to a sitting position, his face twisted in what seemed to be anger as he shouted, "Stop! I want to mentally prepare myself!"

This was definitely not how Jaeyoung had expected the night to go. As he froze, blinking in surprise, Sangwoo slipped away. He heard a door slam shut a moment later.

Jaeyoung turned and stared at the bathroom door, slightly bewildered. After a few seconds, he walked over, knocked gently, and pressed his ear to the wood. Silence.

"You okay…?"

"Just…give me a moment."

There was the sound of running water, but it wasn't loud enough to be the shower—if Jaeyoung had to guess, Sangwoo was washing his face at the sink. He turned around and slid to the floor, sitting with his back against the wall and staring blankly into the darkness.

It took a moment, but Jaeyoung's arousal eventually subsided. Climbing to his feet, he fumbled along the wall in search of a light switch, hoping to pour himself a glass of water.

When he finally managed to find one and flick it on, he found himself standing in a small apartment—so clean and sparsely furnished that it felt almost uninhabited. The bedroom only contained a bed, two desks, a bookshelf, a clothing rack, and a small dresser. The kitchen area was equally as minimalistic, with a microwave, a shelf, and a small refrigerator. Inside the fridge were seven cans of Black Holic, a few eggs, a carton of milk, and two bottles of water.

Jaeyoung grabbed one of the bottles and chugged it as he walked back to the bedroom. After glancing around for a place to sit, he settled on the bed. A navy comforter lay draped over white sheets, their placement neat and precise.

So this is where he sleeps, Jaeyoung thought, feeling another rush of blood to his nether regions. He forced himself to look elsewhere.

The bookshelf had to be the most boring thing he'd ever laid his eyes on. It only held giant programming books, without a single work of fiction in sight. As for the clothing rack, a couple of jackets and six shirts hung on the upper tier, and below them were two pairs of pants. Every single piece of clothing looked familiar.

Jaeyoung had suspected it before, but now he was sure that Sangwoo must follow a specific rotation when dressing himself.

Next, he examined the desks, only one of which had a lamp on it. He assumed that was the one reserved for studying. The other, a larger office desk, had a monstrous desktop setup sitting on top, complete with dual UHD monitors that had to be over forty inches wide. Even the accessories—a mechanical keyboard, gaming mouse, and speakers—were from high-end brands. A transparent PC tower, probably packed with top-tier components, sat nearby.

I guess this weirdo never learned to do things in moderation… Jaeyoung mused. The PC setup alone was probably more expensive than everything else in the apartment combined. He couldn't help but chuckle quietly at the contrast between the simplicity of the clothing rack and the extravagant PC—it was so…Sangwoo.

"Hey, Jaeyoung?"

The sound of Sangwoo's voice had him instantly springing to his feet. He rushed over to the bathroom. "Yeah? What's wrong? You feeling okay?" he asked through the door.

"I'm feeling a bit more sober now."

Sangwoo's voice was calm and almost emotionless, and Jaeyoung suddenly found himself dreading what he would hear next. *Please don't reject me, not after everything…* He anxiously curled his hands into tight fists, waiting until Sangwoo spoke again.

"I wanted to do it, I really did… I did so much research… But I don't know if I can."

Jaeyoung stayed silent, hanging onto every word.

"Please…leave."

"What?"

He gaped at the door in disbelief. If Sangwoo was uncomfortable with the idea of having sex with another guy, he would have understood—in fact, he was familiar with that discomfort himself, and it was likely magnified tenfold in someone as rigid as Sangwoo. But what pissed him off was that Sangwoo had been an enthusiastic participant in their activities just minutes ago. Despite that, here he was now, claiming that he couldn't do it anymore.

Countless responses formed and dissipated in Jaeyoung's mind. Finally, he opened his mouth.

"It's not like I kicked down your door," he said. Even he could tell that his voice was chilly and sharp. "We agreed on this, remember?"

Sangwoo hesitated for a moment, then said, "I knew you would be angry, but I can't—"

"*Angry*? I'm not mad at you. I simply don't understand where this is coming from."

"The thing is, I don't think I can perform like the people in the videos."

Sangwoo's voice sounded calm and collected. To Jaeyoung, he might as well have been saying: "Sorry, but I don't give a shit about your feelings."

Jaeyoung's breathing grew ragged. The desire and ecstasy that had been simmering in his heart were nowhere to be found, replaced by burning rage.

"Oh, so you don't wanna see me anymore, game be damned?"

"That's right. I momentarily lost control of myself. Please leave."

"You've gotta be kidding me!" Jaeyoung shouted, fury erupting.

He was starting to see the pattern here—for a while, everything would be fine, then Sangwoo would suddenly cast him aside without warning. Of course, he'd fallen for it every time like the complete sucker he was.

"You must be the most inconsiderate asshole I've ever met!"

"I will ask you for a second time. Please leave."

"No," Jaeyoung snapped. "No more hiding. You want me to leave? Come out here and tell me to my face!"

His only reply was silence.

It was infuriating, the way Sangwoo managed to ruin everything whenever Jaeyoung managed to fool himself into believing everything was absolutely fantastic. But this incident…it was worse than all the others combined.

Jaeyoung spent the next few minutes hurling every single cuss word he knew at the closed bathroom door. He knew he was acting pathetic, pouting and sulking like this after being denied sex, but he didn't even care. Unfortunately, it didn't make him feel any better, and the fact that Sangwoo had stayed completely silent the whole time didn't help.

Abruptly, he heard Sangwoo bang on the door from the inside. "Of course you're not worried! You'd just lie there!"

"What the hell are you talking about?" Jaeyoung snapped. "Come out here and explain, unless you want me to stay here all night!"

"No! Then you'll kiss me, and… And touch me! And then I won't be able to think logically!"

"Then don't think! Who cares? Stop trying to be so rational!"

He could practically hear Sangwoo seething. "That doesn't even make any sense! You've ruined everything for me!"

"What don't you get about that?!" Jaeyoung shouted in frustration, slamming the back of his head into the door with a loud thud.

As he slid limply to the ground, he wondered if he was being an idiot getting involved with Sangwoo. After all, that complete weirdo was someone who refused to venture past life's well-trodden paths, only staying in familiar, safe territory.

"You know what? Never change, asshole. Just keep following your stupid routine, wearing your stupid outfits, eating your stupid meals, making your stupid plans…!"

"That was the goal until *you* interfered."

Apparently, Sangwoo was planning on dumping the blame on Jaeyoung for their current situation instead of taking any sort of accountability. But…he was technically right, wasn't he?

Jaeyoung's head throbbed. It was painful to admit it, but he *had* been the one to barge into Sangwoo's life. And with the intent of turning it upside down, no less.

Still, he refused to admit that their relationship was as one-sided as Sangwoo made it sound. If he was a bug in the weirdo's program, Sangwoo was a glitching brush tool. Sure, Jaeyoung might knock the weirdo off-kilter, but it was a mutual effect. Jaeyoung couldn't get his mind off him, to the point he was dedicating a significant amount of his time and effort to helping the weirdo make his game.

But Sangwoo didn't seem to realize that it took two to tango in a relationship. His world was black and white, with only a perpetrator and victim. He wanted to preserve his precious routine—nothing else mattered in the grand scheme of things.

And that really pissed Jaeyoung off.

"Just…come out of the bathroom, asshole. Let's talk."

"No."

"Don't make me tell you twice."

"Please go."

"You've got ten seconds to come out, or you won't like what happens next."

"That's an empty threat, and I know it. You can shout and cuss as much as you want—"

"Oh, an empty threat? Personally, I think I can *totally* kick down that door."

"Try it, then. Let's see if you're still that confident when you're sitting in the police station."

Apparently, the sole purpose of Sangwoo's existence was to piss Jaeyoung off. Scowling in annoyance, he took a quick glance around the room.

"Your PC looks pretty expensive," he commented nonchalantly. The effect was immediate.

"No! Leave my PC alone!"

Ignoring him, Jaeyoung began the countdown. "Ten."

"I already turned you down!"

"Eight. Too late. Should've done that before I came in here."

"I was too drunk to think straight. You kept giving me those free drinks…"

"Not listening. Seven."

"You can't force someone into having sexual intercourse."

"Five. Just come out. I wanna have a deep, long talk with Sangwoo Jr."

"My erection is gone now."

"Three seconds."

"Oh, for… When I get my hands on you…!"

In the end, the weirdo proved way too predictable for his own good. The bathroom door swung open right before Jaeyoung finished his countdown.

Sangwoo's face was flushed, and he was visibly seething. Jaeyoung could almost see the steam gushing from his ears. His shirt was hanging on for dear life, with only the top three buttons remaining to hold it together. The rest flapped wildly at his sides, making him look downright ridiculous.

Jaeyoung, who'd positioned himself against the wall far enough away that he was safe from getting smacked by the bathroom door, looked up at him in silence.

Sangwoo sounded completely serious as he said, "I mean it. I don't know what I'll do if you don't leave. I've been way too stressed because of you."

Geez, what a weirdo…and that's putting it mildly.

For a long moment, Jaeyoung simply stared at Sangwoo. In hindsight, he'd displayed an uncharacteristic boldness when he'd barged into the restaurant Jaeyoung worked at and demanded to speak to him, especially after pushing him away for so long. The fact that Sangwoo had agreed to become his friend with benefits had also come as a surprise.

In the end, Jaeyoung had simply come to the conclusion that once Sangwoo made up his mind, he never looked back. Thus, it had been natural to assume they'd actually end up going all the way. And that was partly why it made no sense to him that Sangwoo was trying to back out now.

"Sorry, but I'm gonna need an actual explanation. In case you've forgotten, I'm a real living and breathing human being, not an NPC."

Sangwoo stayed silent, staring at the ground with a conflicted look on his face.

"You can't get rid of me that easy."

Sangwoo's head shot up. He glared at Jaeyoung, muttering. "Easy...? You think this is easy?"

"Uh... Yeah? You tried to banish me from your apartment like you were deleting an app. Unfortunately for you, it doesn't really work like that with humans."

"Of course you think this is easy. You're always so nonchalant and confident... You deadbeat piece of trash, you have no idea what I'm going through right now..."

"Maybe you can explain it to me, then," Jaeyoung snapped. "Sorry for being so damn ignorant, but you seemed like you were raring to go until now!"

"I've been trying to tell you, but my mind went blank, and everything felt so weird..."

"What's the problem, then? Isn't that what—"

"*Stop making it sound so easy!*" Sangwoo roared.

Jaeyoung flinched slightly, backing up a few steps. The way Sangwoo was glowering at him made him wonder if he was about to throw a punch.

The standoff dragged on endlessly, Sangwoo's glare so sharp and intense it felt like it could cut. But then, his eyes began to shine with tears, and his face gradually crumpled into an expression that made Jaeyoung's heart sink.

"Sangwoo...?"

He rose to his feet and took a closer look at Sangwoo. There were definitely tears brimming in the younger man's eyes—the muscles in his face were twitching as he fought them back, and he was biting on his lip hard. Without thinking, Jaeyoung reached out to touch his cheek, but was immediately denied access.

"Are you...*crying*?"

Sangwoo didn't say a word. He merely glared at Jaeyoung for a few more seconds, fists clenched, then spun around.

Jaeyoung reached out again, trying to grab Sangwoo's arm and draw him back, but he found himself stumbling back a few steps after receiving a strong shove. He remained relentless, though, charging forward and wedging his arm in the bathroom door when Sangwoo tried to squirrel himself away again.

His escape attempt thwarted, Sangwoo grew visibly flustered and shriveled into the corner. When he covered his face with both hands and leaned his forehead against the tiled wall, Jaeyoung belatedly spotted the tears running down the smaller man's cheeks.

Ah… That's not fair.

The fight drained out of Jaeyoung's body in an instant, and he felt the walls he'd put up around his heart—spikes and all—disintegrate into dust. The sharp words he'd been about to hurl at Sangwoo quickly dulled and lost their edge. What was he supposed to do when his opponent broke down crying in the middle of an argument?

Somehow feeling even worse than before, Jaeyoung stood there and let Sangwoo cry. The only sound in the quiet bathroom was the younger man's uneven, ragged breathing.

A long while later, Sangwoo climbed to his feet once again. Turning on the tap, he splashed water on his face a few times.

"Feeling better now?" Jaeyoung asked hesitantly.

No response came from Sangwoo, but he seemed to have lost most of the aggressive edge he'd been sporting before. Brushing past Jaeyoung, he collapsed on his bed, then wrapped himself in the comforter until he became a giant burrito. By the time he was done wedging himself in the corner of the bed in a defensive position, only his eyes peeked out.

Sighing inwardly, Jaeyoung grabbed a few tissues from the desk and placed them by Sangwoo like a peace offering before sitting on the edge of the bed, putting as much distance between them as possible.

The seconds ticked by in uncomfortable silence.

"You have no idea what it's like," Sangwoo said abruptly. "I'm not satisfied, no matter how many times I masturbate… The erection keeps coming back, and then I can't think straight."

Same here, dude, Jaeyoung thought, but chose not to comment.

"The only thing I can think about is fornication. My life is falling apart. You may not take it seriously, and you might think it's easy, but I…"

Sangwoo went on to explain exactly how much he was struggling, and how Jaeyoung had ruined his life. Although it was mildly worrisome to hear that he was seriously considering chemical castration, Jaeyoung never interrupted him. As he listened to Sangwoo, his mind was filled not with empathy or pity, but doubt.

Honestly, Jaeyoung was at a total loss. He could explain to Sangwoo that everything he was ranting about was totally normal and rooted in basic human instinct, and that most people experienced the same struggles at some point in their lives, but he had a feeling Sangwoo wouldn't buy it.

He took a moment to choose his words carefully, knowing Sangwoo had a tendency to interpret things in an annoyingly selective and superficial way. Finally, he decided to start with, "Are you…a virgin?"

"No."

"What's all the fuss, then? You're acting like a kid who got his first erection."

So much for not losing his cool. Mission: failed.

Sangwoo sniffled, and his hand slipped out from underneath the comforters to grab the tissues Jaeyoung had brought him. They disappeared, tucked into his palm, and made a reappearance near his neck.

Sangwoo blew his nose noisily, then muttered, "Until now, I have always been able to control my desires. On the few occasions I've felt such sensations before, they didn't particularly bother me. That means you're an anomaly."

"Are you implying I'm not normal?"

"How can you look so…enticing? You're lucky I never acted on every single thought I had about you… Then I'd be imprisoned for life."

Jaeyoung blinked.

"Actually… I can't blame you for being so pretty. I'm the perverted scumbag here. Why did you do this to me? You've ruined everything. This is your fault."

Is he trying to flirt with me or blame me for his problems? Jaeyoung thought, confused. Sangwoo's speech was jumbled, a stark contrast from the robot-level composure he usually displayed.

Then the truth of the words truly hit Jaeyoung—Sangwoo was trying to say his desires, which barely stirred for anyone else, had turned into a raging inferno for Jaeyoung and Jaeyoung alone.

It was a shame that such a confession, which could've been incredibly grand and emotional, had unfolded in such a lousy fashion. Maybe Sangwoo's talents were wasted on computer science—he would do better directing an erotic film.

"Then sleep with me," Jaeyoung said with a sigh. "Can't bash it until you've tried it, right?"

It was his last-ditch attempt at "fornication," as Sangwoo would say. He was definitely a scumbag—the scummiest of them all. Sangwoo was literally crying, and he was still trying to get into his pants.

Sangwoo shook his head, looking completely drained. "I can't cause you that much pain, no matter how aroused I am. And I…I don't know if I can put it into…where excrement comes out. I'm sorry to let you down."

Jaeyoung had almost forgotten how self-absorbed Sangwoo could unintentionally be—the asshole had assumed he'd be topping since he was a man, not bothering to consider that Jaeyoung was also male. He couldn't help but sigh in disbelief.

Why does that idiot always act like he's the center of the universe?

Sangwoo's lack of social skills were so extreme that describing them as an inability to empathize with others wouldn't do it justice. It was more like he hadn't formed a single meaningful connection with another human being in the past twenty-five years, only interacting with people on a surface level.

This is exhausting… Jaeyoung had been looking for a simple fling. He hadn't signed up for a whole emotional rollercoaster. *It's not worth the damn trouble.*

For a long moment, Jaeyoung sat in complete silence, covering his eyes with one hand. Then he said, "All right, I get it. Let's continue this conversation tomorrow when we've both calmed down a little and you've sobered up."

Silence.

"You ignoring me again?"

Is he being serious right now? Jaeyoung whipped his head around to glare at Sangwoo, his temper flaring, only to see that Sangwoo was already asleep with his head propped against the wall.

"You've gotta be kidding me..."

Sangwoo looked infuriatingly innocent in his sleep. Jaeyoung's hands curled into fists, but there was nowhere to release his anger with his only opponent knocked out. Turning away as his shoulders slumped, he contemplated his next course of action.

It was about time he made up his mind. Perhaps it would be better to abandon the game, since it seemed like their collaboration was surely doomed. Sure, he'd already spent hours getting the key assets together, but things would only get busier once the prototype was out.

"This shouldn't be so damn complicated," Jaeyoung muttered to himself.

Until today, he'd lived by a very simple rule—to dive into anything he felt drawn to and quit anything he didn't. But now, the three pillars he deemed most important—work, sex, and social life—felt more like sharp blades, digging into him.

Maybe Sangwoo was right. Maybe the smartest thing to do was to wash his hands of this mess and walk away.

With a sigh, Jaeyoung got to his feet and stepped into the bathroom to quickly clean his face and hands. When he came back out, his gaze landed on the shiniest, most expensive thing in the room—Sangwoo's PC setup.

"No! Leave my PC alone!"

Unfortunately for Sangwoo, it was human nature to want something more the moment it became forbidden fruit. Jaeyoung walked up to the sleek, transparent PC tower and pressed the power button, telling himself he would leave right after. When the LED lights came on, they were rainbow—a stark contrast to the dark, boring outfits Sangwoo usually wore.

It only took a second for the PC to boot up, thanks to the ultra-high specs. There was no passcode—probably because it was Sangwoo's private computer—so Jaeyoung found himself greeted with a black-and-white grid background instead. The way it was laid out across the dual screens made it almost resemble a chessboard.

There was nothing but three folders on the desktop: My PC, Trash, and…

Wait. Jaeyoung's brain stalled out as he leaned in, face nearly brushing the screen. Maybe he'd misread the label.

But no. The last of the three folders was clearly named "Jaeyoung Jang." There was no mistaking it.

He couldn't even begin to guess what was inside. Did it contain information Sangwoo had gathered on his weaknesses? Or a collection of paperwork he'd put together in case of a lawsuit?

Anxiety fluttered in his heart as he double-clicked on the folder. And then…

What the…?

Inside the folder were pictures. Dozens of them, all featuring Jaeyoung. There were around ten videos as well. Some were from as far back as his high school days—a few he didn't even remember taking!—while others were more recent uploads from his social media, neatly organized by date, location, and source.

"So he's been jerking off to me this whole time, huh? What a perv," Jaeyoung muttered.

His disbelief grew as he checked the other files. Everything Jaeyoung liked—his favorite products, styles, athletes, and hobbies—were organized neatly into a document. It even recorded changes to a music playlist of his that had been updated earlier that very morning, which meant Sangwoo had been looking at it only hours ago.

The situation was so absurd, it felt like something straight out of a sitcom—but instead of disgust, a warmth spread through Jaeyoung's chest, reaching every corner of his body. His heart pounded as if it might burst through his skin, and a quiet chuckle slipped from his lips.

Just sexual desire, huh…? I wouldn't be too sure about that, Sangwoo Choo.

He closed the folder and began to poke around the rest of the computer's files curiously. Nearly every game that had been released recently was installed on it—everything from popular MMORPGs to trending PC games. It looked like Sangwoo was genuinely set on becoming a game developer, after all.

As Jaeyoung clicked through various folders, he drifted into Sangwoo's downloads and found five files dated two days ago. They reminded him of what Sangwoo had said in the car—something about purchasing videos for his research. He frowned as he read the file names.

Size kink, fetish play, dildos... Okay, sure, that's par for the course with porn videos. Hold on—incest, gangbang, torture, and bondage...? What the hell?

He played the videos one by one, already scared of what he would see.

The first video featured two men in surgical gowns, standing around a naked man wearing a blindfold. It started off with wax play and vibrators, and escalated to physical mutilation at the end.

He double-clicked on the second video, which started with the scene of a tiny, lean man getting reamed out by another man with a giant cock. That by itself wasn't too terrible, but the small man was subjected to various abuse until he was bleeding.

The third video featured an orgy. The fourth, a gangbang. The last one was so rough that Jaeyoung couldn't even watch to the end. While the yelling and pained cries of the actors were obviously an act, it was too much.

I get it now.

Jaeyoung had a good idea of what had gone through Sangwoo's head while watching these videos. The younger man's whole life revolved around manuals, after all. Knowing him, he'd probably downloaded the top five films based on popularity. Unfortunately, it seemed the site he'd stumbled across specialized in hardcore porn.

For a few minutes, Jaeyoung sat motionlessly in front of the PC. Everything was falling into place. He finally understood why Sangwoo had pushed him away despite the burning desire in his eyes, and why he'd rambled on about needing to say something, about needing time to prepare, only to end up rejecting him.

Jaeyoung now knew how to handle the mess on his hands. He could only hope that it wasn't too late, but he had to be patient. Everyone moved at different speeds, after all—if he pushed Sangwoo too hard when he wasn't ready, the whole thing would go belly-up.

After deleting the five videos, Jaeyoung stood up and walked over to Sangwoo, who was fast asleep. *He can't be comfortable, lying curled up against the wall like that…*, he mused. Gently unwrapping the comforter from around Sangwoo, he repositioned the smaller man properly on the bed and pulled the blanket back over him. Then he crouched beside him, studying his face intently.

If Sangwoo were awake, he'd probably be grumbling at him or chastising him. But in his sleep, he looked completely relaxed—peaceful, even.

"Hey, weirdo."

No response came, but Jaeyoung kept talking.

"You were being a total idiot today, you know that? But you're not driving me off anytime soon."

It was strange—despite the earlier fiasco, Jaeyoung's heart tingled pleasantly as he gazed at Sangwoo's sleeping face.

"Also…" He stroked Sangwoo's cheek with the back of his hand, his thumb caressing the younger man's cheekbone. "We're gonna pick up where we left off next time, so you better not forget how it felt."

Before he left, Jaeyoung couldn't resist pressing one last kiss on Sangwoo's forehead. Even then, he lingered a moment longer, leaning in to whisper, "Make sure to dream of me tonight."

Semantic Error, Volume 1 END